In the Night Café

Other books by Joyce Johnson

COME AND JOIN THE DANCE
BAD CONNECTIONS
MINOR CHARACTERS

Joyce Johnson

In the Night Café

E. P. DUTTON  NEW YORK

PUBLISHER'S NOTE: This novel is a work of fiction.
Names, characters, places, and incidents either are the product of the author's imagination or are used fictitiously, and any resemblance to actual persons, living or dead, events, or locales is entirely coincidental.

Published in the United States by E. P. Dutton,
a division of NAL Penguin Inc.,
2 Park Avenue, New York, N.Y. 10016.

Published simultaneously in Canada
by Fitzhenry and Whiteside, Limited, Toronto.

Library of Congress Cataloging-in-Publication Data

Johnson, Joyce, 1935–
In the night café / Joyce Johnson.
p. cm.
ISBN 0-525-24741-6
I. Title.
PS3560.0379515 1989 88–28277
813'.54—dc 19 CIP

DESIGNED BY EARL TIDWELL

Portions of the novel originally appeared in *The New Yorker,* in slightly different form as "The Fall of Texas" and "Launching Day, 1962."

Portions of the novel originally appeared in *Harper's*, in slightly different form as "The Children's Wing."

For Hettie Jones

I often think that the night is more alive and more richly colored than the day.

I have tried to express the terrible passions of humanity by means of red and green.

—VINCENT VAN GOGH
Arles, September 8, 1888

My house burned down
And I can't go there no more.

—"Backwater Blues"

I

Into Thin Air

It's a good name, you once said, for a vanishing act.

To be called Tom Murphy is to be about as ordinary as grass. America has Tom Murphys everywhere. You told me you found them in phone books in every town the year you got out of the navy and were moving around a lot. Sometimes, having drunk enough, you'd dial each number, standing at a pay phone putting the nickels in. You were nineteen. The war had made you crazy. Strangers would answer suspiciously. You'd ask if a Thomas Murphy was there, and if he was, you'd ask the other questions. "Sorry I disturbed you." Sometimes you wouldn't apologize either, just hang up quickly.

Tom Murphy steps back into a doorway, slips into a crowd, takes a ride toward some fresh start, some different identity in uncountable locations; dies in a rooming house with an empty wine bottle on the dresser, or on an operating table under white lights or a wooden bench in a railway station, or is still alive, eighty years old—it's not impossible. Anyone with the slightest hope of finding him would have to know where he'd gone to, at least roughly. Or have amazing luck, unthinkable persistence.

1

Missing persons don't die. Time congeals around them. They remain as young, as unfinished, as when they went away.

In 1925, there was a Tom Murphy on Tenth Avenue and Forty-third Street. He was a good-looking boy of twenty—blond, blue-eyed, slim-hipped, half Norwegian. The other half was as Irish as the neighborhood. This Tom Murphy was addicted to cars and appropriated them when he could. He was light-fingered, too, when it came to women. He ran around with a lot of girls and got one of them, Marie Dixon, in trouble.

It was late in August when he took his leave of permanent absence—the time of year when tenement families, choking for air, slept on mattresses on rooftops and fire escapes. Summer closed in on Hell's Kitchen like a vise of heat. Grimy children plunged yelling into streams of water from hydrants and begged for pennies to buy shaved ice doused in syrup. Soot from the railroad tracks of Eleventh Avenue—called Death Avenue by some—grayed the sheets and bloomers hanging out over the backyards.

One August day Tom Murphy took a bunch of pretty girls for a ride up and down Park Avenue in a yellow touring car. He sat on the leather seat behind the steering wheel like a Princeton boy on a holiday outing, a straw hat on his head, striped shirt sleeves peeled back to the elbows. The excited girls in their rolled stockings, their bright, flimsy dresses, draped themselves around him, hooting and waving at the sedate pedestrians on the clean, gray sidewalks. The automobile had been stolen for the afternoon.

Tom Murphy was a newly married man by that time. But his bride would have been too pregnant to have come along. On August 16, her mother brought her into Polyclinic, the hospital just across the street from Madison Square Garden. It was famous not for its maternity ward but for its other clientele—boxers carried in unconscious straight from the ring, gangsters whose bullet wounds were treated in its emergency room. The child born to Marie there was a boy.

Tom Murphy stayed around just long enough to see that his son was named after him. A few days later, he borrowed his new brother-in-law's car and disappeared. He was remembered in the neighborhood, with a certain admiration, as a driver of stolen vehicles, though his son's birth certificate listed his occupation as cabdriver. He may also have been involved in the trafficking of bootleg alcohol.

But there was another side to this Tom Murphy. Somewhere he'd learned to play the trumpet. He seemed to have dreams of becoming a musician. It was said he had the trumpet with him when he left.

Everyone told little Tommy Murphy he looked just like his father. When he looked in the mirror, he saw a little boy; he didn't see his father at all. Later he began to see him more and more, as if Tom Murphy were hiding in his own face. Tom Murphy got him in trouble all the time. His mother said bitterly, "You look like him, you act like him." She smacked him to make her point. She'd never wanted him, she told him that. She didn't even like him when he was a baby, when he couldn't have been doing anything wrong.

When her son was born, Marie was eighteen, fast and flighty. Motherhood didn't slow her down. At times a dangerous pitiless glint flashed off her like a knife. She got rid of her wedding ring, marcelled her auburn hair, rouged her small, thin mouth into the arcs of a valentine. She frequented the Arbor dance hall on Fifty-second Street, got a job checking hats in a speakeasy. She met other men, it wasn't hard. She was an I-don't-care sort of girl.

The neighbors thought she acted strangely with the baby. She'd stick him in his carriage, park him out in front of the stoop for hours and forget to bring him in. He'd wail and kick and scream. Someone's kid would have to go running up four flights to bang on the door, wake Marie from her daylight sleep, make her come down and tend to him. She'd rub her eyes and say, yawning, "Come on, what's wrong with a little fresh air?"

Once Marie almost lost the baby. An old German woman who wasn't right in the head passed the house each day on her way to do her marketing. Seeing the baby always out there on the street, the German woman got the idea that he belonged to no one, that he was hers for the taking. A neighbor, looking out a window, spotted her wheeling the carriage away. The neighbor got the child back with the aid of a cop. But the next day the screams of the baby could be heard as usual and the carriage was again down in front of the stoop.

Marie hadn't always lived in Hell's Kitchen. Given the opportunity, she'd remind people of that. She'd speak of piano lessons, crepe de chine party dresses, property her father had owned in Brooklyn. But her father had died and the property had been lost, and she'd moved with her mother and sister to a cold-water flat on Forty-ninth Street with toilets in the yard.

At sixteen Marie left school to become a telephone operator. For two years she'd plugged people into each other. "Number please" nine hours a day on a high metal stool in an enormous room that never stopped buzzing, as if a million flies were trapped in it. A good job compared with some she could have gotten. The telephone company drilled its girls in politeness and enunciation—they expected them to be perfect ladies, of course. They fired her for lack of "moral character," for the big ugly belly she had, thanks to Tom Murphy, that had nothing to do with her diction or the speed of her fingers. "You're through at Bell Telephone, miss," they said.

Men she met at the speakeasy gave her extras—sometimes a little cash or a pair of stockings—but her boyfriends never stayed around. The kid, as he grew older, cramped her style. She could no longer leave him so easily at night with a bottle tied to the bars of the crib. A few times when she couldn't dump him at her mother's, she had to cart him along.

He had memories later of strange, crowded tobacco-smelling midnight places, of smoke and light, of a back room occupied by a large, heavy, green-covered table and his mother making him lie down under it, saying, "You shut your eyes now and stay there. And you keep yourself quiet, or else." And waking up later in the darkness hearing odd cries and noises, thinking his mother was on that green table above him with some man.

Marie brought one new boyfriend home who didn't go away like the others—a cockney seaman with a big bald head and the reddened, belligerent face of a drinker. Frank Crosby worked on a British freighter docked at the North Pier. In Marie he found something so compelling that he decided to jump ship. Marie told her mother that they were crazy about each other, but maybe it was anger that connected them—his the blind anger of the fist, hers darting, glittering, insidious.

"Stay out of Frank's way," Marie told the little boy. "Frank doesn't like kids, so don't get him mad at you."

He asked, "Is he my dad now?"

"You don't have a dad," she said.

In a few weeks Frank drank through all his sailor's pay. Marie began yelling, "Get a job!" She locked Frank out one night, bolting the door from the inside, shoving a trunk against it. Hiding under his blanket, the little boy could hear a tremendous racket, fists crashing against wood, terrible threats of what Frank would do to Marie, and his mother shrieking and laughing, strangely exhilarated.

Then suddenly Frank was back in Marie's good graces. He'd found a job in the Bronx as a super and a free apartment in the basement of the building where he worked that had steam heat and a real inside bathroom. It seemed they'd be coming up in the world if they moved in there with him—and besides, Marie was going to have another baby.

A green truck arrived one day, and everything they had was carried down the stairs and loaded into it. They got into it, too, the little boy squeezed in up front between his mother and the driver. The driver called him Sonny and gave him his first stick of chewing gum, and they left the neighborhood—Tom Murphy's old haunts—for good, the dark red tenements with their broken stoops, the summer sidewalks aswarm with kids, the blue river with its mournful bellowings of ships, the rattle of freight trains down Death Avenue.

There are things that happen to little children that can't be distinguished later from dreams. Sometimes a picture would come into

Tommy Murphy's mind of a room with a brown carpet on which he'd been told to sit and wait, and the memory of someone rubbing his face with a wet cloth and handing him a pink rubber ball to play with and closing the door. The room had furniture with heavy, clawed animal feet that greatly interested him, and he remembered also some patches of light on the carpet, which kept gliding back and forth and seemed to glow with all the colors in the world. The door had opened and a stranger had come in, a tall man with yellow hair who seemed awfully glad to see him. "Well, hello there, Tommyboy," he said, and the man gave him a nickel and lifted him so high he could almost touch the ceiling. He could never figure out where that room might have been, or be sure it had ever existed, or whether the man who'd come in and lifted him up had been his father.

His mother said, "Your dad's in jail, the last I heard. You'll end up there, too, if you don't watch out."

In the new neighborhood, he was drawn to a gang of older boys. They teased him and sometimes made him cry. Whitey, they called him because his hair was so light. "Go home little Whitey, your mother wants you," they'd jeer if he trailed after them on their adventures. They hung out on his roof, where they smoked stolen cigarettes and dared each other to walk the narrow parapet. "I can do it," he told them, but they chased him away. "Get lost, kid. You're too young to die."

He went up to the roof one day when no one was around. The sun was hot and bright, tar stuck to his feet. He ducked under the flapping sheets on the clothesline and walked to the edge, and after staring thoughtfully for a while at the parapet, climbed up on it the way the big boys did, holding his arms straight out from his sides, seesawing against the breeze.

Mapes Avenue glittered six stories below, the slick tops of

cars, the shop windows, the tin lids of garbage cans. He stuck one foot out into blue space and told himself he could make the other foot follow, why couldn't he take a walk in the air? But then he started trembling. All of a sudden he knew what was out there.

The apartment Frank had moved them into was near the boiler room. A buzzer would sound, and other people's garbage would travel down to them on the dumbwaiter. In the winter it was tropical down there, but the sun never reached them even in summer, and there was a thick, damp smell, as if some black river flowed beneath the surface of their lives. The boiler forever demanded propitiation, devouring mountains of coal, spitting ash that would have to be hauled out to the courtyard in barrels. A fine grit appeared everywhere—on their windowpanes, their furniture, their skins. He used to think he could taste it in everything his mother cooked.

He was known to the families who lived on the floors above them as the super's kid, although he did not belong to Frank in the way his little brother Kevin did—Frank had made that very clear. Frank, Marie and Kevin—they were the real family, the Crosbys. He did not even seem to belong to Marie. He was someone they permitted to live with them because he was too young to work; meanwhile they allotted him a bed and food. "You're a lucky boy," Marie once said when he'd angered her. "I could have given you away when you were born."

Most children seemed to take their belonging for granted. He watched the other families in the building, the other mothers with their sons. He noticed that even when these women yelled and got mad, there was a torrent of passionate sorrow, a warmth, as if the worst thing these boys could do to their mothers was to damage themselves by their acts of foolishness, as if the women somehow bore on their own bodies the scrapes and bruises of their children. He liked the Jewish families best, and it didn't matter what Marie said, that they'd killed Jesus Christ in the old days. Their strange customs appealed to him. Every week they gathered around a table with a white cloth on it and burned candles over which prayers were said in their foreign language. Even little kids like him were allowed to be present on these grand occasions, eating their roast chicken as the candles melted all the way down. He would stand in the courtyard and look up, and if the blinds weren't drawn, he could see the golden insides of their rooms, the small flames flickering, casting shadows that lapped at the walls. When he grew older, sometimes he got into their houses—on Saturdays, when Jewish people were forbidden to work. Women would call to him from windows—"Little boy! Little boy!"—and offer him pennies to come up and light their stoves. Their kitchens would still smell of baked bread and roasted meat, and he'd catch glimpses of other rooms—photos of somberly dressed men and women in gilt frames, upright pianos, rows of books behind glass.

In the warm weather, the mothers came down from their kitchens in the evenings to offer each other advice and opinions. Some brought folding chairs and set them up in front of the stoop. Until the sky darkened and the air cooled off a little, they'd stay out there. Then they'd sigh and say they still had to do the dishes. Marie would be out on the stoop with all the rest. Anyone could see she was the prettiest, the slenderest; even the women made flattering remarks about her figure. She'd be laughing and smoking cigarettes and showing off the fat baby. She'd stretch out her legs so her trim ankles could be admired. He felt proud to see his mother there—but also uneasy, as if any minute the others would discover she was only pretending, that something was wrong, something he couldn't name.

For a while Marie was all the rage. A couple of the women were her best friends. She was always finding excuses to take the baby and run off and sit in their kitchens. She'd return excited from her visits, brimming over with things she'd sworn not to tell.

Frank kept warning her, Don't get thick with the neighbors. He got mad when he couldn't lie around the house and drink and know her exact whereabouts. He didn't believe she went where she said. Marie made up to him by telling him bad things her friends had said about their own husbands. She saw nothing wrong in repeating these things to others as well, women for whom she had no particular liking. For Frank's benefit and her own amusement, she'd make fun of all the women in the building, doing hilarious imitations of their voices. For Marie any secret seemed its opposite, something to be broadcast to the world. Implicit in any promise was the forbidden power of breaking it.

One summer evening, Marie went out on the block with the baby in his carriage as usual, but no one spoke to her. A silence came over the women when she appeared on the stoop. They stared at her coldly, then turning their backs to her, resumed their talk in low, angry voices. She walked slowly up and down the sidewalk with little Kevin, smoking her cigarette, but no one relented, no one called out to her. She could have been a stranger or a ghost or someone who was not there at all. She was just canceled out like a dead person.

Tommy Murphy, playing ball in the middle of the street, was surprised to find his mother calling him. "Tommy, let's walk down to the candy store, you and me, and get ice cream." Her voice wobbled, honey-sweet the way it never was. He stopped playing and ran over to her, and she said in the same new, funny voice, "Now dear, you wheel baby." Spots of red burned in her cheeks. His mother looked dead ahead as they walked past all the silent women, and her fingers pressed hard into the back of his neck.

He remembered it because that was about the only time he ever thought Marie had forgiven him for coming into the world. He'd always remember pushing the baby carriage across Mapes Avenue in a daze of joy, wondering if she'd be taking him to the candy store from now on.

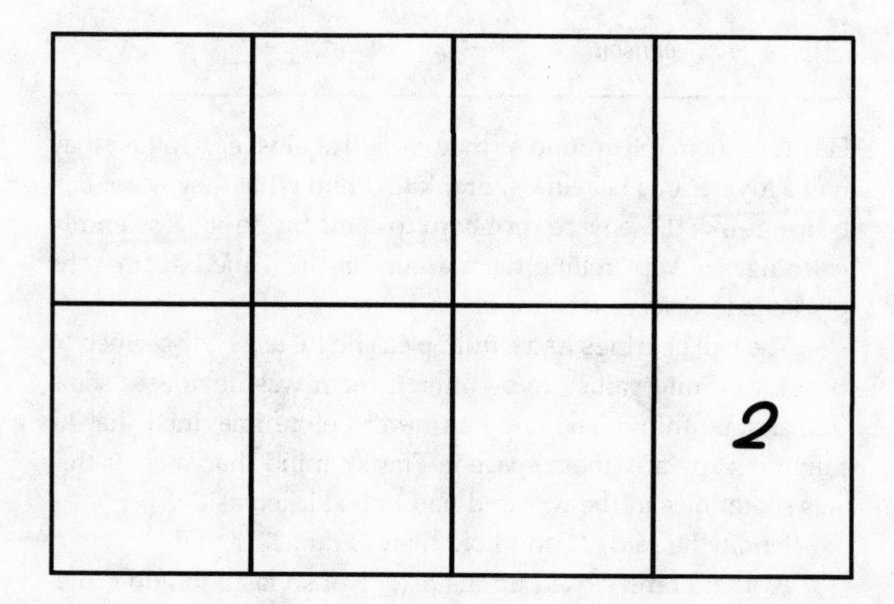

Sooner or later you'd get to a certain story.

"Now listen, this is a really good one. Did I ever tell you how I sold my mother out for two ball bearings? You'll like this. It's got the right elements."

But it never did you any good to tell it.

The boy in this story of yours was seven or eight. Not smart yet, you said. This kid would still believe anything. One day he came home from school and his stepfather Frank was waiting for him. Frank had been drinking. He said, "Come up on the roof with me. I'm going to give you a present." The kid fell for it, though Frank had never given him a thing up to that time.

The roof was covered with deep snow, absolutely smooth—not a single footprint in it. No one went up there in winter.

"What do you think of these?" Frank said, and he opened up his fist. In the palm of his hand were two very small metal balls.

He made them roll around so they clicked against each other; they had a mysterious heaviness. Frank told him what they were. Ball bearings like these were very hard to come by, he said, solemnly belching. He kept rolling them around as he leaned against the blackened bricks of a chimney.

The ball bearings had a dull, pleasing luster. They seemed to possess infinite value. To be offered them was obviously some tremendous thing. The boy had never before imagined that he might occupy any more space in Frank's mind than a chair that was sometimes in the way and had to be kicked aside.

Finally he said, "Can I hold them, Frank?"

At that Frank closed up his fist. "Not so fast. You do something for me and I'll do something for you."

The kid thought maybe Frank needed help that day shoveling snow, but that wasn't what Frank wanted. Sweat broke out on his heavy red face. He started talking about killing someone he called the Italian, choking him with his bare hands in front of all his customers. He only wanted to know if something he had reason to believe about Marie and this Italian was true, so he wouldn't be laying down his life for nothing.

Grabbing the boy by the collar of his jacket, Frank shouted, "You'd better tell me what you know. Don't cover up—or I'll leave you up here all night and lock the door!"

The boy started crying because he didn't know anything. How could he know what Frank wanted him to know?

The Italian was a guy called Al who ran a butcher shop on Tremont Avenue with his brother. Marie bought all her meat from these brothers. Sometimes Marie would ask him to go to Al's for her, and she'd give him a folded-up note telling Al what she wanted. Al had curly black hair and wore a stiff apron always smeared with blood. He whistled while he sawed up chops. After he'd wrapped them up in brown paper, he'd give the string a smart yank and bite the end off with his strong teeth. Al would unfold Marie's note and read it carefully. Looking him in the eye, he'd say, "Well, tell your mama I said 'Hello, beautiful.' Don't forget."

"Al says hello," he'd report when he got home. He could never manage the word *beautiful*, though somehow it seemed the most important part of the message and the one his mother might like best.

Frank said Marie and Al had been seen. They'd been spotted coming out of a house one afternoon in another neighborhood. He said lately Marie had been serving meat all the time. When he warned her they couldn't afford it, she said she'd been getting it at a new place at bargain prices. Frank said, "You know where it comes from, don't you?"

The kid kept crying and saying he didn't know anything.

Frank pushed him down and forced his face into the snow. "The present's too good for you!" He seemed to think it was loyalty to Marie that was making the kid hold out on him. But in his own mind he seemed convinced of the very thing he needed so urgently to find out.

Finally, he said, "Right. I can see you want to stay up here." When he left, he padlocked the door from the other side.

Hours passed on the cold roof. The snow and the sky both turned gray. Lights went on one by one in kitchens across the street, and shouting boys miles below pelted a car with snowballs.

The weird thing was, you said, that kid could not imagine being looked for. It was as if the skin around the ordinary world had cracked apart, and no one noticed that a boy had fallen through. It wasn't worse in this new place, only colder. If Frank ever came to get him, maybe he wouldn't come down.

The sky grew as dark as the ink they made him write with in school, and the snow turned white again. He saw that light never stood still but must always be moving. He thought about this and stopped being afraid, and lay down against the warm bricks of the chimney.

At some point Frank returned and he was hauled to his feet. The man shook him out like a rag and kept yelling, "Had enough?" He made the air smell like the inside of a bottle.

It was as if a radio had gone on in the middle of the night and the words you heard were meaningless because you didn't know the beginning of the program. And you could say back equally meaningless things because nothing mattered, nothing was to be won. You could fill up the air with any old words, any old words that came to you, so he made up a black car that he saw one day on Tremont Avenue and some man at the wheel and his mother getting in fast, looking over her shoulder. And suddenly the man in his mind startled him by saying loudly, "Hello, beautiful," and it wasn't Al the butcher who spoke but his own father. And as the black car screeched away from the curb and roared toward its getaway in the distance, for a moment he saw himself in the backseat.

Frank took the ball bearings out of his pocket and threw them into the snow. The kid went back the next morning and managed to find one of them. He had it a few days, then lost it.

The Italian went on living and selling his meat.

As for Marie, Frank gave her such bad bruises on her face that she didn't leave the house for a couple of weeks.

"And I did nothing," you said to me once, weeping. "I did nothing."

I covered your eyes with my hands. "Don't, oh don't." I held on to you in the dark, frightened, waiting for morning.

Little Whitey

Winter 1964

3

I remember Caroline Murphy saying, that time I met her in 'sixty-four, that it had been very hard to explain death to the children. You had to put it in terms they would understand, she said. "What I finally told them was, Daddy's all gone—just like ice cream."

She was proud of that explanation. I was careful, I said nothing negative. "Of course," I said. "It must have been very difficult." Later I thought about the meaning of ice cream. A Popsicle was what came to mind—it was cold and hurt your throat but you liked it so much you ate it all up and your mother said "All gone," in a loud, approving voice as if it were all right that everything ultimately disappeared.

Caroline had flown up to New York with Tom's two kids just for the weekend. "On impulse," she said when she called me, as if she were a person accustomed to taking impulsive flights. An old flame had resurfaced, she said, and was taking her to dinner and she wanted to meet me while she was in town. Or look me over. After all, wasn't I that girl her husband had gone and married? I'm not sure to this day, though, what she wanted.

"My little nieces have a gorgeous apartment where we're staying and they seem to believe we'll all survive the visit. You could see the children if you came by."

I said, Yes, I'd like to do that, and wrote down the address. It was the first time we'd ever spoken. She could have been talking to anyone, any friend of a friend in a strange city.

By then I knew any unlikely thing was possible, anything formerly unthinkable. That was the principle upon which the universe apparently operated. You could wait on a street corner, for example, for a man who'd died two hours ago; you could walk into your house and find your life swept away. Caroline had never come with the children while Tom was alive. It made sense she would do it now, when it was too late.

"This is Joanna," she told them. "Joanna was married to Daddy."

It couldn't have meant anything to the little girl Celia, who was only three. She sat on her mother's lap eating animal crackers with great deliberation, taking them out of the box one by one. But the boy stared. His blue eyes fixed on me with a million questions.

"Well, say hello or something," Caroline said sharply.

He looked down at the toes of his sneakers. "Hello."

"That one's Tommy," his mother said, pointing him out offhandedly as if I wouldn't have known his name.

The nieces' apartment was all the way east in the twenties. It was on a high floor and had a living room that seemed to hang out in space over the river. The river was a hard gray like the air, the color of January. Tugboats kept passing, as they had the day I'd gone to Bellevue and sat in a room that also looked out on the river, waiting for my name to be called. It had all been done in Swedish modern and potted palms for the benefit of the living who were there to make the final identifications. But when they'd ask the next of kin to come outside, the body would be rolled into a kind of hallway, as if it had no real place. Is this Thomas Murphy? they asked and I said Yes it was him and they said That will be all, thank you very much. And that was all there was to death in the dream I couldn't wake up from, that kept unreeling behind my eyes. In this dream Tom had died, though I knew he'd only disappeared as he'd threatened to do in the dark times. For weeks I'd been seeing resurrections—brown-haired men in bright blue nylon jackets always walking too fast for me to catch up with them, vanishing around corners before I saw their faces. Sometimes a motorcyclist would streak past me into the distant, shifting traffic, bent over the handlebars in a certain familiar way, reckless and unhelmeted. It was only in the dream that there'd been an accident, that I'd seen the body of the rider, stretched out on a steel table, that I'd touched the thick brown hair for the last time.

Tom's son had hair of a different color, so light it could have been made of cellophane; even his eyelashes were paler than his face. Until I saw him I'd never understood Tom's childhood nickname Whitey. Finally, now, I could see little Whitey, exiled among the ashcans, the cement courtyards of the Bronx. Little Whitey had a face I instantly recognized—the face of the child I was never going to have. There'd be other children maybe, but never that one. That one had been lost before it ever existed.

I've been saner than I was in those days. The air buzzed with meaning and I saw everything starkly connected. I kept thinking you had to break the chain, there must be some way you could break it. I looked at Tommy and I wanted to steal him, take him out of there with me.

Right away Caroline let me know how much trouble he was.

All day he'd been pestering her to let him ride up and down in the elevator by himself. She knew what he'd do—he'd push all the buttons. Complaints would be made to the doorman.

He stood there and listened, trapped by being seven years old. He had that eerie dignity that's so amazing in certain children. "I wouldn't," he said. He touched the sleeve of his mother's dress, pressed against her thigh, which annoyed her all the more.

"Don't lean all over me, Tommy!"

I couldn't understand why she didn't want that child close to her then. She'd fend him off with a word or a look, but he'd keep coming back. Didn't she realize how it could multiply? Maybe she knew and knew she couldn't help it and felt anguished secretly. Or maybe I saw it wrong that day because I always blamed her for so much.

"The boy looks like me, acts like me, *is* me," Tom used to say. He'd tell me he wasn't so worried about the little girl. The baby was going to be all right, she wouldn't even remember him. But the boy. . . .

He once said, "I know what I did to him."

He'd had some pictures of the children on him the night he left Palm Beach. But he'd cleaned out his wallet when he got to New York. In a men's room at the bus terminal, he tore up every snapshot, got rid of his credit cards, address book, the keys to his car and the house his father-in-law had paid for—everything that belonged to the old life.

"Don't look back. Someone might be gaining on you," was his favorite saying.

Caroline Murphy was taller than I'd expected; she had a face that was all cheekbones, nervous, delicate angles. One of those lean, fair-skinned women who spend too much time in the sun and look older than they should long before they're forty, as if whole years somehow get burnt up by all that heat and light. She seemed much better at being a widow than I was. She hardly got the door open before she was clasping my hands in hers. "Oh, I'm so *glad* you're here," she said fervently. And you could almost believe she truly was, although it seemed strange to me that we would touch each other. I was reminded that she came of very old blood, on her mother's side at least. She'd been one of those girls brought up to believe that the proper gesture could get you through the most awful situation.

I don't think I hated her. What I mainly remember feeling was puzzlement. I couldn't imagine Tom ever being with this woman, couldn't picture them lying down in the same bed, even sitting at the same table. It all seemed to have been so fatally arbitrary. By accident Tom had married her. By mistake she'd lived with him thirteen years, given birth to these children he'd had to leave behind. It's become possible for me to think of her as a woman who boarded the wrong train and got off in a country she never should have visited. Sometimes I imagine her at sixty, still trying to get back.

At one point she went walking to those windows with the river view. She flung out her arms and cried, "Hello world! Are you out there?" like a character in a William Saroyan play with some sentimental message about living life to the hilt. It made me wish to be elsewhere, like coming upon a stranger in underwear. I didn't want her revealing herself to me that way. I wasn't there to be her friend.

I thought she'd be curious about me, but she wasn't. She asked me very little about the accident, didn't seem to want to know the details. She had certain things I suppose she needed to say out loud to find out whether or not she believed them.

"Weren't you relieved?" she asked me. "Weren't you relieved when it finally happened?"

"Relieved?" I heard myself repeat it like some lesson in a foreign language.

"Oh, it was there, always—the possibility. Anyone who knew Tom could see that."

I said, "Caroline, there were other possibilities." I remember I was trembling. I did almost actually hate her.

"Not really," she replied, drawling out the *really* a little, "though I understand why you'd want to think so. How long were you two married—a year? You'll be more careful the next time. We'll both be more careful. And won't *that* be boring?" She'd rallied up her graciousness again, her hostess tone. "You know what I keep telling myself? That maturity means accepting the necessity of boredom. Just imagine what Tom would say to that!" She was looking straight into my eyes. "I do think about him, you know. I listen for that voice of his, don't you? I even find myself hoping someone else will say the terrible, outrageous thing. But of course no one ever does."

I could feel her pulling at me, demanding some sign that this was more like it, this was what a real widow would say. It could also have been the truth, just like the word *relieved;* the truth was all in pieces.

I remember thinking, All right. You be the widow. I'll hand over the goddam title if it means so much to you. And I imagined stepping out from under it as if it were no more than a black veil and being an ordinary person in the world again. But I didn't want my old life back and there was nothing else to step into. I felt the kind of terror you feel when you look too closely at the future and see nothing but unfilled space.

The children were running in and out of the room while all this talk was going on over their heads. Though you never know what a very little kid understands. A child will remember an atmosphere, the way two women were sitting on opposite sides of a coffee table, an unexplained tension in the air, a sentence or two with no surrounding context. "Weren't you relieved when it finally happened?" The *it* might seem ominous, disguising a darkness, Daddy gone—like ice cream melted down to nothing.

It's the duty of children to enjoy themselves, to be unaware of serious matters. They're commanded to play as if play is the work they must do in order to remain unconscious.

There were toys for the kids in some bedroom, but there weren't enough toys or not the right ones. The boy said, "Why can't we play in here?"

"Because Joanna and I need to visit for a while. Why don't you go inside and draw a picture for her and come out when it's ready. Look at the river and draw a picture of the river."

She said to me, "You know, at home he always draws. Tom used to take the scribbles he did and tack them up in the studio."

The boy was listening. "When did he, Mom? What were the pictures?"

"They weren't pictures, they were scribbles. Just like your sister does now. He saw something in them—your father was always seeing things no one else did. You were only two or three."

"Well, what did he *say,* Mom?"

"Who on earth can remember conversations years later? Only great geniuses and I'm an ordinary person."

"I can draw better now," said the boy.

"That's certainly true. Now take your sister and scoot. Draw or don't draw—it's all the same to me."

He stood his ground, though. "Guess what crayon water is?"

"Oh for some peace!" Caroline said warningly. "Blue. Now go."

He still wasn't leaving. "You've got the wro-o-ong answer," he sang as if he'd won his mother into his game, and then he looked at me. "It's the lady's turn."

Except for "hello," he hadn't yet spoken to me directly. I couldn't manage the tone of half attention he probably expected.

I said something about its sounding like an easy question, but it wasn't. "Not the gray crayon and not the white one, right Tommy?" I said. And I remember how hard it was, how weirdly self-conscious I felt, saying that name.

He gave the perfect, startling Zen answer. "A no-color crayon, of course." I wondered whether Caroline heard the echoes the way I did. "No crayon, no color, no picture," he said with triumphant logic.

"That's no way to talk," Caroline chided him.

I said, "I bet your dad told you that, didn't he? He knew all about the colors of things."

His eyes narrowed and his face looked old for a moment. He was concentrating so painfully. "I forget," he said, not looking at me now.

"You can draw me a picture some other time," I said. "Maybe we'll meet again."

"Yes," said Caroline. "That would be so nice. We'll all keep in touch now that we've gotten to know each other."

Tommy didn't go. I'd been sitting by myself on a blue velvet sofa, and very shyly he came and sat there too. He leaned back carefully against the cushions, his feet dangling in midair, hardly breathing, as if good behavior could make him invisible. Once in a while he'd glance at me hopefully, waiting, expecting something.

"Well, it looks like you just fascinate him," Caroline said.

I remember thinking no one was giving that child anything at all, not even one look around his father's city. At least someone should give him that. And I had that crazy, mistaken urge again to take him out of there, to vanish with him into that same lost space that Tom inhabited.

I started talking about the glories of New York—the stone lions in front of the public library, the Staten Island ferry, the hundred stories of the Empire State Building. I must have sounded like some demented schoolteacher. I wasn't saying anything I wanted to. The city I was describing seemed alien to me. Tom and I had never lived in such a place.

Tommy wanted to know if the building we were in was a skyscraper. I told him it wasn't; it just had a lot of floors, I said. I asked him if there were skyscrapers where he lived and he shook his head gravely, he didn't think so, and then a light came into his face and he said, "I want to see all the tallest skyscrapers in the world."

He had moved closer. One thin little shoulder brushed against my arm. I reached down and took his hand, and I had no right to do so, no right at all.

Caroline's nieces showed up with boxes of cake from some famous French bakery on Madison Avenue. They'd bought their aunt a bunch of small pink roses and picked up a Chutes and Ladders game for the children. The roses were put in water in a cut-glass bowl and a pink linen cloth was laid over a table and the children were taken into the bathroom to have their faces washed. I said I had to be leaving, and Caroline said, "But you *can't!* You have to stay for tea." She seemed to feel very strongly about it, as if it remained to be proven that everything had really been very civilized.

We all sat down around the table and she poured tea into white cups. A washed-out sun was sinking. I saw the sky turn violet over Brooklyn and there were long black barges on the river, and I wanted someone to draw the blinds.

I think the nieces were a little shocked that I'd turned out to be someone young; widows were supposed to be much older. They were pretty girls, implacably wholesome and optimistic. It was strange to think they'd known Tom much longer than I had. He'd taken them sailing when they were little and taught them to swim. "When we moved up here, we thought about calling him, but we felt funny about it," one of them said. They told me Caroline had always been their A Number One favorite relative. All afternoon they'd been thinking about her, and they'd finally decided she should definitely do something special with her hair before her old flame arrived to take her to dinner. They'd been meaning to bring this up ever since they'd met her at the airport. "You can just set it in rollers, you know, and try teasing it some on top."

She seemed a little embarrassed but pleased by all the attention. "I can't be bothered. I've no aptitude for anything like that."

"Oh, we'll do it for you. Please—it'll make all the difference."

"Don't you think she ought to try it?" one of them appealed to me.

"Absolutely," I said, though I had no real opinion. Then I found myself saying, "Sure, take a chance. After all, what's there to lose?" That was what Tom would have said. And if he'd been very drunk, he'd have put it, "Everyone dies. So why not?" But you could never say things like that at tea parties.

By the time I left, the children had been coaxed into the bedroom to watch "Superman" and sure enough, the nieces had gotten Caroline onto a kitchen chair and put a towel around her shoulders. Bottles of conditioner had appeared and a whole arsenal of pink foam rubber. They were working against time. The gentleman from the past was due at seven. I learned he was a stockbroker, conveniently divorced, a man she could certainly have married if she hadn't run off with Tom.

One of the nieces wet a comb and started drawing it through Caroline's hair and I saw a look come on her face of odd contentment.

I kept learning about being a widow in little, distant flashes. I saw that after a very long while, if you had no one to touch you, you might eventually become someone who went to beauty parlors and paid to have strangers do your hair. You'd pay for the sensation of it, the hands of another human being pouring warmth on you, gently smoothing, stroking. You'd close your eyes and lean back into those hands and your face might have exactly that look, I thought.

Life just goes on, you see, any old way it can. Even the dead can't interrupt its flow.

4

I called Caroline afterwards from the subway station at Twenty-third Street. That was the only other conversation she and I ever had. I said, "Caroline, I want to spend some time with Tommy tomorrow." I had to shout it over the phone to her because a train was going by on the lower level, and hearing a silence at the other end, I knew there wasn't a prayer she'd let me do it. I'd been sure she wouldn't all along.

She said, "My God, what's all that noise?"

I said, "I'm in the subway, Caroline," and she said something about the awfulness of subways and how could I bear to ride them? And then she said in a chilly, constrained voice, "Could you possibly pick him up by eleven? I'd like to go out to brunch."

That was all. No questions.

I've wondered ever since if she'd actually somehow been counting on me, wanting to leave me alone with Tommy from the start.

"This is sweet of you, Joanna," she said, as if I were doing her a favor.

She wasn't there when I picked him up.

There are white, glittery mornings in New York when the wind steals your breath and salt runs out of your eyes. It was one of those, not ideal at all for a tour. It worried me that Tommy had immediately taken off his cap—a striped, knitted thing with a tassel on it—he'd stuffed it into his pocket in the elevator. It was babyish, he'd declared, and I'd felt it would be wrong to press the issue.

I wanted him to have his dignity. In fact, I wanted to give him everything—enough to last a lifetime. I remember almost feeling that I could and at the same time thinking I didn't know at all what I was doing. I'd been only a kid myself the last time I'd been alone with one.

We had four hours. I told Tommy, "I'll take you wherever you want." That was a little overwhelming for him, he wasn't used to making choices. He asked for the Empire State Building, but couldn't come up with anything else. He'd become shy with me all over again. I kept thinking he knew as well as I did what the day was really for.

It took ages to find a cab. Finally one came into view, but an old woman tottered into the street under an enormous black fur coat and flagged it down. She called to us to get in with her. "You don't want to stand around with your little boy in an awful wind like this." A wind like this could knock you down, she told us. When I told her we'd be getting off at the Empire State Building, she said, "Well, that's very educational."

She chattered away at us. "Your little boy," she kept saying.

I didn't correct her. Tommy was kneeling beside me on the backseat, staring out the window.

"Is this young man your only child?" she asked.

I said, "I'm not his mother. He's my husband's child." To say it in the present tense made Tom alive for a moment.

Tommy had turned his head. His blue eyes penetrated mine. I felt he was telling me, Don't give away our secret.

The old woman pursed her lips and said disapprovingly, "Well, I thought you seemed young to have such a nice big boy."

I had theories about kids. Superlatives were supposed to impress them—what was biggest or best or had the most of something. Of course, any seven-year-old boy would have to go right to the top of the Empire State Building. "And now for the longest elevator ride in the world!" I said to Tommy when we got out of the cab on Fifth Avenue. I even made him pause on the sidewalk and directed his eyes upward to the bright needle of the radio tower.

He did what I told him, he threw his head back obediently. But now that we'd arrived, he showed no excitement.

"I don't want to," he said. "I don't want to go up." His voice had a blanched-out sound to it, and I should have paid more attention.

"Sure you do," I said. We'd crossed the street and I was starting for the entrance to the lobby to buy tickets.

Tommy pulled me back by my sleeve. "It's too high for me," he insisted.

I made a try at telling him we'd be safe, we weren't going to go outside, but he had such a pinched, stricken expression on his face that I stopped pretty quickly.

"Okay," I said. "Too many floors?"

He gave a forlorn little nod that made me feel terrible. I could see he thought he'd let me down.

I got him away from there, started walking him up Fifth Avenue, though I didn't know where we'd be going next. I hated the way everyone got damaged, even kids, that Tommy would see his tall building and have to think of falling. I remember wishing for crowds, wishing Christmas hadn't gone from all the shops. The mannequins were on uninteresting vacations now in Hawaii or Bermuda, languid and brown under nylon bougainvillea. The wind sent dirty bits of paper scudding along the gutters.

Near Rockefeller Center we found a small broadcasting exhibit where you could see yourself on TV. Sheepish-looking people would show up on a large screen and on a row of television sets in the front window. Tommy said it was neat.

We waited on line and we each took a turn getting on the platform, making blurry gray faces at the camera. Tommy asked me if he could do it alone. "This time I'll be getting on my spaceship and you watch me out there on all the TVs."

I went out through the revolving doors and stood at the window as the line moved slowly forward. When Tommy climbed up on the platform, he waved to me with great solemnity, his arms making wide intersecting arcs above his head. He stretched his mouth into "Good-bye . . . good-bye. . . ."

The day was running out when we got to the zoo. Most people were keeping their children home that day. Bored tigers paced and yawned in their cages; tropical birds on dead branches picked at their feathers or went fluttering at light bulbs. It all seemed shabbier than when I was a child or when I'd walked through there with Tom one day only last spring. Flotillas of babies were out in strollers then, and I'd looked at them with secret hunger, wanting to be pregnant, wanting to be filled with baby—not daring to say it, of course—telling myself, Someday, maybe next year. "Why the hell did we end up here?" Tom had asked me.

I bought Tommy a blue balloon, a box of Cracker Jacks, a plastic samurai sword. Tom would have bought him that sword, I thought. I kept trying to conjure him up, put him here with us.

The seals were enjoying themselves that day. They shot through their pond, flipping themselves over as they chased each other in their brown water; they splashed off their rocks like clowns. When it was cold like this, I told Tommy, and there was nobody much around, maybe they were at their best, because they felt so much more at home.

"I think nobody knows but us," Tommy whispered.

He leaned against me a little, and for a while we watched them, standing together by the black railing with its sign that warned you not to throw foreign objects in the water. "I'd never do anything dumb like that," Tommy said.

All of a sudden he stopped looking at the seals. A man was slowly approaching us, holding a tiny boy by the hand, holding him up, really. The child had just learned to walk and his legs, wadded into his red snowsuit, were still so uncertain that he seemed always on the verge of sitting down. Every few steps the man would have to stop and steady him, stooping because he was so tall.

When they reached the pond, the man swung the child up and sat him on his shoulders. "Seals," he announced to his son. He smiled at us. "That's quite a show they're putting on."

Tommy tried to keep the conversation going. "They're not afraid of us because we're quiet. Animals like it. When you're so quiet, they forget you're looking." He couldn't take his eyes off the two of them.

The man laughed and gave his son a bounce. "The seals like us," he said to his son in his announcer's voice. But there were other things to see and he moved on.

"Did my daddy ever think of me?" Tommy asked.

That was the question he'd been keeping inside him—the one he'd been saving for me, for anyone who could answer. Not Did my daddy love me?, you understand. Nothing as abstract, as adult, as that. What's love after all but a kind of thinking? We hold to each other in our thoughts, we can't let go.

I did the best I could. I said some things that seemed quite inadequate. "Tommy, he thought about you every day. Your dad always talked about you and your sister. I know about all the things you and he used to do."

"Tell me about the *things*!" Tommy demanded. "Tell me all the things!"

What I told him about was fishing, Tom taking him fishing when he was very little, a story I remembered about how he'd caught his first fish off a pier when he was only five. And his dad had rubbed it with black ink to make a print with it, as Japanese fishermen do for their sons, to mark the day for them. "And didn't you give it some kind of funny name?" I asked him.

Then suddenly I came up with the name myself. "Didn't you call him Mish the Fish?"

"Mish the Fish!" Tommy yelled jubilantly. "Mish the Fish!"

I remember something else Tommy said that day. I was bringing him back to Caroline and we were walking up the sidewalk to the nieces' apartment house, hurrying because it was late and the wind was blowing fiercely from the river. He slipped on a patch of ice and fell down hard.

I helped him to his feet and he rubbed his eyes on his sleeve. We looked at each other for a while and my eyes got as wet as his.

"I almost didn't cry," he said. "So I almost made it."

The Fall of Texas

Spring 1962

5

The world was supposed to end on a Saturday night in March of 1962. Some medieval astrologer had absolutely predicted it, and for a while the approaching cataclysm got a lot of play in the pages of the *Daily News*. You never believe such things, of course, but you don't entirely disbelieve them either. People made jokes or decided to have parties. The idea was to go out with a bang.

I was twenty-six. I don't think I've ever felt older. In three years I'd had fourteen lovers. The count may even have been higher. There were the serious ones who took months of your life and all the transitional ones in between when you were trying to recover. Those were the ones you tended to forget, and if you passed one on Second Avenue, you'd give a distant nod and walk on too fast for conversation. I once asked one of them, "Why are we here?" as we were taking off our clothes, and I remember his answer, though not his name. "If you don't know," he said, "I can't help you."

I was living then in a two-room walk-up on East Seventh Street above a linoleum store. My landlord was the linoleum king of the Lower East Side. Linoleum was that man's passion; he was careless about his real estate. I'd moved into his building with a saxophone player named Arnie Raff, who met a rich girl in East Hampton one weekend and moved in with her and never returned—even to pick up his records, which I kept in boxes for a while, then put back on their shelves and played until the music wore out all Arnie Raff associations and became mine. Finally he remembered where his records were, the great sides he'd had ever since he was a kid and had to steal his brother's draft card to get into Birdland to hear Charlie Parker. "Hey, why don't I just come on by and get them?" he said, and I said, "No, you can't ever walk in here again, Arnie. There's nothing you can take out of here." I'd always thought of myself as a gentle person and now here was a piece of someone's life and identity I wasn't giving back, as if I'd hardened without realizing it. It's better to be tough than sad, I thought.

I would have married Arnie Raff, although it seems incredible now. The illusion of kindness was in the chestnut color of his hair and eyes and the warm, Russian-looking moustache over his lips, which hid, as it turned out, a small mouth of real meanness. Arnie Raff was much more bourgeois than I was, which made me feel safe. He yelled at me about my cooking and sanded the floorboards of our apartment and stripped most of the plaster off a wall of brick, as if he meant to live there forever.

After he left, I became aware that the apartment had begun to disintegrate. Little pieces of it kept breaking off or falling down. There was a crack in the ceiling above the bed. I used to lie there and stare up at it. First it looked like the outline of a cloud drawn by a fine black pen, then the cloud began to resemble Texas.

Gradually Texas began to look three-dimensional. It made my various lovers nervous. "That ceiling's going to fall," they'd point out accusingly, as if by inviting them there I'd endangered them deliberately. I believed Texas would fall someday, but I didn't believe it would fall on me. So far something had held it up, and no one I personally knew had ever been crushed by a falling ceiling. I thought when it did fall, I'd be in Rome. A friend of mine had just found an apartment there with an extra bed for me, and at black times I'd remember to say "Rome" to myself as if I were really about to get an airplane ticket and go there. It was the most exotic of the ideas I had about turning myself into a luckier person.

I was home the night Texas came down. The man I was with was married and was always holding up his wrist so I could look at the luminous numbers on his watch in the dark and tell him what time it was. He was a very nearsighted poet who could see nothing without his glasses, and he'd put them on top of a bookcase that jutted out from the wall behind the bed. As I lay in his embrace, I heard a loud ticking as if he were wearing a grandfather clock. The ticking grew louder and faster and he said, "My God, what's that?" and we both sat up. Plaster rained down around us, falling on the pillow where our heads had been, crashing into the bookcase, severing his glasses neatly at the bridge but amazingly leaving the lenses intact. He put on both halves of the glasses and said in an awed voice, "I guess I'd better go. I've never had an experience like this. That was a close one, wasn't it?" I helped him find his clothes and we brushed off the white dust as best we could, and pinching his glasses together so they wouldn't fall off, he made his way home to his wife.

I turned on all the lights and sat up the rest of the night staring at the enormous hole where Texas had been, wondering what it meant to find yourself alive when you'd done nothing in particular to ensure your self-preservation.

That week a card arrived in the mail, silver ink on black paper:

Dance the end of the world away.
Make the apocalypse a night to remember.
R.S.V.P. Regrets only.

You had to pay attention to an invitation like that.

It made me feel hopeful, though by then I'd been to enough parties to know whom you could expect to see—Arnie Raff, for example, or the poet in his new glasses turning up with his wife, or the old painters who liked to dance with you ostentatiously, wheezing for breath while their women exchanged ironies near the wine table.

I took some of the rent money, since the landlord wasn't rushing to make repairs, and went to Klein's on Union Square and bought a dress. A slithery shift of something that looked like silk and was so much brighter than anything I had—all zigzags of purple, blue and green—that I didn't quite know who I was in it. I could imagine wearing it in Rome if the world didn't blow up.

I wasn't one of those who flourished at those famous downtown parties of the sixties. I knew what they were about, aside from abandon and ambition. You put yourself out there to be seen, to be taken up, to be judged in the flickering of an eye. I'd slip into watching and become, I thought, invisible. Then someone would accuse me of checking out and I'd make an effort for a while to simulate presence. Watchers stand alone, which is against the rules of parties. They're like pieces that have fallen out of a kaleidoscope when all the other pieces are being shaken up so new patterns can be formed. It's the kaleidoscopic nature of parties that makes them necessary or things might stay too much the same.

The art scene never stood still for long. There were always people coming and going, surfacing overnight, disappearing into thin air without ever sending a postcard to a friend. People gave up on New York and went to Paris, California, Mallorca, Mexico. Some started dropping out of life altogether, people as young as I was mostly, leaping off rooftops into space, diving from windows and landing so gracefully there was only a little blood around the corners of the mouth.

I remember the tall, beautiful, coffee-colored girl with strange green eyes who'd appeared out of nowhere that winter and was seen at all the artists' parties for a while, the wildest of all the dancers. Her name was Annabel, it was the season of Annabel. She had a little baby named Anton, whom she'd carry everywhere in her arms and put to sleep in back bedrooms among piles of coats and ride home with at dawn in taxis with various infatuated strangers. She moved into a railroad flat on St. Marks Place, where immediately there were surprising numbers of hangers-on, smoking joints and drinking wine while Annabel made big pots of rice and beans, West Texas style, on her three-burner stove as if she were everyone's mother. You could go there on Sundays for brunch and eat bacon and grits and dance to Ray Charles on the phonograph at eleven-thirty in the morning. "Ooh don't go," Annabel would say if she caught you heading for the door. "I hate an empty house worse than anything."

The story went around that Annabel was in hiding from her ex-husband, a remittance man from an old Boston family whom she'd met in Paris while she was modeling. But she never acted like someone who was hiding.

One week, though, at the beginning of the summer, people were asking, "Has anyone seen Annabel?" Nobody had. Annabel left her baby with a friend one afternoon and never came back for him. She told the friend she had an important date. She wore an armful of ivory bracelets and a little green silk shift and new gold sandals. She went rushing off to meet some deadbeat, who gave her an overdose of heroin. After several days an electrician found her body in a cellar on Avenue C.

I realized later that in an indirect way Annabel helped to change the direction of my life, though I might never have thought it if she hadn't died the way she did. We always smiled at each other, but I can't recall that we ever had a single conversation. I was never even sure she knew my name. It surprised me, in fact, to get one of those black-and-silver cards.

She sent out so many—to more people than could ever have fitted into her apartment. Even early in the evening there was a fancy uptown crowd no one knew piling out of taxis in the rain, pushing their way in past Annabel's friends drinking wine out of paper cups on the stairs. In her brief season, this was the big event.

Upstairs it looked like Halloween. Annabel had draped all the furniture in black sheets and lit candles. She wafted from room to room, very high and giggly, a lost child in a silver gown. People milled around in the dark in their wet coats, spilling beer on each other and saying, "Hi, I didn't know it was you," in hushed voices. Somewhere in the back the baby woke up and started crying. "What is this shit anyway?" someone said drunkenly and turned on the lights.

Too much had been expected, of course, so all the guests felt cheated. They also hated being caught with their imaginations down. Where was the gaiety, the wit, the inspired madness with which artists would greet the apocalypse? "Tonight Marcel Duchamp would not be impressed," one of the old painters commented loudly.

From then on it was like a party for someone going away whom no one gave a damn about anymore, not even Annabel, who drifted into a room with one of the guests and locked the door. Later people said she'd been trying to tell the rest of us she saw doom up ahead, but that night no one cared.

I didn't feel much like dancing, so I walked back to where the baby was. I wanted him to stop crying. His head banged against my shoulder when I picked him up. I kept repeating, "Shh, Mommy's coming soon," though I knew that wasn't the case, and patted his bottom, which was very wet. I felt utterly inept. Suddenly he was quiet, so I put him down in his crib. "Go to sleep, Anton," I said, pretending authority, but I heard him wail as soon as I walked back into the party.

People were doing the latest thing, something called the Twist, in which a man and woman rotated their hips in front of each other but never touched. I poured a glass of wine, looked around the room and thought very calmly, There is no one.

A man came up from the street. I noticed him because he wasn't wearing a coat, just a heavy gray sweater and a green scarf around his neck, and I remember thinking he must be cold. He had thick brown hair wet from the rain and a face that had been used a lot, fierce eyes set deep in smashed bone, the right one angled down sharply. He was a very good-looking man, so I decided he would be dangerous, spoiled rotten by women no doubt. For a while he stood near the door at the edge of things, like a player waiting his turn in a game, sizing up his next move. Now and then he'd tighten his lips, pressing them together as if against some oblique thought he couldn't voice to anyone. He caught me staring, so I stepped back a little behind a dancing couple. When I looked again, the party had swallowed him up.

A little later he was standing right in front of me. He took me in, I don't know how else to say it. My tremendous uncertainty, my habit of watching, my ridiculously bright dress. It was as if he could read my bones, it wasn't that he wanted anything. "Why do you hang back?" he said and walked away.

I stood amazed where he left me, wanting to run after him and find out who he was. But his fierceness really scared me. I didn't want him telling me I'd made a mistake, that he'd said all he was ever going to say to me in one question I couldn't even answer, which suddenly seemed the entire painful puzzle of my life.

He was one of those people who'd probably never surface again who kept wandering in and out. He'd disappeared by the time I got brave enough to look for him.

To tell the truth, I wasn't sorry. I thought of his blue eyes and his handsomeness and how the night might have gone.

Down on St. Marks Place in the cold darkness the world was still intact, and I carried his question into the rain.

6

There was a dairy restaurant in those days on Second Avenue where you could sit all night under big yellow globes of light with baskets of fresh rolls and saucers of butter in front of you until the dark turned pale and you could go home. It had the world's gruffest waiters but they understood their customers. They'd forget about you for hours if that was what you wanted. You always knew nothing bad could ever happen to you in Rappaport's.

I went there after Annabel's party. I sat down at one of the long empty tables up front and ordered coffee. There were braids of bread in the window and cheesecakes under a fluorescent light that turned them blue. The wet glass was like a black pool. I could see my transparent self in it marooned behind all the baked goods and occasional ghosts passing through me on the other side, swimming by under umbrellas or with Sunday newspapers above their heads.

I sat there an hour or so watching the rain fall on the avenue. And when I think about it now, it seems that I was waiting, that I even knew who one of the ghosts would be, as if I were somehow dreaming my own life.

I saw the man from the party. He was walking downtown very slowly, still with no coat on, holding up his face like a blind man daring the rain to fall on him. The lights from Rappaport's took him by surprise. He came up to the window and leaned against the wet glass. I put down my coffee cup, almost afraid to breathe.

He didn't see me sitting there. He stared at the cakes, the pasted-up menu, the clock on the rear wall of the restaurant, before he moved on.

That was the week the plasterers came early one morning. They rang my bell, getting me out of bed, two seventy-year-old Ukrainians in stiff white overalls like bakers, carrying buckets and brooms and a ladder. They wanted to know if my mother was home, having the innocent misconception that all young unmarried women in apartments were daughters. I tried to explain that *I* was my mother. They seemed puzzled, but they came in. They whacked at the ceiling with their brooms and the rest of it crumbled like icing. By the end of the day they'd made it solid as a rock. You could hardly see a fault line.

I walked over to the infamous Cedar Bar after they'd gone. The poet, who'd been making himself scarce, would perhaps be there. I thought I'd tell him I had a new ceiling in a lighthearted manner, and thus lure him—or discover he was no longer lurable. The poet and I had never actually *said* we were having an affair, or even that we had some fondness for each other. We came at such matters obliquely. Often he brought along his tape recorder so that we could appreciate his voice for an hour or so giving his latest reading. "You don't mind," he'd say, switching the thing on. How could you complain about poetry? He was small and jaunty like a bright little warbler, and I think he flew around and visited others with his tape recorder.

He was standing with some strangers at the bar when I came in through the swinging doors—two gloomy, serious men with beards who were there with their wives or girl friends. I noticed he had his tape recorder with him. He saw me right away and I smiled at him and walked forward and paused for a moment, but then he decided he hadn't seen me after all. He made a little quarter turn and kept on talking, and I walked on and sat as far away as I could. I'd wait a bit, then leave, I thought. I'd walk past him and call out good-bye in a loud, arresting voice. I ordered a beer and sat without drinking it, picking at the label on the bottle.

A man came from behind me and put a glass and some cigarettes down on the bar. His hand took a position very close to mine. I remember staring angrily at the ring he wore, a ring of heavy, carved Mexican silver with a square of dull red stone.

"Can I buy you a drink?"

"I already have one."

"You don't seem to like what you have."

"It'll do," I said. I meant to sound completely discouraging. But then I looked up at him for the first time, and it was the man from the party. "Oh, I remember you," I said in embarrassment.

"Likewise," he said, and stared at me the way he had that other time. "Do you come here a lot?" he asked me.

I said, "Well . . . in certain periods," though the period when I hadn't was at least a year ago.

I had loosened up the label on the beer bottle considerably, and now I peeled off a big strip of it. The man from the party put his hand on the bottle and moved it away.

"Wine would taste better—if you change your mind."

I said, "All right. I guess I've changed it." I had a strange thought then: *This is the beginning*. I thought that in a while I'd walk out of there with him, that years would go by, just as I'd known he'd walk down Second Avenue in the rain.

He asked me to tell him my name, then he told me his. Tom Murphy.

"An easy one," I said.

He told me right away he wasn't *entirely* Irish; there was Norwegian blood on his father's side. He had his father's name, and he'd given his son that name as well.

At that point I felt deflated. My psychic abilities had proven unreliable. So he was married, of course. So that was that. I asked him how old his little boy was just to make conversation.

It took him time to answer. Somehow the question burdened him. "He's only five." Then he motioned to the bartender and I got my wine.

I found out that he was a painter, that he'd just come back to New York after a long absence. He'd spent a lot of time in Mexico City; the last five years he'd lived in Florida—Palm Beach. He'd looked up a friend from the old days at the Art Students League. That's how he'd heard about Annabel's party and the Cedar. He didn't mention his kid again or say *we,* as married men did. He drank one beer after another very quickly, gulping each one down like someone enormously thirsty. He had a way of wiping his mouth fast on the back of his wrist the way a boy would, and sometimes, when he did that, I'd want to put my hand against his lips.

I told him a lie I momentarily believed—that I'd be leaving New York very soon. I'd never been to Europe or anywhere much, and it was time. A girl friend of mine had a fabulous apartment in Rome—I remember how suddenly it became "fabulous." She was an actress like me, and we were going to get work in Italian movies as extras because she had connections.

"So you won't be here very long," he said.

"I hope not. Just a month or so."

"You can't count on the movies," he said.

"I never count on anything."

"I can tell that," he said, not smiling the way he should have.

And I said, "Really. How?"

The hand with the Mexican ring came down over mine. I could feel the cool wood of the bar flat against my palm, and that shock of warmth over my fingers. Our hands just remained there like that, quite still, as if they'd been welded together, and I don't think we talked for a while.

Meanwhile I'd naturally forgotten all about the poet. His friends evidently left and then he remembered that he knew me rather well. Suddenly he appeared on the other side of me, saying, "Come and have a drink. I'll get a table."

He looked down at the bar and saw the hands. It was a somewhat confusing moment. I said, "Carl, a gentleman has bought me a drink," which I thought had a certain elegance of cadence.

"Catch you later then," he said, and I felt the little invisible threads between us break and he just dropped away from my life. We often ran into each other after that, but it was over. Many things ended that night—a whole period, a way of living I never really went back to.

I left the Cedar with Tom Murphy and we walked all over the Village and all the way down to Chinatown. He told me he'd been wandering around like that ever since he got back to New York, couldn't seem to get enough of it. We looked at ducks hanging upside down in windows on Mott Street and there was the smell of gunpowder in the air; we were supposed to be deciding on a restaurant. We walked back uptown again to an Italian bar on Houston Street, a place called Googie's where you sat on little barrels and the customers were hoods, not artists. "You never got any dinner," he said, though I told him I didn't want any, actually.

He ordered me a hamburger deluxe with French fries. "I have to take care of you now," he said. "When you're over there in Rome, you'll remember the inconsiderate guy who made you walk your feet off."

My trip seemed very real to him—and by this time, to me as well. He was going to look at my apartment, and if it was big enough for him to paint in, maybe he'd take it over while I was gone and I could leave my stuff there. Finally, there in the bar, we talked about being two ships that passed in the night. I even found myself making a fairly fancy statement that maybe those relationships were the most perfect—just that pure first excitement and you said good-bye before things went sour.

He asked me how long I'd had that belief, and I said, "Just for the last ten minutes."

He said, "This is too fast for you, isn't it? We can't slow it down, though."

I never did make it to Rome.

My son Nicky passed through there last summer. His wallet was stolen on the Spanish Steps, and he spent a couple of days sitting up in cafés, walking the streets hungry, waiting for me to wire him some money. It wasn't too bad, he said. Actually it was interesting—being down to nothing in a foreign country.

You would approve of that attitude. And when I think of Rome, I think of you there too at Nicky's age, but that was during the war and so you seem much older. It's as if you never had any adolescence at all. You came into Rome with the troops and everyone was starving and you took everything out of your pockets and gave it away to little kids and drank wine with beggars in the ruins of the Colosseum in the moonlight. You told me you'd been on a minesweeper, and I said, that first night we talked, "But how did a sailor get to Rome?" "Hitched a ride on a tank," you said, as if it were the most natural thing in the world.

I keep sorting through the leftover shards, stories with missing pieces that can never be filled in. The route you took from Anzio to Rome and what happened to you along the way—I knew it for one evening but didn't listen nearly closely enough. It all got drowned in the onrush of love. We were going down the waterfall, and I didn't eat much of the hamburger either. *We can't slow it down,* you said. And there it was—the declaration. But now you seem to have been saying something else—how little time there was going to be.

7

I woke up with you the next morning, and I thought, Found. I remember it, *Found*—as if a string had been plucked in the midst of great silence. I heard the note, then the overtones washed over us, not dying but continuing out there in space. I've never heard it that way again with anyone, though God knows I've listened for it. The sun was in the window and there was an odd, white film over everything, a fine dust, you could see our footprints in it. I lay there astonished with your arms around me.

And later we were having breakfast at the kitchen table. I'd somehow made eggs and we were drinking coffee as if we'd been together a million ordinary mornings. Out of the blue you said, "Look, I can't marry you yet. But I'm going to marry you."

That seemed so wildly extravagant that I trusted it. I'd never met anyone so rashly serious, although in the circles I moved in, speed was of the essence, an entire way of being. Men and women came together so quickly they could be said to have collided the way colors collided on canvases, running into each other, merging. Lucky and unlucky convergences.

Then you told me what I'd guessed. You were still married. You'd left a wife in Florida, a woman you'd stopped loving, Caroline. Who'd been with you in Mexico City in a tiny pink house, where you used to paint on the roof under an awning you'd rigged up and the yard was full of bedsprings and the landlord's chickens and an avocado tree. You said someday you'd go back to Mexico because you'd been happy there, though there'd been times you and Caroline were so broke you'd actually lived on avocados.

I heard other things. The story of a car you'd left behind in Palm Beach—an old, white, custom-made MG. You'd traded a large painting for it—you'd never have a car that great again. "I was dying down there in the palms," you said. You'd kept having accidents, so you knew how it would happen—your death in the MG, skidding off the road one night with too much booze in you and the gas pedal all the way down. "But I never drove like that with the kids," you told me. "I always looked out for my little babies."

All this I took in—the pieces of your particular legend, the circumstances that had miraculously brought you to me, which I was going to learn by heart.

I had once even dared myself, *End it,* so I thought I knew all about that, too. It was a game I'd played the night I learned Arnie Raff had left me—Chianti and aspirin, I wasn't a driver. I lay down on my bed and started swallowing the little tablets, six or seven of them. But suddenly I realized, I don't mean this, and it seemed quite humiliating to want to die over Arnie Raff.

But I didn't tell you about any of this. I didn't say a word about Arnie, the original occupant of the apartment. My real history had after all begun that moment you spoke to me at Annabel's party. I asked you, did you happen to remember walking past a place called Rappaport's on Saturday night?

You were so surprised. "How do you know that?"

"I was in there. I saw you. Where were you going?"

You said, "I was looking for *you*, kiddo."

There was a roll of canvas that had been left downtown and a suitcase and finally it seemed appropriate to get them. By that time it was getting dark outside again. We walked down to Duane Street along Broadway. I remember us radiating light at each other, passing all the decaying iron-columned buildings, the blue-lit upstairs factories where Puerto Rican women sat behind whirring spindles of thread.

Tom's friend who had the canvas and the suitcase lived in a studio behind a rag shop that was going out of business. We had to ring his phone twice from the street, so he'd know he wasn't being raided by building inspectors. He opened the door to let us in. He was a small wiry man with a bristling, flaming red moustache. I'd seen him around the Cedar. A long white scar ran straight from his forehead to a bald spot on top of his head. Tom said very abruptly, "This is Joanna. We're going to be living together from now on." It was the first time I heard it as a fact to be communicated to outsiders.

Since Tom had just been going uptown for a beer the last time Leon Renfro had seen him, Leon didn't know what to think. He took off his glasses and wiped them and said, "Well. . . ." Then he slapped Tom on the shoulder. "Didn't I tell you you'd luck out?"

"There's all kinds of luck!" Tom said, and I saw him turn fierce in an instant. I think he wanted Leon to know right away that the luck was love.

"Sure, sure," Leon said. "Why not?" But he still must have

taken a pragmatic view of the situation. Most people would have, I guess.

He did insist on toasting us, though. He poured the remains of some vodka into a paper cup, and we each took a sip from it as Tom collected his things.

Leon asked me what kind of place I had and where it was and if I had a shower. "You wouldn't mind if I came around sometime to use it? I always bring my own soap and towel."

I admired people like Leon who had stratagems for everything, who even seemed to relish poverty because it made things hard, kept them alert to possibilities. What I hated about being poor was that it took up so much time, you always had to think about it. If you needed practical advice, Leon was definitely the person to go to. He knew how to vacuum electric meters to make them run backwards. He kept his potbelly stove going with big wooden crates he dragged in from the street. He could tell you what days of the week mattresses got thrown out in classy neighborhoods or where the crashable parties were in the penthouses of collectors. Leon got real enjoyment out of the rich but was down on the bourgeoisie. When he wanted to step out, he'd put on his tuxedo from the Goodwill and take a girl friend uptown to the Hotel Pierre or the Plaza. They'd crash some big wedding reception, where they'd hurriedly consume dozens of canapés, passing themselves off as distant relatives.

According to Leon, it was only in America that an artist could live the way he did. You couldn't do it in Paris, where things were much closer to the bone. The stingy French never threw out anything. "You could starve in Paris," he said indignantly. "America's the greatest place for The Artist." "The Artist," he kept saying, as if he were an expert conducting objective research on the subject.

Leon was an ex-marine. The scar on his head was a war wound. Tom had met him at the Art Students League when they were both young guys on the GI Bill. For eight months they'd shared a horrible room with a hot plate in a boardinghouse full of drunks and Jehovah's Witnesses in Brooklyn. In Reginald Marsh's class, they did hundreds of sketches of Serena the model, an elderly Follies girl. Once they even got Marsh to have a beer with them. Tom had been drawing all his life, every time his fingers found a pencil, but he'd only started painting after the war. Even so, he was already thinking big, thinking about Mexico, talking about doing murals like Rivera. Leon wanted to paint apples like Cézanne. On the dresser in their room he kept A&P bags filled with apples that turned rotten before he could render them and attracted mice.

Leon went on to abstract expressionism years before Tom, but never got anywhere with it. Now he was working with chicken wire. So far he alone was on to it. It made a grid, but it was an expressionist grid, and it was also a very cheap material. He had a couple of enormous rolls of it in his studio. He was taking all his old canvases that hadn't sold and painting them over with deck paint—battleship gray. Pieces of grid were going on top of that. And just lately—one day when his sleeve had caught in the wire—he'd had the inspiration to use rag, bits of rag caught like his sleeve, and maybe thread or even yarn.

He led me around the studio, turning on lights so I could look at all his new work on the walls. I saw a lot of gray paint and chicken wire. It all sort of hung there mute, not even ugly in a way that might shock someone into staring. "This is just a preview," he said. "The rags go on next week. You see how they'll work, don't you, what they'll do to the space." I said, Yes, I thought I saw.

Leon turned off the lights and scrutinized me. "Hey, you should talk more. How'll I get to know your thoughts? So what do you think?"

I said, "Leon, they depressed me."

"Exactly!" he cried excitedly. "Of course they did!"

And they had, they'd brought me down, invaded my happiness, reminded me how easily people's lives got wasted. Even when I was young I knew that life could be destroyed by art, though it was worth it, of course.

"When the new wave comes," Leon said, "I'm gonna be up there on the crest."

Tom looked up from the corner of the studio where he was stuffing things into his suitcase. "Fuck the new wave! Throw the art magazines in the garbage!"

"Now Tom," Leon said patiently, "you don't understand the situation. You haven't been *here*."

"Right, I've just been painting fifteen years. Out in the sticks. Don't forget that!"

"Abstract expressionism is through, *finito*. You could be Michelangelo and you couldn't get a gallery."

"I paint what I paint. I'm not going to be one of the fish lying on the beach, panting through my gills for the collectors."

"This is a good man, but an impossible man," Leon said to me.

"Van Gogh was impossible! Pollock was impossible!" Tom yelled.

"The handwriting is on the walls of the museums, man!" Leon shouted back at him in exasperation. It was the title of an article by a new upstart critic that had made all the abstract expressionists furious. It said there was no such thing as an old revolution. I'd read it myself over someone's shoulder in the Cedar. *"The Handwriting Is on the Walls of the Museums."*

Tom yelled that the critics could go on practicing their handwriting as well as their typing. It was all right with him as long as they didn't take up the brush.

Then they both started laughing and Tom said it was just like the old days, they still liked to shout at each other, they could still get excited enough to fight. "Yeah," Leon said gloomily. "But now it's about survival."

"It always was," Tom said.

Afterwards, out on the street, when Tom and I were waiting for a taxi with all his stuff, he said suddenly, "There's only one way to think about all this art critical shit."

I said, "Which way is that?"

He pulled me close to him and put his mouth against my ear. "Red, white and black. Red, white and black."

Next morning you opened the suitcase out on the bed. It was the suitcase of someone who had packed too fast, full of light-colored clothes, not really right for the last days of winter. There was a brown leather cigarette case with the initials T.M. and a knife you'd bought in Mexico City that you used for fishing. "This knife will last forever," you said and showed me the places on the handle where the black stain had worn away. You'd thrown in your staple gun too and a big expensive brush that had never been used.

It alarmed me, that suitcase. What wasn't in it. It seemed that someone who could take so little with him could walk away from anywhere very fast.

I said, "You're going to need an overcoat."

You said, "It'll get warmer."

You picked up the brush and showed how smoothly the bristles flexed against the back of your hand. "Look how they bend. That's what a good brush does."

8

No matter where we shoved the furniture, my place was too small to paint in. We moved the bed anyhow and made a wall, clear all the way to the window. "You could do a really big canvas there," I said. "You could roll it up when it's finished and start another."

"Yeah," he said, "I could always do that—roll 'em up like a rug. We'd be painted out of here in a month. Maybe I'll get me an easel and do *nice* little paintings. That's about what you could do in this place."

"Would that be so bad for a while?"

He laughed and shook his head. "Oh kiddo, you don't know what I do. You haven't seen anything. Maybe you won't even like it."

"Of course I'm going to like it."

He stared at me thoughtfully for a moment. "Yeah, maybe

you will. Because the work is me. You could even write me off—and there'd still be the work."

"How could I write you off? What are you talking about?"

I don't remember what he answered.

Those early days were best, when we still lived on Seventh Street. I hardly remember anything but happiness. It's funny to think how we rushed to get through them, as if they didn't quite count, as if our real life wouldn't begin till we'd moved, found a studio, brought all Tom's paintings up from Florida in a truck, *then* we'd be happy. The future was like that wall we'd cleared, which we'd stare at from bed when our eyes opened, blank and not blank, nothing there but morning rippling across it or stripes of shadow. Soon we'd wake up somewhere else, see a different wall.

Leon said we should try to get a place on the Bowery. The Bowery was our best bet. Who would want to live there but an artist? We searched for the lucky sign everywhere we walked—Loft for Rent on some gray upstairs window, maybe *our* loft. We'd write down the addresses of vacancies, whitening their walls in our minds, filling them with paintings, talking about how great the dusty old glass would look after it was scrubbed down with newspapers—that was the best way to clean windows, Tom said. We'd walk east or west, turning corners at random, ending up in odd neighborhoods without possibilities—old red brick projects down by the river, a market on Ludlow Street with bins of used eyeglasses, forsaken parks where winos lay out on benches under dusty sycamores. I'd suddenly feel my arm being gripped and hear Tom say, very quietly, "You didn't see that—but you don't have to," and I'd know he was steering us out of the way of something. He told me he'd learned to walk like that when he was a kid, to see everything. He said now that he was in New York, all his old alertness was coming back to him.

We didn't have nearly enough money to move. Tom had just

started looking for work. I knew you had to buy large, expensive things for a loft—stoves, refrigerators, water heaters. How could we afford them? I had my Rome fund—three hundred dollars—and my various part-time typing jobs. Tom hocked his watch and his silver ring and got fifty-nine dollars. "Well, that's it," he said, putting all the bills on the table. He was proud he'd come away from Florida with so little, left everything behind for his kids, all the money from his last show, where he'd sold a painting for seven hundred dollars. He said, "It'll happen again, you know, only better because it'll happen in New York." It was always New York that made meaning.

Meanwhile he sometimes felt his life had been rolled back. He said it was like being in Mexico City after the GI Bill ran out and he'd no longer had pesos in his pockets. Still, back then he'd gotten by for a couple of years doing little water colors of churches and marketplaces; he'd sign them with a Spanish name and take them to a shop that sold them to American tourists. Caroline gave lessons in ballroom dancing at a girls' school. Then the tourist shop burned down and that was the beginning of the end. The end of Mexico, the end of the good times in the marriage. Caroline was pregnant with Tommy—she was so anemic the doctor told her she'd probably lose the baby. He borrowed money from everyone they knew and put her on a plane, sent her back to her family in Florida. For six years she hadn't spoken or written to her father. Tom had remained behind in the empty pink house, waiting for her to come back to him with the kid, wondering how they'd all survive.

Then a letter came from Caroline telling him they'd had a son. Mexico was just too hard, she wrote. "It isn't a life that makes sense for me with a baby. It doesn't even make sense for you anymore, and you know it." "And I did know it," he said, "but Palm Beach was no answer." Caroline's father adored his grandson; he'd finally even forgiven her for running off to New York and Mexico and marrying an artist. He'd offered to pay for everything, to buy them a beautiful old house—there was a room on the second floor that had windows on three sides, perfect for a studio.

Tom knew it was the wrong move, but he joined her. He figured he owed his kid a good start in life—a childhood better than the one he'd had. He'd packed up all the paintings he'd done—the early figurative stuff influenced by Marsh and Rivera and the work he'd done since he'd broken away, all the abstractions. They owned so little there was hardly anything else to take. "I think I had two pairs of socks, but who needed socks?"

He used to tell me it was Mexico that taught him black, white and red. "Mexico taught me that."

Tom said Caroline's father was a man who always got what he wanted. None of his children ever got away from him. Caroline had been the only one who'd tried. "The old man crushed them with his money." I couldn't imagine what it would be like to be crushed by money. Caroline's father had bought half a county of worthless swampland in southern Florida, sold it all off acre by acre, got taken to court by some investors and paid off the judge. To a man like that, seven hundred dollars for a painting was laughable, it was nothing.

Harry Theodore Vincent. Harry T., you called him. He'd wanted to set you up in the construction business. Then he'd offered to buy you a partnership in an architectural firm, something more artistic. He was going to confer on you a future of designing lobbies for hotels. I heard his voice once on the phone, rough and not so aristocratic—"Listen, Miss Whoeveryouare. I'd like to speak to my daughter's husband."

You made me think of him in sinister pastels. A large, pink-skinned man with pure white hair who always carried a fresh, green five-hundred-dollar bill folded up small in his watch pocket—"For life's little emergencies, Tommy." Harry T. was from Alabama, from some tobacco farm, as I recall it—but he wore his pale blue suits like a senator, had them custom-made by Tripler's in New York. He liked to go into restaurants and order oysters, and when the oysters came, he'd put on his pink-rimmed glasses and bring the plate almost up to his eyeballs while his wife and daughters watched breathlessly. "They all right, Mr. Vincent?" the waiter would ask. "They don't look fresh to me," Harry T. would be apt to say sternly and send them back.

"I never eat oysters," you told me.

Strawberries—that was the other thing you would never eat because of years of Sunday dinners at Harry T.'s. When strawberries were in season, there was always shortcake, Harry T.'s boyhood favorite, and Harry T. would make a production of smacking his lips over the berries, and you'd see the sweet red juice on his lips and ask the maid to bring you another drink. "Watch out for that booze, boy," Harry T. would say, his eyes twinkling. He'd made his first killing back in the twenties running rum from the Bahamas. He was a man who knew a thing or two about thirst.

You told him once you thought your father might have been involved in New York in that line of work. He'd put his arm around you—"You and me, Tom, we're both upstarts." And you'd had tears in your eyes. You were taken in, at that moment, totally. Family was what you always craved and never got.

I'd leave you each Sunday and take the F train to Forest Hills. I had sad little Sunday dinners of my own. I'd walk along Queens Boulevard from the station and when I could afford it, I'd buy my mother lilacs from Spyros the Greek because she was crazy about flowers but never bought them for herself unless company was coming and company never came. Even when my father was alive, she'd never had people over.

When I was little I'd picked bouquets for her—dandelions and clover—she'd never told me they were weeds. Everything I did then was wonderful. If I wrote a patriotic poem about the war effort, I was going to be another Emma Lazarus. If I whirled on the red oriental rug to the music from the radio, I was going to be Pavlova. Daddy's heart kept him home from the war—he'd tiptoe in and take a picture. My aunts kept scrapbooks of my achievements. They typed up my clever sayings and showed them to their friends. It was a cult of The Child, and if I'd died at the age of twelve, it never would have ended.

My mother felt my wonderfulness should be offered to the world. So Daddy took lots of pictures of me in his store in front of the same velvet curtains where little boys sat for blue-suit bar-mitzvah portraits or war brides corsaged with gardenias posed with their soldier grooms. I'd lean upon an imitation alabaster column and Daddy would bring a braid of hair forward and brush at my bangs and arrange my hand so that it supported my cheek. "Look wistful," he'd say. Or "Look as if someone just gave you a wonderful present." He'd fuss with his lights and I'd work on my wistfulness or my joy, telling myself, Don't blink, don't blink, so I wouldn't at the wrong moment. I knew the whole future of the family depended on getting the right shots—on me, though I couldn't have said why.

Daddy made shiny prints of me in four different poses, and Ma and I began taking the subway to Forty-second Street and Broadway all the time and sitting around in office after office because show business mostly had to do with sitting around, like waiting to see the doctor. Now and then you'd finally get a minute with a jaded producer—some old man in a striped suit. "Too tall . . . too short . . . too young . . . too old," the producers used to tell us, hardly looking.

"Not Swedish enough, sweetheart."

"What do you mean, not Swedish enough?" my mother

demanded indignantly, mortifying me by holding up one of my blond braids.

"I don't see Swedish. Okay?"

"Ma, let's go!" I whispered.

But Ma had iron in her that day. The part called for a blond eight-year-old girl. Well, her daughter was blond and eight, she said—shocking me because I was really nine. My mother said Fair was fair. That was how little she knew about show business. She said nothing would make her walk out of there until the man had seen for himself what a beautiful talent I had. And she straightened the red Woolworth's bows at the ends of my braids and said, "Don't let anyone scare you. Show him what you can do."

Someone finally put a script in my hands, all typed up on onionskin. It was about a Minnesota farm family whose entire wheat crop had been eaten by locusts and I had to be a little girl dying of scarlet fever in fifteen lines. The first words came out with a squeak, but then my mother's will got into me, and I read, hardly hearing what I was reading. Maybe it was fear that carried me out of myself, fear of revealing myself as just a nine-year-old little Jewish girl and not being as wonderful as my mother said. I was all mixed up about the lies you had to tell the men in offices, whether such lies counted as real ones or not. I never knew whether it was me who'd landed that part or Ma.

I met a great actress once, and I asked her, "Did you always know you could do it?" And she said, "I just knew I could execute an intention." But all the years I was acting or making the rounds trying to get parts, I never had that feeling, not even the eighteen months I played that little Swedish Minnesota girl on Broadway. It was the lights I liked that bathed you and got inside you somehow, and the stage was a clearing in the forest at night and the audience, dark, rustling like trees. And I liked staying up long past my bedtime and eating dinners in the Automat with all my matinee makeup on and the Great White Way that wasn't white but brown because of the war and the theaters jammed with young servicemen on furlough who'd been given free seats, so even acting was patriotic. I used to tell my mother I was going to marry a sailor.

You and I once figured out that at least a night or two you were on furlough somewhere in those crowds around Times Square. You'd have been looking for a girl, a grown-up girl of course, not one in pigtails. We used to speculate on the chances we'd actually walked right by each other. "I'd have noticed *you*, babe," you said. You said there should have been a voice that said, "Stop right here," so we could have promised to wait for each other another seventeen years.

I think I might have been ready even then for a promise like that. It was me my mom and dad both seemed crazy about instead of each other. Maybe that made me lonely from the start.

Daddy always rinsed out his own coffee cup in the sink and came and went in our house like a shadow. He'd smoke one cigarette, put the ashes quickly in the garbage, then he'd be gone leaving no traces. He wasn't supposed to smoke at all because of his heart. He spent half his life in his darkroom and his hands were always peeling from the chemicals. I loved to run downstairs to his store. I'd say, "Let me see the negatives, Daddy." Because it seemed quite wonderful to me that dark could be light and light could be dark, as if a world of night existed where everything was in reverse.

Daddy could turn old brown-and-white photos of dead people into pale, almost flesh-toned ones by tinting them with a fine brush, but he never let me watch him do that because it made him too nervous. Every now and then he'd put a Closed sign on his door and disappear for most of an afternoon, and if we'd ask him where he'd been, he'd say, irritatedly, "Just experimenting, just experimenting." Once he called my mother and me downstairs to the store and showed us his latest "experiments"—photos of the most ordinary things, the Italian vegetable stand around the corner, old ladies gabbing on a stoop, a boarded-up doorway with a colored boy leaning against it. "But Jules, these are so *ugly!*" my mother exclaimed.

My mother loved beauty, she wanted to be around it all the time. That was why she'd set her heart on having me on the stage, so we could always have beauty together. She'd never been able to find it on Queens Boulevard. She never spoke against my father, she just said, "I hope you never throw yourself away on anyone." So naturally, later, I threw myself away as much as I could and never quite got myself back.

You used to tell me I blamed my mother too much. Other kids didn't have mothers who wanted the best for them. "Look at me," you'd say. "You could have had someone like Marie."

I'd say, "Okay. But my mother went to extremes." I just couldn't let go of the argument.

"So the theater—all of that—it never should have happened?"

"I *loved* the theater. But it was wrong. It wasn't the best start."

Then you'd ask me, "What would have been right? Who's got the answer to that one?"

"You know where I was when I first knew I was going to paint?"

I said, "Where?"

"Right here. Right here on the Bowery."

"On this street?" It was one of those days we were searching for lofts. We'd gotten down as far as Rivington.

Tom took a look around, then said, "Yeah. It could have been. That's what I'm trying to figure out. Without the el, it's all different."

"What were you doing on the Bowery by yourself?"

"I had important business. I was looking for something that belonged to me. You think you were the only little kid with business? I used to get down here from the Bronx on the el, sneak under the turnstiles. I never had the nickel."

He asked me if I remembered how the el had cast a great shadow all along its route, how the tracks had been held up in some places by walls of blackened stones and how the trains had run at exactly the level of the third stories of houses, so you'd find yourself looking into hundreds of rooms.

He used to keep running away on the el, usually to his grandmother. She'd let him stay with her until the truant officers came around uptown and bothered Marie. His grandmother had a room on Forty-seventh Street where even the bed was covered with feathers and veils that she sewed on hats for people. She had a huge orange cat, Bobbie, that slept all the time on the windowsill. Sometimes she'd stay drunk for days and forget to buy food and he'd even have to help her get out of her corset. "She and I just took care of each other," he said. One time she told some rich woman she made hats and that she had her grandson with her, and the woman had given her a little child's ring with a bird carved into it. "It was supposed to be the Bluebird of Happiness," he said, "and I damn near believed it was."

Marie said the ring was real silver and took it away to keep for him. She said he'd only lose it. He kept asking for it back, and finally she told him she'd hocked it for two dollars. She wouldn't tell him where the pawnshop was, but he'd seen lots of them under the el along the Bowery. He made up his mind to find that ring and steal it back, even if he went to jail.

For weeks he went down there, searching the windows of the pawnshops, staring through the iron gratings at watches and knives and musical instruments. "Finally I knew," he said. "I wasn't going to see that little bluebird ring. I never believed there was such a thing as Never before that. I stood on a corner and I looked over at the el—the dark, awful stones of the el. That's what Never looked like to me.

"I think it was September," he said, "and very, very late in the afternoon, and suddenly the stones changed, they turned red as if they were burning deep inside, and light was falling—falling through the tracks—down onto the street in shafts. The el wasn't beautiful, but it was beautiful. I saw something that day," he said. "You understand?"

"I have to buy me some paint, kiddo," he told me one morning, looking embarrassed. I lent him fifteen dollars. "As soon as I get my hands on some dough, you're getting it back."

I had to go to a job that day. When I came home, there was canvas tacked to the wall opposite the bed and he was priming it with gesso. Now and then he'd step aside and give it that quick, sizing-up stare of his as if something that wasn't on there yet had flashed out at him. He seemed like a dancer, so quick and light on his feet with the can of gesso in the crook of his arm and the big brush in his hand that he'd brought all the way from Florida. I couldn't take my eyes off him. I forgot to start dinner or put the groceries away. The truth was, the sight was almost painful because it reminded me I hadn't found my own work yet. I still hadn't entirely given up on the theater.

The gesso had to dry overnight, he said.

He got up so early the next morning, I was still half asleep. I heard the shade go up, then knew he was moving in and out of the room. He came over to the bed and touched my hair. He said, "Stay there, kiddo."

The paint hit the canvas with a sound like rain.

9

In those days, I was a crackerjack typist—one hundred w.p.m. I typed envelopes, theses, just about everything. I'd stick cards up all over the Village: *Speed-of-light satisfaction. No job too big or too small.* If I ran out of clients, I'd be a Kelly Girl and go around to various offices. I didn't mind that too much because it was interesting to work in different parts of the city. I'd eat a tunafish sandwich at my desk and walk around on my lunch hour, learning about places like Varick Street and Coenties Slip. I could usually type faster than any of the other secretaries and sometimes they'd ask me to stay on permanently. I'd say, No, I didn't want a regular job. It was because of the acting—I always had to leave an opening for it—but also I was afraid, afraid offices would get me and I wouldn't be free anymore. I'd somehow be stuck in a role I'd never meant to choose, an office girl who wore nylons all through the hot weather and a dictation pad on her knee, when I wanted so much more for myself, when my real life hadn't even started. As a Kelly Girl I saw things I didn't like in other people's offices—tyrannies, cruelties—but the beauty of being a Kelly Girl was that none of that had to do with me. I could walk out and go to acting class, hang out with artists at the Cedar. I could tell Kelly Girls to send me to a different job. I was temporary, I had no stake in any office.

Now and then on my lunch-hour walks, I'd see something that would make me want to take a picture of it—a mirror high up on a blue-tiled wall that had once been part of someone's bathroom, a high-heeled red satin shoe smashed onto the cobblestones of Canal Street—ghosts that somehow seemed full of meaning I couldn't have expressed in words. I was always a little surprised by such moments. I liked to think my father had looked out for such things on those afternoons he closed the store. In acting class, it was always someone else's thoughts, someone else's imagination, you had to make real, make your own. Something in me resisted that. I often felt I was only acting as if I were acting. I was getting very tired of as-ifness.

My mother still bought copies of *Show Business* every week. She followed the theater the way gamblers followed the racetrack. If she happened to see a casting notice that read: *Blonde, 5'3"-ish, 20–30,* I'd hear from her immediately. My phone would ring and she'd say excitedly, "Now I want you to take this down." It gave her enormous satisfaction to think I'd probably never hear of these wonderful opportunities if it wasn't for her.

One night she called and got Tom. "That was a man," she said disapprovingly.

"True enough," I said. "I'll bring him over sometime. You'll meet him."

"Well, please don't get yourself all involved."

"Don't worry," I said. I had a policy of making light of my involvements.

My mother's explanations for my lack of success in the theater changed from month to month. I didn't have the right clothes, the right hair, know the right people; I was too retiring in my personality to put myself forward. All these failings in her view were correctable. She would gladly bend the world for me. All I had to do was put myself back in her hands. Our old partnership was what she missed, even the hardships she still complained about—how she'd had to collect me right after school and take me to dance lessons, drama lessons, voice lessons, theaters, rehearsals, casting calls. "It was terrible," she'd say. "I was never home. We were always going, going. I should have had my head examined."

"Your poor father never got a hot meal," she'd say. But she'd never taught me how to cook.

In a way, Ma was absolutely right—without her the theater didn't seem to work anymore for me. It was all mixed up in whatever I learned that day she found me dancing so remarkably to the radio in the living room: You had to make yourself into something special, something more. No one could love you for what you really were. I still made the rounds of producers' offices, but Ma had been the audience I'd played to.

I can see myself whirling, whirling, on her red oriental rug, knowing nothing but the music pouring into me. Then all at once someone is watching, and the being watched changes it. I see myself trying to imitate what I had done before, the movements that had been so charming to the grown-ups.

That day you let me watch you paint, you said, "Stay there," because you knew I wanted to. But then you forgot me, there was no one in the room for you at all. Nothing but the bare white field. You were alone with it, you had always been. No mother or father had ever put a crayon in your hand, taken an interest. I lay there in bed. I saw the whole thing. How the field changed with the first red sweep of the brush, how black obliterated red, how white obliterated black, how white could disguise itself as pinks and grays that had no name. A hundred paintings bloomed before you found what was hidden in that field.

You stood back and wiped your eyes with your sleeve. You laughed and lit a cigarette. Time flowed on before you returned to me.

"This one's yours, kiddo. You want it?"

You dipped the smallest brush in black and painted *Thomas Murphy* on the lower right-hand corner. "The name always finishes it," you said.

Leon dropped over to take a shower. He brought his own washcloth and bar of soap and a towel from the Plaza Hotel. He sang loudly under the water, "I went down to the St. James Infirmary/I saw my bay-uh-bee there. . . ." Tom went running to Second Avenue for beer and I opened another can of Progresso kidney beans and added it to the chili he'd taught me how to make. Kelly Girls hadn't called me for a couple of weeks. Whenever we were broke, we'd enter a Mexican period.

The three of us sat around drinking Millers at the ugly table with the green enamel top that had been left behind in the kitchen when I moved into the apartment with Arnie Raff. I remember Leon kept getting up, walking into the bedroom. He was the only one besides me who'd seen the new painting. He'd go in there and take another look at it and come back and thump his beer down and say in a very dry, critical voice, "Yes, well, that white *still* knocks me out." The table was in a delicate condition. It trembled on its loose leg when we laughed. We were all a little smashed, excited. Leon and Tom kept talking about red and white. The white was a force—it rushed in, wiping out everything. But the red did get through, you couldn't subtract the red. "It's that little red," Tom said, "that makes it. I was going to take it out but I left it in."

Leon wanted to hear about the paintings down in Florida, how many of them were like this white one. He acted as if he'd forgotten everything he'd said before about the galleries being hopeless. He said Tom had to take slides around to the galleries right away. "Get them to everyone. Just walk in there. Fuck 'em!"

Tom was quiet. "Yeah, Leon. I know." He got up out of his chair and walked to the refrigerator for another beer. When he sat down again, he said, not looking at Leon, "I guess I should have stopped as I was leaving to find a guy with a camera."

Leon was horrified. "You mean you didn't come up here with slides! You left everything you've done down there!"

Tom said he was going to get all the slides made after he'd had Caroline ship the paintings up to him. "You have to be sure the lighting is perfect," he said. But I could tell he didn't want to talk about it.

"We don't even know where we're moving yet, Leon," I said.

"In other words, you got nothing. Ain't it romantic?" Leon reached for the beer and poured it slowly into his glass, watching it foam against the sides. "What about the wife, Tom? What if the wife won't let them go?"

We'd had that part of it all figured out, of course. How we'd find a place and Tom would write Caroline and tell her when a truck would be coming. Once the work started selling, he'd be sending checks for the kids all the time. He was going to tell her in that letter that he wanted a divorce and that he hoped it would be a positive relief to her. She was always saying how much she wanted peace and he'd certainly never brought her that.

Whenever I thought of Caroline in those days, I'd see a sort of Florida postcard on which a woman in a two-piece bathing suit was stretched out beside an aquamarine pool as if permanently on vacation. When the letter came, she'd prop herself up a little to read it, scanning it through her dark glasses almost indifferently.

I know I believed in Caroline's indifference. I was actually quite grateful for it, since it had brought Tom and me together. "Marriages wear out," he'd said. "One day you look around and find there's nothing left." Though such a thing could never happen to us.

Just before the end, he'd told me, Caroline had been spending a great deal of her time doing crossword puzzles—not just the ones in the paper, she'd send away for books of them. It would be two A.M. and he'd find her still sitting up in the living room with her dictionary and Roget's thesaurus and her little teak bowls of peanuts. He'd come in drunk from God knows where and she'd be filling in the blanks and hardly look up. Once he'd shouted at her, "Don't you want to know where I've been?" He'd been with another woman and he was going to tell her. He had the crazy notion that maybe a fight would save them, because nothing else would. He said she'd actually looked back down at the page and asked if he knew a six-letter word for something. Now no one was shouting in Caroline's house; no one came in drunk and disturbed her "golden silence," which was a term she started using against him after she'd read one of his books on Zen.

"Kiddo, the paintings are me," he'd say. "She knows they're my life. That's why Caroline's not going to want any part of them."

It would make no sense for her to hang on to his work, he told Leon.

Leon sighed. I remember what he said. "Things don't have to make sense, man."

But then they even started joking about it. "So what'll she do? Keep them on the chance I'll die famous?"

"Yeah," Leon said. "Maybe she'll do that."

A million schemes always ticked away in Leon's brain. He loved to put them in action, even for others, because he had so many. He said, "Listen, I'm going to sell that white painting for you. I know a guy . . ." And he really did—a young stockbroker just starting a collection. Leon had run into this wealthy young man at some opening, introduced him to a few artists and had twice been taken out to fancy dinners. "Leon, is it okay if I come to you if I need advice on my art investments?" the stockbroker had asked. "Well, naturally I told him, 'Feel free—as long as it doesn't distract me from my work.' I'll call him," Leon said. "I'll bring him over. We could even get him here tonight."

I had a quick glance from Tom, as sharp as a poke in the ribs.

"How about it?" Leon was saying.

I still hadn't spoken up, so Tom told him. "The painting's Joanna's."

"A nice gift, Joanna." I was sure Leon thought it was a dumb gift, not a nice one.

"That's right," Tom said, in a tone that meant, Okay, that's the end of it.

Leon wouldn't give up, though. "Big shot, giving away paintings! I see it's steak we're having tonight, not beans." When anyone did something deliberately impractical, it threatened Leon's whole system.

"Eat your beans," Tom said in a dangerous voice. "We can all see what's on the plate." I saw him take a tremendous gulp of beer.

Leon held up his hands. "Hey," he said, smiling. "I'm trying to get you a thousand bucks."

"I told you whose painting it is."

"Let Joanna decide if she wants to sell it then," Leon said patiently. "Women are the ones who've got sense."

"Thanks a lot, Leon." I was looking at Tom, trying to read him. Finally I appealed. "What do you want me to do?" He just shook his head with a funny, bitter smile and I knew he wasn't going to tell me.

I wasn't used to being given things. Arnie Raff gave me a

frying pan for my twenty-fourth birthday. French red enamel. I said, "This is beautiful, Arnie," and didn't even know why I felt disappointed. But that white painting—to be given something like that was almost too much, almost a burden. Tom told me he wanted me to have it because it was the first one he'd done in New York and he didn't have anything else to give me. "You'll always have this," he said, as if even then he was thinking it was going to outlast him. I remember feeling I was too young to own something that was going to last forever.

Really that white painting seemed to belong to itself, as if it were something live that had been born into the world, something totally unownable. Of course the world doesn't work that way. Paintings are owned by people like Leon's stockbroker. A very distinct picture of him came into my mind. He was sitting at our kitchen table, plump in his gray suit, prematurely bald. A light shone on his scalp as he wrote a check; he felt pleased with himself, important. It seemed inconceivable that I could prevent his arrival. I couldn't help thinking of that thousand dollars Leon had mentioned and what it would mean to us, how Tom could even get his studio. I had the idea maybe he really wanted me to say yes but hated to admit it, so it really was left up to me.

I put my hand on his arm, bunched up his blue sleeve a little in my fingers. I said, "Listen, maybe we should."

"Oh," he said coldly, "you think so?"

"But if we could get a thousand—"

He jerked his arm away. "You keep the money then—for yourself."

All of a sudden he was on his feet. "Go on! Tell Leon to make the fucking call." He turned and walked out of the kitchen. I heard the front door close before I even knew he was leaving.

All our later fights would start that way, come to a boil very fast. Something would set him off, something I wouldn't even think of.

Leon sat there with me and we waited for Tom to come back. "He's just taking a walk around the block," Leon said. "He's always been like this—hotheaded. You could kill him sometimes. Caroline used to give him hell."

I asked him to tell me what kind of person Caroline was. He said, "Oh, she's not so bad." He told me he was the one, in fact, who'd met her first. She'd run away from some fancy girls' college in Virginia to study dance with Martha Graham and had just started modeling at the league. Her family had detectives out looking for her. He walked into a life class one day and there was this nervous, skinny blonde who managed to look like a debutante even though she was naked. The teacher kept yelling at her because she couldn't hold a pose. Later he found her in black from head to toe sitting on the steps outside the league, smoking, looking all red-eyed as if she'd gone into the dressing room and cried. He told her not to let the teacher get her down, and she said it was just that she'd never modeled before and she could see it was going to be terribly boring. He said, "What's your name," and she thought a moment and said, "Veronica Christian."

"I made her a little speech," Leon said. "I said, 'Veronica, I should obviously take you out and raise your spirits, but I happen to be financially embarrassed at the moment, so all I can do is invite you to Brooklyn for filet mignon.' She said, 'You can afford *that*?' and I said, 'Yes, I can, if you're game.' So I took her to an A&P before we got on the subway. I was wearing a big raincoat from the marines—I slipped a couple of filet mignons under it. She said, 'Well, really, darling Leon, shouldn't we have mushrooms and wild rice?' and stuck them under her sweater. That was how she talked. Classy, like Katharine Hepburn with a southern accent. I was very entranced," Leon said. "I could hardly wait to get to Brooklyn. I snuck her past the landlady, got her into the room, turned on the hot plate, poured us some wine, and Tom walks in. 'What's for dinner, Leon? Who's this?' Once she set eyes on him, I could have been a boiled potato. Three weeks later she's taking the bus with him and eloping to Elkton, Maryland. You know," he said, "as Veronica, she was sort of great. She should have stayed Veronica. Maybe they'd still be crazy about each other."

Then he got all red in the face. "Listen, that was a stupid thing to say. I'd better call it a night." And he did.

I cleared the table, washed the dishes, scrubbed out the chili pot. I thought, Tom will be back when these dishes are done. But I finished too soon and the minutes kept dragging by. Even then I didn't have much faith in fate's benevolence. Whoever walked out the door could be gone for good. I remember washing the kitchen floor around midnight, the awful speckled brown linoleum where the roaches always danced no matter how many got stamped to death. I kept thinking of Caroline and how he'd left her, how he could just leave me and never even come back for the white painting. I thought if I sat down at the table and did nothing, I'd be just like her.

The bed shook and when I opened my eyes, the room was full of cold gray light. You were sitting on the edge of the mattress unlacing your boots, very slowly, as if each little hole required thought. You got them unlaced but you couldn't manage to get them off. You kept bending over them, tugging and tugging. I was so relieved and grateful you were back that if I'd yelled, it wouldn't have been sincere. I raised myself up on one elbow and said, "I'll help you." My voice sounded strange to me, foolish; it seemed to be just trying itself out.

"Don't talk to me," you said. "Don't help me."

I stayed balanced on my elbow. My eyes filled with tears. "Why can't I help you?"

You didn't want to answer. You mumbled something to yourself. "When hungry, eat. When tired, sleep." You gave up on your boots and lay down on top of the covers. You'd never kept yourself so far away from me. Every night we slept in each other's arms, our legs all tangled, your hands holding my breasts.

It kept getting lighter. I saw the white painting float up from the dimness, the red so dark it could have been black; it was only remembering it that made it red.

"Put it out on the street," I heard you say. "It's yours."

Around noon you woke up angry. Like a child I trailed after you, asking you to tell me what I'd done. I went into the kitchen to make coffee and started crying because I'd failed to love you perfectly, and you came in and found me and still said nothing, just took a beer out of the refrigerator.

Finally you did tell me. You were still pretty drunk—you'd never gotten sober. Maybe I should have discounted everything you ever said to me in that state. But I never did because it always seemed to me you knew things then you didn't otherwise—things that sometimes seemed unbearable because of the awful truths in them.

I was trying to explain about the painting, how I'd only wanted to sell it for your sake. You stopped me and said I was one of those people who could love but had no experience in accepting love—I'd never learned a way to do that. "I'm the only one who's ever loved you. Isn't that right?" you said.

I said, "How do you know?" and you said, "Because you're just like me."

But you still hadn't lost your anger. "I had nothing to give except that painting. You knew that, and you wouldn't even take it. Am I that poor? Is that what I am now—nothing?"

When the white painting dried, you took it off the wall and did one that was mostly red. Leon brought the stockbroker around to see it. The stockbroker said it was great, but he'd bought a new couch that was a certain shade of orange, so he didn't want it. He said it wouldn't do.

You told him, "Sell the goddam orange couch."

The stockbroker thought that idea was outrageous. "You don't understand," he said. "It's Italian."

10

One morning on Seventh Street I woke up and looked around that small room. It was already getting crowded with rolled-up canvases. I stared at your brush marks on the walls. The floor-boards were dappled with color; the May air smelled of turpentine. We were living inside your painting. I had a thought that took me by surprise. *I am in my life.* My real life had surrounded me. What I wanted was exactly what I had.

That was the moment, I think, when I finally gave up on the theater. It wasn't even painful. It just made sense. I saw it was what I had to do. I just decided to give you what you needed. I wanted to do it so quietly, though, you wouldn't even catch me at it.

So I lied to you, I acted. I said I was sick of the theater because I never got to work. But I had to be out in the world more, I wanted some kind of career.

You were a little hurt. "I thought you liked it here with me."

An employment agent sent me to a place called Lester and Leaper, which she said had a very creative atmosphere. Lester and Leaper published illustrated, encyclopedic books on brilliantly inconsequential subjects. *The Complete Book of Pickles and Pickling, The Worldwide Toxic Mushroom Guide, Songbirds of the Western Hemisphere.* Mr. Leaper was seventy-two. His secretary was leaving him to marry the mushroom expert. I was hired to replace her. Her name was Melanie; I gathered her predecessor had been called Gloria. "You're not engaged, are you, Gloria?" Mr. Leaper asked me suspiciously. Without a qualm I said I wasn't. *Engaged* didn't seem to exactly apply to me.

There was a high marriage and engagement rate at Lester and Leaper. The work was fairly routine and there was no one around to flirt with, so girls got married to escape. Secretaries would turn up on Monday mornings with rings on their fingers and suddenly refer to "my fiancé." Old girls who'd left would periodically drop in to show off their infants. It was the kind of office where people would create excitement by passing around homemade brownies. For each person's birthday there'd be a surprise party with the same pink-and-white cake ordered from Schraffts. Mr. Leaper would make a gallant speech of congratulation, putting on his glasses to read the correct name off the cake.

Mr. Lester was twenty years younger than Mr. Leaper. He was morose and not at all as nice. He'd stalk around desks, muttering about inefficiency; he played golf several afternoons a week. His secretaries were always the most glamorous and got very quickly married off. I was told that at a low point in the history of the firm, Mr. Lester's father had bought him many shares in it, because they both believed Mr. Leaper would retire any minute. But this was fifteen years ago, and Mr. Leaper was still going strong. His only problem was names. Sometimes a woman named Frances Patterson would appear, who was even older than Mr. Leaper. She was Mr. Leaper's widowed sister, who had once been married to a well-known explorer. She'd been one of the original editors in the company and a suffragette. Now she devoted herself to travel. When she came in, I'd have to drop everything and find hotel rooms for her in Cairo or Java.

I had a little cubicle with a geranium plant that had arrived even before Gloria. It was incredibly spindly and gnarled and I kept picking off the dried leaves and putting them in my ashtray. There was a window that looked out on a wall and a sliver of Park Avenue South. If you'd see someone with an umbrella, you'd know that it was raining. Across the avenue there was a parking lot that always looked empty with a sign that said Park Fast in enormous yellow and black letters. Now and then I'd look up from my typing and just stare at the word Fast.

It was orderly and mild at Lester and Leaper. I'd said I wanted to be out in the world, but I never felt I was. You could spend an entire lifetime in that office with your birthday party to look forward to every year and nothing too great or too bad would ever happen to you. I liked it more than I expected to. I liked it uneasily.

You'd get up when I did every morning. You'd walk me to the stop for the Third Avenue bus. Sometimes we'd go to Rappaport's first to have coffee. You'd buy a newspaper on St. Marks Place to take back with you. Later you told me you read the want ads every day—it shamed you to see me go off on the bus. When the Third Avenue bus came, sometimes you wouldn't let go of my arm. You'd say, jokingly, "Oh, don't take that one." Once you rode all the way uptown with me. You were on your way to a gallery on Madison Avenue that had advertised for someone part-time. But when you saw what paintings they were selling, you just walked out.

I'd sit on my typist's chair and little pictures of you would flash up in my imagination. I'd see the empty rooms of the apartment, but then the door would open and you'd walk in with the paper under your arm. Or you'd be standing in front of one of the paintings, smoking, your eyes narrowed on something unresolved. Once a day, in the afternoon, I'd call you. There were times when the phone would ring and ring. My mind would start searching for you, trying to force up other pictures. I'd suddenly think you could be anywhere. I think I knew you were in danger, that I'd somehow left you exposed to yourself. But it wasn't a conscious thought yet at all.

You used to say, "Don't I always tell you everything?" But you didn't. You said things to me about the children you didn't believe yourself. You'd see a little kid on a two-wheeler, and you'd say, "Tommy has a bike like that. He wants to stay on it all day. He wouldn't like it up here." Mostly you didn't talk about them, though.

If the subject came up, there was a word you always used: *surgical*. You'd made a surgical break; it would leave no scar tissue. You said you either had to live with your kids or be strong enough to allow them to forget you. That was the way you were about everything: either/or. I didn't try to make you change your mind. I told myself you knew more than I did about kids. I was scared that if you ever went down to Florida to see them, you wouldn't leave them a second time.

I asked you once if you thought about what would happen when they were older. "When they're sixteen or seventeen they'll want to know you."

"Yeah, it'll happen," you said. "They'll come looking for me. By then they'll be able to handle it."

We both failed, we both were lying all the time when we were so sure we were being honest.

On those long afternoons when I couldn't find you, were you thinking of them?

You turned up one day at Lester and Leaper. The receptionist said, "There's someone at the desk to see you," and when I walked into the waiting room, it was you. It was a shock to see you there, so threatening to all that mildness. For some reason you were wearing a strange, wrinkled tan suit that didn't fit you very well. You stepped forward and kissed me right on the mouth and because the receptionist was staring, I laughed and said, "I know this person." You said, "Let me see where you work."

I didn't really want to take you inside. We passed two desks and I had to introduce you: "This is my friend, Tom Murphy."

"Friend?" you said loudly.

I hated that you had caught me in my office personality.

You wouldn't sit on the visitor's chair in my little cubicle. You went to the window and frowned out at the view. You wanted to get me out of there, to have me come downstairs.

I tried to explain I couldn't do that. Secretaries didn't just leave the premises unless it was lunch hour. It's a rule everyone understands about work, but as I tried to explain it to you that day, I suddenly felt you were right. It made no sense. Why couldn't a person go where they wanted to?

"Come on," you said roughly and pulled me up off my chair and I had to walk out with you. We went down in the elevator to some hamburger place off the lobby where there were no customers because it wasn't lunch hour. We sat in a torn, gloomy booth and you said very sadly, "I feel terrible. I put you in that place. Wasn't it me that put you there?" By then I'd realized that you'd been drinking. I asked you what was going on. I said, "Where did you get that awful suit?"

"On the Bowery," you said. "For seven dollars."

"Forgive me," you said, taking my hand, though I didn't know what I was supposed to forgive you for. "This has been a significant day," you said, and when I asked you why, you told me it was because you'd finally gotten yourself a job, just like me. Market research. "You didn't think I'd do it, did you?"

So that was the reason you got the suit. "All us working fuckers got to look the same."

Chrystie Street

Summer 1962

11

At the Cedar, everyone was talking about a sculptor who was quitting, giving up art. Others had quit, always very quietly, but the way Howard Stricker was going about it was odd and spectacular. He'd been building a boat in his studio, a twenty-five-foot catamaran. He planned to launch it in the East River in a few weeks' time. Then he was going to sail it by himself all the way down to Key West. He said he would live on rice and fresh fish. What he was going to do with his life after he reached Key West he never told anyone. People hadn't paid much attention to Howard Stricker before. They didn't exactly admire him now, but they were awed by his craziness. No one believed the boat would float. A bullet would be faster, one painter said.

Leon said we should definitely look at Howard Stricker's studio, which was downtown on Chrystie Street between Grand and Hester, just around the corner from the Bowery. He said he'd seen it and it was cheap and big and that Howard Stricker was said to be looking for key money so he could finish his pontoons and leave on schedule. Tom called him one evening and he told us to come over.

Howard Stricker had worked in stone and had stubbornly kept sculpting the human figure as if he lived in some century of his own. He was forty years old and it was said he'd never sold one piece. I don't know whether his work was good or bad, because when he'd decided to build his boat, he'd taken a sledgehammer and a power drill and broken up everything he'd done. When we met him, he referred to this with a kind of pride. "It took three days," he said, "but of course that was much less time than it took to make them." The broken pieces were all upstairs, so no one who took the studio would have to deal with them. "It seemed better to put them there," he said, "than out on the street."

Above the studio were two empty floors where there'd been a fire thirty years ago. Howard Stricker said, "You can use them for storage, burial purposes, plenty of room for whatever." He got a flashlight and took us up to see them. The windows were gone, he told us, and that tended to make the whole building cold in the winter. Birds had gotten in up there, pigeons, you could hear them chortling in the dark. When Howard Stricker turned his flashlight on, a couple of them got scared and flapped up to the ceiling. I saw piles of white stones like fragments from some ancient ruin. After we started living in the studio, I never went up to those floors myself, though Tom rummaged around there all the time.

The studio was two enormous rooms as gray as a cellar. You could see that at first Howard Stricker had tried to fix the place up, had even been ambitious. He'd constructed a high platform for a bed and built a big stone fireplace and there was a wall outside the bathroom made of dull-colored chunks of marble embedded in cement. At some point, though, he'd lost interest. There was an old three-burner stove and a refrigerator from the forties that hummed loudly above our conversation and a sink encrusted with whatever he was putting on his pontoons.

We saw them that night—long, slender things. They did have a grace. Tom was quite taken with them. He told Howard Stricker they looked like Brancusi birds. But it worried me that you could see each seam in the wood. I thought they had an awfully homemade look.

Howard Stricker said he'd hoped he'd be through by now, but he'd run out of money. He'd been advised to put many coats of some terribly expensive acrylic sealer on his pontoons and he had to buy more wood to make a deck and a small cabin by August. He said he'd seen such boats in the South Pacific when he was in the service, and it was beautiful the way they skimmed the waves; the tension between the pontoons made a perfect balance.

He seemed to like having us there. I had the feeling he never had much company. He drew sketches for Tom of the pontoons' inner structure and made us some muddy coffee that he poured out of a pot through a strainer. He said he'd invite us to the launching.

Finally Tom asked, "Well, what would it take to reimburse you for all the improvements here?"

Howard Stricker thought it over, staring at us. "Four hundred dollars," he said. "I could get more, but that would be enough. Rent's seventy dollars a month. No one's supposed to live in this building. The health inspectors will come around and bother you, but don't pay them any attention." He left the room so Tom and I could talk about it.

Tom was tremendously excited. He walked up and down in the front of the studio, trying to measure it off. "There's so much space here, Joanna. Look at the length of those walls. You could paint anything, make something huge. This is our kind of luck, kiddo. Everything from now on is going to happen just like this."

I believed it, too, though I think part of me was skeptical. There was all that grayness. It was almost as if the walls were imbued with Howard Stricker, as if his loneliness and failure had somehow eaten their way inside them. But I believed in our luck.

I had a dream one night after that in which I saw Howard Stricker's catamaran floating quite nicely on a deep green sea as still and flat as a lake. It was sort of like an oversized sled with its deck high up on runners. People sat on the deck calmly drinking coffee. Then the sea boiled up into enormous waves. The boat was thrown about, tipped over onto its side. All the people on the deck spilled off like toy figurines and I found myself with them in the terrible water.

Tom said what I'd seen in my dream was what sailors called white water. He'd run into it himself on a minesweeper in the Ligurian Sea. "It was like being trapped in a tin can with the hand of God shaking it. There were times you'd get real religious out there. That was only the beginning of the trouble we had. About a week later we hit a mine. That was what we were out there for, that was the deal. A thing like that could happen any minute."

"What happened to the ship?" I asked.

He was silent for a moment. "Oh, the sweeper went down. For a while everything burned. You'd never think water could burn, would you? I had this life preserver. I floated on my back, just looking up at the sky for hours, waiting, not thinking of anything really. I mean my wonderful youth in the Bronx, and all of that, didn't run through my mind. I just emptied out—ready. Finally a destroyer came along and picked me up. See, it wasn't my turn. I guess I was meant to be here like this, looking out the window at Seventh Street twenty years later."

Howard Stricker's launching was on a Saturday at the end of June. He'd been working day and night to finish the pontoons; all the rest would have to be done at a boatyard in Coney Island. Tom said he'd help him. He went to the Cedar and rounded up a couple of artists, Bruno and George, who came along not because they knew Howard Stricker but just so they could tell their drinking friends what they'd seen. We all rode down together on the Third Avenue bus.

It was one of those bright blue afternoons that make you think of trees and the seashore and wonder what you're doing in the dust of the Bowery. All the way downtown Bruno kept making wisecracks. "So you can't get a gallery, you jump in the river. Well, I hope that guy has had swimming lessons." No one laughed, though, so he finally just kept quiet.

When we got off at Grand Street, Tom said, "Let's do this with some wine," and George said, "Great. This is some far-out opening all right." I guess it was Howard Stricker's vernissage in a sense.

Howard Stricker didn't have much to say to anyone. He wasn't thinking about anything but protecting his pontoons. He kept lashing rope around them in different ways, then not being satisfied and starting again. They were too long to go around the bends in the stairway, so he was going to lower them out the front windows on some pulleys he'd made. "I'm hoping for the best," he said, looking up at Tom, wiping some of the sweat off his face. He sent Tom and Bruno downstairs to wait for the pontoons on the sidewalk.

From there you could see how fragile the operation was. The pontoons dangled awkwardly, trussed up in the air three stories above the pavement. They lost their gracefulness when you saw them like that. To me they looked more unreliable than ever. I found myself thinking again about those seams where the water might get in.

Howard Stricker's launching caused a commotion on Chrystie Street. Italian housewives were hanging out their windows and a crowd of sidewalk superintendents gathered, the men from the garage next door and even some bums who stumbled over from the strip of park across the street, where the greenest green was the green of broken bottles. The bums were rubbing their rheumy eyes and poking each other. "Lookit that! What's those wooden things?" If you looked in their direction, they'd shout, "Hey! Got some change?" They gave each other wise, significant glances when they saw Tom's wine. "How about that now?"

Howard Stricker had rented an old flatbed truck. After the pontoons had been loaded on it, and the little platform he'd built out of scrap wood to hold his outboard motor, he ran upstairs for the last time and came down with a duffel bag and a box of tools. I remember seeing him stand very still on the sidewalk, staring up at the windows of his studio before he got on the truck. Then he reached in his pocket and handed Tom the keys. "Well, it's your place now."

He wouldn't drink the wine. "Nothing for me," he said in that curt way he had, as if words were just exhalations that got wasted.

Tom turned to the bums and held out the bottle. "Go on," he said. "Take it." They must have been startled by such good fortune, but they grabbed it right away.

The truck took us all the way across Grand Street to the launching place on the East River Howard Stricker had picked out, where it didn't take long at all to attach the three parts of the boat to each other and lower the whole thing into the water.

Then Howard Stricker swung himself down off the pier and crouched over the motor on his little homemade platform as the current began carrying him away from us, ostensibly toward Brooklyn. There was a breeze from the north and the river was running fast. The pontoons skimmed the surface just as he'd said they would.

We all went wild, even wisecracking Bruno, waving our arms, yelling, "Bon voyage, Howard! Bon voyage!" He heard us and scrambled to his feet with a funny, stunned smile on his face. He was a man walking on water who couldn't believe it.

Tom said, "Come on, Joanna," and we said good-bye to the others and started making our way back across Grand Street. I had the idea he wanted to spend the rest of the afternoon in the studio now that we had the keys, but when I asked him if that was where we were going he said, as if he were tired, "No, kiddo. Not today."

"Well, I wouldn't really want to go there right now either," I confessed.

He didn't seem to want to talk, and after we'd walked on a bit I said, "What are his chances?" Which was the question I'd been holding back since the beginning.

We were standing on a corner waiting for the light to change. "In a heavy sea," Tom said, keeping his eyes on the light, "that boat will snap like a pretzel. If he doesn't leave before September, he'll never make it around Hatteras."

"But hasn't he thought of that?" I wanted to save Howard Stricker. I wanted someone to talk him out of going, to tell him to be very careful.

"Oh yeah," Tom said. "He's thought of everything."

We got rid of Howard Stricker's grayness with whitewash. Even the floors we painted white—we didn't care about its being impractical. We put every dime we had into the place and ate chili every night. There was nothing left over for Tom to spend on canvas for a while.

One night we went out when we were tired of working. We had hot-and-sour soup in Chinatown and wandered all the way down to Wall Street. It was one A.M. Wall Street was deserted, though a light burned here and there. Tom spotted an empty U.S. mailbag that had been left out in front of one of the buildings and bent down to inspect it. He grinned up at me. "What about it, kiddo?" It was made of perfectly good heavy canvas. No one was watching, so we rolled it right up and took it home with us. It was probably a federal offense, but it made us awfully happy. We felt the streets had given us something—that, too, was a sign of our luck. Tom cut up the bag and made two small paintings. They were the first he did in the new studio.

We picked up a round table the same way—another gift from the streets. We found it abandoned outside an old bar in Little Italy that was modernizing itself into green Formica. It had dark rings on the wood from its previous life, and later there was a black spot where a cigarette of Tom's burned into it. I was thrilled to get that piece of furniture. It had a real bohemian chic, I thought. Someone gave us a spider plant and Tom hung it over the table from the ceiling. I can see that table and two blue Mexican chairs half facing each other, set at an angle as if Tom and I have just pushed them back a little and walked away.

I remember whiteness. Whiteness, especially in the mornings, looking down from the high platform bed. Everything seemed afloat, unanchored. The spider plant was singing, trembling toward the light. I wish I'd thought to take a picture.

For years my mother kept the boxes I couldn't open. "Leave them," I'd say. "I don't need anything." She said I was being foolish. "You don't remember what's here. We could at least give this stuff to Goodwill."

So finally I got a knife and cut the tape on one of them. There were some chipped yellow plates wrapped in newspaper—they seemed neutral enough. She was right, I'd forgotten things. I worked my way through the box quite calmly, with curiosity. At the bottom was something round and heavy, also wrapped in newspaper. As I tore away the paper I saw that someone had wrapped a stone. It was an ashtray Howard Stricker had left, made out of a polished piece of granite. Tom used to keep it on our round table. Someone had actually wrapped it, cigarette ashes and all.

Can you imagine? Ashes.

I hadn't told my mother I was living with Tom or moving with him to a studio, I just told her I was thinking of changing my phone number.

"What are you doing that for?" she asked suspiciously.

I said it was because some nut kept calling me. For a few weeks after that, she kept wanting to know about the nut and whether he'd called again and whether I'd reported him to the police and whether I'd gotten a chain for the door. Finally she said, "Well, I think you should change your number," and I said, "Yes, that's the simplest way to take care of that nut."

Just before we moved, though, I called her and told her I'd like her to meet this man, this artist Tom Murphy I'd been seeing lately.

"What kind of name is that?" she said. "Irish? Catholic?"

"Names don't matter to me," I said sternly.

"Nothing matters to you. I know."

"Well frankly, Ma," I said, "this man matters." It was the first thing I'd told her in a long time that was the absolute truth.

She didn't say anything. I guess she just stood there in her old pink chenille robe in her avocado kitchen wondering about everything I wasn't telling her. From the time I was eighteen and first started sneaking to Greenwich Village and hanging out with people like Arnie Raff, our entire relationship had been based on alibis.

"I'm going to make roast beef," she said. "It's nicer than chicken."

When you've been at war so long with a person, you forget they might wish you well. They might even be happy for you.

The night Tom and I went out to Queens, the whole house smelled of furniture polish and my mother's best china was on the table—I hadn't seen those gold-rimmed dishes since my father died. My mother brought out wineglasses and put little cork coasters under them that showed Mexican peons asleep under sombreros. "Would you like some sherry?" she asked us. It was strange to feel like a guest rather than a daughter.

We sat on the living-room couch with our sherry and our coasters and our feet on the red oriental rug. Tom said, "I bet this is the rug you danced on when you were little."

My mother was delighted. "Oh, that was certainly her favorite occupation. She couldn't keep still if you turned on the radio. I'm surprised you remember that," she said to me.

I said, "Sure I remember it. I remember a lot."

"She was just a tiny little thing, but she *insisted* on dancing lessons—toe, tap. We gave her the best instruction in everything. It seemed very important at the time."

"But nothing's wasted, Mrs. Gold," Tom said quietly.

"Oh yes," my mother repeated doubtfully, "nothing's wasted. Isn't that the wisdom of the East?"

My mother was taking painting lessons in the neighborhood that year, watercolor. Her teacher was Japanese. She brought out some studies of pots and flowers painted on rice paper. "There's some really nice color here, Mrs. Gold," Tom said. He pointed out the places where my mother ran into trouble with perspective. He told her how Vincent Van Gogh had built a special frame to help him get the perspective exact and how he'd carried it with him everywhere when he was learning. My mother wanted to know where she could get a gadget like that.

"You know how I dried these watercolors?" she asked him. "I didn't want to leave them out on the table because of the cat. So I stuck them to the refrigerator overnight with magnets."

"That's certainly not very Japanese, Mrs. Gold," Tom teased her.

"But it works!" My mother was laughing, flushing like a girl. "You should try it."

She wanted to know whether Tom did still lifes too, or did he do figures? He told her he'd started out that way, of course, but now he was an abstract expressionist. My mother was disappointed, though she still maintained her smile. "I've heard of that," she said politely. "Is that what people are buying now?"

I assured her some abstract expressionists had made millions. I tried to create the impression of a boom.

"I hope you'll return to still lifes again one day," my mother said. But she liked him, I could tell.

In the kitchen she took me aside and whispered, "You know, I never trusted the other one," meaning Arnie. "Even though he was a Jewish boy, I always felt he had something up his sleeve.

"Come to the table," she sang out and brought out the roast on a platter. She was picking up the knife to carve it herself, but Tom said quickly, "Let me take care of that for you." The brightness went from my mother's face; there was a wet look in her eyes. "You know we have no men in our family," she said to me. "That's really terrible, isn't it?"

And although we were going to wait till Tom had his divorce to tell her we were getting married, I nearly broke the news that moment. "Ma, I'm going to marry this man. You'll have grandsons." I thought of our sons, I think, for the first time, that they'd really be possible, that the children we'd have would fill in the empty spaces. Maybe it was even Nicky who flew into my imagination and took root there.

I remember we were all dressed up that night in clothes we wouldn't have worn otherwise. Tom had gone out and bought a white shirt and a necktie, and I'd ironed a pink cotton dress from the bottom of the closet that made me look like a milkmaid. I saw how even our costumes divided us from Ma, just like my lie about the phone. I wished we could all just be real to each other.

Maybe Ma knew, though; maybe she did sense what was in the air. Suddenly she started talking to Tom about my father as if she'd never said to me, "Don't throw yourself away on anyone."

"My husband was very talented artistically. He could have worked for the magazines, but because of the family he thought it wiser to have a business. He did the biggest weddings, you know, all over the borough, the fanciest affairs. He was in demand, let me tell you. His customers were always thrilled because he made them look so natural. He just spoke to them in a very quiet way until they relaxed totally. There's quite an art in that."

When Tom said he'd like to see my father's work, my mother sighed and looked embarrassed. "Oh, most of it's gone. I couldn't keep those files. What could I do with all those pictures of strangers? When the Viennese bought the business, he cleaned out the shop. Did you show him the shop?" she asked me.

I told her I had. We'd stopped and looked in the window.

"Well, that work isn't good—everyone smiling with so many teeth like morons." My mother stopped and demonstrated. "There's no sensitivity, but he makes a living. He has an assistant, a nice Puerto Rican. My husband never had that. I pleaded with him but he wouldn't listen. So . . ."

She caught her breath and leaned toward us over the red gladiolas we'd brought her. "Joanna may have told you—he went to a wedding and never came back." That was how she always put it when she explained to anyone how my father had died. It had become her tragedy; the wedding was an irony that somehow made it worse.

"It was this time of year, the big month. He'd worked every weekend, a man with a heart condition. The affair was on an estate—Oyster Bay—in a big garden. In the morning the temperature was ninety-nine. I said, 'Don't go. You'll kill yourself.' 'They have tents,' he said, and he went."

I said, "Let's change the subject, Ma!" And I heard the way my voice sounded, cold, heartless.

We did take one trip to Coney Island to look up Howard Stricker, inquiring around various boatyards till we found him. This was toward the end of July. He'd built some of his deck, but had made no progress on his cabin. To raise more cash he'd been working as a maintenance man on the Whirlwind and some other rides. He couldn't get over it that we'd come all the way out on the subway to see him.

He was living in an army tent on his half-finished deck. "What a suntan, Howard!" we said. It really was a terrific one, deep and even. It made him look younger, as if there was more life in him. For the first time I thought it might really be okay, that he'd probably make it to wherever he was going.

He offered to cook us some brown rice on his camp stove, but Tom said, "No, forget that," and found a place to buy us all hero sandwiches—really great ones with cheese and salami and tiny hot peppers.

"Certainly this is the opposite of brown rice," Howard Stricker said, chewing thoughtfully.

The three of us sat on the deck on wooden crates, the pontoons rocking in the swells of water beneath us. The boatyard was on an inlet on Gravesend Bay. All that separated us from the Belt Parkway was a strip of gritty sand with some marsh grass growing in it. Cars whizzed by with a sound high-pitched like wind, but after a while you forgot them. You could just look out at the shine on the water.

A crowd of gulls flew in, arriving suddenly out of nowhere. Tom stood up and started flinging pieces of Italian bread at them, throwing hard like a pitcher. They'd swoop and rise, swoop and rise, making their loud harsh squawks. There was one all the way out who wouldn't come in. The feast its friends were having didn't interest it for some reason. It was keeping its distance in the middle of the waves, bobbing up and down by itself.

"See him out there," Tom said. "That one's the wise one. He's beyond everything."

"Sometimes you get one like that," Howard Stricker said.

12

Right around the corner from where we lived, Grand Street turned into the street of brides. Four stores there sold cut-rate bridal gowns. The mannequins were very old. They had Celluloid marcelled hair, yellowish complexions. Tom used to say they looked like flappers who'd achieved sainthood. They had nylon veils and bouquets of dusty paper lilies—they held them up in the windows, smiling their mysterious waxy smiles.

Tom used to kid me about those white gowns. "How about that one, kiddo? You'd look great in the one over there."

We'd decided we'd definitely get married in the fall as soon as he got his divorce. One day we'd just take a cab downtown and do the whole thing at city hall. Afterwards we'd have breakfast in Chinatown. It was funny to think how we'd wake up that morning in one state and lie down at night in exactly the same bed in another. I used to wonder whether becoming someone called wife would make me feel different. When I was still a virgin I'd had similar thoughts about sex. Sex, of course, had seemed a far more drastic experience. I think what marriage meant to me was the sealing of a love affair. I didn't have a concept of it as an institution, never gave a thought to property and all of that.

Caroline had more of a grasp of such things. Maybe not at the start when she was trying out wildness and pretending to be Veronica. I think it was something that came to her bitterly, after Mexico. As love got chipped away, the institution became meaningful. Later she could be a widow and fail to mourn. Or maybe, after Tom left her, she continued to want him; maybe that was always the problem. Even now I know next to nothing about Caroline. I know what she did, but not how she felt.

Those first months with Tom, I used to think of her as "Florida," "down in Florida"—more of a previous address than a person. "Any day we'll hear from Florida," I kept telling myself after Tom finally wrote her in July, giving her the name of the lawyer Leon had found him who was going to take a painting in exchange for his services. It was the only word she'd had from him in four months. I know I didn't make the effort to imagine "Florida" receiving such a letter.

Weeks went by without an answer. Then, slowly—through her silence—Caroline became clearer to me. She was striking back at Tom. Silence was all she had. It reminded me of holding on to Arnie's jazz collection—a last stubbornness.

The letter came at the beginning of August in a cream-colored envelope. For a second I thought someone had sent us a formal invitation. It lay on the broken tiles under the mail slot in our downstairs hallway. I'd walked in with a shopping bag of groceries. I bent down and picked up the envelope and when I saw who it was from, I almost wished it hadn't arrived.

We had been happy, and I knew all at once that it would

change. It was like weather, great masses of air suddenly shifting so that even the light looks different. You know you've been in a certain period when it ends.

I took the cream-colored envelope upstairs. I gave it to you as soon as you came home. You ripped it open and started reading the letter right away. I went to the sink and washed dishes because I couldn't bear to watch you.

When I asked you was the letter okay? you said it was perfect. But I didn't think your voice sounded good.

"Everything's fine. She's getting herself a lawyer. If they taught you how to write such letters in finishing school, this one would get an A."

You folded it up small. You shoved it under the stone ashtray on the table.

"Thirteen years," you said, as if you'd never added them up before.

I remember August seventh was a Monday, and I couldn't seem to get you to wake up. You told me you weren't going into work. "I can't cut it," you said. You lay on your back with your arm crooked over your eyes. I asked if you were feeling ill, but you said you weren't. "I can't cut it, that's all."

At first I thought it was your job. Lately your supervisor had been bugging you—"What's the matter with *you*, Murphy? Been up all night with a sick painting?"

We'd been riding the bus uptown together to our offices every morning. It felt strange that day to get on it alone.

You'd been working on a new painting all through the weekend. This one wasn't coming fast like the others. Maybe because there was no red in it and so much black—black strokes that kept getting denser and denser, crowding out the white. "I'm narrowing my palette," you told me. I thought I knew what was really keeping you home—all that black coming in, taking you by surprise.

I felt very sure you were painting when you didn't call me at the office. I felt proud of myself for not phoning, not breaking in on you, learning how to be an artist's wife.

When I came home, though, and took a look in the studio, I saw that the painting hadn't changed at all.

I didn't hear your key in the door till I'd warmed up dinner enough times to be mad at you. I was convinced you'd been at the Cedar. Then you told me how you'd spent most of the day—walking in and out of toy shops. When I heard that, it scared me.

You leaned against the refrigerator, watching me fuss with a pot on the stove. "Don't bother with that for now." There was something left out in the studio that you wanted me to see. You said you'd actually bought something.

I went in with you and saw a large package on the floor, all tied up in ribbon and gift-wrapped in red-and-blue-striped paper. You told me, "Go ahead. Open it," and I said, very puzzled now, "You bought something for me?"

"Go on," you said. "Tell me I've done something crazy, tell me anything you want, kiddo."

I took the wrapping off very carefully in case it had to be used again. The package came from a toy store on Fifth Avenue, the best one in the city. It was a blue sailboat lying in a nest of white excelsior, a sort of miniature galleon with tiny brass cannons mounted on the deck and bright flags on the rigging. "It's wonderful," I said. "This is for Tommy, isn't it?"

"He's six today."

"Why didn't you say something?"

"There it is," you said. "I just said it. What am I going to do with this thing? What the hell am I going to do with it?"

I said the only thing that came into my mind. "I guess you'd better take it to the post office."

You didn't see how you could do that, though.

You showed me a birthday card you'd bought for Tommy, a funny one with sixes and blue elephants all over it. You'd thought of putting it inside the package with some kind of message, but all you'd written so far was, *I love you. Dad.* How could anyone write a letter to a six year old that would have to say, *I love you but I can't be with you.* How could Tommy be expected to understand that? And maybe the card would never reach him, maybe Caroline would throw it away. Or maybe the whole idea was wrong in the first place, too confusing. A kid doesn't hear from his father for months—and then a goddam package arrives. And where do you go from there anyway? What's supposed to happen after that? You'd even missed his birthday by now. "I've fucked it up for him," you said. "I'm hurting him. Every day I'm hurting him."

I remember pushing my brain to find a fast way out of it. I wanted to fix it somehow—as if all it came down to was a question of whether or not to mail that package. Maybe that would take care of it for now, and then we could go back to what I thought had been our happiness, because I was afraid to understand what it was to lose one's children or that August 7 would come around every year of our lives. I needed to believe you and I were enough for each other even if the rest of the world was out of control. "Florida" wasn't just Caroline, you see, it was the kids—the way all our lives were bound up together, a knot you couldn't untie. I remember advising you to send the package special delivery. "Then it will get there the day after tomorrow."

You were staring at me with such grief. "The day after tomorrow is too late."

You asked me what time it was. I thought it was eight-thirty. "I've got to call Tommy," you said. "He'll understand that, won't he?"

I said I didn't know. Maybe it wasn't the best thing, I said.

"He'll be up," you said. "He holds out. No one can put that kid to bed. He likes to grab the phone—'Hello, this is Superman. Hello, this is Mickey Mouse.' I'd have to yell at him, 'You wacky kid!' 'No, you're the wacky kid, Dad!' "

"Don't do it," I said. "Please don't call down there."

"What are you talking about? What are you afraid of? Caroline?"

I said, "I'm afraid of you."

You said it would be all right because it had to be.

You walked past me into the other room and I heard the phone being dialed, heard you give the number to the long-distance operator. Then there was silence, and I knew the phone was ringing and ringing in Florida.

I remember going all the way to the front of the studio and standing at the open window, and if there'd been a fire escape, I think I would have climbed out onto it. It wasn't quite dark. The sky was still a kind of burnt-out red. A bottle crashed somewhere down the block and I heard the summer bell of a Good Humor truck. Bums were yelling in the park. They seemed to be fighting over a pair of shoes.

A man was shouting. "You bitch! You bitch! Coldhearted fucking *bitch!* You want me to come down there and choke you!"

13

I stayed where I was, shut my eyes and steadied myself with my hand against the window frame. It was like those moments after an accident, when time weirdly slips back on you—you tell yourself, Nothing's happened. I could still hear the bums yelling down below. Caroline must have hung up on him. I knew what she'd said to make him shout that threat at her. I knew the gist of it even without the words.

If it had been me instead of her, what would I have done, hearing that voice ask that favor over the phone, ask *me*—of all people—for a way out of pain, just wanting to get past me to the kid. Could I even have thought of the kid at all? Suppose it had been Nicky. Would I have put Nicky on the phone? When they say everyone's only human, they mean anger and craziness too, people who've loved each other turning into mortal enemies, clawing at each other's soft spots.

"Are you afraid of me now?" he said when I walked into the other room, where he still sat holding the receiver.

I remember trying to act as if everything hadn't come apart for good, as if you could press a button and turn everything rational, even though insanity, I knew, would always win. Everyone goes to extremes, I said, and I tried to convince him that the words he'd shouted at Caroline could be taken back, that she could be made to see he didn't mean them.

But of course he'd meant them, he insisted furiously. He could see I didn't understand and he wasn't blaming me, he wasn't. It wasn't in me to be hard the way she was. "She *knows* what she's doing to me."

Suddenly he reached out and seized me by the shoulders and I saw that he was weeping. "They should have been your kids!" I told him there was no point even thinking that, but I was crying, too.

Then he said, all right, he'd do it, he'd call Caroline again, but only because he still had to think about Tommy. It had nothing to do with her, and maybe he could make her listen if she didn't just hang up on him again. Over and over he kept calling, but he was only reaching operators, and the operators would sing their song of "Sorry, the line is busy." It was clear she'd taken the phone off the hook.

Finally he told me to go to bed. "I don't want you sitting up with me." He switched on a small lamp next to the phone and lay down on the couch with a pack of cigarettes.

All through that night I'd half wake up, yellow burning against my eyelids, and think I'd hear him, speaking very low, still giving the number to the operators.

When I got up to go to work, Tom was asleep on the couch in all his clothes, the empty cigarette pack crumpled on the floor. I turned off the lamp and let myself out of the house as quietly as I could.

At the office I did a lot of staring at the Park Fast sign. I called Tom at ten. There was no answer. Every time my phone rang after that I felt dread and wished I'd stayed at home.

He called me in the middle of the afternoon. There was a lot of noise in the background as though heavy vehicles were grinding by, and he was shouting over it to me, telling me he'd had to take some money out of the bank.

"Tell me where you're calling from!" I cried.

He was in an Esso station, he said. I remember he was very precise about where he was—standing in a phone booth on a highway just outside Easton, Pennsylvania. He said he'd found a truck that would take him all the way to Florida.

"I'm taking Tommy his present. What do you think about that, kiddo?" Sometimes when he'd just finished a painting his voice had that same sound—a kind of defiance and elation, as if he was giving the world notice nothing could ever change what he'd arrived at.

He said the truck was leaving and he'd see me next week, and I never got to tell him what I thought.

When I came home later, sure enough the package was gone. I could see he must have wrapped it again, put the striped paper back around it, tied it up with the ribbon.

If he'd even had five minutes with Tommy, I think he could have lived with it.

That was the night I heard from Harry T., who had been to see his lawyers and a judge who was a personal friend, and had also informed the Palm Beach chief of police that his daughter's life had been threatened. Harry T. took pains to make me understand what an influential and popular man he was—though he didn't show me his charming side and I never would get to eat oysters with him in Palm Beach's finest restaurants.

He addressed me as Miss Whoeveryouare. "You get him for me," he said. "You put that son of a bitch on the line."

I'd never run up against anyone like Harry T. No one with such conviction that *he* was the Authority and knew what was right and therefore had to be obeyed on the spot. I could imagine him waving a gun if he found it appropriate—backed up by lawyers, judges, restaurant waiters, maybe even God. I saw why Caroline had run away from such a father.

At first I tried to sound like a Kelly Girl, someone who really didn't know the ins and outs of the business. "I'm sorry. He's gone out. . . . I don't know exactly what time he'll be back. . . ."

But then Harry T. started thundering about "whereabouts," demanding "whereabouts." I recognized "whereabouts" as a police kind of word. It was the place they'd come and corner you and take you away in handcuffs.

I said, "Well, this is where he lives, but he isn't home right now, so I really can't get him for you. Perhaps you would leave your phone number."

There was a roar from Harry T. "The son of a bitch *knows* my number! Don't you lie to me, miss. You'd better tell me what he's up to." It was almost as if he had his eye on the very truck that had picked Tom up in Easton.

I lost my Kelly Girl's voice. A large, dry pit got stuck in my throat and I couldn't seem to swallow it. I knew it wouldn't do any good to plead with a man who had no doubts, but I did some pleading anyway. "Listen, whatever he said to your daughter he didn't mean. He was just terribly upset. You know he'd never do anything to her—to anybody. Haven't you known Tom for years? That's not the way he is."

"He's scum," said Harry T., "to put a plain word on it. Dangerous, crazy. A so-called artist. He had my girl hoodwinked. You'll find out for yourself, Miss Whoeveryouare. Why don't you tell him a couple of things if you hear from him. Tell him, don't even think of setting foot in the state of Florida. Don't call to speak to little Tommy. I'm taking legal steps to protect my grandchildren. He won't be seeing those kids again. He's not even going to get near them."

You used to say it all came down to timing.

Take the way the two of us had met—happening to turn up like that at the end-of-the-world party. Or even the fact that you hadn't died at nineteen on the deck at Anzio when the guy next to you got hit. His blood was all over you, but you were alive—you could have been standing where he was.

Maybe you should have played it safe, you admitted later, and never gone back to Florida, but you were counting on one thing. That the kid was still crazy about the two-wheeler you'd given him, that he still pedaled it up and down the sidewalk, where sometimes you'd even found him in his pajamas, his mouth smeared with Skippy peanut butter that he'd helped himself to in the kitchen. A couple of mornings when you hadn't made it home the night before, he'd been waiting for you when you got out of the MG. "Let's go for a drive, Dad. Are you going to play with me now?" It had been hard for him to understand when you told him you weren't up to it. You'd stood there blinking in the sun with your hand over your eyes, so drunk you hardly knew what you were saying, without the slightest memory of the roads you'd just been on, the swerves and curves under the palms and the mangrove trees.

Driving past the house the first night, you actually saw the MG. It was parked in its old spot in the driveway as if no one had moved it since you'd gone, like you'd come out any minute and get into it, instead of being on the wrong side of the street in a rented Chevy. You let the Chevy roll to a stop. You turned off the lights and sat listening to the insects thudding against the windshield. Across the street all the windows were black; everyone was up there on the second floor in the air-conditioned dark. The baby would be on her belly in the white crib. Maybe Tommy was talking in his sleep, kicking off his sheet—it always landed on the floor.

You saw that Caroline had put flowered drapes over the windows of your studio. You were trying to remember the last painting you'd done up there before you left, but you couldn't quite see it, couldn't quite bring it into focus—the way you couldn't quite see the faces of your children. You thought of the face you couldn't see at all, the one that belonged to the tall man you were still pretty sure must have been your father, though Marie used to swear you'd only dreamed about him. You imagined your own face dissolving slowly like a bar of soap dropped into water—that was the way it must be for Tommy by now.

Early in the morning you came back in the Chevy and circled the block. You kept doing it every twenty minutes or so. You had the birthday present on the seat next to you, which was where you were going to put the kid when you opened the door and called to him and told him to get in. You were going to tell him you were just making a surprise appearance because you'd missed his birthday, that it was a secret from everyone else. The day was just going to be fun for him—nothing emotional. You couldn't do that to Tommy. You'd take him out to the marina, the pier where he'd caught his first fish. "I'll bet you can do it again, Tommy," you'd say. "I'll bet you can catch an even bigger one."

You remembered a pay phone there at the bait place. You'd call Caroline and tell her you had Tommy; you'd get him back in time to go to bed. Though even that was kidnapping, if they wanted to get technical about it.

But you also thought of going all the way—you did keep coming around to that. Taking Tommy with you. Just stealing the kid and the Chevy and driving till you could no longer pay for gas.

"I could have done it," you said, after you told me that last thing, looking me straight in the eyes. I always knew you loved me enough to want me to know everything.

And what about us? I remember thinking, but I kept the words inside me. I saw there was no Us right then when it came to Tommy.

You used to test me with guessing games, but I was never much good at them. There was always some obscure Zen answer I'd end up missing.

Once you held out your fists and asked me did I notice anything unusual. "Take a look at the knuckles," you said.

But I didn't see anything out of the ordinary.

You blamed it on my sheltered life. If I'd grown up in the Bronx, I might have known what to look for. All your knuckles were flattened, except for one on your right hand.

You said in a proud, sad voice, "Well, they didn't get that way from holding paintbrushes." You'd broken them all yourself, getting into fights, smashing them against people's heads. "One of these days I'm going to smash the last one."

There was no fight when it happened. It was that morning you were cruising in circles waiting for Tommy. You were taking the Chevy around the corner the fifth or sixth time. When you saw the patrol car blocking the road, you drove your right fist into the dashboard.

"I smashed the last one," you said when you called me from Florida.

By the time I heard from you, I couldn't think beyond wanting you back, couldn't think at all beyond my need of you. I'd keep walking into your studio and turning on all the lights, telling myself you'd surely come back because you'd left all your paintings behind—there was even the new black one you still had to finish. I couldn't believe just in myself as the reason, despite what you'd tried to teach me. I'd take off my clothes and put myself to sleep in the sheets that had your smell, superstitious about changing them.

I never got any wiser from loving you. All the time we were together, the two things I believed never canceled each other out: That love was bound to make everything all right. That no matter what I gave you, it wouldn't be enough.

Six days—that's all you were gone. They'd locked you up down there in Florida, but only kept you overnight. Caroline wanted you a thousand miles from herself and the kids and decided to drop the charges. A patrol car drove you to the airport and they shipped you back on Pan Am, all expenses paid. Harry T. bought the ticket.

You sent me a telegram with the flight number. It came early in the morning, and I called in sick and didn't go to work and went out to the airport and waited. I'd washed my hair and put on the dress I'd worn the night I met you. I wasn't sure who you'd be after so much had happened to you. It was as if I'd have to win you all over again.

I remember standing at the arrival gate very scared because everyone was coming off the plane except you, one stranger after another. You were the last one to walk through, and people turned their heads and gave you edgy, disapproving stares, seeing only wildness in you, trouble. You hadn't shaved for days; there were black-and-blue marks on your face; your right hand was wrapped in a dirty bandage. You raised it in the air when you saw me and tried to smile, and I ran forward and you said, "You're beautiful." You said, "On the plane I kept thinking you wouldn't want me. Why would anyone in her right mind want me?"

It was late afternoon by the time we got home. You said you'd had moments when you thought you'd never see the place again, that you'd blown it permanently. You talked about blue—the pure, terrifying blue you'd seen from the windows of the plane. "It's the blue of emptiness."

I told you there was no emptiness now. "Not now. Don't think about it." I stood on my toes to reach your bruised lips and started kissing you into silence, closing your eyes with kisses, too. I pressed into you with my whole being and heard you cry out as if I'd hurt you, and we swayed together in the middle of the floor like dancers before the advent of the Twist and distance.

I remember what you said to me that day, after we'd made love. "What are we doing here, laughing or crying?"

V

The Red Harley 220

Fall 1962–Summer 1963

14

At first he was going to show me how he could keep going, how he could pick up right from where he'd left off.

He even made an attempt to retrieve his job, though I'd warned him not to count on it. When he walked into the office two days after he got back, the supervisor at the market research place said he was amazed someone who took off without notice would have the gall to show his face: "I don't know how we'll get along without you, Murphy, but we will fill the gap."

"Fill it and stuff it!" Tom shouted, and that was that.

No goddam office would ever trap him again, he swore to me. He'd only tried it out because I wanted him to. Now he'd find his own way to support us. An argument seemed to be going on inside him with someone he was mistaking for me. "Maybe I'm not what you need. Maybe you want a nine-to-five type—some guy who has to get permission to walk around the corner."

The things I wanted I couldn't express to him—days with a shape I could count on, the life we'd had that ended on Tommy's birthday. He was painting in the mornings now that he wasn't working, but in the afternoons he'd get his thirst and head for the Cedar. He seemed to forget everything once he was up there. Finally we had a terrible fight because I'd cooked too many dinners he didn't show up to eat. He'd had a lot to drink and he got very mad when he walked in and I told him it was midnight and why hadn't he called me? He threw our clock out the back window because he thought I spent too much time looking at clocks.

The following day when I came out of work, I found him waiting on the sidewalk in front of the building. He presented me with an old alarm clock he'd bought from some bum on the Bowery. It had giant dented brass bells on its sides, but it didn't work at all, and we laughed about the whole thing. We made promises we'd both go back to the way we used to be with each other in that time, only six weeks ago, that seemed so fuzzed over now, like history.

He wanted me to know I was the one he'd always come home to, no matter how late it got uptown, so I had to promise him to quit being scared and jumping to the wrong conclusions. Already he was getting over what had happened in Florida. He still had me, after all. He still had his work. And even some of his afternoons at the Cedar hadn't been wasted. Lately he'd been hanging out there with a terrific young kid named Billy Cutty, an art student who'd come all the way from Phoenix on a motorcycle. Billy had found himself a deal renovating a loft that was going to be turned into a dance studio. It was more than he could handle by himself, so Tom was going to be his partner. This was a sign that the old luck was running again. "Everything's ahead of us, kiddo."

Tom's divorce lawyer, George Steinbock, came over for breakfast one Sunday to pick out a painting for his fee. Artists' divorces were sort of his hobby—"a kick," as he put it, because they allowed him to build up his collection. His other clients were businessmen, dentists, even a famous ballplayer. Leon said he'd made a fortune from them. George Steinbock had just bought a town house on Perry Street. He wanted a work of art that would cover a wall in his new dining room—floor-to-ceiling if possible. He'd made measurements and written them down in his memo book. To help him make up his mind, he'd brought along a girl friend he'd spent the night with. "Edwina has a great eye," he said.

Edwina's eyes were behind dark glasses. Judging by her thinness, she was some kind of model. Her dress was so slippery it kept catching on parts of her bone structure and her nipples. She yawned and asked me where the little girls' room was when George announced he had news about Tom's case.

"They've agreed to settle out of court, so it's just about wrapped up now."

He was sitting across from Tom at the round table. I was passing around a basket of bagels. "Oh, I'll have a poppyseed one," he said.

My head was spinning, I couldn't look at Tom. But the poppyseed bagel gave me hope. Would someone select a bagel as he was about to tell very bad news? Though I knew the news couldn't possibly be good. George Steinbock had already told Tom what the attempt to see Tommy had done to his chances.

"There's a positive side and a down side. Do you want to hear the down side first?"

"Sure," I heard Tom say in a flat voice.

"Well, they won't grant you visitation rights. It's no go there." George Steinbock was cutting his bagel in half. He flicked a crumb off his cuff. "Of course, we expected that. It's no surprise."

"There's a surprise?"

"In a manner of speaking." The lawyer paused as if he needed to gather breath. He took a sip of his coffee. "The paintings. I'm asking them to send us a list, a complete inventory. Your wife wishes to retain them."

Tom got to his feet. He was gripping the edge of the table. "You hear that, kiddo?" he cried out. "The paintings, too! She's taking the kids and all the fucking work!"

"I wish you would sit," George Steinbock said, sounding tired. He put down his coffee and waited. Then he went on, enunciating each word, as if he were forcing himself to speak to someone who didn't understand English. He said the list would be coming by registered mail next week. He said that after all, the paintings were of undetermined value. It wasn't a situation where the work of an established artist was involved. He said actually Tom was getting off lightly. That was the good news, which perhaps he should have mentioned earlier. The other side was making no financial demands—no alimony, no support payments. George Steinbock even had a theory that the trip to Florida had had some positive effect. "Your wife believes you're a dangerous person. She wants no further contact with you in any form. That's the best possible outcome." He leaned across the table and said to Tom, "Look at it this way. You have no further obligations. It leaves you free."

"Free," Tom said. He was shaking his head and there was a strange glittery look on his face as if he was about to laugh. "Everything I've made, everything I've worked my guts out for, that's what they're taking from me. Did she figure that one out herself, or was it the old man's idea? Maybe I'm the one who isn't going to settle out of court."

George Steinbock said sharply, "You'd better settle. Desertion, attempted kidnapping—that's what they'd claim. You don't want to stand up before a judge."

"Oh yes," Tom said, his voice trembling. "I appreciate your efforts. Free—that's something, isn't it?"

I remember saying I was going to make scrambled eggs if anyone was interested, and George Steinbock saying, yes, he'd be interested in eggs, as his girl friend finally walked out of the bathroom, her glasses off, in the full glow of all her makeup. She said she never ate breakfast as a rule. She took the chair next to Tom's and her skirt shot straight up her skinny thighs. She said, "Don't you think being up in the morning is a terrible shock to the system?" He gave her a stare that had all his fury in it. "What's going on here?" she asked. "Have I missed something?" And he said, "You always will."

He rested his arm on the back of her chair and bent over her, his mouth almost against her ear. "I love what you're wearing, what you aren't wearing. . . . My life has just been ruined by a woman who used to look like you."

"Too bad your life is ruined," she said, grinning up at him, rearranging her long bare legs.

I walked away, got eggs out of the refrigerator and started breaking them against the rim of a bowl. I'd broken about half a dozen when I remembered George Steinbock was the only one who wanted any.

Now Tom was telling Edwina he thought he'd fix himself a drink. "I can see you're the only person here who'll join me."

She gave a little shriek. "What makes you so sure of that?"

"Experience. You want references? George will tell you who to write to."

You went to get some Jack Daniel's you had in the studio, but as it turned out, there wasn't much left in the bottle. I remember being glad it was Sunday, because all the liquor stores were closed. It was the only thing I was glad about.

I told myself we'd be okay until tomorrow. Maybe you'd take

your pain more or less straight. It seemed better to me that way, only because I wouldn't be so frightened for you, though I knew the pain would be worse. I always felt utterly selfish when I had such thoughts, utterly wrong to want to protect myself from you when you fell into that darkness where you needed everything and nothing I had, nothing I was, could be of use. I remember feeling jealous of Edwina and being ashamed because that was so ridiculous. I should have been the one to join you. I should have been the one with a drink in her hand at eleven in the morning.

You lifted your glass to her. "To beauty," you said. And it hurt me, even though I knew you were being ironic.

George Steinbock said maybe he'd come back some other time. Maybe this wasn't the right moment to pick out his painting.

You demanded to know what was wrong with today. "You think I've been finished off by my wife? You think there's an amount of shit I can't eat? Listen George, you can get a truck and come back here, grab every last painting in the studio, clean me out. Do you think that would make me give up?"

George Steinbock said that certainly wasn't his intention. I could tell all he wanted was to get away fast.

You told him he ought to take two paintings, since after all they were valueless. "Take two, and I'll do six more. See, that's what Caroline doesn't understand. All those years—and she doesn't even know who I am."

You said George had to make his choice right away before you took back your offer. And you made him go with you into the studio without Edwina. "This is between my lawyer here and me."

Edwina asked to borrow a comb. Then she wanted ice. "Your boyfriend never put any in my drink. He's a little nuts, isn't he?"

I told her you were pretty upset. She said divorce did make people very weird. She'd been divorced three times herself.

George had handled her last one and had gotten her terrific alimony. "What about you?" she asked.

I shook my head. "Never."

"Why not?" she wanted to know. "Didn't anyone like you?"

You were the one who liked me. You said I was the kind of woman who needed to be married—at least you could do that for me. "I'm giving you my name," you said. "Next time, though, you'll pick yourself a better bet."

It made me crazy whenever you talked like that. "What do you mean—next time?"

"In your other life." You'd turned your head, so I couldn't see your eyes.

"Well, this is the one that counts!"

It kept coming up, that philosophical difference. The day we got married, though, you told me we'd both had such hard times, you'd decided God had finally taken pity on us.

I'd asked to have that Friday off from work. October 5. We made love when we woke up. Before we left the house, we remade the bed. Everything new—the pink sheets my mother had bought us, a Hudson Bay blanket, your kind of red, cadmium light, with a black stripe along the border. It lasted for years, then the moths got it.

There are pictures of the wedding—not the kind my father would have taken, just my mother's amateur snapshots. We're smiling as if we'll never stop, holding hands as we stand on line for the ceremony at city hall. Afterward, we're with Leon, the best man, at the French restaurant where my mother insisted on taking us because she was scandalized by the idea of Chinatown. I'm wearing the enormous white orchid she gave me, but I'm not at all embarrassed by that bourgeois flower. Your hands and mine are on the table, clasped together, as an elderly waiter stands by with a bottle of champagne and a white towel. The Eiffel Tower can be seen behind us with fireworks painted on the navy blue sky, and the two of us have that oblivious glaze that only shows up on the faces of people in love, as if there's light just beneath the flesh. But the color's so poor in these photos that everything's more orange than it really was.

Later, when we went home, you started a painting—two looming red shapes joined by a single mysterious gray stroke. You said it was you and me going down Grand Street.

15

The first night Billy Cutty ever parked his red Harley 220 in front of the Cedar, he'd asked a stranger at the bar, "Say, how do I get to meet Jackson Pollock?" That person had been unkind. "Just go to the cemetery in Amagansett and walk to the biggest rock."

"Shit, I was *fourteen* when the guy popped off. How was I supposed to know? Wish he'd hung on, though, so we could have had a few beers," Billy used to say.

He told Tom and me he was twenty but made us swear to keep the secret. For everyone else, Billy's official age was twenty-five—he wanted people to take him seriously. He was growing himself a moustache, waiting for it to droop over the corners of his mouth. He'd touch it every now and then to see how it was coming along.

Billy didn't understand people liked him because he was so amazingly young. He had the long legs and goldenness of the boy cowhands in movies, the rash, overeager ones old-timers took along into Indian territory.

Billy had been doing construction work and sketching old boots and steerhorns and Chianti bottles in some cowboy academy of art in Phoenix before he and his Harley came into our lives. If he hadn't seen some reproductions on some postcards from the Modern, he'd never even have known there was a Jackson Pollock. "Phoenix is the dumbest hick town," he said. "Well, in those days, I was what you'd call a hick, I guess." Now he was drunk on New York and abstract expressionism and the mistaken idea that any strokes that ended up on canvas could be declared art. When Billy was just walking around or hanging out in artists' bars, he felt he might be an undiscovered genius. But he'd always get sick to his stomach, he told Tom, when he picked up a brush.

"Well, give it up, Billy," Tom said to him once. "Forget it. Right now."

Tom described to me how Billy had gone pale. " 'I can't, man. I've gotta keep doing it.'

"So I said, 'Look at me. I'm sick every day.' "

Whenever Billy came down to see us on his motorcycle, he'd take a long, hungry look at whatever was up on the walls of the studio. It alarmed me the way he'd walk up to paintings almost as if he were going to climb inside them. "How'd you do this one? What made you thin out this black?" He'd sound jealous and suspicious, on the lookout for a trick hidden somewhere, a marked card in the deck.

One time he asked Tom, "How long is it going to be before I can paint like you?"

"First you'd have to be me, Billy."

"Okay," Billy said with a grin, "I'll be you for a day or two."

"I used to be like Billy," Tom told me. "All excited because I'd just invented painting and obnoxious because I didn't know a thing. You wouldn't have given me the time of day, because I wasn't sophisticated."

I did wish Billy would get tired of us and wouldn't visit us so often. He said he loved my chili and spaghetti, but apart from that, there seemed no subjects he could talk to me about, because I was a wife, not a potential girl friend for him. Billy hardly ever slept in his little storefront on Sullivan Street because "older women" of twenty-seven were always bringing him home for the night. "Well hell," he'd ask Tom. "Was that love or what?"

Billy always wanted to hear Tom's war stories. He wished he hadn't missed out on all of that action. When Tom told how he'd lied about his age in order to join the navy, Billy couldn't get over it. "Your folks let you do that?"

"My folks? Oh yeah. My mother said, 'Be sure they get the address right. I don't want to miss out on the insurance.' "

Billy thought that was some kind of joke. "Whew!" he said. "Tough lady!"

Billy's mother had gone to bed and cried for a week because he was leaving Phoenix. His father was a Chevrolet dealer who hated artists and said New York was full of Jewish Communists and queers. We were among the kinds of people he didn't want his son to meet. He was waiting for Billy to have some sense knocked into him; then he'd take him into his business as a partner. "I'll never get that kind of sense," Billy would say. Even when he was little, he and this man had always fought. It worried him that he didn't seem to have the right feelings about him. "I try to fake it, but he knows."

It took a while for Billy to tell us exactly what he was faking. Finally it came out, one of those nights when the three of us were sitting at our round table after Billy had eaten three helpings of everything. His real father had been a fighter pilot who'd been shot down over the Philippines two weeks before Billy was born.

Tom was awfully rough with Billy when he heard about that. "Why all the secrecy? Why the hell didn't you say so before?"

Billy shrugged and clammed up for a while. Then he said his dad didn't like him to talk about it. "He always tells everyone I'm his boy. I mean, Dad's the one who brought me up—"

"Dad," Tom interrupted him coldly. "Let's not hear any more about *Dad*, Billy. Your dad is the dead one. Don't mix them up."

It was the only time I ever saw Billy at a total loss for words. He was running his thumb over his moustache, smoothing the fine gold hairs against his lip.

"You'll always be in trouble, Billy. There's no one who can take the pilot's place."

I came home from work one evening and found Billy Cutty's red motorcycle standing by the curb. You were squatting down beside it next to him, tightening something on one of the wheels with a wrench. When I was halfway down the block, you stood up and called to me, wiping your hands on your pants.

"How do you like our bike, kiddo?"

"Our bike?" I had no idea you meant what you were saying.

"Fucking right, it's ours. Looks great, doesn't it?"

"I told you you should have warned your old lady," Billy said.

Later you teased me about the way I stood back from it, keeping myself awfully quiet as if the bike were some wild animal that was going to bite me. I stared at its dented red fenders, the tilt of its handlebars, the jumble of nameless parts that made it run. It seemed flimsy to me. It gave me the same funny feeling I'd had about Howard Stricker's boat.

"I don't know what I think," I said.

You'd bought it from Billy that day for two hundred and fifty dollars—a bargain. You still owed him seventy-five. Billy was getting himself a secondhand panel truck, something he could use to haul lumber.

"Billy's teaching me how to ride it."

"Nothing to it," Billy said. "Hell, you can ride it already."

"Come on, Joanna," you said. "I'll take you for a spin."

I said, "No thanks. Maybe later," which struck Billy as hilarious.

"Tom, you sure are in a lot of trouble *now!*"

The two of you were both laughing, ganging up on me, a little high on beer, with that red Harley so gay and dangerous and your hands black from the grease you'd been putting on it.

"Right now I think you're out of your mind," I said. "But I'll probably get over it." I knew I was being very square, the way old ladies were supposed to be.

"Tom," said Billy, "you can go down to Mexico on that thing. You can go anywhere. Just don't ride it when you're real loaded, though."

"I'm not going to sit around the Cedar getting loaded now that I have the bike." You looked right at me, not at Billy, when you said it.

I said, "Tom, promise me that."

"Promises are for children," you said.

It took a few days to talk me into it. I can still recite the reasons we needed a Harley 220 to improve our lives. We could park it anywhere. We could run it on practically no gas. The main thing, though, was the quality of the experience. On a bike you could be at one with the road, instead of insulated from it inside a machine. I'd never wanted to be at one with the road, but Tom said I was going to love it. "We have to have wheels," he kept telling me, as if that were the only thing we'd lacked so far. "You're looking at our freedom, kiddo."

When I'd go downstairs, I'd glance at the red Harley—its chain, its wheel spokes, its handlebars, all the bits of old metal our lives depended on. If you leaned, the bike leaned; if you resisted its motion, you'd throw it off balance. "It's your ass going down the middle of the road," Tom said. But he liked it that way. He said that was the way it always was anyhow.

That first night he showed me how to get on it behind him. The place where I had to sit was called the buddy seat, and I was supposed to wrap my arms around him. All the time we moved we'd be locked together in that embrace. I said, "Oh, I see. It's a machine for lovers."

"Yeah. Why do you think I bought it? Hold on now," he said, and without any warning we were jolting over the cobblestones, wobbling around the corner toward the Bowery. I was clutching at Tom's waist as if I could somehow slow us down. "Jesus Christ!" he yelled. "I'm doing the driving. All you have to do is sit."

"I'm trying!" I yelled back. I didn't know whether I was excited or scared to death.

"Try harder, kiddo. Or we're going to have a spill."

I seemed to need a lot of rides to learn how to be a passenger. I used to wonder whether other women picked it up just like that. He'd get a little mad because it seemed I didn't trust him. He said he could feel the fear in my body; he didn't have to look over his shoulder to see it on my face. It reminded me of when I was little and afraid of dogs. I had a baby-sitter who once warned me that dogs could smell my fear, and I was always very frightened of the smell after that, much more than of the dogs themselves. I'd go up to strange dogs and make myself pet them just so the smell wouldn't be on me anymore.

The thing was, though, I did trust him. I trusted him with me but not with himself.

We went places that fall. On the weekends, when it always seemed to be Indian summer. We'd get up very early and put on our warmest clothes and go downstairs to the bike. Next door the garage would just be opening. All the men there knew us by now.

They were Italians like everyone on the block except us. Sometimes they'd want to know did we ever hear from Howard Stricker? "That was some weirdo," the owner once said, but with respect. We were weirdos, too, but we couldn't help feeling they thought we were all right; we seemed to entertain them with our oddness. One guy, Ralph, would always stand on the sidewalk, seeing us off. "Listen you two! Don't get caught in the rain."

I remember hurtling out over the Brooklyn Bridge in astonishing rushes of cold air, the steel beneath our wheels singing its one long high note. And the highways that took us out of the city, all ablaze the farther we went. Red/yellow. Red/yellow. For a while you could fill your mind up with those colors. Or with the roadbed beneath us which had to be watched so carefully—all those patches of things that could have done us in. Oil slick or sand, spills of gravel, the shiny places that were wet when we came up on them fast. We kept saying we had to buy helmets, but we never did.

I was always freezing, trying to warm myself, my breasts bruised into you, skidding on the blue nylon of your jacket. I got to know the back of your neck by heart, the places where your hair grew thickest and curled a little. "You smell brown," I remember whispering into your ear when we'd stopped for a light in some town in Westchester. I'd close my eyes and hold you even tighter when you speeded us down that narrow path between the lanes of cars. Death Alley, it was called, like the avenue in your old neighborhood.

On the roads, I'd see other couples clenched in the same embrace. This was how we looked, too, I'd tell myself, surprised. Daring and fatal. I would never have been the girl on the buddy seat if it hadn't been for you.

Motorcycle riders would salute each other, holding their right palms up against the wind. It was always done so solemnly that at first it made me want to laugh. Then I began to think maybe we did all belong to the same thing—a secret society traveling the lanes cars wouldn't dare to enter, coming out on our machines to burn up time.

Now it seems crazy that I came to be so unthinking, accepting the danger of those rides the way I accepted the cold. Being like you, I used to feel, instead of like me. Didn't we move out there as if we were one body? I was sure that if we died, we'd die together. But how could we die when we were so alive?

Our red Harley had a sound I think I'd instantly recognize even today. It was much too elderly and low-powered to roar like the Hell's Angels bikes. It made a kind of dry, apologetic sputter like an old smoker who couldn't stop coughing. Out on the road I'd forget it, lose it, my ears would fill up with wind. It was a sound I always listened for in the loft, when I was alone. Sometimes I thought I heard it, even when I hadn't. It was inside me, that dry sound, far away as if in the distant reaches of the Bowery, then coming closer, closer, as the bike turned the corner at Grand, loudest of all before the engine was shut off just under our front window. Then there would be silence and I'd know Tom was opening the downstairs door. "I made it home, kiddo. Made it one more time."

Promises were for children, but we were grown-ups. And he never made ones he knew he couldn't keep. He'd go uptown to the Cedar, sure he'd only stop in for a couple of beers. Then suddenly it would be very late and he'd think, Why take the bus when he had the bike? When he was very drunk, he used to say he could almost ride the Harley in his sleep, that he was in fact a *great* driver, had always been a great driver, and didn't I realize that by now? And he'd tell me again about the white MG spinning off the road, all the times when something could have happened and didn't, and wouldn't. Because he drove the way he painted, with the same hands, the same eyes. "The instinct's *there*, don't you see? Don't you know anything? Haven't you learned a little from me by now?"

Sometimes, though, he'd let Billy ride him home. Billy knew how to ask. "I really miss that old bike," he'd say. "Why don't you let me take a turn at the driving?"

16

I was afraid of Christmas that year, but didn't know how to ignore it. On Christmas Eve I ran out just as the stores were closing and bought the last turkey on Mulberry Street. It was sixteen pounds, much too big for the two of us. I'd never cooked a turkey in my life. I had cut out a recipe for chestnut stuffing from the newspaper; next morning it took me ages to get off the shells.

The hours went by, hushed as if both of us were holding our breaths. I kept on chopping and stirring and Tom worked in the studio building stretchers. A little snow would come down every now and then and whiten the railings of the back fire escape. There was a mission for homeless men around the corner and I guessed they were having turkey, too—I could hear them singing "Deck the Halls," "Adeste Fidelis." Tom went out to get cigarettes. He said he'd never seen the Bowery so empty.

"I came right back, didn't I?" he said. "Today I'm not drinking. I can do it."

I told him I knew he could. All he had to do, I said, was stay busy so he didn't start having bad thoughts. But it was nothing I knew or believed.

He went back to his stretchers. The electric saw went on and off for the rest of the afternoon, and the turkey kept getting browner. I could see it was going to look like the ones in those magazine pictures of families gathered around holiday tables, with the little wide-eyed children holding out their plates.

We nearly did get through that day except for the fight we had about Billy as I was taking the turkey out of the oven. Tom wanted me to hold everything. He was going to go and find him. Here we were with all this great food for the two of us, and maybe Billy was just sitting in his little place on Sullivan Street that didn't even have a phone or a refrigerator.

"But the turkey will get ruined," I said.

"No it won't, kiddo. I know about birds. Just leave it where it is and turn off the gas." I saw him reach for his blue nylon jacket, the one he always wore when he was on the bike. He was going to ride uptown and be back in no time. If he didn't find Billy in the storefront, he'd take a look in the Cedar.

"I don't want Billy here tonight."

I didn't even mean it, but a dread was upon me. He'd get on the bike and he wouldn't come back. I thought about the patches of snow on the streets, the drinks he'd probably have in the Cedar. I was going to keep him alive by making him stay home.

We had to be alone, I kept insisting. Couldn't we even have Christmas by ourselves?

He thought I'd gone nuts. He didn't give a damn about the fucking bird. Was I jealous of Billy, jealous even of a kid? He'd never seen that in me before. He said it was like finding a flaw in a diamond. It spoiled something.

He threw his blue jacket on the floor and left me alone in the room. My hands were shaking as I set the table. I kept calling him and finally he came, but we sat there like two people on the verge of divorce. "Would you pass me some of that?" was about all we said. Afterward, when I stood at the sink soaking the dishes, the quiet still had that terrible hum.

I knew he was right. I'd been awful about Billy. But I'd kept him home.

You gave me a camera that Christmas. An old Leica—with a cracked leather case. But the lens was perfect. I'd never had a really good camera, never even knew I wanted one. I was still just taking pictures inside my head.

The Leica came from the Bowery. You'd never lost your habit of looking in pawnshop windows. Weeks before, walking on Rivington Street, you'd spotted it. You often saw incredible items up for sale on that block, even right out on the sidewalk. Once an old black wino wearing one shoe had offered to sell you a hard-boiled egg. He'd displayed it in the palm of his hand, a fine-looking egg, white and uncracked. He wanted a nickel. You gave him a quarter and put the egg in your pocket. "I bought you this egg," you said when you came home.

You were always turning up with little gifts that you'd hand me with embarrassment, because you couldn't seem to learn about being practical. You had an eye for silver. I used to wear an old chain you gave me. The catch had been broken, but you knew how to mend it. "You'll never lose this now," you said. Silver lasted, wouldn't change. Maybe that was why it attracted you.

You took a risk, getting me that camera. There it was, asking to be used. You'd even bought some rolls of film—allowing me no excuses.

"Oh," I said politely, almost as if I didn't want it, "this is a really fancy one."

I think I was lodged in your mind the way you were in mine. You were studying me all the time, doping out my secrets—the things I'd never ask for or dare to give myself.

Your secrets were harder, not always the kind to be brought to light. Not long after you'd finished all those stretchers, I came across something in your studio I wasn't supposed to see. It was a Saturday morning—you'd gone out to buy paint and I'd taken it into my head to surprise you. By then we'd both forgotten the fight we'd had on Christmas. I cleaned the two big studio windows; then I wet the broom and started sweeping. Sawdust was everywhere, bits of two-by-fours and plywood. I pushed the broom along in a professional manner, making neat little piles.

I was having an attack of happiness. The wet wood smelled sweet to me as it dried in the sunlight, and everything seemed calm and good. I wanted to make everything ready for you.

The broom turned over a small plywood triangle. For some reason I bent down and picked it up even before I noticed the writing on it. Five words in thick carpenter's pencil. NOW I WILL HANG ME. Paintings got hung, I thought. Maybe that was what it meant. I put the triangle in a bag of trash, buried it under orange rinds, empty cans.

I dug it out and read it again before you came home. The letters seemed to come unjoined when I'd stared at the words long enough.

I wasn't going to show it to you, but I had to. I said, "Hey, can you tell me what this is about?"

You said you'd just been fooling around. You didn't remember when it was you'd written on that piece of wood.

17

In the spring we started going on trips again. If it wasn't too cold, we'd get on the bike and Tom would head for water—Brighton or Rockaway, the gray, wide beaches. At that time of year even their trash cans were empty. In Sheepshead Bay one Sunday we found a pier where there were always four or five boys fishing with drop lines. "What do you catch here?" Tom asked them. They all said flounder. Tom bought himself a rod and we started coming back. I'd help him cut up the clams he used for bait, but I never got the hang of casting out. He'd catch crabs, blowfish—anything but flounder. We just came to be there really. We'd sit in the sun with our eyes on the line as it pulled against the blue. We came for the stillness. Sometimes out there I'd know he was thinking about Tommy. He'd talk to the boys with the drop lines, let them try out his reel. "No one fishes more seriously than kids," he said.

We used to go to a clam bar right across the street that always filled up in late afternoon with red-faced men in windbreakers who'd been out since dawn on party boats. Tom would strike up conversations about how the bluefish were running and whether the tides were right. They'd try to figure him out. How come he knew so much? "I did a little fishing down in Florida." "Marlin?" they'd ask him eagerly. "Yeah, I've gone out after marlin."

Once a group came in who seemed to have caught nothing but beers. They were very loud in ordering their Bluepoint Specials and getting the waitress to pay attention to them. They all worked together in some insurance office. Someone was retiring after forty years, and the firm had rented a boat in his honor.

One of the younger insurance men started staring at us. Even when he saw that I noticed, he couldn't tear his eyes away. Something about us seemed to fascinate him. He was heavyset and Irish-looking in an ugly tan jacket; he'd gotten a very bad sunburn out on the water. He had sort of a military haircut that made him look belligerent from a distance. It alarmed me when he got off his stool at the bar and made his way over to our booth. He stood in front of Tom for a few moments, shifting his weight from foot to foot. He cleared his throat and said, almost in whisper, "Tommy?"

Tom was shaking his head. "Do I know you?" Then I heard him say, "Oh my God."

"Joanna, this is my little brother," he told me. "This is Kevin."

Later Kevin said he'd been confused because I didn't look at all the way he remembered Caroline. He'd met her once years ago just before she and Tom went to Mexico City. Kevin kept grabbing Tom's shoulder and saying, "Can you believe this?" He called over a couple of his friends and introduced us. One of them said, "You never told me you had a brother."

Tom wasn't talking much. After a while, I had the feeling he was waiting to get up from the table and drop out of sight for another thirteen years. Kevin kept on asking questions, though.

Where had Tom been living? What happened to Caroline? How long had he been back in New York?

Finally Kevin got quiet himself. "All right, Tommy. Say we didn't run into each other. Would you have tried to look me up?"

"I don't know, Kevin," Tom said. "I don't know at all."

Even so, Kevin wanted us to leave the bar and go home with him right away. We had to meet his wife, see his kid.

Tom said, "Too fast, Kevin. I'll call you. We'll get together."

"You won't do it," Kevin said.

"Sure I will. Write down your number. I've got no problem seeing you."

"Glad to hear it," Kevin said, forcing a smile.

Kevin and his wife Grace lived somewhere near Idlewild, which hadn't become Kennedy Airport yet. When we went out there on the bike the following Sunday, we got lost for a while riding through blocks of two-story red brick houses that all looked the same. Kevin had a small backyard, just a square of grass, a clothesline full of little overalls and a lilac bush. We ate barbecued chicken under Kevin's lilacs as planes kept roaring right over us, dropping down in the sky to make their landings. Grace said she'd always been scared that a plane would crash on their roof. She wanted them to move much farther out on Long Island to a place that would be better for raising children. They had a three-year-old, a tiny asthmatic boy. Kevin held him on his lap, making him open his mouth for little pieces of chicken; sometimes his son would whimper and try to push his hand away. "A couple of times we nearly lost this one, but we pulled him through," Kevin said proudly. Grace couldn't have another baby, so they were trying to adopt. A Catholic agency was sending over a social worker to inspect them. That was another worry they had—that they'd fall short of perfection, that somehow they wouldn't be judged suitable. It seemed strange how little sense they had of how good they were, good in ways that Tom and I could never be. They had a terrible amount of patience, they obeyed all the rules. I could see this even in the way the appliances shone in Grace's kitchen, the jars and pots lined up like soldiers. Kevin and Grace were ready to worry about us, too, the way families worried about their own.

It really upset them that we rode around on a motorcycle. "What made you get a thing like that, Tommy?" Kevin asked. He wouldn't hear a word about its advantages. It must have been the insurance man coming out in him, I thought. He'd told us he'd been a cop in East Harlem for a few years until Grace made him give it up, but he seemed much too sweet-natured to have ever arrested anyone. Kevin had a friend in Rockville Center who sold used cars. This man could be absolutely trusted, he said. He wanted to take Tom over there to talk to his friend about trading in the bike. "I'll bet your wife's got her heart in her mouth, sitting on that little seat."

"Not anymore," I said. "I love it." I'd have told anyone that if they'd asked me. I lived for those Sundays, those trips we took that always somehow brought us back to ourselves even after one more week had collapsed on us. I only felt fearless when I was riding on the buddy seat.

Kevin didn't believe me, though. "Sure, Joanna," he said, laying his hand on Tom's back. "Well, now that I've found this guy, I want to keep him in one piece. So why don't you use your influence?"

Tom wasn't annoyed. He was laughing. "Listen, I'm not about to buy a car. Anyway, you're just my little brother. Look who's giving who advice!"

You didn't want to talk about old times that day. I remember you warning Kevin about that. "Let's keep it light," you said. But there kept being silences heavier than the air in Kevin's backyard.

You and Kevin were strangers really. All you had in common were memories of that basement apartment in the Bronx.

Kevin said he'd been sure for years that somewhere he'd run into you. He'd have you over to his house and Grace would cook you a steak dinner; then you'd have this talk you said you didn't want. "You're my only brother," he said. "That means something."

"I don't know what it means, Kevin. I haven't been a brother. More of a writeoff. Isn't that true?"

"I used to think you couldn't stand me."

"You were all right. To me you were just this little baby. I knew you shouldn't hate babies. I wasn't going to turn out like them."

"They're pretty pathetic now," Kevin said. "I notice you haven't asked about them."

"That's right," you said. "I'm not asking."

"You have no intention of seeing them then?"

"I can't come up with one good reason, only a few bad ones."

"They never treated you right, Tommy," Kevin said. "I could never understand it. I guess even back then they were kind of crazy."

"Let's talk about the Yankees," you said. "Fishing. Insurance. What's the insurance business like?"

"Well, maybe you'll never have to meet my mother-in-law," Grace remarked as I was drying dishes in her kitchen.

I admitted to her I couldn't help being curious. I wouldn't have minded seeing Marie just once.

"You don't want her in your life," Grace said fiercely. "You don't want her near you."

She said Marie had made a lot of trouble for her years ago before the marriage, told Kevin a lot of lies about her. "Just for spite," Grace said, as if she were still puzzling over it. "Just to cause harm. I never knew there were people like her. Everyone was nice in my family. She said some woman had told her I'd had a baby and given it away in Chicago, because I went there one summer to stay with my aunt. Why would anyone make up such a story? I never even had a boyfriend in high school before I started going with Kevin. And Kevin really believed her. He used to tell me how beautiful his mother was. She's not beautiful now, never was—not what I call beautiful.

"Kevin and I are all right now, though. And you know why? Because I never have to go with him anymore to see her. And they never come here. Maybe that's terrible. Kevin says I should feel more pity. But that's the way it has to be."

Kevin had moved his parents out of the Bronx, Grace told me, found them a small apartment in Marie's old neighborhood in Hell's Kitchen. He sent them a check for the rent every month. His father had lost a leg to diabetes—"All that drinking," Grace said. "It caught up with him." Kevin had gone with his mother to the doctor, when the doctor wanted to explain to her what meals to make for Frank. But Kevin didn't think Marie paid much attention. Sometimes she didn't cook anything for days. Sometimes when Kevin went to the apartment, it was so filthy he'd have to spend hours cleaning it, carrying out all the garbage. "You can't talk to him when he comes back from there," Grace said. "You have to give him room for a while. Go and mow the grass, I tell him."

This is what I did one day on my lunch hour. I took the subway uptown and walked around Hell's Kitchen. I had the Leica with me. I was still getting used to it, getting over feeling I was an impostor taking pictures. Give yourself permission, you used to tell me. I'd been practicing that, stealing bits of life here and there, learning to be fast, indistinguishable from the city's rush. Only the mad and the lost seemed to stand still, so that someone like me might pause and record them.

I passed the hospital where you were born and went farther west, through long brown blocks where even the stones looked bruised. Bodegas sold mangoes, dark twisted tubers, candles for the dead—wax rainbows in cheap glass. Boys hooted after me in Spanish. There was a burnt-out car near Tenth Avenue, then a wheelless one with a big blue-eyed doll's head hanging by string from the rearview mirror. The head had a look of stupid amazement, so I took its picture, establishing my credentials so to speak.

Maybe the Irish were all indoors that day. I didn't see any. Still, it was Marie's zone. She could have stepped out from any chalked-up doorway in cracked five-and-ten bedroom slippers, cursing the terrible decline of the neighborhood, cursing the filthy spics, the sons who were ungrateful, the bums she'd spread her legs for.

Don't look that woman in the eye! That's what one would warn oneself. Take her in quickly. Don't even let her see you turn your head.

Too many clothes for this warm afternoon, slip sagging under the garish coat, riotous red lipstick on askew. Pathetic. Maybe a social worker could decide that, professionally—or someone with Kevin's kind of goodness. My Leica, though, would do its job without pity. All I'd have to do was get too close to her, endure the furious glare for a moment, step in and out of the electrical field.

Then I'd come back to you armed with that picture. "Look at this," I'd say. "This has nothing to do with you."

18

Howard Stricker had told us not to pay attention to housing inspectors, but one of them discovered us. He knocked on our door one morning—luckily, I'd already gone to work. Right away he told Tom he didn't approve of our setup. "Do you live here?" he asked, casting his eyes up to our platform bed. "No one should live here."

Tom said, "Why would I live in a place like this?" He told the inspector we lived in Queens with my mother.

"So what about the bed?"

The bed was just for taking naps, Tom said. Some nights he'd work very hard and want to lie down for a while.

"With girls, maybe?" the inspector said with a leer.

He kept turning up after that. The late morning was his favorite time, just when Tom was painting. "Have to check out the conditions here," the inspector would say. He'd give the walls a few raps and squat down to examine the plumbing. Taking a chair in the studio, he'd jot things down on his clipboard. "Hey, you got any coffee?" Tom said the inspector felt free to indulge in art criticism. "I don't know about this one," he'd say, walking up to a painting and shaking his head. "Guys like you get good money for this stuff?"

Leon said he'd heard about this inspector from other artists he knew. "Bribe the bastard," he advised us. "He's just coming around with his hand out."

When Tom offered him a hundred dollars, the inspector acted deeply offended. "Not me. I don't take bribes."

"A gift," Tom said, and made it a hundred and fifty, which was about all we could have raised since there hadn't been any carpentry work for a while.

"What do you think I am?" said the inspector. "I see you still got the bed. That looks very bad. You're asking for it with that bed, in my opinion."

For a day or so, we thought about getting rid of the bed. The mattress was new—a gift from my mother. Where would we sleep, though? I went to a camping goods store and brought home a foam rubber mat, so thin it could be rolled up and hidden. "Fuck that," Tom said. "We live here. We're not a couple of gypsies." He stayed up all night and constructed an ingeniously hinged rack that went around the bed. He said he'd just shove some canvases up there every morning. On weekends we wouldn't have to worry because the inspector would be off duty.

On his next visit, the inspector took note of the rack. "Busy, busy, making improvements around here," he commented. Then he condemned our stove, our refrigerator and our hot-water heater. "Too old," he said. "These are fire hazards. You're just working here, so what do you need them for?"

Tom showed up at my office that day as I was about to go out for lunch. "Surprise," he said. But he wasn't smiling. "Come on, kiddo. I'll treat you to a sandwich and some iced tea." When we were in the elevator, he put his arm around me.

He told me the news in the Greek coffeeshop around the corner. He said he'd called Leon again for advice. Leon thought the guy might settle for three hundred, but just to be on the safe side we'd better get rid of the appliances and buy new ones.

I ate at that coffeeshop every day, and all the waitresses knew me. The one who brought us our order glared at Tom. I'd burst into tears and she probably had the impression I was being jilted. Tom said he'd never thought a refrigerator and a stove would break my heart. But it was more than that—more than the money we didn't have and couldn't get. If we couldn't stay in the loft, where would we live? If we had to move to a small apartment, Tom couldn't paint. If he couldn't paint, I'd lose him. I saw very clearly what all this was going to lead to. So I sat there sobbing, "I'm sorry. I'm sorry for doing this," as Tom kept ripping paper napkins from the holder and handing them to me. But I couldn't tell him the true cause of my grief.

We decided not to do anything. There really wasn't a thing we could do. We just kept stacking paintings around the bed in the mornings. We continued to wash in our illegal hot water and cook on our illegal stove. We waited to see what would happen the next time the inspector came. Weeks went by with no sign of him. At first we thought he was on vacation; then we began to hope he'd been transferred to a new district. Even so, we never really felt rid of him. The inspector remained with us. He was like a force we couldn't keep out. It was as if the world had decided people like us were somehow in the wrong. We had to be hounded supposedly for our own good, saved from the very conditions that made our existence possible.

One evening after work that summer, I ran into Arnie Raff on the main floor of Bloomingdale's. There he was, just a few feet away, all dressed up in a white suit with a little striped bow tie. His moustache was gone—instead there was a strange bluish space between his nose and upper lip. I checked myself for evidence of emotional disturbance and found none, so I walked up to him and said, "Hello, Mr. Raff."

He looked stricken either by panic or guilt, but then he seemed to realize I meant him no harm. "Well, hello there," he said, and we carried on one of those catching-up conversations in which no one really listens to the other person's news. We could have been two former classmates who'd known each other slightly in high school.

"What are you doing in Bloomingdale's?" I asked, since it was a place Arnie's principles wouldn't have allowed him to be caught dead in when we lived together on Seventh Street.

He said he'd come there to buy perfume, perfume for someone's birthday.

I said, "Oh, are you getting it for your wife?"

He conceded that he was. "I'm surprising her." But he didn't know what kind to get. "What do I know about perfume?" he said, imitating the rough, sullen air of the old Arnie.

I actually ended up accompanying him to various perfume counters. I was sure he'd never tell his wife who had smelled her present.

We kept opening bottles and passing them to each other for sniffs and spraying the contents on each other's wrists. I acted as if I really cared how different kinds would smell to her. He seemed to be in awe of his wife, who he said had spent her summers in the south of France when she wasn't in East Hampton; he was also proud of the fact that she collected valuable wines—she didn't *drink* her collection, he explained; she just liked owning the old bottles with their labels. And now she's collected *you*, Arnie, I almost said. Finally he settled on a tiny hundred-dollar bottle of the stuff I assured him smelled the best. "Probably she'll hate it," he said gloomily.

"Arnie, do you remember that frying pan you gave me?" I asked. "I still use it."

Arnie frowned. "What frying pan? I don't know what frying pan you mean."

I couldn't believe he had forgotten something of such symbolic importance. "Red," I said. "My twenty-fourth birthday."

"Okay," he said. "I admit I made a few mistakes."

"Water under the bridge, Arnie," I said, with a wave of my hand.

He told me I was looking good, but that was because he wasn't looking at me. "Things have worked out for you, haven't they?"

"Yes they have. I'm terribly, terribly happy," I told him.

Happiness that had terror in it. I still remember that choice of words.

And what was I doing that evening so far uptown? It must have been one of those black periods when I'd come home to Chrystie Street knowing I wouldn't find you there, knowing you wouldn't even necessarily be at the Cedar if I called. You were just out—caught in some barroom time machine where the numbers on the clock never shifted until suddenly the bartender served the last round, and even then it was as if you'd just come in.

It was very hot on Chrystie Street those summer evenings. But the air in the stores I used to visit after work was perfectly chilled. I'd pull things off racks, carry them into dressing rooms. It was quite exhausting trying on so many outfits. Sometimes I'd be looking at myself in a three-way mirror and my eyes would fill. Before I came out, I'd have to put on a lot of mascara.

"Why are you always going shopping?" you asked me, puzzled because I never made any purchases.

"These are the best times we'll ever have."

I remember you saying that in a sad voice, and I didn't know what you meant, because the better times seemed like a brightly lit station so infinitely far away we wouldn't see it till we were almost there; meanwhile the black tunnel we'd entered went on and on.

I was learning to be very good at waiting. Great at it, in fact. It was like learning to ride on the buddy seat—one of my main accomplishments. Waiting things out. That was how I was going to save you.

I developed techniques, I could dispose of whole hours, though I never became a crossword fan like Caroline. I learned to work a sewing machine—everyone was still wearing shifts, which took very little work and material. The sewing would wear me out, and I'd lie down on the couch and pretend to sleep, setting the clock next to me. The numbers would glow greener and greener as the summer light faded from the room. It was like being a child again, put to bed too early. Glass would break in the park, kids would go by on roller skates. Around midnight the iron gate over the garage would come down with a crash.

When I'd hear you come in, I'd sit up, a little dazed. "Tom? Want something to eat?" But you hardly ever did.

"Well, it's there if you want it."

Well, I'm there if you want me.

Sometimes it was easiest to just stay very late at the office, outlasting the old woman who came to empty all the waste baskets. One of those nights, on its way downtown, my bus stopped at Tenth Street and you got on, very smashed. To find you on your way home so unexpectedly seemed almost a miracle. You stood next to the driver, fumbling for change. You pulled your pockets inside out. Pennies and nickels rolled all over the floor. You were laughing and saying, "Oh shit, oh shit," because you didn't have the balance to pick any of it up.

There was a big Chinese family on the bus traveling down to Mott Street. The kids were pointing at you and giggling. I knew they were saying "drunk" in Chinese, and I hated them for it. I got up from my seat and walked down the aisle to the front of the bus and paid your fare. "Oh," you announced to all the passengers, to the world, "let me introduce my wife. This gorgeous, generous woman is my wife."

Despite everything, I knew you meant it. You had the most beautiful smile on your face. I put my arms around you and kissed you in front of all those Chinese strangers. I bent down and started to pick up the change you'd dropped, but you wouldn't let me. "Leave it there," you said. "Leave it for the poor."

You told me it wasn't women. "It isn't women, if that's what's worrying you. I'm not off somewhere picking up broads. I always come home, don't I? I mean, here I *am*, baby, whatever that means. Whatever good that does you."

"What is it then?" I asked you. "Tell me. Why can't you be here?"

"Tomorrow I'll stay home. I won't go out, won't drink. Just leave me food—no money. You can call and check up on me all you want." Then you gripped my arms so hard the red marks were still there the next day. "Listen," you said in a threatening voice, "I'll only leave you once."

In the morning you were contrite when I told you what you'd said. The sheets were as drenched as if you'd had a fever. You asked for some coffee and I brought it to you. I sat myself on the edge of the bed, but you pulled me down and lay on top of me, looking into my eyes.

There was always another chance in the mornings.

Our worst battles took place in cabs with the driver's contempt in the mirror.

"Make the light!" No matter how drunk you were, you'd yell

that out when we got to Grand Street, bitter that you'd had to be retrieved, reeled in by me.

Billy kept track of you. We'd conspire to get you home. The phone would ring on Chrystie Street—"Maybe you'd better come up here, Joanna. I'll try to keep him from leaving." Somehow he'd steal your key ring from your pocket, so you wouldn't be able to start the bike. Then he'd lure you out to the curb, where the cab would be waiting. When I opened the door, he'd wrestle you onto the backseat. "Give me the fucking keys, Billy!" You seemed to be dying of thirst, like a man who'd come in from the desert too late—all the beer, all the wine in the world wouldn't have been enough.

"It doesn't make any sense." I used to keep pointing that out to you. None of it made sense. I was still trying to keep you alive—that was really what we fought about. I was simply going to keep coming for you and waiting for you until you'd see there was nothing you could do that would shake me loose. I didn't have any other plan. I thought we had time—maybe not forever, but years. I wonder how many years I would have stuck it out.

"I'll only leave you once." I never questioned that. You'd lost too many people by the time you got to me. I could only leave you if I meant it to be for good—you'd never try to get me back. Maybe I'd get one call, long-distance, the way you called Caroline once in the middle of the night months after the divorce. Maybe you'd ask me the same thing in that same low, deadly voice. If I knew what I'd done. "Did you *know?* I want to know how cold you were when you worked it out."

I couldn't imagine being cold to you. Hating you, but not being cold.

I hit you one night. Maybe it was hate. One of those nights I'd dragged you home from somewhere in a cab. We were standing out on Chrystie Street and you wouldn't come upstairs. You were insisting I look at the moon. Of all things, the moon. But I wasn't about to grant you that. "I'm going to stay out here until God strikes me down," you said, and I hit you right below the eye and ran down the block. I got to the corner, but there was nothing there. Just the hot, still air, the useless burned-out globe in the sky, the bums snoring under the bridal-shop windows. I didn't know what I was running to. That was why I came back.

Grand Street

Fall 1963

19

Summer couldn't seem to end itself that year. At the Cedar Bar, the weirdness of the fall became a topic of conversation. The leaves should have been turning, but they weren't. We noticed this even in the bums' park across the street, where the sycamores wouldn't yellow. Dust just kept falling on the dry green leaves.

I didn't appreciate the warm days, even though it was nice not to have to wear a coat. I knew I'd feel easier in the cold weather, when Tom wouldn't be riding around so much on the bike. I used to look down our block as soon as I turned the corner, praying I'd see the red Harley outside our house. There were still too many nights when it wasn't there.

If Tom was home already, the television would be on. When I came in, it would be the six o'clock news and he'd be on the couch asleep. He was trying to cut down on his drinking and it made him awfully quiet, as if he could only hold on to himself by hardly speaking. We'd eat dinner with Jackie Gleason on full blast. It seemed funny that we should come to this—just a couple watching TV like millions of others tuned to the same channel. It was like the fate I'd always feared, that ordinariness would overtake me.

Tom wasn't painting. He'd walk through his studio just to get to the front door, without ever turning on the lights. On the wall in there was an unfinished canvas he couldn't look at, one of the black-and-white paintings he hated now. He said he hated everything he'd done the past few months. He'd worked like a madman, not like an artist. That was why those paintings were no good. They'd all end up on the floor, he said, as soon as he had the guts to rip them off their stretchers. I begged him not to do it. What if months from now he felt differently? But I knew in my heart that he was right. Sometimes he'd talk about all the other paintings he'd lost, the work no one but fools would ever see. He told me you could lose everything you had by trying to replace what had been taken from you. "That's the way they rob you twice, kiddo. Some people know that, have that in mind."

For a while he kept himself occupied making shelves and a kitchen counter from scraps of wood Howard Stricker had left behind. He said he wanted me to have my own darkroom. He was going to build it as soon as he got some cash. In fact, Billy had told him a big carpentry job was coming up—enough work for a couple of months. With a job like that, he told me, he wouldn't have time to drink, wouldn't have time to paint either, even if he wanted to.

"Don't you like me better when I'm not painting? Look how handy I am around the house?"

All my adult life, I'd been lugging shopping bags home from supermarkets, but now Tom wasn't going to let me do that anymore. Every Friday he was going to meet me after work at the Grand Union on Spring Street. He was very serious about it. Somehow he'd manage to show up there even if all afternoon he'd been drinking. On those days he never realized how long it took us to get home. He'd stumble along carrying those heavy bags with the rest of the loud world darting around him—housewives charging back to their kitchens from the fish store, kids screaming "Throw me the ball! Throw me the ball!" playing the last furious game on Mulberry Street before dinner. He'd always stop right there and watch them.

I remember we kept buying tomatoes from an old man with a pushcart who always cheated us a little. They were the best and worst tomatoes, deep red, bursting, three pounds for a quarter. He'd load them onto his scale so fast there was no telling which ones were rotten. One night he informed us there was going to be a *festa*. "A good week for the saint," he said with a wink, fanning himself with a fistful of dollar bills.

Workmen had been going around the neighborhood that Friday, putting up the wires for colored lights. They'd strung one of them high over Grand Street, though I didn't take any notice of it at first. We were standing on the curb waiting to cross when I felt Tom tap my arm.

"Look up! Look up over there!"

A dead bundle of feathers was hanging throttled against the sky. Just an instant before, he'd seen a pigeon fly straight into that wire.

For days we talked about it. Tom kept saying it was one chance in a million. It had only been a question of the wire having the right amount of slack. But why had that bird flown into it when it had an entire sky to itself?

In mid-October we had all our relatives over for Sunday dinner—part of our campaign to be normal. We invited my mother and

Kevin and Grace and their kid. Tom took over most of the cooking. He promised me that even if Kevin brought him a bottle, he'd only drink Coca-Cola. Before everyone came, I scrubbed every visible surface in the kitchen, but still it would never look like Grace's.

Kevin and Grace always got very nervous whenever we suggested they should come and see us. Tom said it was shyness. Their lives were so different from ours, they probably thought they wouldn't like our place and were afraid they'd say the wrong thing. Once when we'd gone out there, Tom had tried to give them a small painting. Kevin said stiffly, "Well Tommy, this is really an honor." He'd called to Grace to come in from the kitchen and they'd had a little argument about where to hang it. Of course it would have to go in the living room, and they kept taking down pictures of flowers and Jesus and ducks flying over lakes and trying it out unhappily. At last Tom said, "Listen, this isn't the right painting for you. I'll do another one sometime that you'll like better maybe." "Oh, it's very nice," they said, but we could tell they were grateful to be let off the hook.

When they finally saw where we lived, they were sort of shocked, though they did find things to admire like the marble fragment wall erected by Howard Stricker. Kevin walked around with Tom, looking carefully at everything; he had his little boy riding on his shoulders because Grace didn't want him on the floor getting splinters. He kept asking worried, practical questions, like weren't we too cold in the winter? Tom laughed and pointed out the loft bed. "Well, you see, all the heat rises up there." He had a can of Coke in his hand, and it didn't seem to bother him to pour his brother a glass of Scotch. He even showed everyone where my darkroom was going to be.

My mother got on the warpath right away. "What do you need a darkroom for?" she asked me.

I'd told her I'd been fooling around a little with photography; I wasn't ready yet to tell her it was serious. "It just costs too much to have things developed," I said.

"Don't you let her do it!" my mother appealed to Tom. "She'll ruin her hands."

I said I didn't care about my hands. I didn't give a damn.

"What if you get offered a movie role? It could happen."

"Ma!" I said. "It's not to be discussed. Okay?"

"Darkrooms are unhealthy," she insisted. "I know about such things."

"Let's all move to the table," Tom said loudly, and started dishing out the olives and red peppers we'd brought home from Little Italy.

My mother didn't mention the darkroom again. Instead she started telling Kevin and Grace about my great career on Broadway. Grace couldn't hear enough about it. She must have thought I was crazy not to have bragged to her about it before. My mother made it sound as if I'd practically been another Shirley Temple, as if I'd been too good for all the parts I never got, as if producers had come to her begging on their knees and she'd had to proudly turn them down. Sure, I said, the truth was, we'd had a great glamorous time of dragging around to a million offices and eating all our dinners in the Fifty-seventh Street Automat. But Kevin and Grace were under my mother's spell. She even wanted to show them all the yellow, flaking clippings that had my name in them and invited them to her house for that purpose. From where they lived, she said, it would only take them twenty minutes to drive over. It was her last stand, but I didn't see that. I only knew she was sucking all the air out of my life.

I threw down my fork and said in a choked voice, in front of everyone, "Whatever I do, whatever I become, I'll never be as great as I was when I was nine years old." It was the way she'd made me feel for a long time, but I'd never been able to just come right out with it. It was as if even now, when I was twenty-seven, I still believed my mother would have no use for me if I couldn't do all the great things she expected. When I was little, I actually used to fear that someday she'd lose interest in me, the way she seemed to have lost interest in my father.

After I'd spoken, my mother's eyes looked teary. I tried to make a joke, but it came out wrong. "Excuse me," I said, getting up to go to the oven. "The *star* has to check on the lasagna."

Tom put his arm around my mother's shoulders. "Your daughter's great with the camera. She's a natural. So I want her to have her own little setup here."

A natural. The moment he said it, that word cut through everything. He could have been saying it for her benefit, but he never told lies about people's work.

He kept his arm around her. "I'll make her wear gloves, Mrs. Gold," he said.

My mother went home that night before dessert. She said she had heartburn. She said it was from the spices in the lasagna, but no one gets heartburn from oregano. I didn't hear from her for a couple of weeks. "Call her up," Tom said, but I didn't, I couldn't.

Grace phoned to invite us to their house for dinner. "How's your mother?" she asked.

I said we'd been out of contact for a while. Suddenly I felt awful, as if we'd be out of contact forever, both of us stubbornly not calling.

Grace said my mother seemed the kind of determined person who'd never take no for an answer. "Does her birthday happen to fall in January or February?" she asked me.

"January twenty-eighth," I said.

"That's what I thought." Grace sounded very pleased. She told me that every morning, right after she did the breakfast dishes, she looked at the astrology column in the *Daily News* and did horoscopes for herself and Kevin. "I really like to keep an eye on the future."

"Not me," I said. "I don't want to know."

"You'd rather have everything just come at you?"

"I don't know. I suppose so."

"Tell me your birthday anyway," Grace said. "Just for fun."

But I wouldn't, even though I didn't want to seem unfriendly. "Oh Grace," I said. "We don't believe in all that."

I proved I was less stubborn than my mother because I was the one who finally called. I expected reproaches, but I didn't get them. Instead she asked how my darkroom was coming along. That was an extraordinary concession on her part—to speak of it as something real, something that would be built and come into use and existence. She'd always acted as if other people's needs were unfathomable, out of control.

There was a tiredness in her voice that day, and I asked her why. She told me she'd been reorganizing the house, making a clean sweep of everything she didn't need, giving away my father's clothes and all the old leather suitcases with his initials on them. "They're not even lightweight, like the ones they make now. I wouldn't want to be hauling one through an airport."

"You planning to fly somewhere, Ma?" I asked her. And she said, "Well, I might. I'm going to be sixty and I've never been anywhere to speak of."

"You could have gone years ago," I pointed out.

"I was worried sick about you. . . . How could I leave the country?"

"Nothing was going to happen to me, Ma."

"Oh," she said. "I'm not so sure."

"But now everything's fine," I told her. It was only a little lie. There are certain old habits you can't ever break.

My father had been another nontraveler. My mother used to complain bitterly about his luggage collection. She couldn't figure out what it was for, since she could never get him to take a vacation with her. He had a predilection for leather goods—expensive wallets, cigarette cases. He'd just buy suitcases that appealed to him and put them in the backs of closets. Right after he died, I'd helped my mother put his suits in a couple of them. "Where did your father think he was going?" she'd asked me.

He'd packed one suitcase himself. My mother found it soon after we talked on the phone when she was going through stuff in the attic. She called me because she wanted me to come out with Tom to pick it up. "This is going to interest you very much, Joanna," she said. It was full of my father's prints, packed between layers of cardboard—the photos he used to take for his own pleasure, the ones my mother once told him were so ugly. Perhaps she'd always felt guilty about that, because she said she couldn't bring herself to go through them; she was leaving that to me. It would be a very nice idea to send the best ones out to photography magazines. "After all, your father subscribed to them for years."

When Tom heard about my father's prints turning up, he said, "Listen kiddo, maybe you're going to be disappointed."

"Maybe I won't be," I said. I was convinced I was going to discover something extremely important, something that would tell me who my father really had been—not just the quiet, worn-out man who always had to be in his store, finishing his dinner long before I finished mine, then slipping away again, giving me a quick kiss on the forehead if I ran after him, a whiff of his smoker's breath.

The night we brought the suitcase home in the subway, I opened it in Tom's studio and stayed up for hours looking at all the prints. Before I showed them to Tom, I wanted to be sure how I felt about them myself.

My father had been an orderly man, always very methodical. Once when a woman came to the store to see if she could get a copy of an old wedding picture, I heard him tell her he'd never misplaced a negative. It was like him to have packed very carefully, so that dust wouldn't get on any of his work. He must have counted on the suitcase being found one day, imagined someone pulling those photos out from all those layers of cardboard, finally appreciating his art.

I laid the prints out on the floor all around me on sheets of newspaper, respecting my father's fear of dust. My mother had been wrong—they weren't ugly. They just weren't photographs anyone who hadn't known my father would have cared about. I think I knew that very quickly, even though I didn't want to. I looked at each one for a long time, searching for what wasn't there, as if my father, in his self-effacing way, had known what he was doing in obscuring the magic I was trying to find. But the photos were no more than they seemed to be at first glance; they could have been done by anyone with a good technical mastery of the camera.

My father had tried out artistically posed portraits, still lifes of flowers and bowls of fruit, all the usual subjects. There were even many studies of a nude—I was thankful my mother hadn't seen those. She had long, rather thin black hair and small breasts with very sharply pointed nipples, a Spanish-looking face. This woman never looked happy, just sort of sour and depressed, uncomfortable about the whole business. Her bed had an old scratched-up metal headboard and the spread she usually lay on had bouquets of ostrich plumes printed on it. Sometimes it was pulled to one side and rumpled, as if her lover had gotten up moments before and left her lying there. Once the woman had a small, dark child in her arms who never appeared again. Then she seemed to put on weight and look older, and the ostrich bedspread was replaced by one with a flamingo-and-palm-tree pattern.

My father seemed never to have visited this woman at night.

There was a window next to the bed, covered with lace curtains, and a filtered afternoon, courtyard light came in, like the light of a particular kind of sadness, the illumination of a lack of joy. Often a lamp beside the bed had been turned on as well, but that was always a mistake. If my father had waited for the light from the window to fall across the woman exactly the right way, he might have had one perfect picture that made up for all the others. Maybe the woman would grow impatient and complain that she was cold, or it would get late and he'd have to hurry back to the store from his "walk." Or maybe he just never saw what the light could have done.

I had the feeling I shouldn't be having thoughts of that sort—part of me in despair over my father's stunted life, the other part of me thinking he should have gotten the light right, angry with him. I looked up and saw the empty stretchers that now stood in a corner of the studio, all that was left of Tom's summer of work. My father had never been able to say, "All these shots are going to end up on the floor."

20

It was the beginning of November, still that quiet time, those strange days that were too warm. We used to wake up early the way we did in the summer, always surprised how dark it was. "We've still got an hour to make love," Tom would whisper. We heard noises on the stairs one of those mornings; at first we thought some bums had spent the night in our building. Tom always chased them out because we were afraid of fire, but the worst they ever did was leave their smell behind or some empty bottles we'd have to throw away. Tom put on his jeans and went to our door to take a look. When he opened it, he found the housing inspector sitting on a step on our landing drinking coffee out of a container. The man had actually been waiting for one of us to come out. He seemed delighted with his cleverness.

"Gotcha! And you said you didn't live here. Where's the wife? She in there, too?"

I was still in bed. I heard voices, then our door slammed. I climbed down and ran over there. "Tom!" Then a crash on the landing made all our dishes rattle. *"Tom!"*

"Stay inside, kiddo!"

Later Tom told me he'd knocked the coffee out of the inspector's hands. When the man charged at him, he'd let him have it really hard.

I could hear them scuffling, banging against the banisters, all the way down the stairs. "Don't ever come back here!" Tom was yelling. I still thought he must be fighting with a bum, a crazy one. I rushed to the front windows. When they came out, I saw that his opponent was someone wearing respectable clothes, a bald, heavyset man in a tan raincoat. Now the bald man and Tom were circling each other in the middle of the street. A driver stopped his car and blew his horn at them. All of a sudden, Tom broke forward, his fists moving very fast, and the bald man wobbled and sank, looking almost foolish, as if a chair had collapsed under him. I saw blood on his chin and on the collar of his tan coat. Tom was holding him down, shouting into his face.

"I know who you are! I can find you. You give me any trouble, and you're dead."

I was more frightened by those words than by anything else that had happened. I still hadn't figured out what the stranger had to do with us.

When Tom let him go, the bald man got on all fours; it took him a few tries before he was able to stand. Then he ran up the street in sort of a zigzag pattern and disappeared around the corner.

The whole thing had happened in minutes. For a while I was sure the police would be showing up. I even thought I could hear their sirens in the distance. But Tom was laughing when he came upstairs. "Well, you finally got to see the great inspector." His left hand was bleeding, but he wouldn't let me take care of it. He walked up and down, sucking the blood off his knuckles.

"You saw all that, didn't you? The moves? See, I never forgot the old moves. He knew I was ready, that son of a bitch. Either I was going to get rid of him or one of us was going to die. I tell you, I was ready either way."

"To die?" I cried. "What are you talking about? What are you saying?"

You couldn't understand why I wasn't just excited about your victory the way you were. "Why do you have such a round, long face?" you teased me.

"What if something had happened to you?"

"Everything's happened to me already, kiddo." And you told me to get dressed and go to work and not to worry. "It's only another Monday."

I remember how it felt, going to the office that day—those orderly cubicles, those low, polite voices murmuring into phones. There was going to be a shower for the receptionist, and a big flowered greeting card came around. Everyone had to sign it and contribute three dollars and a witty remark. A couple of people had even written rhymed couplets. I sat with the card in front of me and couldn't think of a thing, so I just wrote, "Best wishes, Joanna." Whenever my mind drifted away from my typing, those two figures in the street started circling each other.

That evening, when I got off the bus at Grand Street, I was almost afraid to walk down our block. I had the feeling I'd find our whole building gone, just an empty lot between the garage and the Italian butcher shop.

But the moment I was on Chrystie, I saw our front windows all lit up. It was the first time in a couple of months. You'd turned on the big fluorescents, the ones you only used when you were working. I could even hear music as I ran up the stairs, a Lightning Hopkins record Billy had given us that spring. You were crazy about a song called "Last Night Blues." For weeks you'd listened to it over and over, moving the needle back to the right groove. The last bars were playing as I came in and a wall was covered with an enormous piece of canvas. You'd nearly finished slapping gesso on it. All that white seemed to glow. It looked beautiful to me just the way it was.

I remember a thought that came at me out of nowhere. That if the inspector hadn't come, the lights wouldn't have been on, there wouldn't have been any canvas stretched across the wall. That maybe when you painted, it was like saying, "Either I was going to get rid of him or one of us was going to die"—somehow it was the same kind of feeling.

But I didn't want to know that about you. It made me think there was nothing to hope for—nothing but a life of furious, burning moments.

You came over to me and kissed me, holding the wet brush at arm's length away from us. "Last painting blues," you said.

You kept telling me we'd heard the last of the inspector. I didn't let on I was trying to prepare myself for losing our place—it was a fear I couldn't get rid of, that somehow our days there were numbered. Numbered days. I thought I knew how it would happen. A letter would come from the housing department, with some kind of form to fill out, and all the information we'd give them would go against us. Whatever would be done to us would be done by some typist we'd never even see. I always expected to find the letter when I went down to get the mail.

I was taking notice of FOR RENT signs again. There was a new one on a loft building on Rivington Street. Riding uptown behind you on the bike, I said, "Look at that. Maybe we could live there." The words just slipped out. You didn't say anything to me till we got off the bike in front of the Cedar. I was going to walk inside, but you laid your hand on the back of my neck and stopped me. "Wherever we go, we'll always be together." That was all you said. I never met another man who said "always."

When the job Billy promised you came through, you took your whole first check and spent it on lumber. "You're looking at your darkroom," you told me. You were going to start building it once the pace slowed down, maybe after Thanksgiving. And you measured it off on the floor, drawing lines with blue chalk, so I'd get some idea of how much space I was going to have. The blue lines were still there the day I started putting things in boxes and the landlord came by and told me that even if I'd wanted to keep the place, it would have been impossible. He showed me the notice from the housing department that you'd never have to see, and I was glad that at least you'd died believing that you'd won.

You'd even become sort of famous for a while around the neighborhood. A lot of people had looked out their windows that morning the inspector came. "That was some fight you had," strangers would say, stopping you on the street. "Hey killer," said the men in the garage.

For about a week that month, I thought I was pregnant. I kept looking for the red stain that wouldn't show itself, trying to remember how or when we had been careless, which night or morning the accident could have happened for which we were now going to pay the price. This baby made no sense at all, but I wanted it. That was the most dangerous part, the part that made the baby real. What if wanting had that much power?

I knew of course exactly what would have to be done, where I could find the old doctor in Reading, Pennsylvania, who'd probably raised his prices if he was still in practice. I'd gone to him once when I lived with Arnie. I'd tried to see it as a test of courage, a trip a woman like me would have to make sooner or later. I was twenty-two. I couldn't think of another choice. I still remember the bus ride back over the Jersey marshes, staring at the miles of flatness, the thick reeds standing in the rank water, the feeling of returning emptied—emptied and freed—bewildered by the way one state seemed to contradict the other.

I'd told Tom about it once. He said he'd never let me go through that again. "We'd just have the kid," he said.

I'd begun to think that was the only way it would ever happen. It had to be left up to chance, like gambling, while we raised the odds against it, warded it off. It would be the thing that would save us or the last straw. I guess I believed it would be the last straw.

Tom asked me that week why I seemed a little down. I said I was depressed and didn't know why.

"Maybe you're just getting your period," he said.

He took me to Chinatown to cheer me up. Now that he was making some money again, he wanted me to have a break from cooking. The job he and Billy were on was going to last a month, maybe it would even stretch longer. He was proud of how many nails he'd hammered that day—three hundred and fourteen.

I thought of having the baby and how Tom would feel if he had to hammer nails and saw wood all the time in order to support it.

He kept having the waiter bring us different dishes and asking me why I was eating so little. That was the night he told me his work was about to go into a new phase. He'd been thinking about the old Japanese scroll painters, how they'd sometimes increased the size of their strokes by tying bunches of sumi brushes together. He was going to find a way to do the same thing, but on a much larger scale. Didn't I see how everything would become more crucial? You'd know with the very first moves whether a painting was going to make it. He was going to start experimenting with sketches, using housepainter's brushes on small sheets of paper—but even huge canvases could be just as free. "No brush is big enough for what I want to do next," he said.

I left the table while he was paying the check. I went into the ladies' room and looked again for the red stain that would tell me we could go on just as we were.

It wasn't till the next day that I discovered my body had been playing a trick on me. I'd only been pregnant with a mistaken idea. I remember thinking, Well, that was my last chance—and getting disgusted with myself for being so melodramatic.

When Lee Harvey Oswald shot President Kennedy, you said the president was just like the bird we'd seen on Grand Street, the one that flew straight into the wire.

Like everyone else in America, we lost a week to television. We didn't even go uptown to the Cedar at night. Nothing could tear you away from the black-and-white pictures on the screen. You couldn't shake the thought that any little detail could have deflected the president's death. You even related it to the new sketches you'd tacked up all over the studio. Small things could become enormous. If the sun hadn't been shining in Dallas, if the president hadn't been the kind of man who felt invulnerable, if he hadn't decided to ride in a convertible that day . . .

Finally, there was the funeral. You were holding my hand when the three-year-old boy in the coat with the velvet collar saluted his dead father. You stood up suddenly and turned off the set.

Kevin called only a couple of days later, right around dinnertime. I ran up the last flight of stairs because I could hear the phone ringing and ringing in the studio. When I picked it up, Kevin didn't say hello, just "Can you get Tommy? Where's Tommy? I've been trying him all day." Kevin always called him Tommy, as if the two of them were still little kids. When I told him Tom still had the carpentry job, he said, "Oh Christ, I forgot." He sounded awful.

"Kevin, is everything okay?" I remember being scared he'd tell me something had happened to his kid.

"To tell you the truth, things aren't so great." He paused and then, lowering his voice, said in a strange, embarrassed way, "I had to take my father to the hospital this morning."

The man who had locked Tom out on the roof was dying. That was what ran through my mind, those two things connected. But for Kevin's sake, I said what you say when you hear that kind of news, that I was sorry.

Kevin said the doctors had amputated his father's right leg, but it had been no use. "He's going fast. That's the way it is. Something could happen any minute. Mother's here with me. You'd better tell Tommy that."

He told me the best place for Tom to look for them was in the waiting room on the sixth floor of Polyclinic. He kept coughing, clearing his throat. "If Tommy doesn't want to come, I'll understand. But something like this—you know how it is. . . . Honest to God, I didn't know who else to call."

Mother's here with me. Those seemed the most unbelievable words. They brought her so close, made her seem like someone I knew. But what else could Kevin have called her?

"You know, your mother's up there with Kevin," I told you when you came home from work. I asked you what you were going to do, dreading that you'd go. I wanted life to just leave us alone. That was the kind of person I was turning into.

But you said right away, "Kevin can't get through this by himself."

I knew all your stories about the two kids who'd had to share a fold-up cot in a tiny room in that basement in the Bronx. Sometimes, for no good reason, Frank would come in and turn on the lights. He'd drag the older one out of bed and start beating him with his belt and his fists. The little brother had learned from the older one not to cry; instead he'd pee and completely soak the mattress. There were times the older kid would get punished for that, too, in the mornings.

"See, Kevin was always too tenderhearted," you said once. "I could never get him trained."

As for you, you believed you had a rock in your heart where forgiveness should have been. Maybe it was a birth defect, you used to say, something you'd inherited from Marie. Or maybe you were cursed with having too good a memory. "It's the guys who remember everything who have to drink. That's why you always hear the best stories in bars."

At one A.M., when you called me from a pay phone, Frank was still alive. "I saw the old man. I saw Frank. They've got plastic all around him like meat in the supermarket. He didn't even know I was there. Lucky for him."

I could hear a jukebox. It was the very end of November, and someone was already playing "White Christmas." You said you'd made Kevin come with you to an Irish bar on Eighth Avenue. Kevin needed a few drinks, needed something. "It isn't the death that's getting to him. It's that *no one's* dying, no one you could have called a person."

I kept expecting you to say something about Marie, but you didn't. Finally I couldn't help asking, "Did you see her?"

For a few seconds all I heard was more of "White Christmas." I guess you were deciding you'd better make a joke of it. "Sure, for about five minutes. It was some reunion—hearts and flowers. A very moving experience."

"Tom," I said. "Was it bad?"

"Go to sleep, kiddo. Don't wait up."

It was dawn when I heard your key in the door; then you stumbled against something out in the studio. You were carrying a big paper bag that you threw all the way across the room before you hoisted yourself up on the bed. You sank down next to me, and after that, you didn't move, didn't even try to take off your coat. I could feel the cold on the hard corduroy, on your face. The only thing you'd tell me was that after Frank had died, you and Kevin had taken a cab up to the Bronx and spent a fortune driving around the old neighborhood. I got you out of the coat, pulled blankets over you. You kept shuddering in my arms even after you fell asleep. Once you woke up and said, "Don't go anywhere."

"My mother gave me a present," you told me later that morning. "Want to see it?"

It was a pair of shoes, heavy black shoes with no laces. You'd brought them back with you in the paper bag; they'd even traveled all the way to the Bronx.

The shoes had belonged to Frank. "He won't be needing them where he's going, so you can wear them," your mother had said. "Go on. Take them," she'd said, smiling, pushing the bag at you. "You were always after me to get you shoes."

We decided the only thing to do was get rid of them, get them out of the house. We went for a walk and left them next to a garbage can on Hester Street and the Bowery.

21

I used to need to keep proving to myself you'd really intended to live. I only trusted concrete, tangible evidence. The fact you'd just had the Harley repaired and bought new tires. A roll of canvas you brought home after the job ended, the first week in December. I didn't trust love. I knew you would have wanted me to think everything was going to work out—to have left me with that. So that roll of canvas seemed more reliable.

There were some days that were still warm when they should have been cold; we saw bums still sleeping in the park. That was why, even though we talked about getting ready for winter, you never got around to putting plastic up over the windows. You made me play hooky from work and we took the bike for a last trip to Sheepshead Bay, sat on the pier in the sun eating fried clam sandwiches. We had it all to ourselves; the kids with the drop lines were in school. If we ever got rich, we'd buy a boat, you said.

Nothing fancy, It would have to be something sturdy with plenty of room, maybe an old Nova Scotia fishing boat we could live on in the summers. There was a change, suddenly, that we both felt—as if we'd come out from the weight and the darkness, and here it was, a radiant blue-gray Tuesday, from which we could see clear ahead to the rest of our lives.

You said it was like a great temporary gift—something we'd had and lost and found again, without even looking for it.

"Not temporary," I insisted. "Not temporary." We were having our usual philosophical difference, and you reminded me that nothing stays the same.

"Oh, there you go," I said. "Not temporary."

You hadn't gone to Frank's funeral, which was very small, just Kevin and Marie. Grace, too, had stayed away. You said you felt incredibly free of that part of your life—it was as if you'd cast it off with Frank's black shoes. Maybe, without knowing it, your crazy mother had given you something you'd needed.

"I'm going to stop drinking," you said. "That's over, too." You were going to see if you could get through an entire week without any alcohol; you hadn't been able to earlier in the fall. After work, you'd come uptown to meet me and ride me home on the back of the bike.

Billy came over for dinner one night, full of gossip about some artist from L.A. you'd missed seeing in the Cedar Bar, and a party he wanted us to crash with him that was going to be full of millionaire collectors. He had news to tell us about himself. A gallery was going to show two of his paintings.

"Hey Billy," you said. "This is the beginning."

Billy looked a little abashed. For weeks, he said, he'd had something to tell you. It would probably make you mad at him, but when you saw the show, you'd find out anyway.

I'd figured out Billy's secret even before he said, "Tom, I've had to give up on abstract expressionism. I'm young, you know," he pointed out, as if no one had ever noticed it. "There's all this new stuff I've gotta try."

I had the feeling he expected you to rise up and shout that you were disowning him. It wasn't that he wanted to be disowned; he just wanted to be sure that it mattered to you a lot that he was no longer under your influence. But all you said that night was, "Well, you don't need anyone's approval, Billy."

You were holding my hand under the table, and your fingers kept tightening around mine, but we were careful not to look at each other as we listened to Billy describe the new work he was doing. I remember it related to the Lone Ranger comic strip and the end of the real Wild West. His latest painting was two huge cowboy boots, standing toe to toe against a flat sunset-orange background. The gallery dealer had said it represented a dialog of great intensity.

That was too much for you, of course. "Oh yeah? Better watch out for bullshit—it can swallow you up."

"I told you you'd get mad," Billy said happily.

Just before he left, he asked you for a favor. A guy had asked him to do a twelve-foot mural for a new bar in the Village. He'd roughed it all out and could paint the whole thing in an afternoon. But his place was too small and he'd have to borrow someone's studio.

"Sure," you said. "How about Monday?"

That weekend there was an anniversary of Pearl Harbor; a special program, "Victory at Sea," ran for two straight days on television for hours and hours. You sat in front of the set with the blinds drawn and watched the whole thing. I kept making pots of coffee and feeling shut in. I didn't care much for all the endless footage of old battles, the sounds of explosions and artillery fire. I went out and walked around Little Italy, bought a lot of food, decided to make a leg of lamb—something different, ambitious. I was busy washing lettuce for a salad when you called to me to come quickly.

"They're showing Anzio!"

I said I'd be there in a minute. I could even have turned and watched the screen from where I was standing, but I still had the water running.

You saw your sweeper, the one you'd been on during the invasion. It was just a glimpse, but you recognized it. "Jesus Christ! There it is!" I heard you shout. And I did turn then, but it was gone. We kept hoping the camera would come back to it, but the show moved on to a different part of the war. And even now, I don't know what kept me from looking sooner. It seems like some failure of love, some need I had to hold myself back from you a little.

I sat with you, though, the next day and watched the end of the show, the victory part, the part where all the soldiers and sailors came home jammed onto the troopships and all the foghorns and whistles were blowing in New York harbor and military bands were playing and people were going nuts on the docks, making V signs and waving little flags, welcoming their boys. There was a whole sequence of shots that just showed people embracing.

You said, "No one was there. No one was there for me." Tears ran down your face, and I started crying, too.

I remember some things as inconsequential as specks of dust. Bits of shell in an order of scrambled eggs—like having chalk in the mouth.

It was Monday. The morning. There were bits of shell in the eggs. The short-order cook in the diner on Grand Street had the radio on. An announcer said Frank Sinatra's son had been kidnapped and that it was the first day of Chanukah, the Jewish festival of lights.

"I feel full of light," you said.

We paid the check and you walked me to the corner. The bus came right away.

There was one call from you later. Around three, when I was at the office. You surprised me by saying you wanted me to know where you were in case I happened to phone the studio. "Billy's using the place, so I got out of the way. I'm up here at the bar."

I said, "Oh," trying not to sound disappointed because of your promise about staying away from alcohol. But you said you'd only had one drink, a beer. "I didn't even finish it. What do you think of that? I walked away and left the glass."

Your voice was warm, very buoyant, the way it was when we first knew we loved each other. You'd never called me like that just to let me know I didn't have to worry.

We were going to my mother's for dinner that night. You said you'd pick me up right after work. "I'm going to do the whole bit now—go home, shave the face, put on a suit for the old dame."

"You don't have to go that far," I said, laughing.

"Ah, what's the difference? . . . Okay, kiddo. See you later."

"I'll wait for you on the corner," I said.

Winter blew in suddenly that afternoon. The sky darkened around four, and well before five, snow had started falling. Limp, white flakes that clung to people's sleeves—I remember thinking the crystals looked magnified like the cutouts kids pasted against schoolroom windows. Everyone was saying this snow wasn't going to stick, but they lacked conviction. People left work earlier than usual, putting up umbrellas, hurrying along Fourth Avenue to the subway.

The snow kept eddying down. I remember standing on the corner of Twenty-ninth Street watching it blow against the black and yellow letters of the Park Fast sign. A woman from my office saw me and said, "What a night." I'd been waiting for Tom about a half hour by then, and I said something about my husband coming uptown on the Third Avenue bus and she said it would probably take forever. I didn't have the awful fear that would always seize me in the future whenever anyone was late unexpectedly. I just kept standing on that corner, thinking he'd show up any minute, but the minutes kept going by, flying past me, piling in drifts, and at six I went to a booth across the street to call the studio, and got the dime back because there was no answer. I kept calling after that, every ten minutes, putting in the same dime, though I couldn't think of a reason he'd be there, and what if he came to the corner and didn't know where I was?

Finally, I called the Cedar. When the bartender shouted, "Tom Murphy!" I knew he had to be alive; he was there, after all, somewhere in that crowd. But when the bartender came back, he said he hadn't seen him, not since around three, come to think of it, so I asked for Billy, who'd only just walked in and said, "Well, you know how he gets. Should I tell him you're mad at him if he turns up?" Billy said he'd left the studio a couple of hours ago; he'd last seen Tom around noon.

I knew there was something I had to make sure of then, just as if I'd always known. Tom would have parked the bike in front of the house. He would have run upstairs to change for a few minutes, then gone right out. All I had to do was see the bike.

I ran out into the street and stopped a cab. "I have to go to Chrystie Street." The driver said, "Where? Where's that? Is that in Manhattan?" When we got to Grand and the Bowery, I told him, "Make the light." I tried to say it the way Tom did. I had the driver let me out at the corner and I ran the rest of the way to our house. But the bike wasn't there.

A man from the garage was shoveling snow. He stopped what he was doing and stared at me. "What's happened?" I cried.

"Oh honey," he said. "You'd better go upstairs."

Upstairs there was nothing. Nothing and no one. The light

was on over the round table, and the clothes on the chair were the ones we'd taken off the night before and the bed was still all rumpled up. I went to the refrigerator—I don't know why—and opened it and saw the remains of the leg of lamb that I'd been saving, wrapped up in foil. I kept thinking the phone would ring, but it didn't. I went downstairs again to make the man in the garage talk to me, but all he'd say was, "Honey, call the police."

It had happened at three-thirty on Grand Street and the Bowery, whatever it was that happened. He really had been on his way home. There at the crossing he suddenly rose up from his seat, almost as if he was trying to get off it, and the Harley hit the back of a truck. No one could ever really explain it. The traffic was heavy, but not moving fast. The bike itself was hardly damaged. But he'd hurt his head falling from it. He lay in the street until the ambulance came. The last thing he said was, "I'm Tom Murphy."

I've always thought about him giving his name, maybe even knowing how close to home he was. The rest of it, too—dying alone. Maybe he was thinking about that.

VII

The Children's Wing

22

I remember people kept finding me apartments and I'd go and look at them on my lunch hours. A super would take me up the stairs and let me in. It would always be two small rooms that were supposed to look great when they were plastered and painted, but meanwhile you could see the brown marks, ghosts of mirrors and pictures that had hung there, chests that had once been shoved against the walls. I'd walk around, pull open a closet, listen to the way my steps sounded on the bare floor. "Thanks," I'd say. "I'll think it over." But already I'd have the thought, I've lived here before.

I couldn't start my life till I had an apartment, so finally I decided I'd better go to Paris. Even my mother thought it was a good idea—she gave me the money for the trip. It was February by then. Everyone said, Don't go to Paris in February, but anyway, I went. I bought a one-way passage on the SS *America*. I'd always felt Europe had to be approached little by little; you couldn't just land there all at once.

I had to go where no one knew me. I craved rudeness, normal indifference—no one lowering their voice to ask if I was taking care of myself. I had to see if I could start over from nothing. I stood on the deck as the SS *America* pulled away from the pier and waved to my mother and Kevin and Grace. I could feel the vibrations of the engines and it was very cold. There was a gray sheen of ice on the river like tarnished metal.

It was true I'd picked the worst time of year to cross the Atlantic, but that seemed right, as if the test of myself was already starting. I'd climb the steel stairs and let myself out on a deck where passengers must have sunned themselves in good weather in wooden lounge chairs that were all chained down. The wind would make the tarp that covered them snap and rattle like a drum, but I'd manage to fight my way to the railing. I'd hang on as the world kept tilting, wondering if I'd get to see white water, if white water was actually white. I'd never asked Tom that. Once a sailor came and chased me downstairs. "You shouldn't be up here," he told me.

There was something absurd about being a passenger—as if you could do anything because nothing counted. You believed you were being carried forward, but the waves couldn't tell you where you were or how far you'd come. Maybe only sailors knew the truth.

I met an Englishman who was going home after seventeen years in America. He'd been in the British navy during the war, then had lived in Montana raising sheep and trying to write novels about his experiences and drinking a lot, I gathered, though he was drying out now, and marrying a couple of times. The sheep had been the most successful part of his life, but now he didn't even have them anymore. He was taking nothing back with him but his American accent, which really wasn't so American, but I didn't tell him that. The skin around his eyes was stretched very tight and he had a way of smoking cigarettes down to the last quarter inch, singeing the tips of his fingers. He was a humorous man, who'd say things like, "To what do you attribute your continuing state of good health?" as each day we sat with each other in the vast dining salon that emptied more and more, as if the ship had been struck by plague. We'd laugh and cheer as entire courses flew off the tables and had to be swept up. It was our mutual failure to get seasick that had made us notice each other to begin with—or maybe it was some aura we both had of people who knew something about hard times.

He'd asked me why I was going to Paris in February, and I'd told him I was on my vacation. "That hardly needs saying," he responded dryly. But the next day I found myself saying my husband had been killed in an accident in December. It was the first time I'd told that to a stranger. I kept thinking I saw little bits of Tom in him.

He didn't say, "I'm sorry," or "That must have been terrible." He just took a couple of seconds to digest the fact, then said he was thinking about where we could possibly make love, since neither of us had a private cabin.

We ended up on the floor of a locked shower room with some German businessmen pounding on the door, shouting *Heraus,* impatient to come in and use the facilities. They were standing in the corridor looking daggers at us when we came out. We kept sneaking in there the rest of the voyage, both of us too driven to care about comfort or what other people thought. It was as if there couldn't be enough of sex for either of us, or just ordinary human warmth, flesh against flesh. The Englishman got off at Dover and I went on to Calais. "We must write each other," he said, but we never did.

In Europe all the colors were different. No one had ever told me that. Washed-out olives, browns, grays; a silver sky. America had redness, I realized. From the train on the way to Paris, I saw Van Gogh's black crows standing in a field pecking at old straw.

At first I had a room near the Opéra that didn't make sense—each wall a different chalky paint, maroon velvet drapes on the windows, murky roses on the bedspread engorged like human organs. It seemed I'd ended up in a bed like the one my father had photographed. I walked around all day dizzy, went to museums and saw nothing that registered, spoke only to waiters. I'd wake in the middle of the night on Chrystie Street thinking I heard Tom's key in the door. That was Hôtel Opal, where one morning, sitting on the awful flowered bed drinking coffee, I suddenly thought, It can be no worse than this.

I moved to a much poorer but better hotel, this one in Montparnasse, where I should have been all along. Everyone had told me Montparnasse was where all the artists were. I think that was why I'd stayed away at first. The hotel was full of young American women in distress, always a few weeks behind with the rent. The concierge had no mercy. She threw out a girl from Detroit because she claimed she'd found menstrual blood on the sheets. I helped Clarice, the girl from Detroit, put her things into suitcases. She was weeping pathetically and saying, "But this is my *home*." It was a room just like mine, a bare pink cell, with one forty-watt bulb over the bed and another over the sink—clever wiring had been done by the concierge's husband so you couldn't get the two to work at once. Clarice had hung strings of beads on the walls, thrown a lace tablecloth over the bed, bought a geranium. So it was home, as I too had come to understand it.

Sometimes, in Paris, I could go for almost a whole day without being reminded of everything I'd lost. I could always hang out with the other women in the hotel, but I liked to wander off alone and have little experimental encounters. I'd practice my halting French on students who gave me the eye on the Métro, sinister Algerians in the cafés, questionable *artistes.* I didn't think of risk. What was there left to risk? I'd gotten very old again, so incredibly old I'd fallen back into innocence. I started carrying the Leica everywhere, shot anything that caught my attention. I no longer had to give myself permission. I told everyone I was a photographer—it didn't feel wrong to say it.

People warned me to look out for myself and my Leica in certain neighborhoods. The concierge said it was unwise for a young person to walk unaccompanied along the Seine in the evenings because *clochards* lived under some of the bridges. "Which bridges?" I asked her. She told me the ones, and I took my camera and went in search of the *clochards.* I had no fear of them because I was sure they were just like the bums on the Bowery, but more resigned to being vagabonds since they allowed themselves to grow fantastic hair and beards and be more outlandish in their dress. I photographed them for months until the images seemed to just repeat themselves. I'd always intended to get shots of the bums asleep on Grand Street under the bridal shops, but I'd been too shy because of Tom. When he was teaching himself to paint after the war, Bowery bums had been his first subjects. He said he used to think any of those old bums could be his father. He'd give a dime to every one who posed for him. He'd always ask their names, but often they wouldn't tell him. They'd turn mean and suspicious and say, "What business is it of yours?"

I saw a *clochard* one day who had eyes as fierce and blue as Tom's. It took all my courage to ask him, "Voulez-vous me permettre de vous photographer pour dix centimes?" He squinted at me as if I was the crazy one, and said, "Je m'en fou," as rudely as any more respectable Frenchman.

Clarice was my closest friend for a while. I lent her some money, helped her out as much as I could. She was only nineteen, the same age I was when I'd left my mother's house. In London, she'd had an abortion and been reported by her landlady to the British police; she'd had to flee England on the midnight ferry. She had a mass of tangled auburn hair, enormous green eyes, holes in her black fishnet stockings—the look of a disoriented pre-Raphaelite angel. Her beauty exposed her to constant danger. Even the concierge's husband, the stingy electrician, had tried to get her into bed. Clarice's parents had threatened to stop sending checks. She wanted to find work, but had no talent whatsoever for speaking French. Meanwhile a friend had taken her in, an "older man" whom she was fending off; she was sleeping on some pillows in his studio. Clarice claimed she only got homesick for things like maple syrup. Once she asked me to go with her to Inno's, the big supermarket in Montparnasse, in search of it. "Avez-vous le sirop qui vient de les arbres?" I asked the shrugging clerks.

The two of us would spend afternoons in the Sélect, where one man after another would become smitten with Clarice's charms. She'd ask me to translate their desperate offers. "Pas parlez," Clarice would say with a scared giggle, shaking her head, then undoing everything with a beatific smile.

She reproached me for staring out at the street too much, looking right through her almost, not even hearing what she was saying. Other people had noticed that habit of mine, and come to the conclusion I was unfriendly. The first few times it happened, Clarice's feelings had been hurt, but then, since I was always so nice to her, she'd decided not to take it personally.

Up till then I'd really thought I'd been doing very well. I told Clarice I'd work on my habit, though I couldn't promise anything, since it seemed to be something unconscious.

Why do you hang back? I didn't tell her Tom had once asked me that.

Clarice said, "Is there someone you're looking for out there, Joanna?"

23

I went to bed for a while with a lot of different men—anyone who asked me, almost. I didn't feel any of the old despair, never asked myself the question "Why are we here?" Because I knew what we were here for and it was not for love.

I thought if you could close your eyes, if it was dark enough in the room, you'd forget whom you were with entirely, and just by chance one stranger might make the right moves—"the *moves*," Tom used to call them—the moves that would remind you of someone else, as if a dead man could live for a moment inside you, like a match being struck then going out.

But bodies don't remember the way the mind does. You can repeat certain words to yourself. No way you can replay the moves.

My son Nicky was born in Paris, but he came back to the States with me when he was two. When Nicky was four, going to nursery school in the Village, he always wanted me to tell him about the time he couldn't remember, when he'd lived in a different country and been able to speak another language. He remembered a bridge and water and his father holding him up with hands around his waist, saying, "Jolis bateaux," but nothing of rue St. André des Arts and being carried up and down the flights of worn stone steps, and the long narrow room with the skylights where the three of us lived—a jumble of cameras and books, reels of film, dismantled sets, and all the cheery, pastel baby things that always seemed so out of place. "We are invaded now by plastic," my husband Mikel used to say to his friends. It wasn't Nicky but the things that came with him that threw him into a state of visual despair. Mikel had a very idiosyncratic aesthetic—dust-colored and austere, not subject to compromise. He refused to concede that the films he was making then demanded far too much patience from audiences. They had a beautiful, gritty light but very little movement; rain falling into a puddle could be construed as an event.

Mikel and I weren't married when I discovered I was pregnant. We hadn't even called ourselves lovers. We'd simply declared ourselves friends who had sex, and I suppose that remained the truth, although we tried for a while to lose sight of it.

When I first met him, Mikel was infatuated with Clarice. The address she'd given the cabdriver the day she was kicked out of the hotel was his studio on rue St. André des Arts. Soon after she moved in, Mikel put her in one of his films—her face filled the screen for twenty-eight unrelieved minutes, her puzzled eyes straining to stay open, her tongue occasionally moistening her lips. He told her it was an experiment, an attempt to prove that beauty could be boring; he said he hadn't proved it. She said he drove her crazy by staring at her all the time, following her to cafés where she was meeting other friends and brooding at tables by himself. Mikel was a powerful-looking man with prematurely gray hair, which made Clarice think of him as middle-aged, although he was only thirty-five. She'd mistakenly thought it was fatherliness that made Mikel offer to put her up. Finally, she wrote to her parents and asked them to send her an airline ticket back to Detroit. The day it came, she cashed it in and checked into a hotel on rue de Seine.

Mikel picked me out as the woman he could tell his melancholy feelings to. He could never have talked with a man about the pain Clarice had caused him. He was horrified, humiliated and rather fascinated by the intensity of it. If the girl had only gone back to America, he could have gotten over her, but why had she moved to a hotel around the corner? Every time he left his studio, he had the expectation of seeing her. He'd escape to obscure arrondissements, call me from cafés no American would ever visit and ask me to meet him there, making me write down precise instructions for the Métro. He trusted me because I was, after all, another mourner; finally he decided we could even go to bed without doing lasting harm to each other. We were both in need of some consolation.

Mikel was a little eccentric, and maybe eccentrics should never marry. But there was so much I really liked about him. It wasn't hard to see through the pride he took in preserving his loneliness, the pride Clarice had threatened. The first time I met Mikel he told me he had been an exile and an orphan since the age of ten. His parents had been well-to-do Jews in Czechoslovakia. They had smuggled him out of the country in 'thirty-nine to live with an aunt and uncle in Lucerne. Soon after the Nazis came, they had vanished. Mikel's father had inherited a factory that sold china and glassware all over the world. He told me his mother had been very advanced and free. When Mikel was two, she had hired a French nursemaid to take care of him and run off to Dessau to study art with the Bauhaus. She had been a famous potter whose work was much in demand. In the flea market at Clignancourt, Mikel had found a cream pitcher he was convinced his mother had designed for his father's company. It had a pattern of small red and yellow rising circles separated by thin black lines.

Mikel hardly ever went to museums or other people's films, but the flea market drew him every Sunday. It was a beach where fragments of the past constantly washed up. He liked to arrive shortly after dawn when the vendors were setting out their wares. He seemed to be afraid of missing something, although he made very few purchases. Being there with Mikel was exhausting because he moved from booth to booth with such concentration. I'd tell him I was freezing and he'd emerge from his obsession and take me somewhere for cognac and coffee. Once he presented me with a paperweight; it was made of thick, chipped glass—you looked down through it at a cracked brown picture of a hotel. He called me over when he found it, very excited. "Look, this was made before the war. I have seen this hotel in Prague."

I remember telling Mikel about Rivington Street that Sunday. I said I'd once known someone who'd bought a hard-boiled egg there from a bum. Mikel knew all about Tom. I didn't know why I couldn't say his name, why it suddenly seemed that it would have been wrong.

Mikel went on his annual visit to his Lucerne relatives that August. I stayed on in Paris as shutters closed over shopwindows and familiar faces disappeared from the cafés. Busloads of perspiring tourists rolled through Montparnasse. It was funny how proprietary I'd come to feel, as if I really lived there now. I'd promised my mother I'd come back in the fall, but I'd sold my first photos to a French magazine in July and I'd moved into a new, much nicer room with a view of the Luxembourg Gardens. I found myself missing Mikel, although I knew I'd been seeing far too much of him. It was almost pleasurable missing someone who would return, not the other kind of missing that was bottomless, that I could never see an end to, a permanent hole cut out of the world.

I walked over to the Right Bank one morning, all the way to the Galeries Lafayette, where I intended to buy myself a pair of summer sandals. I remember standing on an old wooden escalator that went up little by little, painfully creaking and jerking; suddenly, between floors, I was attacked by the strangest feeling—a violent pang of something like hunger that made me so light-headed I thought I was going to fall. I got off the escalator and looked for a place to sit, and as I was doing so, the thought that I was pregnant hit me. I knew, I was sure. I wasn't scared this time, just stunned by the unexpectedness, the thought that it would happen now. Why now, I wondered bitterly, and not before? Evidently nothing was enough—some final cruel trick had to be played out. Why couldn't I have had Tom's child? Then suddenly I thought of this child as mine. I hadn't lost everything. Fate had given me a child. Once Nicky was born, I felt he had always been with me, as a wish, a possibility, finally claiming his own time.

I didn't write Mikel; I waited till he got back to Paris to tell him. By then I'd made decisions, worked things out. I remember making a speech that seems completely wrong and thoughtless to me now. The child was mine—my desire, my need, my fault, even, if anyone was to blame. I kept assuring Mikel he had nothing to feel bad about. I was going to have this baby, live very far away with it in New York, support it totally by myself. I said I hoped he'd wish us well.

I listened to myself being very clear and brave, I thought, about what was right. I wasn't prepared at all for Mikel's anger. What kind of man did I think he was, he demanded, that I expected nothing from him? Did I think, because he was European, that he would have no serious feelings, or was that what American men had accustomed me to? What a crazy thing, to deprive him of his own flesh and blood while hoping for the sweet sentiments of bad movies. "And how do we call this idiocy?" he yelled.

I told him I didn't know what to call it, but I couldn't think of an alternative. How could I raise a child in Paris by myself? By then I was crying, because everything Mikel was saying made me wish I could love him. But a door had flown open and I was going in, even knowing it was wrong.

We were having this awful conversation in a café, and Mikel sat glowering at me across the table and let me cry. Finally, he said we should get married at once. He'd never believed that lovers required marriage, but children did. I was rubbing my eyes, and he made a rough, exasperated gesture and pulled my hand away. He told me it had never been demonstrated to him that families worked, but neither did loneliness.

"The joke is that nothing works," he said a few years later when we decided to split up. "Nothing."

24

Mikel's studio seemed wonderfully Parisian to me until after Nicky was born. It was an open seventeenth-century attic—Mikel wouldn't spoil it by putting up a wall. It had a romantic little balcony. You could step right out onto it and see chimneys and silver flashes of the Seine between rooftops. But there was no running water. Buckets had to be carried from a tap three flights down. I used to think if we'd had a wall or two or American plumbing, our marriage might have lasted longer. Mikel greatly admired Nicky, but he left him entirely to me. The soft spot on babies' heads alarmed him; he'd pick Nicky up as if he were made of glass.

Mikel put Nicky and me into one of his films. He stood on the balcony shooting down into the courtyard below. A winter scene. I looked like an Italian peasant woman at a funeral with a black wool scarf around my head, and Nicky was gaily grabbing at the ends of it as I held him with one arm and fumbled for the key in my pocket. I had no idea this moment was being immortalized. It was late afternoon and I was extremely tired. As I remember it, I'd walked out with Nicky around eight that morning intending never to return, after hearing Mikel's usual complaint that the presence of the baby made it impossible for him to do any work that wasn't shit. I'd wheeled Nicky around the Louvre for hours; he'd napped on my lap in cafés. I was amazed to learn that Mikel had been frantically watching for us, that he'd even considered calling the police.

When I left Paris and took Nicky back to the States with me, the idea was that Mikel would join us. He would look for work as a cinematographer, and we would make one last stab at remaining together. For six months he stayed with us in an apartment on East Twelfth Street that always smelled of chocolate because it was above a bakery. Mikel did find a job filming commercials, but he hated it, and hated New York. He said the Village was a pitiable imitation of Paris, that Americans were always imitating things, either what had been done in previous decades or in other, more interesting countries. I told him I'd never aspired to be the wife of a snob. He ran into a Hungarian sound engineer who shared his views and they would sit in a coffeehouse on MacDougal Street talking French and German and having "European evenings." Mikel was offered a much more attractive job on a feature film in L.A., and decided he was much better off out there altogether. L.A. was so strange and original and had tropical vegetation and didn't remind him of other places. He didn't urge me, though, to fly out there with Nicky. After we got divorced, he lived for quite a while with a nice actress from Galveston, Texas. I met her once. She looked a little like Clarice.

Nicky was only three when Mikel left us, but he knew exactly what it meant. He kept asking me when Daddy was coming, forgetting what I'd tell him, waiting for one of my answers to be the right one. When the phone rang, he'd say, "That's my dad," and I'd say, "No Nicky. It's someone else." In a way, it was surprising, because Mikel had never spent much time with him. He'd just continued to admire Nicky, sort of from afar, almost as if he were someone else's child.

A couple of years went by, and Mikel didn't see Nicky at all. He said he was too busy establishing himself out on the Coast; he couldn't take a week off for a visit or turn down work. He sent checks every month and postcards for Nicky with pictures of coyotes and bears, and once a letter came, explaining to me how Mikel could never, even if he was around, be one of those fathers who sweated in the sun tossing baseballs to small boys; nor could he communicate with a four year old in an amusing manner. So he was looking forward to Nicky reaching an age when he could be taken on trips to interesting places.

When Nicky was six, he spent five weeks with Mikel and his girl friend in California. He came home with circles under his eyes, but he said it had been great—every night they'd taken him to the movies. Once the three of them had gone to a nightclub, where a ventriloquist had engaged Nicky in conversation with his dummy. The next day, Mikel and his girl friend had bought him two Charlie McCarthy dolls, whom Nicky called the Double Charlies. He would make the Double Charlies have long dialogues with each other, and he slept between them for ages, until they fell apart. Mikel had had Nicky memorize his phone number. I told him that now he could call his father whenever he felt like it. It made him very proud, giving the number to the long-distance operator by himself.

We never had much stuff in that apartment on Twelfth Street. My mother said it looked as if Nicky and I were only camping out there. We could have packed up and moved out in a couple of hours, leaving behind us all the clothes that didn't fit and the toys Nicky no longer played with. He used to race his bike from room to room, ringing his bell. I tacked my photos up on the walls, the crayon drawings he brought home from school. I didn't have any of Tom's paintings in that place. I'd tell myself I didn't want to have to explain about them to Nicky. The things he had to understand about life were complicated enough.

The paintings were safe where they were. Leon was storing them for me in his studio. For a couple of years, I called up gallery people and curators, but no one wanted to come and look at them because they'd never heard of Tom. Leon had made a rack where the canvases on their stretchers leaned against each other gently. They used to remind me of sails without wind. It seemed wrong not to keep trying to get them shown, but Leon said there was no use. The bottom had dropped out of the market for abstract expressionism just as he'd known it would. Once we talked about how frustrated Tom would have felt if he'd still been alive. He'd have turned his back on the whole scene, Leon said. He'd never have changed his work just to make things easier. "The man would have been impossible," Leon said. "You know that, don't you?"

I said, "I guess I do. I guess I do know that."

Leon wanted me to go out with him. He said he was even extremely popular with little kids. We tried it for a while, but my heart wasn't in it.

I never asked to look at Tom's paintings. Leon would call and say, "Come on down. I'll take them out of the rack for you," and I'd reply, as if I were only trying to be considerate, "No, it's okay. I don't have to see them."

I could never tell Leon that the paint on those canvases wasn't just paint to me. Moments had been caught there, moments that had somehow left their tracks. You could follow those tracks and I knew where they would lead you. To a place where there was nothing, no movement at all.

Sometimes my memory would land me suddenly on Chrystie Street. I'd see the two big rooms undismantled, everything still in its place. Certain paintings would come to me the same way, or a look of Tom's—so clear and then gone. As Nicky got older, I'd try to recall him as a baby. I'd been so weary when we lived in Paris, I knew I hadn't been conscious enough. I wanted to always be able to see all the faces Nicky had grown out of. But the pictures blur more and more every second you're carried forward. You seem to get left with memories of memories.

We'd been living on Twelfth Street about six years when Leon called me one day and said he could no longer keep Tom's paintings. We'd been out of touch for quite a few months. I hadn't known he was giving up on getting his work shown in New York and that he was taking a teaching job in Milwaukee. New York had gotten so expensive that even being poor was costing him too much money. Leon said he'd tried to find me another artist with extra storage space, but nothing had worked out, so now he was borrowing a friend's truck to bring the paintings up to me. I'd just have to keep them in my apartment until I decided what to do next. The truck came the following Saturday afternoon. Leon carried all the paintings up the stairs for me. He arranged them as neatly as he could in a corner of the living room, downed a cup of coffee and gave me a quick good-bye embrace. "Look me up next time you're in Milwaukee."

Nicky was staying over at a friend's house that weekend, so I was alone after Leon left. I sat in the living room for a long time like a paralyzed person, staring at the backs of stretchers. Leon had turned everything to the wall. I thought of the painting Tom had done on the old mailbag we'd found in the street. It was mostly red, that was all I could remember. I had the awful feeling I might no longer be sure which one it was. I walked across the room and started pulling the smallest paintings out. I found the one I was looking for right away.

When Nicky got home the next day, he said, "What's going on here, Mom?"

I'd moved most of our furniture away from the walls and polished the floor. Tom's paintings were hanging all over the place. It was the first time the room had looked beautiful. Nicky wanted to know where so many paintings had come from. He said he really liked them, but he couldn't tell what they were supposed to be. He seemed to have the idea they were like very hard books only grown-ups could understand. I told him the paintings were just themselves, that there was nothing hidden in them, and that he would see them better and better every day. I said the man who painted them had been someone I loved.

Then I said, "I never told you this, Nicky, but I was married to that man before I met your dad."

He asked me where was this person now, and I told him he'd been killed falling off a motorcycle a long time ago. "Wow," Nicky said.

He stopped asking me questions, and I was relieved. He didn't seem to be at all troubled about what I'd told him. A few days later, though, there was something on his mind. "Were this man and you going to have a baby?"

I had a very hard time formulating an answer. I told Nicky that when you felt about someone a certain way, you couldn't help wanting to have their child.

Nicky thought this over a long time. He had one last question. "Mom, if he hadn't died, would I have been born? Or would there have been a different me?"

25

I used to worry about failing Nicky, harming him in ways I couldn't help. I had changed once he was born. I knew I had to keep going for him no matter what. Even sadness seemed a self-indulgence, something that had to be ruled out because it could rub off on him. Nicky had to be saved from everything dark and hurtful, everything unthinkable. I'd clutch his hand in mine and hurry him across streets, always on the lookout for the mad driver coming out of nowhere.

Even though he missed his father, I had the feeling Nicky was happy. He considered he and I had a pretty good time of it. Across the hall from us on Twelfth Street lived a child we both felt sorry for. Every night we'd hear his parents screaming at him and at each other. The boy, who was older than Nicky, shocked him once by saying he hated his life. Nicky was only seven—it was the first time he'd come up against despair. "No one should hate their own life," Nicky said indignantly.

He was always healthy. I guess I took that for granted. But one morning, when he was ten, he woke up with an excruciating pain in his back. In a few days he could hardly walk, and no one could figure out what was wrong with him.

What happened to Nicky seemed to have the terrible speed of an accident. It made no more sense than that, although a doctor told me boys of that age are vulnerable to strange illnesses. I kept thinking I'd allowed myself to become too innocent. I should have been more vigilant, warded off fate. I thought Nicky would die because Tom had died. But once he was in the hospital he started slowly getting better.

I was working in midtown that summer, editing photos for a fashion magazine. Each day I'd leave my office a little early and go to a Chinese takeout place on Forty-ninth Street. After a while it was my regular routine. Nicky would call me in the afternoon and place his order. "An egg roll, of course," he'd say. "And sweet-and-sour shrimps. And Mom, would you bring me a Coke?" I'd never liked him to have soft drinks, but he'd say, "Please, please," trying to sound pitiful, and I'd always get one for him in the end.

When I'd get to the hospital, the other mothers would be there already with their shopping bags. Soon whole families would be gathered around the bedsides of the children, everyone eating out of foil containers or off paper plates, like an odd kind of picnic or a birthday party that had been displaced.

The children's wing was in the oldest part of the hospital. It had a marble rotunda on the ground floor. When you took the elevator up, there was no more marble, just dim green corridors and unending linoleum and muffled fake laughter from all the television sets. The kids pressed those switches the moment they woke up. If you came in the afternoon, it would be soap operas or game shows; by the evening it would be "M*A*S*H" or "The Odd

Couple," reruns of "The Flintstones." There was a lady volunteer on Nicky's floor who called herself The Teacher and came around with little workbooks. No one took her very seriously. She told me once that she was going to bring some literature to explain to Nicky what a biopsy was because he seemed so bright. She was taken aback when I shouted at her, "I'd rather you didn't!"

I kept thinking Nicky's time in the children's ward would irrevocably change him. A permanent shadow was falling across his vision of life and there was nothing I could do. I went to talk to a psychiatrist, who said, "What can I tell you? This will either do damage to your son, or he will rise to the occasion and be a hero." I saw that this was true. There were those two alternatives. Somehow I could accept the logic of that answer.

By August Nicky had seniority in Room K. New little boys kept coming and going, accident cases mostly. They lay beached on those high white beds, bewildered to find themselves in arrested motion. They'd each been felled by some miscalculation—running out too fast in front of a car, jumping off a stoop the wrong way. They'd go home with an arm or leg in a cast and sit out the summer in resentment, listening for the bell of the ice cream truck, driving their mothers crazy. "Hey man, what you break?" they'd ask Nicky, looking at the plaster around his torso with respect. "You break your back or something?"

Nicky would explain his condition like a junior scientist. He'd picked up all the lingo from the doctors—"left lumbar vertebra . . . unknown organism." "You see, in the X ray there's a white swelling on the left lumbar vertebra."

Sometimes I'd look around the room and stare at all those simple broken limbs in envy. I'd wonder if Nicky did that too. Why couldn't it have been something like that? Why had it been necessary for him to learn the awful possibilities, how your own body could suddenly turn against you, become the enemy?

"An organism is just a germ of some kind, an extremely tiny one, you see."

He was the little scientist and he was the birthday boy. When the pain would come, he'd hold on to my hand the way he had at home on those nights I'd sat up with him. The egg roll would go into the garbage with the rest of the Chinese dinner. "Do you see that?" he'd say, pointing to the decal of a yellow duckling on the wall near his bed. "Isn't that ridiculous to have that here, that stupid duck?"

I agreed with Nicky about the duck and Room K's other decorations—brown Disney bunnies in various poses, a fat-cheeked Mary and her little lamb, all of them scratched and violently scribbled over. I could see how they threatened his dignity.

Mikel kept flying in from California to visit Nicky. He was always phoning me to ask how Nicky was and what I thought he should buy for him. There was a game called Boggle that interested Nicky for a week and an expensive tape recorder, which fell off the bed one day and broke, and a collection of intricate miniature robots from Japan. All this stuff piled up around him. The fruit my mother brought him turned brown in unopened plastic bags.

Nicky only liked one thing, really; he could have done without all the rest. A fantasy war game called D&D that had been all the rage among the fifth graders. I never even tried to understand it. I just kept buying the strange-looking dice he asked for and the small lead figures that he'd have to paint himself—dragons and wizards and goblins—and new strategy books with ever more complicated rules. "I want to live in a fantasy world," he told me. I remember it shocked me a little that Nicky knew so explicitly what he was doing.

He refused to come back from that world very much. There were nights he'd hardly stop playing to talk to me. He'd only look up when I was leaving to tell me the special colors he needed. The nurses complained because there was always model paint on his sheets, silver and bronze from the armor of his warriors. If I'd encourage Nicky to get to know the other kids, he'd look at me wearily and say they didn't have the same interests.

"Maybe you could interest them in what you're doing."

"Mom . . . I can't. I'd have to start them from the beginning."

Still I was grateful to the makers of D&D, grateful he had a way to lose himself. If you walked those green corridors, you'd pass certain quiet darkened rooms where there were children who weren't ever going to get well; there were parents on the elevator with swollen faces who'd never look you in the eye. A little girl in Room G died during visiting hours. I could hear her as soon as I got off on Nicky's floor, a terrible high-pitched, rattling moan. It went on and on, and there were doctors running down the hall with machinery.

I walked into Nicky's room with my Chinese takeout shopping bag. He was staring at all his figures lined up in battle formation; he didn't say hello. The other kids weren't saying much either. Their parents hadn't come yet. One little boy asked me, looking scared, "What's that noise out there?" "Oh, someone's very sick tonight," I said, and I closed the door. I just shut that sound out. Then I felt I'd done something wrong, that we all should have acknowledged it somehow, we should have wept for the child who was dying.

I used to try to get Nicky out of bed for some exercise. We'd walk up and down outside his room very slowly, the IV apparatus trailing behind us like a dog on a leash. Some nights we'd sit for a while in the visitors' lounge, where there were brown plastic couches and ashtrays and tattered magazines, and Nicky would drink his Coke and go over his strategy books.

A mentally disturbed boy appeared there one night. He was

tall and had a man's build already, muscled arms and shoulders. He looked eighteen or nineteen years old, though I later found out he was only fifteen. He had a face that could have been beautiful, but you didn't want to see his eyes. They were all red and enflamed, emptier than a statue's. I thought of the word *baleful* when I saw them. The boy with the baleful eyes. He was wearing dirty jeans and an old gray T-shirt. I thought he might have come in off the street.

Nicky and I were alone. This boy walked right over and stared down at us. I spoke to him softly, trying to sound calm. "Are you looking for someone?" I said.

He started shaking his head, grinning. "Who? Looking for Mr. Who. Have you seen Who?"

I said I hadn't seen him.

"Are you a nurse? You're not a nurse."

"The nurses are outside the visitors' room," I said. "Just down the hall."

He sat down next to Nicky. He rapped on Nicky's cast with his knuckles. "Hello, Mr. Who. Want a cigarette?"

Nicky was sitting very still. "No thanks. I don't smoke," he said in a small voice.

The boy laughed and stood up. He took out a pack of cigarettes and some matches. He lit a match and held it up close to Nicky's face for a moment. Then he lit his cigarette with it and stared down at us a while longer. "My name is Joseph," he said. "Do you like me?"

"I like you very much," I said.

He studied me a long time, almost as if I were someone he remembered. Then he threw the cigarette on the floor and drifted out.

Earlier that day a boy from Nicky's room had gone home. When we got back there, we saw that the empty bed was taken. A small suitcase stood beside it and a nurse was tucking in the blanket, making hospital corners. A little while later an intern led Joseph in, dressed in pajamas. "Mom," Nicky whispered, "they're putting him in *here.*"

"Don't worry about it, honey," I told him.

I went out to the nurse on duty at the desk and made a complaint. They had no right to put a boy like that in with sick children. The children would be frightened, they had enough to contend with. A boy like that should be put in a special place. "It's the only bed available," the nurse said. "There's no private room for him now. Try to understand he's sick too, he needs care. We're going to watch the situation very carefully." When I told her about the cigarettes and the matches, she said, "My God. We'll take care of that."

"Where does he come from anyway?" I asked her, and she told me the name of some institution upstate.

My telephone rang in the middle of the night. A nurse said, "Hold on. Your son insists on speaking to you."

Nicky got on the phone, all keyed up and out of breath. "Mom, you have to give me some advice. You know that guy Joseph?"

"What's the matter, Nick?" I said.

"Well, guess who he's picked to be his friend? He keeps getting off his bed and coming over to talk to me. It's too weird. I don't know what to say to him, so I just listen."

I wanted to go straight to the hospital and bring Nicky home. I said, "I guess you're doing the right thing, honey." I asked him if he was scared.

"Not so much. But it's hard, Mom."

"The next time he bothers you, just pretend you're asleep. Maybe he'll go to sleep, too."

"Okay," Nicky said. "Can I call you again if I have to?"

I turned on the lights and sat up and read so I'd be sure to hear the phone. I called him back early in the morning. Joseph was sleeping, Nicky told me. The nurse had finally given him some kind of pill.

I went to the office as usual but I couldn't get much accomplished. Around three I gave up and went to the hospital. They were mopping the corridors and a game show was on in Nicky's room. A housewife from Baltimore, Maryland, had just won a walk-in refrigerator and a trip for two to Bermuda. "Yay! It's the fat lady! I knew it!" a kid was yelling to the others. I found Nicky propped up in bed painting a dragon, making each scale of its wing a different color. I looked around for Joseph, but I didn't see him.

"I'm concentrating, Mom," Nicky said.

"Is everything okay?" I whispered.

With a sigh he put down his brush. "Joseph is taking a walk. That's what Joseph does. But don't worry—he'll be back." And then Nicky said to me, "You know, sometimes he seems almost all right. I ask him questions and he tells me very sad things."

"What kinds of things?"

"Stuff about his life. He doesn't go to school, you know. He lives in a hospital with grown-ups. He thinks he's going to live there a long time—maybe always."

When Nicky was four, I used to take him to a nursery school on the way to work. It wasn't convenient, but I never minded. The place, as I recall it, was always yellow with sunlight. Green sweet-potato vines climbed up the windows and there were hamsters dozing in a cage. In the mornings the teacher would put up the paintings the children had done the day before. You could smell crayons, soap, chalk dust. And all the little, perfect children pulling off their coats had a shine about them, a newness. Sometimes the thought of that bright place would get me through the day, the idea that it was there and that Nicky at least was in it—as if I'd been allowed a small vision of harmony.

I thought of it again that afternoon at the hospital. We couldn't get back to it; it was lost, out of reach.

In the institution Joseph came from, they must have kept him confined. In the children's wing, he roamed the corridors. A nurse found him standing in a strange room and had to bring him back. "Joseph, you stay in here," she admonished him. He walked up and down, banging his fists against the beds. He poked at little kids and chanted at the top of his voice, "Hey! Hey! What do you say today!"—which might have been a form of greeting. The kids said Joseph took things; they said he'd beat them up if they asked for them back.

He stopped by Nicky's bed and watched him paint the dragon. He pressed down on it with his thumb. "Hey, the mad monster game!"

"Wet paint, Joseph," warned Nicky.

Joseph took the dragon right off the bed table. "Joseph, you creep!" Nicky yelled, his eyes filled with tears.

I went over to him and held out my hand. "I'm sorry. Nicky needs his dragon." It was odd how Joseph inspired politeness.

He stared down at my open palm as if puzzling over its significance. "That wasn't Nick's," he said.

Joseph stood by the door in the evening when the families came, when the bags of food were opened and the paper plates passed around. I went out to get Nicky a hamburger and a chocolate milkshake. When I came back, the room smelled of fried chicken and everyone was watching "The Odd Couple." Joseph lay on his bed. He had put his arm over those red eyes, as if the light was hurting him.

Nicky tapped my arm. "Do you see that, Mom? No one came for him."

I said, "Maybe there's no one to come, Nicky."

"Someone should."

I handed him his milkshake. He peeled the paper off the straw and stuck it through the hole in the lid of the container. For a while he twirled it around. "Mom, I think you should get him something. Can you?"

I went down to the machines in the basement and got Joseph an ice cream sandwich. I put it on his dinner tray. I said, "Joseph, this is for you." His arm stayed where it was. I touched his shoulder. "Do you like ice cream?" I said loudly.

Mrs. Rodriguez, who was sitting at the next bed beside her son Emilio, shook her head at me. "Loco," she whispered fiercely. "Muy loco. You understand? No good here. No good."

She wasn't wrong, I couldn't argue. The ice cream sandwich was melting, oozing through its paper wrapping. I went back to Nicky and took him for his walk.

Later, out in the corridor, we saw Joseph. He took a swipe at Nicky's cast as we passed him and yelled after us, "Dragon Man and the Mom!" There was chocolate smeared all over his mouth.

The next day I bought an extra egg roll at the takeout place. It seemed I'd have to keep on with what I'd started, though I had no idea at all how much Joseph remembered. I kept thinking of him lying there alone during visiting hours. What I really wanted was to walk into Room K and find him gone, some other arrangement made, so I could remove him from the list of everything that troubled me.

When I got to the hospital, some of the other parents were there, earlier than usual. They were standing out in the corridor near the head nurse's desk. One of the mothers had her arm around Mrs. Rodriguez, who was wiping her eyes with some

Kleenex. They gestured to me to join them. "The supervisor is coming to talk to us about our problem," someone said.

"What happened?" I asked Mrs. Rodriguez.

She blew her nose; it seemed hard for her to speak. "Joseph! Joseph! Who do you think?"

Joseph had somehow gotten hold of some cigarettes and matches. He had held a lighted match near Emilio's eyes. "To burn my son!" cried Mrs. Rodriguez. Emilio was only eight, a frail little boy with a broken collarbone.

I put down my shopping bag and I waited with the others. When the supervisor came, I spoke up, too. Irresponsibility, negligence, lack of consideration—the words came so fluently, as if I'd turned into the kind of person I'd always distrusted, someone with very sure opinions about rightness and wrongness and what was best for society.

The supervisor already had his computer working on the situation. "Just give us an hour," he said.

In Room K, an orderly had been posted to keep an eye on Joseph. He'd made Joseph lie down on his bed. The children were subdued; they talked in murmurs. Even the television was on low, until a parent turned up the volume. There was an effort to create the atmosphere of the usual picnic.

Nicky looked wide-eyed, pale. "Did you hear what Joseph did to Emilio?"

I leaned over him and pushed the wet hair off his forehead. "Nicky, don't worry about Joseph anymore. They're going to move him in a little while to a room by himself."

I started opening containers from the Chinese takeout place, and there was the egg roll I'd meant to give Joseph. I angled my chair so that I wouldn't have to see him. It was as though life were full of nothing but intolerable choices.

"Eat something," I said to Nicky.

In a loud, dazed voice, a kid in the room seemed to be

talking into a phone. "Hey Grandma, guess who this is? I'm gonna see you soon, you bet. I'm gonna get on a plane and fly. Yeah, I'll bring my little bathing suit. Gonna see you, Grandma. Gonna see you."

"Mom," Nicky whispered. "Can you hear him?"

We saw the removal of Joseph; everyone did. Two nurses came in and walked over to him. "Joseph, it's time to get moving now," one of them said. "Let's get your personal things together."

They got him off the bed very quickly. One took his suitcase; the other had him by the arm. The orderly positioned himself in front of them. Nicky turned his face into the pillow when they started walking between the rows of beds. I was holding his hand and he kept squeezing my fingers, not letting go.

As he passed by us Joseph broke away from the nurse. For a moment he loomed over Nicky and me. He kissed me on the top of the head. Then they took him out into the long dim corridors.

When Nicky was thirteen, he told me he couldn't remember much about his childhood. He wanted to, but he couldn't. The whole subject made him very angry. "What I remember," he said, "is Joseph."

Nicky got well but he got old.

The Night Café

There are lives you could draw in fairly straight, long lines. For others, it's all starts and breaks. Except for Nicky, that's the way it's been for me.

A lot of time—isn't that what marriage is supposed to come to? So I really never found out about marriage. Not long ago, I came to that conclusion, even though, of course, I married twice. I'll never know what happens when two people spend so many years together, for better or worse, the way my parents did. I wonder if I could have done it, who I would have been by now.

I used to believe Tom and I would have stayed together for life—which we did, in a sense, although his life was much shorter than mine. He would have stopped drinking, we would have had a child, his kids would have grown up and found their way back to him. I believed everything promised by those last days we had. But maybe nothing was really being overcome. He would have worn me down, driven me away. Time was only going to bring us another kind of ending.

Maybe that afternoon when he was riding home, all of a sudden he knew it. That was what he saw ahead when he rose from the seat of the bike with the back of the truck right there in front of him and his foot pressed down hard on the pedal, as if with the beat of his thought. That was all it took, and he might even have been surprised to have lost control, that the foot had come down like that with so much weight, when he'd only been playing with a very old, familiar idea, when he wasn't even sure he hadn't meant to keep going.

When I was as young as Nicky, living in the first of all my terrible apartments, I remember wanting a little yellow rush-seated chair like Van Gogh's. I kept my eye out for such a chair in stores that sold secondhand furniture. But I could never find one exactly like it.

Tom once told me he couldn't bear to read Van Gogh's letters. I'd read them myself around the time I met him and had found a certain line: *Empty chairs—there are many of them, soon there will be more.* Van Gogh was writing about those who had died, or would die. He hadn't painted his own chair yet, the yellow one with his pipe on the seat. He did that after he came out of the madhouse, when I think he must have been seeing with that purity that comes to people after pain. The chair, the real one, was white. Van Gogh wrote his brother merely that he was trying for an effect of light by means of clear color, as if the painting were the humblest exercise. He didn't tell his brother he saw his own death.

After I read the letters, I lost my desire for the little yellow chair, but the painting became more beautiful to me. Maybe I'd been drawn to it in the first place because the darkness was always there, painted into the sunny yellow.

If I were a painter, I wouldn't paint empty chairs. Instead I'd paint windows of places I've left, places where I no longer live—the way they look when you see them from the street and you know you can't go up there, can't even cross the threshold. The key is lost. You know someone else is inside there, taking your place. I've looked up from the sidewalk the way Howard Stricker did long ago.

When Nicky was little and we lived on Twelfth Street, Seventh Street wasn't very far. I used to walk by there almost daily, Nicky in his stroller, warm in his padded snowsuit. Somehow I felt protected by having Nicky with me. I'd give myself excuses for taking this route—I almost believed I was on my way to a better vegetable stand. But when I'd come to the linoleum store, I'd always slow down and look upstairs. I used to see an empty flowerpot on the window ledge, one I was sure I'd left there.

Many of my best photos are of windows. It's an obsession of mine, almost a signature. I especially like the black windows of the old warehouses down by the Hudson, the symmetrical rows that catch fire from the sunsets over New Jersey. I'm always rather fascinated, too, by shop windows that reflect the street outside them, the way the windows of Rappaport's did. I wish I could sit in Rappaport's again on a rainy night with my camera, but of course it's gone out of existence.

It took me eighteen years to go down to Chrystie Street, and I've never walked that block. I saw the windows of our studio just once from a cab. I was on my way to a dinner party in Brooklyn and there was a great deal of traffic on the Bowery. I suddenly told the driver, "Why not take Grand Street?" because I knew he would turn into Chrystie. We went by the building very fast, but I could see the top floors had finally been renovated, though the big windows of the studio looked the same as ever. The front of the place was absolutely dark, but a light was burning all the way in back. I said to myself, Tom's home. And I believed for that moment that he was.

Clenched Fists, Burning Crosses

A Novel of Resistance
by Cris South

The Crossing Press/Trumansburg, New York 14886
The Crossing Press Feminist Series

For Jennifer,
with love

An earlier version of Chapter 7 originally appeared in *Feminary.*

The Crossing Press Feminist Series

Cover design by Beverly Rosen
Book design by Allison Platt
Typesetting by Elaine DiStefano
and Martha J. Waters
Cover photograph by Alma Blount
Photograph of Cris South by Barb Lewis

Library of Congress Cataloging in Publication Data

South, Cris.
Clenched fists, burning crosses.

(The Crossing Press feminist series)
I. Title. II. Series.
PS3569.074C4 1984 813'.54 84-16975
ISBN 0-89594-154-6
ISBN 0-89594-153-8 (pbk.)

Acknowledgments

Thanking those women who read, believed, critiqued, suggested, argued, cared, cried, fought, and supported the process of this book, and me, seems like an impossibility. The book probably would have happened eventually, but it would have been longer in coming. Although it was a long, hard process, their encouragement made it a positive experience and, often, an exciting one.

So I would like to thank Diana Rivers, Maureen Brady, Boone, Ayana, Robin Divine, Patricia, Judith McDaniel, Sue Brown, Liz Snow, Helen Langa, Eleanor Holland, Tia Cross, Candace Burt, Susan Waldrop, Barbara Bradford, Jane Ollenberger, Merryl Sloan, and Jennifer Mayo for their readings and reactions, not to mention invaluable suggestions. Some of these women read along constantly; some read periodically; some read only once. But they all kept me believing in myself.

Then there was Elly Bulkin, who kept telling me to write (and to send her a copy of) a manuscript she had never seen. I want to thank one woman who asked not to be named, who believed in what I was doing and sent money to help the project along. Special love and thanks to Mab Segrest for retreating to the beach with me for a month to write and heal.

Very, very special thanks go to Catherine Risingflame Moirai, Merril Harris and Minnie Bruce Pratt for their tremendous belief in what I was writing, in me *as* a writer, and for their constant willingness to go through each line, word by word, over and over and. . . .

Last of all, thanks to Nancy K. Bereano for establishing a warm working relationship between editor and author, and for being a friend in the middle of the crises. And there is a special hug and kiss for Dorothy Allison and Barbara Kerr for making me laugh as I finished this book.

All those wonderful women.

Cris South

The Klan and the Nazis are our enemies and must be stopped, but to simply mobilize around stopping them is not enough. They are functionaries, tools of this governmental system. They serve in the same way as our armed forces and police. To end Klan or Nazi activity doesn't end imperialism. It doesn't end institutional racism; it doesn't end sexism; it does not bring this monster down, and we must not forget what our goals are and who our enemies are. To simply label these people as lunatic fringes and not accurately assess their roles as a part of this system is a dangerous error.

From "Revolution: It's Not Neat or Pretty or Quick" by Pat Parker in *This Bridge Called My Back* (Kitchen Table: Women of Color Press)

1

"The Klan rally was attended by an estimated one hundred twenty men, women and children. Many of the men wore T-shirts with the words *WHITE POWER* imprinted on them. There were guards posted around the site of the rally, supposedly to keep out troublemakers and undesirables. When asked who these undesirables were, the guards refused to comment.

"David Burke, leader of the American Nazi Party in this area, was quoted today in an interview as saying that his party is in complete support of this latest rise in Klan visibility and mobilization.

"Also in the news today, teachers talk strike in Boston. We'll be back with that story after. . ."

Jessie turned off the television set with one hand and gently pushed the cat out of her lap with the other. The Klan, the Klan. They were certainly getting into the news a lot these days. She stood up and stretched her stocky, muscular body, groaning softly as joints popped and cracked. Glancing at the ceiling, she tried to envision a thirty-foot-tall burning cross. She shook her head. Maybe it would all die down. Surely no one in this day and time would take them seriously. They were a bunch of clowns, trying to get attention. They were like little kids playing dress-up—robes, hoods, and dramatic crosses burning. Jessie snorted. The less said about them, the better.

She walked to the front door and into the yard. Kelly ran in tight circles in front of her, eager for a walk. Jessie grinned as she rubbed the setter's head.

"Later," she promised the dog. "I've got to hoe the garden."

Clouds were building on the horizon, grey and black thunderheads which promised rain soon. Jessie picked up the hoe and started around the house.

"How're you, Jessie?" Mrs. Carpenter approached laboriously, leaning heavily on her walking stick, her white hair standing on end in the wind.

"I'll do. How are you?"

Dorothy Carpenter stopped a few feet from Jessie and wiped her face with a tissue. "Hotter'n hell today."

"That it is," Jessie agreed.

"Been to the mailbox?"

"Yeah. Nothing there."

"Well, no news is good news."

"I suppose," Jessie smiled. It was like talking in code. She leaned on the handle of her hoe and waited, watching Dorothy as she scanned the sky suspiciously.

"It's gonna rain cats and dogs," she said. "Can't rain enough. The well's gonna run dry for sure if it don't. Dry as a bone, that's what it'll be."

"It's held up pretty well so far this summer."

The old woman eyed Jessie. "So far. Lots of summer to go yet. You fix that leak? I been hearin' the pump runnin' some today."

"I fixed it. I washed dishes. That's probably why you heard the pump."

"I told Ben to get himself down here and fix that for you, but he said you could manage."

"He was right. Just a washer. Only took a couple of minutes to fix."

"Can't understand for the life of me why a girl like you'd want to live in an old, broke-down place like this anyway. And all by yourself, too. Don't you git scared stayin' in this house and nobody with you?"

Jessie looked at her and shrugged her shoulders. "I haven't yet. You just worry too much."

Dorothy Carpenter's eyes narrowed quickly at the mild reproof. "You should, too. Lotsa meanness. Ain't safe for a woman to be livin' alone."

"You and Mr. Carpenter are just up the hill."

"Shoot," she snorted. "Somebody yell *fire* and I'd burn up 'fore I could get to my feet. And Ben'd burn 'fore he heard you. You keep that dog of yours in the house nights?"

"Sure do," Jessie answered, nodding her head.

"That's good. Guess she'd bite, wouldn't she?"

"She probably would."

"You just remember to keep that old gun loaded and your doors locked. Y'know, I used to be a good shot in my time, but I cain't see good enough these days to hit the broad side of the barn. Pretty useless, I guess. And Ben, he don't see no better than he hears. Not much good for nothing either. You're smart not to have nobody hangin' on you. Well, I guess I'd better get on back home, or he'll come lookin' for me to make him some dinner. You'd think he could at least make himself a sandwich when he gets hungry. Useless old man. My hip's killin' me today. You come and set later if you got time. Gets lonesome up there with nobody to talk to."

"Maybe later," Jessie agreed. She watched Mrs. Carpenter begin the long, slow trip back to her house at the end of the driveway. The elderly landlady reminded Jessie of her own grandmother. She picked up the hoe and headed towards the garden.

Jessie flopped down on the grass and rolled over on her back, lifting her T-shirt to catch the breeze and dry the sweat that ran down her chest. She wished the garden were further from the road so she wouldn't have to wear a shirt at all. But it was too close to risk it, much as she was tempted to try on days like this one. And Ben Carpenter, it wouldn't do to forget about him. In spite of being elderly and slow, he could move his large body very silently and had sneaked up on Jessie more than once. Jessie didn't trust him. He had hugged her too many times for Jessie to believe his "grandfather" claim.

Clouds were still building in the sky, but so far there had been no rain. The young plants in the garden were growing too slowly in the dry heat, and the ground was beginning to crack like clay pottery around the edges of the large plot. She might have to start hauling water from the creek, bucket by bucket, if the weather didn't turn soon. Already she was saving her bath water and bringing it out, a panful at a time, and pouring it around the tender plants. Not nearly enough to do much good though. The leaves were yellowing and beginning to go limp. The hay around the plants and between the rows helped keep in some moisture, but the ground was being baked completely dry by the steady July heat. There had been no rain to amount to anything since early in May. She leaned on an elbow and broke off a brittle grassblade and stuck it in her mouth. She could see the tree line along the bank of the creek, on the other side of the pasture. A long damned way to haul water.

The sound of the car in the driveway broke her reverie. Jessie rolled onto her stomach and lifted her head so she could see over the tall unmown grass. Kelly dashed by her with an excited yip, tail wagging madly. She could see Denny holding out her hands to fend off the leaping dog while she tried to make her way into the house. Jessie rose to her knees and waved her hand in the air.

"I'm by the garden," she called out, and then sat down again. It was too hot, too hot to do anything except sit and think about the heat.

". . . c'mon, Kelly. That's enough." Denny's voice grew louder as she approached. "Dammit, Kelly! You're drooling on me again! I hate it when you do that. Stop it!" Denny sat down beside Jessie, a disgusted expression on her face. "I can't take it when she drools all over me."

"Setters drool. That's a fact."

"Yeah, I know," Denny answered flatly as she pulled some dry grass and tried to wipe her bare legs, "but I wish she'd turn her head or something. Look at me!"

Jessie laughed outright. "Any time you want to try to teach her that, you have my blessing."

Denny tossed the grass aside. "I came out to work in the garden. I've been spending too many hours over books and behind the cash register. I turned it all over to Dianne this morning and told her not to look for me again until Monday. Hell, by the time I get back, she'll have everything right, the books balanced, and an order ready for me to call in. She knows more about that restaurant than I do, and I'm the manager."

"And she probably figured most of it out by trying to cope with things when you were away."

"Probably. Some good news came through last week though. Janice, you know, the woman who owns The Food Patch? She is definitely going to open another place this fall, and she wants Dianne to manage it for her."

"That's great."

"Dianne is thrilled. It means a lot more money for her, which I know will help since she has a child to support. I feel happy for her and sad for me. I like working with her and hate to see her go."

"But she deserves better than what she's got working for you, Denny."

"I couldn't agree more. Waiting tables is shit work no matter how you cut it. I think she'll do great. She's much better at it than I am, that's for sure."

Jessie glanced again at the sky. The thunderheads were close now and building quickly overhead. She slid the hoe across the grass to Denny and then rose to her feet, relieved by the cool wind preceeding the oncoming storm. "I didn't hoe the last two rows, but that's about all I left. If you feel real industrious and it doesn't pour on you, you can always mulch with the hay. I'm going inside and taking a fast bath before the storm gets here."

Denny nodded absently as she stepped over the rows of plants and began to hoe near the fence. Jessie, glad for the break, headed into the house. A bath would feel good. Then maybe she could talk Denny into staying for dinner. Most women didn't want to drive so far out into the country, even for a meal. She hadn't had any company in a long time.

Ben Carpenter spit a stream of tobacco juice on the ground. Dorothy shifted her position in the cane-bottomed chair, lifting her hair off the back of her neck with one swollen hand.

"Think it'll rain?" Ben asked his wife.

"Yep," she answered as she pulled the sticky cotton fabric of her dress away from her damp body.

"Huh?" he persisted, cupping one hand to his ear and leaning his head in her direction.

Dorothy sighed. It hurt her throat to have to yell so much. "I said yep, I think it'll rain." She frowned in disgust. Wisht he'd buy himself a hearin' aid, she thought silently.

"Whose car's that down there?"

"One of Jessie's girlfriends," she hollered back at him. He nodded and was quiet for a moment.

"I cain't figure it out," he said finally, his words accompanied by wheezing sounds as he spoke. "She lives down there all by herself and only some girls comin' to see her. Never talks about no man. Think maybe she just don't have no boyfriends?"

"Ain't nobody been to see her lately." Dorothy struggled to her feet. "Maybe not. But you're the one what told her not to be havin' men hangin' around the place. Reckon if she does have boyfriends, she ain't about to let us see 'em."

"Huh?" Ben cupped his ear once more.

Dorothy snorted as she reached for her walking stick and headed towards the house. "I said I'm gonna start supper cookin'!" She walked away, swaying from side to side as she coaxed her lame hip along. "Ain't good for a blessed thing," she muttered to herself as she reached up to open the screen door. "Not one blessed thing. Cain't hear, cain't see. Just a pack of trouble, him wantin' to be waited on and me with my bad hip!"

With a grunt of effort, she pulled herself up the two steps and disappeared inside the house.

Jessie slid the cue stick gently through her fingers until it bumped the ball. For a moment she thought perhaps Laura had been wrong. Just because this style worked for her. . . The white ball glided smoothly over the green felt and touched the side of the eight ball. Corner pocket. C'mon. She held her breath. The black eight teetered on the edge for a long moment. Then, almost in slow motion, it dropped into the pocket. Laura laughed from her perch on the barstool, a deep sound that seemed to rise up from her toes. She nodded her head emphatically.

"I told you. You just have to relax and kiss that ball. Just like loving a woman. Works every time," Laura said, her brown eyes dancing delightedly. Denny laughed as she leaned her stick against the side of the pool table.

"I guess this means I buy the beer," she said, pulling a crumpled bill from her pocket.

"I guess you do," Jessie answered, smiling. It was the first game she had ever won, and she did not attempt to disguise her smugness.

As Denny passed she patted Jessie on the shoulder. "I expect another game. A tiebreaker. I'll be back in a minute."

Jessie put quarters in the slot and waited for the balls to drop. She racked them slowly, arranging their order inside the blue plastic triangle, alternating high and low numbers, eight ball in the middle. Laura stood up, stretching her arms over her head.

"I could have sworn you weren't paying any attention to what I was telling you the other night," she said to Jessie, "but you are doing all right. My money's on you for this next game." Laura winked and walked away.

Denny reappeared with two beers and set them on a nearby table. Picking up her cue stick, she chalked the rubber tip carefully, her face set in concentration.

This time Denny played seriously, and the game moved faster. When Denny sank the eight ball, Jessie still had four balls left on the table. She shook her head ruefully and put her stick back in the wall rack.

"That does it for me. I owe you a beer," Jessie promised.

"I won't forget," Denny laughed. She dropped her arm around Jessie's shoulders and led her to an empty table. "Let's sit down and finish our drinks. I haven't really seen you in a couple of weeks. What's going on in your life these days?"

Jessie sat down and lit a cigarette, ignoring Denny's look of distaste. "Mostly, I've been working to get everything together at the shop."

"How's all that going?"

"I've drummed up some small accounts. I don't think I could do it all by myself, and I'm sure glad I didn't try. With Laura handling graphics, design, and scheduling, and me running the presses and hustling, it's still almost more than we can deal with."

"Well, the word is definitely around. A lot of liberal and left-wing political groups are looking for printers like you who they can trust not to botch their work and miss their deadlines. I think you'll do okay. Just takes a little time."

"I hope so. I'm sure nervous enough about it." Jessie studied her beer for a moment. "Denny, do you know Kate Robbins?"

Denny was startled by the abrupt change in the topic, and she peered at her friend in surprise. "I know who she is. Why?"

"Just wondering," Jessie answered with a casual shrug of

her shoulders. "I'm supposed to have dinner with her."

Jessie's tone caught Denny's full attention as she tried to decipher the meaning behind the words. "Yeah? Where'd you meet her?"

"At a battered women's shelter meeting a few weeks ago. We've had lunch a couple of times, and she asked me to dinner."

"At her house?"

"At her apartment." Jessie glanced at her. "Why?"

"Just curious," she answered with an enigmatic smile. Denny tried to be casual as she adjusted her glasses, pushing them back up her nose with one finger. "Want to tell me about it?" she asked.

"What's to tell? I'm just having dinner with her."

Denny grinned and moved the conversation closer to home. "Are you attracted to her? You're acting awfully cool about this."

Jessie shifted uneasily in her chair. "Yeah, well, a little bit. But that doesn't mean. . ."

"Is she attracted to you?" Denny's grin was spreading even wider as she waited for Jessie's answer.

"Hell, I don't know. Maybe. I didn't ask her."

"There are signs, y'know, Jess, certain signals that let you know. . ."

"Well, I don't know very much about that," Jessie answered defensively, feeling she was definitely losing control of the conversation.

"Calm down. I'm not attacking your virginal lesbian self, sugar. Just making an observation." Denny looked as though she might burst with delight over the unexpected turn the evening had taken. She leaned back in her chair and draped an arm over the back, her gaze never leaving Jessie's face.

"Cut it out, Denny. This is the very first time I've ever been attracted enough to consider doing something about it, and I think I have the right to be a little uptight. Tell me what I'm supposed to do!"

"About what?"

"About Kate Robbins!"

Denny laughed out loud. "Just relax and go have dinner with her. You can't plan these things. They never go right if you plan them. Have dinner and enjoy. What will be and all that." Denny shrugged and grinned. "Then I want to hear every detail."

Jessie glanced around the room trying to find some part into which she could fit comfortably. Finally, she sat down on the floor by the fireplace and leaned her elbow on the edge of the wood coffee table. The space around her was totally foreign to her, crowded with plants, mismatched furniture, canvasses in various stages of completion leaning against the walls. In one corner there was a tall work table which was covered with tubes of paint, jars, brushes, and cloths. Jessie twisted her head in an attempt to see the paintings better. She didn't think she could just look through them without Kate's permission, but she didn't want to ask. What if she hated Kate's art work? What would she say then? Besides, she didn't know anything about art. She didn't know how to talk about it, what to comment on if asked. She wondered if Kate ever showed her work.

When Kate came back into the room, Jessie busied herself with staring at the contents of her wine glass. She was very ill at ease, even after nearly two hours alone with Kate. It had not occurred to her, as she had readied herself for this evening, that she might not be able to think of anything to say. Now she found herself wishing she had suggested they go out for dinner. Perhaps some neutral territory would have made talking less difficult. At the very least, there would have been some distractions to fill the long silences. She shifted her position a bit, her crossed legs rapidly growing numb from lack of circulation. She was afraid to move around too much, not wanting Kate to notice her uneasiness.

Kate was puzzled. She eased her lanky body down as close to Jessie as she dared place herself. She was a little afraid that if she got too close, the younger woman might bolt from the room. She helped herself to some more wine and tried to refrain from looking at Jessie. The evening was certainly proving to be a surprise, she thought silently. She was baffled, remembering how easily Jessie had talked when they had had lunch together. Had she done something to put her off? Kate didn't think so.

Kate leaned back and sipped her wine, watching Jessie covertly. The warmth she felt spreading through her body had little to do with the alcohol she was taking in. She wanted this woman, and she had thought Jessie felt the same way. Maybe

Jessie was simply very shy.

"You said you are a writer," Kate said. "What sort of writing do you do?"

Jessie glanced at her quickly, then looked away. "Not very much these days. I'm too busy trying to get the business on its feet."

"Well then, what sorts of things do you write when you have the time for it?" Kate patiently rephrased the question.

Jessie shrugged. "Some poetry, but mostly fiction. It takes a lot of time to write. At least, for me, it takes blocks of uninterrupted time. I haven't had very much of that lately."

"What kind of fiction?" Kate leaned over and refilled Jessie's glass. She wanted to touch her.

"I've done some short stories, but I have trouble keeping them short. I think I want to write a novel, but I just don't have the time. Maybe when the business really gets going. . .I don't know."

"Have any ideas for a novel?"

Again the shoulders shrugged. "Not really."

Kate stared at the plants on the shelf above Jessie's head. Well, that subject had been exhausted pretty quickly. She groped for another one with which to replace it.

Agnes, Kate's old grey cat, wandered into the room and walked over to Jessie, cautiously sniffing her pant leg. Jessie, relieved to find any diversion, leaned over to pet her. Agnes immediately sat down, delighted to have such unexpected attention lavished on her by a total stranger.

Kate seized the moment to stare openly at Jessie. Jessie sat with one knee drawn up, her chin resting on it, her muscular body seeming tense and somewhat out of place in the crowded room. Kate felt the urge to run her hands over Jessie's wide, solid shoulders.

Minutes passed in silence as Jessie rubbed Agnes, her hands touching the soft fur, rubbing deeply into the muscles. Agnes arched her back and purred, pressing up against Jessie's fingers. Kate watched. Not particularly beautiful hands, but strong—hands that seemed very knowledgeable about touching. Sensual as they stroked the small cat. Kate set her wine glass on the floor and reached out to catch Jessie's arm, pulling it to her so she could hold her hand. She ran a finger over the back, tracing the veins which shone pale blue under the skin.

"You know, Jessie, I asked you over because I really wanted

a chance to get to know you better. I wanted time to talk more with you. But also because I am very attracted to you." Kate's tone was matter-of-fact.

"I wasn't sure," Jessie answered, staring at Kate. She did not withdraw her hand.

Kate quietly considered Jessie's response as she continued to rub the hand she held, fully aware of the faint flush that arose on the other woman's face. She waited.

Jessie cleared her throat carefully. "Kate. . .I'm feeling very self-conscious right now."

Kate glanced up, a puzzled expression on her face. "Why do you feel that way?"

Jessie refused to meet her gaze. "I. . .well, I've never met a woman I was so attracted to before, and I don't know exactly what to do. I mean. . ." Jessie fell silent, still staring at the cat who stood up indignantly now that she found herself so suddenly ignored.

Kate didn't understand. "I don't get it, Jessie. You talked about being a lesbian. . ."

"I really feel that I *am* a lesbian. It's just that I've never. . ."

"Oh, baby," Kate whispered. She reached out and put her arm around Jessie's shoulders. "So that's it. It's okay. I'm even more delighted and flattered that you're here with me."

"I'm glad you are," Jessie said a trifle bitterly. "I just feel silly."

"I don't think you're silly." Kate kissed her lightly on the cheek. She could feel the tension in Jessie's body. She wanted to laugh, but she was afraid she might offend the other woman.

"Maybe I should just go home."

Kate leaned around so she could see Jessie's face. "I really don't want you to leave."

"I don't know what else to do," she burst out in frustration. Jessie ran her fingers through her short, dark hair. "I can't even carry on a decent conversation with you."

"We don't have to talk. I don't mind sitting quietly with you. But I want you to stay tonight. We don't have to make love. We can just sleep together. I want to be close to you."

Indecision was in Jessie's eyes. She hesitated for several long moments. "All right," she said finally.

"Good," Kate answered, smiling. "We can talk in the morning." She stood up and offered her hand.

Jessie lay without moving, without opening her eyes. Something was not right. The morning sun never fell on her face. And the smells were all wrong, the sheets odd against her naked skin. The feeling of disorientation nearly overtook her until she remembered—Kate.

She could feel the heat from Kate's body and sensed that the other woman was also awake though still and quiet, perhaps waiting for Jessie to open her eyes. Jessie remembered drifting off to sleep the night before, her back pressed firmly against Kate's breasts and belly, Kate's thighs curving under her buttocks, pubic hair tickling lightly whenever Kate inhaled. It had been very wonderful, soft and peaceful, and Jessie had relaxed into the quiet rhythm of Kate's breathing, finding sleep almost too quick and close. But now it was morning, and Jessie lay on her back, feeling the weight of Kate's arm across her stomach, feeling warm breath against her ear.

Jessie slowly moved her hand up to rest on Kate's arm. Then lightly, holding her breath, she stroked the soft skin, feeling the downy hair rise slightly under her fingers. She was acutely aware of the pleasant fluid heaviness in her thighs and stomach. Her breathing quickened suddenly when she felt Kate's mouth move against her ear, soft tongue flickering lightly. Then a quiet laugh made her finally open her eyes.

"I didn't think you were really sleeping," Kate whispered.

"No," Jessie admitted.

"Still feeling awkward?"

"Yeah, a little."

"I. . .want. . .you," Kate said slowly. She paused over each word, her mouth against Jessie's ear, the sounds seeming to slide into Jessie, leaving a warm trail through breasts, belly, and finally falling into a moist heap between her thighs. "You don't have to do a thing."

Jessie felt completely immobile for several moments. Then her stomach rippled involuntarily, and her hand moved up, almost without her knowledge, along Kate's arm, over her shoulder and down her side, coming to rest on her hip, tugging slightly as Jessie coaxed Kate closer.

Kate moved until she was over Jessie, their thighs pressed together, light and dark pubic hair mingling, stomachs touching at the slightest stirring or intake of breath. She held herself up on straightened arms, watching Jessie's face, watching as Jessie's hazel eyes darkened when Kate's long hair brushed over her ribs and breasts. Kate held back, wanting to be quick, feeling her own impatient rhythms rising, but she restrained herself. She teased gently, moving her body in concentric circles as she leaned down to give light, tantalizing kisses, only to pull back once more, listening to Jessie's breathing as it quickened and deepened, rubbing until the younger woman groaned softly and arched up to meet her. Jessie grabbed her with strong, certain hands, pulling Kate down to the full length of their bodies.

First time, Kate thought, as she felt herself tremble. She forced herself to move slow, slow, easing down a trail of kisses, light, insistent, coaxing. She paused as Jessie's hands found her breasts, touching tentatively, and she pressed forward against Jessie's fingertips.

Jessie almost reached to stop her as she felt Kate begin to move down her body. Men had done that, and Jessie had hated it. Then she heard Kate groan softly as she slid her face between Jessie's thighs and pressed her mouth to the wetness there.

"You feel so good," Kate murmured softly, "so good."

For some reason that Jessie didn't understand, the words released her tension. She felt herself relax, drawn into the dance of Kate's mouth and tongue. She held the back of Kate's head, her fingers curling tightly in the long, touseled hair, suddenly pulling Kate closer, wanting to take her inside and hold her there. Her body felt lighter, lighter, and then she came, suddenly, with a burst of color behind her eyelids and a soft, damp spring against Kate's face. Not thinking about gentleness, she pulled Kate hard against her until the last shudder broke and ebbed away. Jessie caught Kate's head between her hands and pulled her up.

"I need you to hold me."

Kate moved her body to fit around Jessie and wrapped her arms around her, feeling Jessie vibrate and then slowly begin to relax.

Jessie opened her eyes to find Kate watching her. She turned on her side and lifted her hand to touch Kate's still damp face. She was hesitant, careful, suddenly realizing that she had never touched anyone's face before and understanding why. It was an intimate gesture, a gesture she had never felt inclined to make. She let her hand drift down, cupping Kate's breast, marveling at the shape and weight, feeling the nipple harden against her fingertip. Then down the smoothness of Kate's belly, the springy, thick pubic hair. She heard Kate's breath catch as she slid her fingers into her, rubbing lightly, attentive to the motion of Kate's body, letting Kate show her what and where and how. She watched the expressions on the older woman's face as she touched, wondering if she, too, had had those same expressions, wondering if she would even know when Kate came. But the certain knowledge was there, and she followed the rhythm, feeling the pulsing under her fingers, following it down as Kate closed around her fingers, hard, trembling. Then she leaned down and rested her face against Kate's breast and listened to her breathing slow and quiet, like the calm after a storm.

2

Jessie had made a huge, unthinking mistake.

She knew that now as she sat on the porch step, a can of beer clasped between her hands. She stared out at the pasture, oblivious to the grazing cows who passed slowly by the barbed wire fence ignoring her as they searched out tender grass.

Laura had been furious. At first, Jessie could not comprehend the reason for Laura's anger. The more she failed to understand, the madder Laura got. Finally Jessie had stopped talking. Laura had shoved the newspaper article across the table at Jessie, headline glaring: *KLANSMEN SAY ORGANIZING WILL CONTINUE.*

"Don't tell me they shouldn't be taken seriously," Laura had said through clenched teeth, her body rigid as she leaned towards Jessie. "Don't tell me they're clowns and the way to control them is to ignore them. They exist because people want them to exist. White people! And only white people can stop them. Did you even read this article? I can't believe you did."

"Of course I read it," Jessie had replied. "Why else. . ."

"*Why* is a damned good question! Is it because I'm black and we're friends? Is it because I'm the only black woman you know and you're doing a trip on me?"

Laura took a deep breath and leaned back in her chair. Jessie stared at her in stunned silence. Laura continued, her voice quieter.

"I want to tell you something. I know your intentions are good. But there are lots of folks out there with good intentions.

And good intentions are absolutely worthless. Let me give you a little piece of reality to think about. In the early 1900s, my grandfather and grandmother bought fifteen acres of land in northern Georgia. They were farmers. The Klan paid them a visit. They burned my grandfather's house to the ground and rode through all the crops. Two years later, because my grandparents wouldn't leave, they came back. They burned the place again. They tore up the crops. But this time, they beat my grandfather and left him a cripple for life. He was a young man with a wife and five kids. They had to move into town and my grandmother had to do maid's work to support the family. Some local white men visited my grandfather and told him that they had heard there was some mischief brewing, but they hadn't taken it seriously. *Mischief!* Then those good-intentioned white men offered to buy granddaddy's land from him. They bought it for twenty-five cents on the dollar.

"So you think about that. They are not a bunch of clowns. Have you ever seen that film, *Birth of a Nation?* Check it out. It still plays around from time to time. Just go to the graduate library, and read all about the hearings that were held about the Klan. Read the testimonies of black women and men. Get some goddamned information before you start making conclusions. As far as I'm concerned, Jessie, you don't take them seriously, then you're as bad as they are!"

With that, Laura had left.

You don't take them seriously, then you're as bad as they are. Jessie lit a cigarette. Sick, she felt sick. She had gone to the library, but she hadn't been able to read very much. The accounts were horrible, endless testimony in volume after volume: stories of beatings and rapes, torture, men killed outright, women beaten bloody and left to die, people terrorized, crops and homes destroyed, black people fleeing for their lives.

Then she had checked through the newspaper files for more current information. It was there, some of it obscure, but it was there. She had spent the entire day reading the accounts, some on yellowing pages, some on microfilm.

She had come home intending to call Laura and apologize, but she found she could not pick up the telephone.

Jessie threw away the cigarette butt with a disgusted flick of her wrist.

"It was a stupid, ignorant thing to say," she blurted out suddenly. Kelly looked at her mildly. "Stupid. Stupid!" She glared at the dog. "Sometimes I don't believe I should ever open my mouth! Stupid!" Jessie turned and stormed off towards the garden. After a moment of uncertainty, Kelly stood up and loped after her.

Jessie leaned over to pick up another armful of wood. She stacked it on the porch, loosely, so the air could circulate through it. It would be dark soon, and the breeze was cool. She wiped the sweat from her face with the bottom of her T-shirt. Jessie sat down on the step and picked up the file to sharpen the dull maul. Tomorrow she would can beans, and maybe some peas, too. Tomatoes were coming in so quickly she could not keep up with them. She shuddered at the thought of another tomato sandwich. Next year, she would know better than to set out ten tomato plants at the same time. Next year, she would know a whole lot more about everything.

There were chickens to do soon. She watched them as they pecked around the yard oblivious to her. One of the roosters strutted around the hens territorially as he jerked his head from side to side, his comb flipping wildly. Jessie kept a cautious eye on him. He had taken to attacking without warning or provocation. Many of the hens were laying now, giving her up to ten eggs a day. Mentally, she scheduled killing three of the roosters. She didn't need five roosters.

She needed to borrow Hollis' truck so she could pick up the old freezer she had bought from Mrs. Anna Washington. A lot of her vegetables could be frozen. And there was that new farmers' market with all of that fresh fruit. She wanted to make applesauce and jam. Jessie sighed. There was just not enough time.

She stood up and stretched. Kate would be coming soon. Jessie gathered the tools and headed to the woodshed with them, conscious of the sudden burst of energy that had come when she thought about Kate. She laughed. Time enough for *some* things.

Jessie ran warm water into the bathtub and stood silently watching the whirlpool current that formed as the water deepened. She had seen Kate several times but still felt shy with her, especially when they made love. Kate took the lead there, and

Jessie wasn't entirely satisfied with that. She understood why Kate felt like she should take the lead, why Kate would feel a certain amount of responsibility, but she didn't like her own passiveness.

Jessie peeled off sweat-soaked clothes and lowered her body into the water until it lapped at her chin. The last time she and Kate had made love Jessie could feel a tension in Kate's body, as though something was being held back, restrained. Kate probably thought she would frighten Jessie if she let the passion go, if she showed how she felt. Jessie splashed water on her face, wishing she knew how to let Kate know that not only was it okay, but that she wanted it. She *wanted* it.

This would be the first time Kate had ever come to Jessie's house. Briefly, Jessie wondered what Kate would think of the ramshackle old place, the dog, the cats, the chickens, the garden. Last night, Jessie had heard a bobcat scream from the woods down near the marsh. Maybe Kate wouldn't want to know that, at least not during her first visit.

Jessie eyed her body through the water. Kate said she was beautiful. Jessie closed her eyes. Her body was many things, but she never thought of it as beautiful. After all, she had been told often enough that it was not even acceptable—stocky, wide-shouldered, a slight bulge at the waistline, ample hips and thighs. She never thought of herself as fat. No, fat did not fit. But definitely chunky, in a nice solid sort of way. Of course, she didn't mind Kate thinking she was beautiful. She just didn't fully believe her.

But Kate, Kate *was* beautiful, in every conventional sense of the word—willow thin, long blonde hair, blue eyes. Men stared at her whenever she and Jessie went out together. They would wink at her and try to engage her in conversation. Jessie had never seen a woman more capable of cutting a man cold than Kate, however. She had a real technique, acidic and very effective.

Jessie sat up suddenly and reached for the washcloth. What are you doing, she thought to herself, sitting here daydreaming about her when she'll be here in half an hour? And what did it matter that Kate was beautiful? Would it be any different if men found her ugly? Or just unappealing, as they seemed to find Jessie? Jessie soaped her body slowly. It disturbed her that she was so attracted to such a conventional-looking woman and had not been attracted to other women who very much looked like dykes.

What did that mean? What the hell, she thought tiredly. You don't have to have a reason for everything.

Kate stood on the porch, sipping wine from the glass Jessie had handed her. The moon was almost full, and the pasture behind the house was clearly visible. Jessie leaned against the door frame, one hand holding her wine glass, the other shoved into her pocket. She, too, stared out at the pasture, seemingly lost in some faraway thought. Kate watched her quietly.

Jessie was something of an enigma to Kate: intense, quiet, almost impenetrable at times, but given to wild flights of fancy, soft whimsical humor, with a gentleness that sometimes belied her exterior toughness. But Jessie *was* tough, and hard. Kate felt that as clearly as she felt the tenderness in the younger woman. Balancing the two notions of the woman who was now her lover was very difficult. She had never before met anyone quite like Jessie.

Kate knew she was a dominating sort of person, used to having her way and the upper hand in her relationships. She tended to barnstorm through life, through ideas, and through lovers. She had never considered her lovers to be her equals, although she had often wished they were. Now she was quite aware that she was involved with someone who she instinctively knew was her equal in every way, and it made her very nervous.

Kate did not yield to the slow, soft motion in her body, the quiet rising of want. She continued to stand near the steps, outwardly still, wanting Jessie to make the first move this time. The thought surprised her. She never waited for anything, and she certainly never waited for sexual overtures. For all her brashness, Kate knew Jessie was shy. Still, she waited, wanting that new balance, wanting Jessie to come to her.

Jessie had yet to really let go with Kate, to drop the guards and fall completely into the lovemaking. Kate wondered if she ever would.

Jessie's want was not so easily stilled. She finished the wine much faster than she had intended and then automatically reached for a cigarette. As she started to light it, a sudden breeze flicked out the match. Kate glanced at her, her attention caught by the flare of flame in the dark. All you have to do, Jessie thought, is go over to her. Just go over.

Kate was caught off-guard when Jessie's arms closed around her and pulled her close. There was still a bit of tentativeness in the gesture, and Kate held herself still in the circle of Jessie's arms. She could feel the hard muscles of Jessie's body, ridges of stone under the soft clothes and skin, the body of a woman used to physical work. Jessie's hands were calloused and scarred. She was strong; Kate knew that, too. For a moment, Kate felt a breath of fear. Jessie held her gently but more firmly than before, her face resting against Kate's neck. Yet, for a brief second, Kate was afraid of the strength. Only in a man's body had she ever felt that power.

Jessie was surprised by the sudden rise of wanting. The sensation was completely new and disconcerting—almost like a roughness, a need for immediate contact, a need to be able to feel Kate against her, to press her body into Kate's until skin merged. She wanted to *take* her, fiercely. The thought surprised her. Uncertain, she turned Kate to face her and pulled her close, closer, until her arms ached from tautness and her breathing deepened, rasped in her throat. She could go no further until she had some sort of sign from Kate that it was all right.

"You're very strong," Kate said quietly.

"Yes."

The silence was long. Jessie almost backed away. She felt a rejection, but she couldn't understand exactly what it was or where it came from. Then suddenly, she felt Kate exhale a long, pent-up breath. Kate tightened her grasp on Jessie and kissed her firmly.

"Hey, Jess?"

"Yeah?"

"I have a sort of strange request."

"What?"

"If we went into the pasture, do you think the cows would step all over us?"

Jessie leaned her head back so she could see Kate's face. "The pasture?" she asked in a puzzled voice. "Why on earth do you want to go. . ." She paused, then began to grin. "Are you sure you want to go out there?"

Kate eyed the meadow. "Is it safe?"

Jessie followed her gaze. "Probably. The cows are most likely in the woods for the night. I could get a blanket and a flashlight."

"Why don't you?" Kate grinned.

"Okay. But the bugs are going to eat us alive."

"I'll take my chances."

"Then I'll get a blanket."

When Jessie returned to the porch, she was no longer nervous. She was in her territory now—the pasture, the grass and sky, even the cows. She threw the blanket over her shoulder, switched on the flashlight, and reached for Kate's hand.

"C'mon. There's a stand of trees on the far side where the grass isn't so tall. Even if the cows come out, the trees should keep them away. They're pretty skittish, and if you so much as look at them hard. . ."

Jessie's voice ambled on as she hurried Kate through the gate and through the tall, wiry grass. She could hear Kate breathlessly trying to keep up, but she did not slow her pace. She felt light, and she could have walked all night. A sudden low noise drifted to them on the wind. Jessie could feel Kate start in fright.

"It's okay. That's a barred owl. Probably hunting down in the marsh. There are lots of owls around here."

"I've never heard one before."

"I love the way they sound," Jessie said softly as she stopped walking and began to spread the blanket. Kate watched her, some of her earlier bravado vanishing. She felt the meadow stretching out around her.

"I thought you were going to spread the blanket under the trees. Aren't we going to be trampled out here?"

"We're close enough to them. Anyway, at this time of year the meteor showers start. You can lay on your back and watch them, all different colors." Jessie stepped back and inspected the blanket. Then she turned to Kate who was watching her intently.

"I have to admit that I'm a little nervous," Kate said.

"About what?" Jessie asked as she put her arms around Kate.

"About being out here in this openness."

"Nothing will bother us. The only thing we might see would be a rabbit, or an owl flying overhead."

Jessie's mouth was insistent. Kate's nervousness disappeared as Jessie unbuttoned her shirt and pushed it aside impatiently. She pressed her mouth against Kate's neck, then moved down to her breast. As they lay down on the blanket, Kate could feel the grass against her ankles, cool and vaguely damp. Then she forgot the grass and the meadow as she sank into wild, impatient rhythms that matched Jessie's fierceness, pressing into Jessie's hands and mouth, urging, coaxing her, and finally tangling her fingers in Jessie's short, dark hair and moving her down, holding her there, there.

"There's another one," Kate exclaimed delightedly.

Jessie lit a cigarette and stared up. "I missed that one. They sure are beautiful."

"So are you," Kate said.

"Yeah, well," Jessie replied, embarrassed. "I won't be so beautiful with all these chiggers."

"What in the world are chiggers?"

"You've never heard of them? Well, they are also known as redbugs, and they are these tiny, tiny little creatures who bite and burrow into your skin. The bites itch worse than anything."

"Sounds awful."

"I have a feeling you'll know for yourself by morning. It takes a while for the itch to start."

"I hope not. I hate to spoil this moment, but I'm getting very cold."

"We could go in."

"I think I need to."

"Okay."

They dressed in silence. Jessie suddenly felt self-conscious as she pulled on her jeans and slipped into her shirt. Had she been too rough, too. . .uncontrolled? She felt a surge of embarrassment. What did Kate think?

Jessie groaned and tried to open her eyes, still locked at the edge of a dream. The sound didn't fit. Somewhere there was a pounding noise, almost like a hammer on a block of wood. She stretched out her hand but could feel nothing. The noise was not pleasant.

Jessie finally woke to Kate shaking her. "Jessie, someone's at the door. Do you want me to get it?"

Jessie sat up quickly, reaching automatically for her jeans. They were not in their usual place on the foot of the bed. Stumbling hastily to her feet, she finally located them in a heap of clothing on the floor. She tugged them loose and pulled them on, swaying and tripping. Nausea rose; she had gotten up much too quickly.

"I'll get it," she muttered. "It might be Ben Carpenter, and I would never be able to explain you if you weren't fully dressed." She shrugged into her shirt, paying no attention to the detail of getting the correct buttons into the appropriate holes. Shirt askew, hair standing on end, and barefoot, she left the room.

"All right," Jessie said as she fumbled with the dead-bolt lock on the door. Her hands would not cooperate, and it took three attempts to slide the bolt free from the tumblers. When she opened the door, Denny and Val stood on the porch.

"I was asleep," she explained.

Denny glanced at her. "That's pretty obvious. What are you doing still in bed? It's almost eleven."

"I got to sleep kinda late," Jessie mumbled as she tried to smooth down her hair with the palm of her hand. "This is really sort of a bad time. I mean, I'm not awake and. . ." Her voice trailed off as Jessie noticed her shirt and set to matching buttons and buttonholes. Denny looked at Val who was trying very hard to hide her smile.

"Well, it's high time you were up. Got any coffee?"

Jessie followed Denny into the kitchen, still fumbling with her shirt. Denny took down the coffee pot and calmly began measuring coffee into the drip basket.

"Look, it's great that you two came all the way out here to visit but I. . ."

"We're not here just for a visit," Denny explained patiently. "We're supposed to have breakfast and plan the benefit dance, remember? You moved the sugar again, Jess."

Jessie grabbed the sugar bowl and thrust it at Denny. "Damn. I forgot. Look, uh. . .I'll make breakfast. I think I have enough of everything." Jessie jerked the door to the refrigerator open and peered inside. When she emerged, she was clasping milk, eggs, cheese, and butter to her chest. She kicked the door closed with a bare foot and set things on the table. "I can make omelettes." Jessie reached for a frying pan.

Kate stepped into the kitchen, hair touseled, sleepy-eyed, heading for the bathroom. She was wearing Jessie's robe.

"Hello," Denny said, a note of delight in her voice. Jessie

flushed furiously as Denny glanced at her, her gaze teasing wickedly.

"Oh, Kate. This is Denny Stevens and Val Berns. Kate Robbins." Jessie gestured vaguely between the three women and turned back to the frying pan, her face a deep shade of red. Somehow, her privacy felt very invaded. She wasn't ready for this.

"I knew the face but not the name. Hi, Kate," Val said as she offered her hand.

Denny nodded, still grinning. "Good to see you again, Kate. We were just starting breakfast before we settle into a meeting. Want to join us?"

Kate nodded and smiled. "Sure. Let me get some clothes on and I'll help."

She disappeared in the direction of Jessie's bathroom. Denny made no attempt to hide the giggle as she turned back to the coffee pot.

Jessie dropped a heavy hand on Denny's shoulder. "One word out of you and I'll toss you out of here on your ear, Denny. I mean it."

"Me? I thought I was being perfectly polite," she protested.

"Not one word," Jessie repeated grimly as she left the room.

Val touched Denny's arm, and they both burst into muffled laughter.

Jessie finally relaxed when Val and Denny drove away some two hours later. She poured another cup of coffee and dropped into a chair on the porch, propping her feet on the ledge. She lit her first cigarette of the day and inhaled deeply.

Kate came up behind her and slid her arms around Jessie's neck, slipping her hands inside the partially open shirt to cup Jessie's breasts. "Your friends are very nice."

"Yeah, they are. But Denny does give me a hard time."

"Bad kind of hard?"

"No. Just teasing the hell out of me."

Kate sat down in a chair opposite Jessie. "Will she give you a hard time about me?"

"Probably."

"Well, I guess it would be hard to resist the temptation to tease, especially after my fatal entrance wearing your bathrobe.

I thought you were just making breakfast. If I had known they were here, I would've been a lot more respectable looking when I came in."

"You looked fine. It's just that I've never had a lover before, and Denny knows that. I was feeling a little self-conscious."

"Well, she can only get so much mileage out of it."

Jessie glanced at her, grinning. "You don't know Denny. She gets light years out of every story. And each time she tells it, it gets more stupendous."

"Does it bother you?"

Jessie laughed as she shook her head. "Not really. I'm just mentally bracing myself. Denny knew I was interested in you, and I haven't seen her since I started seeing you."

Kate's eyebrows went up slightly as she helped herself to a cigarette from Jessie's pack and lit it, her gaze never leaving Jessie's face. "Really? You haven't told me about *that.*"

Jessie ran her fingers through her hair. "No, I guess I haven't."

"Are you going to?"

"If you'd like."

"C'mon, Jessie. I love these kinds of stories."

"Well, it's just that I was attracted to you and was trying to find out about you, what you were like. You know." Her smile was self-conscious as she continued. "So I asked Denny because it seems like she knows everybody in these parts. She zeroed right in on it and told me I should by all means have dinner with you and then come back and tell her everything."

"Did you? Go back and tell her everything, I mean."

"No. I haven't seen her. I'm sure she's been wondering."

"Looks like she got her confirmation this morning."

"But the next time I see her, she really will want all of the details."

"And what will you tell her?"

Jessie glanced at Kate, her expression teasing. "I don't know. Maybe I'll tell her it's none of her business."

"Or?" Kate asked, also smiling.

"Or maybe I'll tell her you are an incredible lover."

"What? No lurid details?"

"I'm sure Denny's imagination can supply more than I ever could. I'm equally sure she will put it to good use."

"You don't take them seriously, then you're as bad as they are."

Laura's face loomed over Jessie, her voice angry, her eyes narrowed. "Why do you want to be friends with me, white girl? Who do you think you are anyway?"

Jessie couldn't speak. When she opened her mouth, only whispers emerged, whispers no one else could hear. Laura turned and began to walk away. When Jessie tried to follow, her body would not move.

Laura kept walking, and Jessie felt herself sinking down into some kind of thick wetness. It slicked her body, and when she raised her arm, it dripped in gelantinous drops down her chest.

She woke with a strangled cry, coming up from the bed as though she would leave it. Kelly sat beside her, tail thumping the floor, a low whine in her voice.

Jessie reached over and rubbed Kelly's head. It did little to quiet the large dog's nervousness. Jessie could hear the distant rumble of thunder. Abruptly, she swung her legs over the side of the bed, grabbing her jeans and shirt as she stood up. She started to pull on the shirt. The night was hot, heavy with humidity. Jessie glanced at the clock. Three o'clock. She threw the shirt onto the bed. She could be safely naked in her own house in the middle of the night.

Barefoot, Jessie went into the kitchen, took a beer from the refrigerator, and found her cigarettes. Kelly padded closely behind her. She pulled the door open and curled her body into the battered armchair on the porch, the light breeze cool on her skin. She popped the top on the can, lit a cigarette, and pulled Kelly's head into her lap. Far away, there were small jags of lightning, thin shards of yellow-white. Usually Jessie loved storms; Kelly always hated and feared them.

But Jessie paid little attention to either the storm or the dog, causing Kelly to push even closer for attention and reassurance. There was little Jessie could do to help Kelly's fear, but her inattention added to it. She rubbed the dog's head absently, her thoughts far away.

Laura. Jessie had known her for about two years. The beginnings had not been easy. Jessie had come into the lesbian community thinking of herself as a lesbian, looking for a group of women with whom she could share ideas and work, women whose political notions paralleled her own. She was adamant about not wanting to work with men. So she approached the lesbian community where, for a while, she was viewed as something of an oddity, a woman who kept to herself and volunteered little or no personal information. Jessie had been afraid she would not be accepted if the women in the community knew her lesbian identity was strictly political, and her personal reality did not, at that time, include sexual relationships. Women speculated about her to one another; she heard some of the gossip. A few asked her about lovers. Jessie never lied, but she rarely volunteered much information. The few women who did know were very close friends and quite accepting of her, even if they didn't completely understand her reticence about sex.

Laura had come onto the scene quietly at first. She had been very clear that her reasons for working with white women had everything to do with the lack of a black lesbian community in the area. White women seemed a bit unnerved by her presence, by her extensive political experience as well as by her color. Their response to her was awkward.

If Jessie was considered odd because of her intense personal silence, and Laura was odd because she was black, they were both considered a little weird and hard to deal with because of their head-on approach to organizing. Individually, each was quick-tempered, assertive, stubborn, and impatient. Jessie could remember more than one occasion where they turned meetings upside down when one or the other got angry over prolonged process or nitpicking politics.

Because they usually agreed with one another, Jessie and Laura often found themselves working together. With almost no outside help from the community, they had organized a march to protest the rape of a local college student, a march that had drawn much publicity and media coverage. By the end of the event, Jessie and Laura were friends. It had happened slowly.

One night, after a particularly long and involved meeting with a local anti-nuke group, Jessie and Laura decided to go to the bar together, having discovered they both enjoyed playing pool. The tension of the meeting was still between them, and their conversations were testy.

Finally, exasperated by Laura's ongoing string of derisive, anti-white remarks, Jessie had slammed the cue ball across the table without aiming and glared at Laura. "Dammit! Will you please stop talking about those 'damned white girls'? I am a white girl, and I feel like you're taking all this out on me. If you have a problem with me, then say so. Stop all the 'white girl' crap."

Laura leaned across the table and glared back. "Fine. Just as soon as you stop talking about 'women of color.' What color? I am a black woman. Every other woman there tonight was a white woman. Talk some reality, thank you very much."

"All right!" Jessie shouted.

"Good!" Laura snapped as she made her next shot. Abruptly she straightened and eyed her companion. "You know what I think we both are?"

"No. What?"

She smiled. "Mean bitches." Laura's voice was calm and content. "Mean damned bitches. And you know, I love it."

Jessie watched the lightning, her beer almost gone. The thunder had ended, and Kelly had fallen asleep, her head still on Jessie's lap. Tiredly, she rubbed her eyes. She would call Laura tomorrow. They had to talk soon.

3

The knock on the door startled Jessie. Immersed in a book, she had not heard anyone coming. She paused before opening the door.

"Who is it?" she called. The .22 rifle was loaded and leaning against the wall. She glanced at it, hating the fact that she found the presence of the old gun comforting. Kelly pressed against her leg, tail wagging but an alert expression on her face.

"Val and Denny."

Jessie opened the door, relief flooding through her. She didn't care for the fact that she was nervous about living alone for the first time in the year she had spent in the house.

Denny stepped inside and almost tripped over the gun. Replacing it against the wall, she looked at Jessie. "What's this for?"

Jessie motioned them towards the living room and locked the door behind them. "You know that button Val gave me that has *STOP THE KKK* on it?" Denny nodded. "Well, I wore it into Pete Davis' store the other day, you know, the store up on the highway? There were a bunch of local guys hanging out as usual. Pete read the button out loud, and you could've heard a pin drop in there. All the men stared at me, and one guy came over and sort of leaned against the counter beside me, looking at me hard. When I went out, I noticed that they all had rifles in the gun racks in their pickup trucks. Just as I was leaving, Davis asked didn't I rent that old farmhouse down at Ben Carpenter's place.

Everyone in the place heard him. It's got me a little scared. I keep watching for men in white sheets."

Val sat down on the sofa, her expression thoughtful. "I've been in that store a couple of times. I think you have a good reason to be scared. Place gave me the creeps. It reminded me too much of the Klan hangouts in Mississippi and Georgia when I was down there several years ago. They weren't your usual good old boys. Something different about them."

Jessie sat by the desk. She could hear thunder in the distance, and Kelly was pressed tightly to her thigh, trembling at the sounds. She stroked the nervous dog absently with one hand while she closed the book she had been reading with the other.

"So what brings you out here tonight?"

"Just a visit. We wanted to pass along what we had heard about the march planning. We tried to call, but you didn't answer."

Jessie's interest rose sharply. "What's going on with that?"

Val tucked her long legs beneath her and accepted the beer Denny handed her. "It is definitely going to happen. The newspaper today reported a Klan spokesman as saying they would not tolerate any interference with their rally and warned us that it's happening on private property. They have a point there. They have the law on their side if we go on to posted private property without the owner's permission, which he isn't likely to give because he would have to be a Klan supporter himself."

"So what was decided?"

"I can't believe Val and I sat through another one of those meetings last night," Denny said, sipping her beer. "There were a lot of rash statements being thrown around, but I think most of the people are beginning to settle down. It's just that there were so many damned men. It's been a long time since I've done any political work with men. The gay guys were okay. But the het men are harder to work with, some of them anyway. A whole lot more men than women."

"But there are women involved?"

"Oh yeah," Val answered, "just not nearly enough to suit us."

"And the straight men were so resistent to input from dykes," Denny interjected. "I'll give credit where it's due to those who did listen, but there weren't many of them."

"The general layout for the demo is pretty simple. We're supposed to meet at the Cary town hall that night at seven o'clock. Then we'll carpool everyone to the edge of the farm where the Klan rally is happening. The idea is to prevent people from walking alone and exposing themselves to individual attacks. We're going to carpool back afterwards. The news media will be there. The Klan is hot stuff these days. We'll demonstrate at the edge of the farm, staying off private property. Then we go home."

"Sounds almost ridiculous when it's actually described like that," Jessie said.

"Yes, it does," Denny answered quietly, "but I'm pretty nervous about it. I think some of the men may show up with weapons."

Val looked at her. "There's no way to stop that unless there's a body search of each and every person before the march. People won't submit to that. If they are going to be armed, I just hope they have the good sense to keep the weapons out of sight."

"I don't know," Denny replied dubiously. "I don't think the Klan will just have their rally and ignore us. Those men talking guns were scared. If a Klansman threatens them very much, there's always the distinct possibility they might pull out those guns."

"But there's not a whole lot the Klan can do if we don't trespass," Jessie said in a firm voice. She hadn't considered the fact that people might be armed.

Denny glanced at her. "There's plenty they can do. They aren't known for obeying the law. That's why we felt it was very important that no one walked around alone."

"You said we, Jessie. Have you decided to come along?"

"Yeah. I think so. I feel like I need to do something. Every time I hear the news or pick up a paper, there's the Klan. And every time I see it, I think of Laura."

Val looked up, a frown furrowing her face. "Say, is everything okay between you two?"

Jessie sighed. "No. It's not okay. Not terrible but not okay."

"What's going on?" Denny asked curiously.

"Oh hell. It's all my fault. If I would ever learn to stop and think before I opened my mouth. . .Laura was over here for breakfast a few weeks ago, and I showed her a clipping from the campus newspaper. It was an expose on the Klan. So I blithely gave my ignorant opinion that they are clowns and the best way to deal with them is to ignore them." Jessie heard Denny's quiet moan. She continued, "I know, Denny. I know."

"So what do you think now?" Denny asked as she sat down beside Val, her hand resting on Val's arm.

"I think I'd better keep my mouth shut until I know what I'm talking about. Laura's been pissed at me before but never like this."

"She probably had her guard down, Jess. You and she have been friends long enough for her not to constantly expect you to say things that can hurt her."

Jessie rubbed her face with the back of her hand. "Well, after that run-in with Laura, I took her advice and went to the library to read some of the testimonies from past Klan investigations. It made me sick. It was actual transcripts, and what was being said was horrible. The fact is, I haven't wanted to see any of that so I didn't. What Laura said to me stopped me dead in my tracks. Those men at Davis' store made it a very personal point to me, too."

"What are you going to do?"

"We are talking. It's just that this is going to take some time to work through."

Val sipped her beer. "Take it to heart and go on, Jessie."

"I know," Jessie muttered, rising and heading towards the kitchen. "I *know.*"

The old woman eyed her as Jessie shifted her rear on the hard cane-bottomed chair. Dorothy Carpenter pushed her glasses up then clasped her hands around one bony, pale knee and leaned forward.

"Yes'm. I asked Papa why did he go through the men's ward. And do you know what he tole me?" She didn't wait for Jessie's answer but plunged ahead, intent on her story. "He tole me that he just wanted to see what they was doing there. He just wanted to look around for a spell, I reckon. They was crazy, ever' last one of 'em. I don't ever want to go back to one of them hospitals. But I guess if I need it and cain't help it, well, then I'll just have to go and be done with it. But I don't think I'll ever go crazy. Takes an educated person to go crazy, and I reckon I'm not smart enough for it." The old woman fell silent, watching the birds in the driveway in front of her house.

"Why did you and your father go to the mental hospital in the first place?" Jessie asked.

Dorothy Carpenter was a storyteller. Jessie had spent many hours on this porch listening to Dorothy weave her tales, some told straightforwardly, some highly embellished and recounted with a tiny, wicked smiled on her face. But this was by far the strangest Jessie had heard.

"We was there to pay a visit to my aunt. She'd been there goin' on eight years, and I reckon she was crazy. Least that's what they said. I remember it like it was yesterday. Her lyin' there, not sayin' a word to nobody. Sometimes, she knew folks. Most of the time not. Or else, she didn't care to. I 'spect that myself. But she kept her hands clenched into fists with her thumbs inside like this," Dorothy demonstrated with her own hands, "and her fingers clenched down tight over her thumbs. Been like that the whole eight years. Nobody could open that woman's hands. It like to made me sick to look at her, sick to my heart and soul. She was a pretty woman 'fore she got put in there. But her skin was as white as pastry flour, and her eyes didn't seem to have no color to 'em.

"And her hands, Jessie, I wisht you coulda seen her hands. Her thumbnails had done growed clean through her hands and was stickin' out the other side. The nails of her other fingers had growed into the meat, too. Nurses said they had tried to open her hands and cut them nails but they couldn't do no good with 'em. Finally, they just gave up tryin'. I guess a woman clench her fists long enough, ain't nothin' nobody can do about it. Reckon it could happen to any of us."

"They grew through her hands?" Jessie asked incredulously, not wanting to believe the story. Mrs. Carpenter glanced at her, sensing the disbelief.

"That's what I'm tellin' you, ain't it? Woman, I seen it with my own eyes! And she let a man do it to her!" Dorothy leaned forward, her hands flashing in agitation as she spoke. "She was a young gal and she got with child and had to get married. After the child was born—pretty baby girl it was—that man of hers pointed her and the baby in one direction, and he took off in the other, and she never saw him no more. She let some no 'count man drive her plumb crazy. Her mama had to raise that baby girl. I don't aim to go crazy. But if I do, ain't gonna be on 'count of no man. This'n here," she pointed at Ben who was dozing in his chair, "he done tried for near forty years. He tried long and hard. If forty years ain't enough to make me crazy, then I guess I won't ever be. Here I set. I just as soon shoot myself right square in the head as let a man do somethin' like that to me."

Jessie leaned back and lit a cigarette. Her landlady went on, switching to a new tale, one that was light and humorous. Jessie smiled automatically in the appropriate places, but she wasn't really listening. The image of the woman's clenched fists wouldn't leave long enough for her to appreciate the next story.

She thought of the clenched fist: rebellion, anger, power. She had used it herself in demonstrations and rallies. Anger. She thought of her mother, standing in the kitchen, angry with her father, her fists clenched as she cried silently by the sink. She thought of how her fists clenched automatically when threatened, when in pain. Abruptly, she shook the image from her mind and stood up. She had to go home. Jessie tried to ignore the look of disappointment on Dorothy's face.

"I have to go and cook dinner. I haven't eaten today."

Mrs. Carpenter nodded, her face quickly cleared of any expression. "Maybe we'll see you tomorrow then."

"Probably." Jessie smiled and started down the driveway to her house. The light was fading rapidly with the approaching storm clouds, and she still had work to do. There was wood to be cut. The last of the vegetables from the day's picking had to be cleaned and stored for canning. Kelly leapt out of the shallow ditch and nipped playfully at Jessie's elbow. Breaking into a run, she raced the dog home. Kelly reached the porch yards ahead of Jessie and turned to bark triumphantly.

Jessie rubbed the dog's head as she cast an appraising glance up at the purple sky. She wondered what would have happened if that woman had ever had a chance to use her fists.

"Who are all these men?" Jessie whispered to Val who sat next to her.

"A strange mixture, isn't it?" Val said.

"Are they all planning to participate?"

"It's beginning to look like it."

Jessie leaned back in her chair and crossed her arms. The number of men in the room made her uncomfortable. When Val had called and asked if Jessie wanted to come to the meeting, it had seemed like a simple thing to do. Now she wasn't so sure. For every woman she could see, there were at least five men. The room was hot, and the open windows did little to relieve the stuffiness of too many bodies in a too small space. Jessie rubbed her eyes with the back of her hand. She was tired. She had stayed at the bar much too late the night before and had gotten up early to finish the canning she had postponed. Where she wanted to be most at that particular moment was in bed sleeping, not in the middle of a meeting.

Jessie searched through the crowd for familiar faces. There were a few—women she had seen at other meetings or at parties. Mostly the room was full of strangers. She watched the expressions on the faces of the women she could see from where she was sitting. They appeared to be listening, but they exchanged looks of distrust and disbelief.

". . . All I'm saying is that we can't take it for granted. They will be armed. It's a Klan rally and *they* are always armed. They post guards and everything. I think it would be stupid for us just to walk up to the fringes without being armed, too. What if they start shooting at us?"

Jessie finally located the owner of the voice, a young man with short hair sitting near the door. She nudged Val and pointed him out. Val nodded, a frown on her face.

The man continued. "Look, it's impossible to predict what might happen. They might ignore us. But I don't think so. I think they might simply start shooting. And I, for one, do not intend to stand there and be a helpless target."

Another man jumped up from his chair, a look of incredulity on his face. He ran his hand through his long hair and then slapped his thigh. Anger or frustration? Jessie couldn't decide.

"I can't believe this! It sounds like the showdown at the OK Corral. This is not the 1800s, man. This is *now.* And the quickest way to get those people to shoot at us is to show a weapon of any kind. That's crazy. You would be putting other people's lives on the line with your gun!"

"The constitution gives me the right. . ." Short-Hair doggedly persisted.

"Fuck the constitution! It's only a piece of paper. It does not give you the right to screw around with the lives of other people!"

There were murmurs of agreement from around the room. A

woman rose and raised her voice so she could be heard over the noise. "I am not willing to participate in a demonstration where people are carrying weapons. I thought we were trying to prove a point here. If we go in carrying guns, then we aren't any better than they are. We will endanger ourselves and everyone who participates. We could easily provoke an attack."

Short-Hair leapt up, pointing a finger at her. "I think it's time you started living in the present! The pacifist sixties are over! People do not respond to the nonviolent theory anymore. This is a violent society, and we have to protect ourselves. Anybody, and I mean *anybody,* who takes to the streets unarmed is a damned fool!"

"Then I'm a damned fool!" she shouted in return, "but I do *not* intend to arm myself, and I do *not* intend to let men like you set me up to be shot at because you can't deal with your own fear and need for violence!"

Another woman rose, her face flushed angrily. "You won't get any women to participate if that's your plan."

"We don't need the women, darlin' " he sneered.

The long-haired man threw up his hands in disgust. "Oh shit, man. You are a damned fool. A stupid, damned fool. What do you mean, we don't *need* the women?"

"Just what I said! We would make a greater show of force if the men were there with. . ."

Shouts of "sit down" were heard from others in the room. Short-Hair stared them down. "Those men at that rally will laugh at the women. They will not laugh at men. They are men, and they will have to respect a show of force by other *men*! As for the dykes in here. . ."

"Do some research, prick!" roared one large woman as she pushed her way through the crowd towards him. Short-Hair backed away a step or two when he saw her size. She stared down at him, not lowering her voice in spite of the fact that she stood less than a foot from him. "There are women in the Ku Klux Klan, too. Women don't just sit back and sew the bedsheets together anymore, fool. They participate. Did you see the latest issue of *Southern Exposure*? Didn't you even notice that that person on the cover with the child was a woman? A woman in Klan drag with her grandson, for chrissakes? You just glanced at it and assumed it was a man, didn't you? Well, it wasn't a man. There are a lot of women in the Klan. And besides, a lot of Klan violence comes down on women in this society, especially black women and Jewish women. So you can take your bullshit and stuff it! You need us! And we aren't going to leave to pacify your male ego!"

The cheers came not only from the women. Men clapped, too, as she continued to loom over the very silent short-haired man. Jessie nudged Val with her elbow. "Who is that?"

Val laughed. "Her name is Moon. That's all she answers to."

The long-haired man held up his hands to try to restore order in the room. Gradually the noise level dropped. When he was able to speak and be heard, he turned to face Short-Hair. "I think it would be best for all concerned if you left, man. Just pack it in and go."

Complete silence reigned as everyone stared at Short-Hair.

"You can't throw me out," he sputtered in confusion.

"The hell we can't. You said we don't need the women. Who we don't need is *you.* We don't need your disruption or your violence. Just get out."

The crowd echoed him, loudly. Finally, the short-haired man grabbed his backpack and started towards the door. "You cannot stop me from participating in the demonstration!" he yelled as he left.

The long-haired man sighed. "I don't know about everyone else, but I could use a short break. What do you say?"

Standing in the yard, Jessie lit a cigarette. She stared at Val. "I can't believe this. Have you been sitting through meetings like this for the past two months?"

"They haven't been anywhere near this eventful. I don't know who that guy was making all the noise. I haven't seen him before."

The large woman who had shouted down Short-Hair suddenly loomed over them. "I think he's an agent."

"Moon!" Val's shout was one of undisguised delight. The two women wrapped into a crushing hug. Jessie watched, grinning. It wasn't often she saw another woman as tall as Val Berns.

"It's been a while since I've seen you," Moon said to Val.

"It sure has. How are you?"

"Okay, whatever that means," Moon answered, shrugging her massive shoulders. Val turned to Jessie.

"Jessie, this is an old friend of mine from at least fifteen years ago. Moon, this is Jessie Pyne."

Jessie held out her hand. "It's good to. . ."

"The hell with shaking hands." Moon laughed as she grabbed Jessie in a hug that almost enveloped Jessie's whole body. "Good to meet you, too, Jessie Pyne. Yeah, Val and I go back to Civil Rights days in southern Georgia. Say, Val, I hear Laura is living around these parts, too. Is that a fact?"

"Yep. In Durham."

"I have to look her up. I've missed my daily fights with her." Moon looked at Jessie. "We didn't really fight, but goddess, did we ever have some great arguments! Nobody's made me think like that since I left Mississippi."

"I can understand that."

"So you know Laura, too? Lucky you! So how do I get in touch with you, Val? I want to have dinner with you real soon."

"I'm in the book. Durham, Alabama Avenue."

"Alabama Avenue?" Moon laughed loudly. "Okay. I'll call this week. Take care of yourself. See ya, Jessie."

Moon pushed back into the building. Jessie crushed out her cigarette and shook her head. Quite an impressive woman.

Val looked at her. "I'll tell you about Moon on the way home. You ready to go back inside?"

"I guess so."

Val stirred her coffee, then sipped. There were circles under her eyes and she looked tired, even though she smiled as she talked. "So Moon came to Jackson, Mississippi, from Georgia. She was all heat and ready to take on the world. There was a group of whites who were trying to find a way to work with the blacks in the area and having some difficulty. We all felt, blacks and whites, that a visible, strong all-black movement was essential. And yet many of us whites wanted to do whatever we could. So some of us started working as support groups, mostly staying in the background, except when we could serve some specific purpose with our whiteness and visibility. Things like gathering information, sometimes managing to get into meetings, things like that. We couldn't do much though because we were so obviously outsiders. Most of us weren't even from the South, and our accents gave us away pretty fast.

"Moon came down. She was very outspoken and pushy. She also overstepped the bounds frequently. She was an open lesbian, a fact which freaked almost everyone out. Moon was very big on security and thought what we called security was totally inadequate. She and Laura clashed hard several times, but the security thing united them. Laura was going crazy over the number of workers who were harassed or caught out alone and beaten up, some very badly. Finally, the group told them to work it out and shut up. They refused to do it until everyone agreed they would follow whatever guidelines and procedures were drawn up. The argument went on for days. In the end, the two of them literally talked everyone else into it. What Moon and Laura came up with was a fairly simple check-in and buddy-type system so that we got the most self-protection possible no matter where we were. They also tightened up security around conversations and meetings so that very little of our planning got out to the public. We were hassled less and got a lot more work done. We knew where everyone was almost every moment, and that made us feel a lot better. We also didn't have any more incidents of workers being caught and beaten up. I think we were just lucky that no one was killed.

"About a year after she arrived, Laura and Moon became lovers. No one understood it, and it caused a hell of a lot of problems for Laura. Moon was sort of ignored, and she didn't think who she slept with was anyone's business anyway. Laura, on the other hand, was challenged on the basis of the entire black liberationist politic."

"How did she stand up to that?" Jessie asked.

"It was rough on her. Moon wasn't black, and she wasn't a man, and Laura caught fairly constant hell for a while. But they stayed together for almost two years, until Moon wanted to move on and organize migrant workers and Laura felt very strongly that she needed to remain within the black Civil Rights movement. They parted as close friends, but I don't know how much contact they've had since then."

"I'd sure like to get a chance to talk with her."

"You probably will. She doesn't usually breeze through a place. She tends to do what she calls 'squatting' for a while, so I expect she'll be around. I'm glad she seems to be fully recovered."

Jessie glanced at her. "Recovered from what?"

Val signaled for the check. "About twelve years ago when Moon was in Mississippi, she was shot by the Klan and left for dead. One of the workers found her and got her to the hospital. There was a lot of nerve damage to her left arm and hand, and the doctors weren't sure she would ever have full use of them again. But she seems to be okay."

"The Klan, huh?"

"Yep. The Klan." Val looked at Jessie. "They seem to come into almost every conversation these days, don't they? I'm beat. Let's go home. Want to stay in town tonight? It's awfully late."

"That would be great."

Jessie followed Val out of the coffee shop. The Klan. The Klan. Why had they arrived so hard in her life?

What the hell was happening? Jessie ran.

Which direction? *Where?* She heard pounding footsteps behind her, and she tried to increase her speed. Hands gripped her shoulder and jerked her hard to the side. She felt herself slipping. Painfully, her shoulder struck the pavement and she rolled. Under something. A truck. She was under a pickup truck. She felt a body slam into her, and Denny shouted into her ear.

"Are you all right?"

Jessie nodded and slid further under the truck, seeking safety between the wheels. Denny shook her. "Do you know where Val is?"

"No," Jessie answered, trying to catch her breath. "I lost sight of her when everyone started running."

"Jesus," Denny muttered.

The shouts and screams were close now. Jessie suddenly panicked. She was under a *truck.* What if the driver. . . She started to wiggle away, but Denny grabbed her and pulled her back.

"Where the hell are you going?"

"We've got to get out from under here. We could get killed lying under a truck!"

"We're safer under here than out there." Denny clung to her.

Jessie tested her arm as best she could in her cramped position. It seemed okay. Bruised and sore, but okay.

Then she saw the woman fall just on the other side of the wheels. A black woman, young, on the ground. Suddenly, all

Jessie could see were hands and feet, hands pounding, feet kicking. The woman was silent, and still.

Jessie struggled to pull away from Denny. "Let go!"

"Jessie. . ."

"Let go, goddamit!" Jessie broke free from Denny's grasp and rolled out from under the truck. The woman was sprawled on her back, unmoving, blood all over her face. One man still stood beside her, his leg drawn back. Just as Jessie jumped to her feet, he kicked out, into the side of the woman's head. Then he looked at Jessie, his gaze daring her to interfere.

She took a step forward, not knowing what to do. The man stepped over the black woman's inert body and grabbed Jessie by the shirt. He shoved her against the truck and laughed as he ground his knee into her pubic bone. When he let go, Jessie doubled up, gasping from the pain. Only supposed to hurt *men,* she thought fleetingly, as she saw him disappear into the edge of the woods. She dropped onto her knees and bent forward in an effort to minimize the pain.

The sudden silence was as frightening as the gunshots and screams had been. Jessie held herself very still, taking deep breaths and feeling the pain subside a bit. Then she realized that she was leaning over the woman. She felt Denny beside her, but she could not tear her gaze from the woman's face. Finally she reached out and felt for a pulse. There was the tiniest flicker beneath her fingertips.

Val dropped to her knees beside Jessie, appearing out of nowhere. Her breathing was labored. She touched the woman's face.

"Oh hell. Oh *hell*," she said, over and over, like a litany.

Denny touched Jessie's shoulder. "Are you all right? Did he. . ."

Jessie shook her head. "I'm okay. I got a knee in the cunt. Get an ambulance, Denny."

As Denny ran down the road, Val pulled a bandana from her pocket and gently tried to wipe the blood from the woman's face.

"What happened, Val? What the hell happened?" Jessie asked.

Val shook her head. When she spoke, her voice trembled and cracked. "I don't know. I saw two men with guns. They fired them into the air. Then all those men burst out of the woods with heavy sticks in their hands. They started chasing people, clubbing them with the sticks. Some people tried to fight back, but most of us just ran. I think a lot of people are hurt. This was stupid. We should've been watching for something like this!"

Jessie instinctively jerked back when she saw the boots beside her. A tall, uniformed highway patrolman stood over her, glaring down from under the round brim of his hat. He touched the black woman's leg with the toe of his boot, a look of disgust on his face. "Stay with her," he ordered, as he moved away. Jessie bit off an angry retort. The pulse in the woman's neck was fainter now. *Be here,* she thought silently to the woman. *Be here.*

Jessie sat in the armchair, staring out the window, watching the afternoon sun drop behind the trees. She ached with exhaustion. Her mouth was coated from too many cigarettes and beers, and she needed a bath. Still, she sat.

In spite of the afternoon heat, she was cold. She wrapped the light blanket more tightly around her. She could hear Val and Denny talking in the kitchen.

One man shot to death. Old Short-Hair himself. A white woman badly wounded with a knife. The black woman had died on the way to the hospital. Lots of other injuries. The black woman's name was Etta. Etta Thomas.

Jessie glanced at the clock. Time for the news. For the first time in hours, she stood up. She turned on the television set and stood in front of it. The newscaster looked alien to her, far removed from the reality of her world, too tidy in his dark jacket and carefully combed hair. He gave his report in a modulated, neutral tone of voice.

"Violence erupted last night during an anti-Ku Klux Klan demonstration at Jennings farm outside Cary. Two people are dead, one woman is listed in critical condition, and at least fourteen others are reported seriously injured from a battle between Klansmen and demonstrators. Police reports say. . ."

His voice droned on and Jessie listened. She heard Val and Denny come into the room, and she could feel them standing close behind her, also listening to the report. Jessie finished her beer and lit another cigarette, ignoring the rawness of her throat. There were few pictures. The news people had packed up their gear and were leaving when the whole thing started. The demonstration was over. Everyone had been heading back to the cars together, just as planned. The photographs being used by the television station were taken by a bystander.

As she listened, Jessie slowly became aware of her surroundings, the quiet breathing of her friends, the sound of the frogs starting to sing, Kelly's panting. She tossed the blanket onto the chair and went into the bedroom. As she reached for the rifle, she noticed that her fists were tightly clenched, the nails pressing half-moon indentations into the palms of her hands. Abruptly, she grabbed the gun and the box of shells and went outside.

Her hands were shaking, and her stomach was knotted with sickening tension. She picked up a beer can from the window sill and set it on the grass. When she had walked about fifty feet from the can, she lifted the rifle and took careful aim. Then she fired.

Reloading, she quickly sent fifteen shells into the can and the ground around it. Over and over. She stopped only long enough to shove the .22 caliber shells into the magazine, and then she fired in almost continuous bursts, taking three or four seconds to empty the chamber.

If she had had a gun, could she have used it? Would she have? If she had gotten out from under the truck sooner, could she have stopped those men? What could she have done? The sharp cracks from the rifle did not drown out the memory of the men's laughter. Jessie could still hear them as clearly as if she stood beside them.

She reached for more shells and found the box empty. A heavy tiredness settled into her body as she went to retrieve the can. It was ripped to shreds by the bullets.

Val was leaning against the dogwood tree watching Jessie. She wrapped her arms around her chest as if cold, and there were tears in her eyes as she waited.

Jessie passed her on her way back inside the house. Still hugging herself, Val fell into step with Jessie. "I didn't know you could shoot a gun like that."

Jessie glanced at her. "No reason why you should. All I killed was a can."

Val stood by the door. Denny was working on the car.

"Come and stay in town with Denny and me for a few days, Jessie."

"Why?"

"It doesn't feel safe out here right now."

"I don't want to come into town."

Val ran her fingers through her thick hair, an agitated expression on her usually calm face. "It's not safe," she persisted.

"It's as safe as your house."

"Bullshit, Jessie. Look, I am scared. I don't know if I can stay out here with you."

"I didn't ask you to stay, Val. To be perfectly honest, I would rather be by myself right now."

"Use your head, Jessie. You are an eyewitness. It's not safe out here. You're too isolated."

"Dammit, Val. Stop mothering me! I don't need it!" Jessie's voice cracked with strain, and there were tears in her eyes. Val stepped forward and impulsively pulled Jessie close to her. They stood there for a long moment, silently locked hard against each other. Then Jessie straightened up and wiped her eyes.

"I think I'm a complete wreck, Val."

"So am I. So am I."

"I'll come and stay tonight. But I have to come home tomorrow. There's too much for me to do to be away from here for more than a day."

"Okay."

"I need to call Kate. She's probably pretty worried."

"Probably."

Jessie sighed. "Let me get some things together and feed the animals. Then I'll be ready."

"I'll take care of the chickens," Val volunteered. Jessie nodded and disappeared into the house.

Jessie's mood was foul. She cursed the press and slammed reams of paper. Nothing in her day was going right. She had messed up several plates, could not get the ink and water balance right on the press, and now she had dropped a rag into the rollers which had fouled the gears. She sat down on the stool and lit a cigarette, taking deep breaths, trying to calm herself. If she kept on like this, she might as well close the shop and just go home.

Laura came into the room and stood staring at the press. The rag protruded like a snake's tongue. Calmly she reached into Jessie's shirt pocket and removed a cigarette.

"You quit smoking," Jessie reminded her.

"One every week or two is not exactly heavy-duty smoking," Laura answered mildly. "I posted the closed sign on the door. We're going home."

"There's too much to do for us to. . ." Jessie began.

Laura silenced her with a gesture. "Ridiculous. You aren't getting anything done anyway, Jessie, and you know it. Besides, I can't stand hearing you yell anymore. I've been listening all day."

"It hasn't been a good day," Jessie said defensively.

"I know. You need to go home and relax a while. Go work in your garden. Get rid of some of this tension. Otherwise, I'm afraid you might really wreck the press."

Jessie threw a rag on the floor. "People are so damned full of advice these days!"

"What's eating you?" Laura demanded. "I'm a partner in this little venture here, and I have a right not to have to listen to your tantrums all day long!"

Jessie turned to face her. "What's eating me is a picture I can't get out of my mind! The picture of a woman dying flat on her back, in the middle of a road, with blood all over her face! *That's* what's eating me, Laura."

"So what are you going to do about that?"

"If I knew what to do about it, it wouldn't be bothering me so damned much!" Jessie did not lower her voice. "What really gets to me is whenever I think about Etta Thomas, I see your face. It could have been you!"

"Honey, I've known that every day of my life," Laura said softly.

"Well, I just figured it out!"

"I'm glad you finally did."

Jessie stared at her and felt the anger drain away. "Yeah, okay. I get your point. Can we be friends again?"

"We never stopped being friends. I just wanted you to think a little."

"Well, I'm thinking."

"So why don't you think at home? I could stand a little time off myself."

"All right," Jessie muttered. She reached for her pack and flipped off the light switch. Laura propelled her towards the door.

"I'll see you in the morning," she said with finality.

"Yeah." Jessie walked to her car. It was early yet. Maybe she should go home and work in the garden. Suddenly, she felt too restless to make the long drive back to her house. She threw her pack into the back seat and started down the street. She would have a beer, then maybe she would be ready to go home.

5

Jessie stared at the wall, her hands shoved into the pockets of her jeans. The light outside was fading but she didn't notice.

Kate sat quietly on the sofa, her gaze firmly fixed on Jessie's broad shoulders. "Jessie. . ."

"Not now, Kate. Not right now."

It had been going on for a long time, this fight. In some ways, it had started nearly a month ago, right after the demonstration, right after Jessie had met with Val, Denny, Laura, Moon, and some other women to discuss what had happened. They had decided to start a group and to put out a newsletter, open and visible opposition to the Ku Klux Klan. Kate had not liked the idea from the start and had been very vocal about it.

But now the afternoon dragged on with an argument that seemed endless. Jessie felt they had gotten nowhere at all. Kate could not, or would not, understand anything Jessie was saying, anything Jessie was feeling. Jessie had seen it coming; she had simply tried to avoid it. She knew Kate opposed her every Klan-related thought and action. This afternoon was just the culmination of all the disputes and tensions.

Kate rose and approached Jessie slowly, tentatively placing her hands on Jessie's shoulders. The strength in her lover's body still scared Kate a little. She had seen Jessie throw large slabs of wood around as if they weighed nothing. She had felt the barely restrained force when they made love. She had seen Jessie angry and had watched her hit the side of the house with her fist, seeming not to notice the pain Kate knew she must feel, or even the split, bleeding skin on her knuckles. Kate felt inept and clumsy by comparison.

"Can't you understand that I'm afraid for you?" Kate asked softly. "I'm afraid something terrible might happen to you. What are you hoping to accomplish?" Kate turned Jessie around, holding onto her arms. "Jess, these people kill. They don't play games."

Jessie pulled away from Kate's light grip, a touch she felt was meant to restrict more than anything else. She didn't notice the hurt expression on Kate's face as she started pacing the length of the room.

"That's the whole point. I was there. I saw what they can do. It's my whole nightmare, seeing it played over and over. I can't let it be just a nightmare, and I feel that's what you're wanting me to do."

Jessie picked up her beer and downed the last of it with one large gulp. Her hands shook, from memories, from too many cigarettes, from exhaustion. The whole conversation was going in circles with no resolution or end in sight. Kate appeared to want her to just give in completely. Jessie unclenched her fists with great effort, but she did not look at Kate.

Kate sighed and lit one of Jessie's cigarettes. She was running out of words. But Jessie wasn't listening anyhow so what did it matter?

"I'm not asking you to forget anything. No one should forget what happened, including you. But I am asking you to use some common sense."

Jessie slammed the empty beer can down on the desk, her face flushed with anger. "And just what the hell do you call *common sense,* Kate? I don't understand. Everyone goes around thinking this sort of thing can't happen to them. I doubt any one of those three people who died would've thought it was possible either. But they are dead. Two women and one man are dead. I was there, too, but I wasn't a target."

"This time," Kate muttered.

"Kate, I swear, if you don't stop baiting me. . ."

"I'm *not* baiting you! Dammit. You're trying to take on something that's so big no one even knows how many people are involved. And you're trying to do it with a tiny group of women and a newsletter. I admire your courage, but I question your tactics. What are you going to do other than call attention to yourself? I don't think even the Klan would pay much attention to you except that you are a witness to a murder and are expected to testify in court. So you put out an anti-Klan newsletter. What's it going to prove? They already know who you are, and this isn't going to make you any less of a threat to them. John Q. Public does not care!" Kate's voice increased in volume as she spoke. In her mind, she had her own private nightmare; she could so easily see Jessie lying on the ground, beaten bloody or dead. She tried to clear the picture from her mind. She couldn't function when she thought of it. All she could feel was a deep, incapacitating fear for Jessie, and for herself.

". . .that in this little town, there is a junior KKK club in the local high school? And that's a fact. We have got to make some kind of start, Kate. More people will join in."

"Why don't you recruit those people first then? The old adage about safety in numbers is true, you know."

"There are three dead people who very much disprove that old adage."

Kate recoiled from the sarcasm in Jessie's voice. This was going absolutely nowhere, and she was afraid they would only end up hating each other for the seemingly insurmountable differences between them, rather than being able to see what was really going on. Kate dropped onto the sofa and rubbed her tired eyes.

Jessie turned on the lamp, holding back tears of frustration by sheer willpower, wishing for another beer, wishing Kate would simply go home and leave her alone. Everything had seemed clear and resolved until Kate had arrived that afternoon, a copy of the newsletter in her hand.

Kelly, who had been watching anxiously from the corner, crossed to Jessie and shoved her cold, damp nose into Jessie's hand, wagging her tail slightly, seeking reassurance. Jessie rubbed the dog's head in an agitated manner, then tried to send her back to the corner with a gesture and an abrupt command to "lie down." Kelly moved a few feet away and sat, watching Jessie intently, her tail thumping on the floor from time to time as she grew more nervous about the disagreement.

"I don't want to live in a world of constant fear, Kate. I reject that. I think it can be changed. Something has to be done. That's what I want. I want to try."

"But it's not realistic," Kate answered, her patience almost completely gone. "The world isn't fair. It's okay to have a vision of people righting all the wrongs. But you are an idealist, Jess. Sometimes I think your trouble is that you can't see around your own visions long enough to acknowledge the reality. Your anger comes from not being able to have the vision, all the peace and goodness. We all know the world is a lousy place. . ."

Jessie whirled around so suddenly that she knocked a stack of books off the corner of the desk. Kelly whimpered uneasily.

"For god's sake, Kate! What do you think I've been talking about for the last two months? This whole fucking society is supposedly set up on the premise of peace and goodness and freedom. And it doesn't work! Sure, I have ideals. Everyone has to have a few. But my sense of reality is damned clear. Killing people seems like a pretty big reality. And we give our permission to those people every time we keep our mouths shut. My own silence makes me a target for them."

"And that's not enough? You're trying to make it even easier than before!"

"No! They do it because no one tells them they can't. I am not giving my silent consent anymore. I'll go down screaming, thanks."

"So why don't you just wear a sign that says *Shoot me, I'm willing*? I think there's more to be gained by simply staying alive while we try to effect change. Confrontations in the streets will only get people hurt. Have you thought seriously about that? What if we all just walked right out there and became targets? What then?"

Jessie was surprised by Kate's biting anger, but she met the older woman's gaze evenly, fighting the impulse to grab her and throw her bodily from the house.

"They can't possibly get all of us."

"But they can get a lot. What then?" Kate demanded, her eyes narrowed and piercing.

"We get killed every day, Kate! You're working for the battered women's shelter. You should know that better than anyone. But what do you think black people faced when they took to the streets in the sixties? They faced guns and clubs, the Klan, law enforcement officials, firehoses, dogs, and death. But they stayed in the streets. They took the chance!"

"Yes, and some people, like Roy Wilkins, stayed behind the scenes and fought for change from within."

"Are you trying to tell me that Roy Wilkins could have accomplished all that if there weren't also people in the streets forcing confrontations, forcing people to take notice?"

"There's the key word, Jessie, *also.* All I'm trying to say is that there are *also* other ways of doing things, not just one way, not just your way."

"I don't want to take cowardly ways of dealing with this."

There was a long silence in the room as Jessie lit a cigarette and dropped into the armchair.

"Now are you saying that not wanting to march in the streets is cowardly?" Kate's voice was tight.

Jessie's hands were shaking, and she almost dropped the matches. She was stammering over words, anger clashing with speech, her feelings frayed, all acuity gone, destroyed by the long hours of beating her head against Kate's solid wall of resistance.

Kate wanted to grab her and shake some sense into her, make Jessie at least acknowledge the other sides to her own arguments.

"I think we have to take some chances if anything is ever really going to change."

"And no one can do anything any other way?"

"I didn't say that."

"Then tell me exactly what you *are* saying!"

"What the hell good would it do to try it any other way? We have tried almost everything. We have talked and begged and even threatened. What has changed? What is different? If anything, it's worse. What good would it do to hide. . ."

"Hide?" Kate sputtered.

"Yes, hide! Hide behind the powers that be and try to make something out of nothing. They aren't going to give it to us because we're good and we don't make trouble. We have to create something from the bottom up and then let them know we won't shut up and go home until things are different."

"Do you think I am being cowardly for not taking to the streets?"

Jessie stared at her, then turned to put out her cigarette. Rising from the chair and crossing the room, Kate was on her in a flash of a second, grabbing her by the shoulders and whirling Jessie around, her fingers digging deeply into Jessie's flesh. Jessie slammed her hands upward, breaking Kate's grip. She grabbed Kate by the shirt and pushed her back, afraid to be too close, knowing she might hit her if Kate touched her again.

"Don't you ever grab me like that again, Kate."

"You answer my question!" Kate shouted. She moved towards Jessie again but then noticed Jessie's clenched fists and rigid expression.

"Your problem is, Jessie, that you can't stand the fact that we don't think exactly alike, that I see things differently from you. Or that I might, just *might,* be able to see some things more clearly because I'm not in the middle of them. All you want from me is an across-the-board *yes* to everything you think, feel, or say. You will not get that from me! But don't you ever insinuate that I am a coward again. I won't take that from you."

Kate was crying, but Jessie just stared at her. Then she turned and walked into the kitchen. She jerked open the refrigerator door and peered inside, then slammed it with a muttered curse. Stomping into the living room, she picked up her car keys, wiping her own tears away with the back of her hand. Kate still stood in the middle of the room, looking drained and fearful.

"I'm going for more beer," Jessie said.

"I could go with you."

"I don't want you to," she flung over her shoulder as she left the room. She slammed the door and stepped outside. The chilly air stung. She could feel her damp cheeks draw tightly, and she wished she had another door to slam.

6

Beth Parrish pulled the old bathrobe tightly around her as she sat down at the kitchen table and opened the morning paper. She never really read the paper; instead she looked at headlines and pictures, at the display ads and grocery specials. The news was always too full of murders, disasters, crises, and Beth found it depressing.

She sipped her tea contentedly, the silence in the small house unbroken except for the occasional rustle of a page being turned. She loved this time of the morning, the only time she had for herself, to be alone, to be still and quiet. It was her ritual, although she never would have thought of it as such. After the boys went off to school and Hank left for work, Beth would put on her faded pink bathrobe, the terry cloth worn nearly through in places, make herself a cup of mint tea, and sit down at the formica-topped kitchen table with the newspaper and the silence.

She didn't remember exactly when, or even why, she had started taking this time for herself. In her mind, she thought she had simply found herself doing it. Beth frequently didn't remember the beginnings of things, only that they *were* now and therefore must need to *be.* She had not made a conscious choice to continue her morning ritual; she just did it. She never told anyone about it, never shared the secret of the time stolen from her busy day and given to herself as a precious gift. And of course, she had to be careful about it. Hank had come back to the house unexpectedly one morning and had almost caught her sitting at the table, lost in a daydream. Since that day, she had been much more discreet, never relaxing so completely that she might not hear his key in the lock or the sounds of Karen next door coming over to borrow something.

Beth unconsciously stroked the worn pattern of the soft robe. Her best friend in high school had given it to her as a birthday present the year they graduated. She had never understood why Hank hated it so much. Well, it *was* getting pretty ratty and old now, but he had hated it even when it was new. Maybe Hank just didn't like anything that was given to her by anyone other than himself. He always found fault with the clothes Beth's mother gave her from time to time, on her birthday or at Christmas. Sometimes, he even forbade her to wear things he especially didn't like. So she kept the robe hidden away from him, afraid he would demand that she throw it away or that he would do it himself. She didn't want him to get mad over the robe. She hated for him to get mad.

She lifted the cup to her mouth. Hank also hated for her to drink hot tea. He said it was a snobby habit and that Beth was acting uppity. Beth never pointed out to him that he drank iced tea by the pitcher so why shouldn't she drink hot tea once in a while? You couldn't argue with him. When Hank was at home, Beth drank iced tea or coffee. She kept the box of mint tea hidden where she thought he wouldn't find it, behind the flour or shortening, being careful to move it from time to time because Hank would sometimes get these wild notions that he needed to check things out. He would methodically go through drawers, cabinets, and closets for no apparent reason other than to berate Beth about her housekeeping. Sometimes he actually seemed to be looking for something, although Beth knew better than to ask what for. Hank hated for her to question him.

She eyed the paper sleepily as she turned the pages. They were wrinkled from Hank's rough handling at breakfast. Sighing, Beth wondered what it would be like to have a fresh paper, to be the very first one to open the crisp sheets and see the headlines. Startled by this unexpected thought, she glanced quickly around the tiny kitchen, almost expecting someone to have heard what she had not said out loud. She flipped guiltily to the comics. Being the second person to read the paper wasn't so bad. Besides, Hank was her husband, and he was supposed to have the best of everything.

Sometimes, though, it was difficult to always put Hank first. Beth knew that was the way it was supposed to be, but Hank was so hard to please and so much the Big Man. Sometimes, he just acted plain silly, like a big, spoiled kid. Or mean.

Sighing again, Beth started to gather the paper up. There was a lot to do—grocery shopping, laundry, and the house needed to be cleaned. As Beth carefully folded the paper to deposit it in the trashcan, her eye caught a picture on the front page of the local section. It was a picture of a black woman, lying on what looked like a street, with two white women kneeling beside her. One of the white women had her back to the camera, but Beth could see the other one quite clearly, a stocky, intense looking woman with dark hair, glaring at the camera as she held the black woman's hand. Beth looked at the headline, *MURDER TRIAL SET FOR FIRST OF YEAR,* and the column header, *Klansmen Claim Self Defense.* She abruptly folded the section into the middle of the paper and carefully placed it in the trashcan.

Hank motioned Tom and Edgar into the room and towards chairs. The room was cloudy with cigarette smoke and stuffy from inadequate ventilation. In spite of the fact that someone had obviously been smoking heavily, all the ashtrays were clean.

"Glad you could come over. I want to get through this as fast as I can so we don't have to miss any of the ballgame. Hey, Beth! Bring a couple more beers out here."

The men were silent as she hurried into the room and handed them the cold cans of Miller. Her movements were quick and nervous. Hank ruffled her hair casually before taking his beer from her hand.

"Thanks, hon." There was little warmth in his voice.

Beth understood the dismissal and left the room as quickly as she had entered. She went down the hall, checking the sleeping children, pulling up blankets and turning off lights. Then she went into the bedroom she shared with Hank and started to close the door. A thoughtful expression settled over her face and she hesitated. Hank had been awfully agitated lately, and he had spent a lot of time on the telephone with his friends talking in a low voice, glaring at her every time she came into the room. She had overheard snatches of the conversations; they were always about some woman. Whatever it was, Hank was certainly upset.

Beth closed the door resolutely. Obviously, it was none of her business what they were talking about. If Hank wanted her to know, he would tell her. She sat on the edge of the bed and bent down to remove her shoes, glancing at the closed door. Unbidden, the picture from the newspaper flashed into her mind. *MURDER TRIAL SET FOR FIRST OF YEAR.* The woman staring at the camera, the black woman lying on the road. She stared at the doorknob and strained to hear any bits of conversation that might drift down the hall.

"There's trouble," Hank said, watching the faces of the two men sitting across from him. Tom looked bored; Edgar looked puzzled. Edgar almost always looked puzzled.

"It doesn't have to be big trouble. No one wants it to be. I have been asked to deal with it before it has the chance to get any bigger."

"Get to the point, Hank," Tom said in a low voice.

Hank bristled slightly. Tom had a long-time habit of challenging, directly and indirectly, what Hank considered to be his authority. Hank assumed that anyone who had the ear of the head of the state Klan organization also had authority. He had Baker's ear; he rarely let anyone forget or overlook that fact. He also had inside information, access to police records and documents, information that made him a valuable man.

"I take it you've heard of a broad named Jessie Pyne?"

"Sure. She's supposed to testify at John Layton's trial," Edgar answered.

"Well, Baker doesn't want her to testify. But he wants to keep a low profile, too. Doesn't want the organization involved in any way that could be traced. He doesn't want any fingers pointing his way, if you get my drift. Now, in addition to being the only eyewitness to that nigger's death, this Jessie Pyne has also started up an anti-KKK newsletter. She and a bunch of other broads are talking it up pretty big. Ordinarily, Baker wouldn't pay them any mind. But this is not a good time. They're already circulating this thing pretty widely, and they're giving speeches. One of those liberal churches has them slated for some kind of workshops. Folks are beginning to pay attention, which is exactly what Baker doesn't want to happen.

"I have been *asked,*" Hank paused dramatically, "to explain to her that no one ever wants to see another copy of this rag she's putting out. I have been *asked* to explain to her how dark it was that night and how unlikely that makes her identification of whoever killed that nigger. I have been *asked* to explain to her that she just needs to shut her mouth and stop spreading all her stupid lies. I have been *asked* to see that this is done as quickly and quietly as possible. I assured Mr. Baker that I knew two men who could do the job and that everything would be fine."

Beth could hear the low hum of Hank's voice from the living room, but she could not make out any words. With a sigh, she slipped between the sheets and turned off the lamp. Maybe, for once, he would be quiet when he came to bed and not wake her up.

"I can't do that, Tom, and you know it." Hank felt a twist of panic as he felt his control over the situation slipping.

"Well, I guess you'll have to go back and tell Mr. Baker that you can't deliver. That ought to really excite him. Impress him, too." Tom's drawl grew more pronounced as he talked, his enjoyment obvious. "Of course, you probably won't have a job after he gets through."

"Look," Hank struggled to keep the rage out of his voice, "I told him I would arrange to plant a weapon that could be traced back to that Etta Thomas and make this a clear case of self-defense. And John Layton has four men who are willing to swear he was nowhere near Thomas when she was getting her head kicked in."

"Afraid of getting your nice blue uniform dirty, Parrish?" Tom grinned his delight at the turn of events. "Get this straight. We haven't said we would do it. But we have said we won't do it unless you come along."

"I serve a purpose when I stay behind the scenes. There's no one else in this town who can. . ." Hank's chest felt tight.

"Face it, Hank," Tom interrupted. "You're a real chickenshit, and you hide behind that uniform. I always knew that. You think you're really something because you can leak a few things out from the department once in a while. Well, I got news for you.

Time for the boy to become a man. And you aren't the only one who knows Bill Baker. I'm pretty sure your police captain would be very interested to know that one of his sergeants is a Klansman."

"You prick," Hank said softly, his voice dangerously low.

"Time for you to stop beating your meat and your wife and do something a real man would do. Oh, you can still be the brains. You can even be the *leader.* But you're going to be there, old buddy. Right there. You're gonna prove yourself to me, man to man."

Jessie pulled herself out of the battered Volkswagen and walked towards the house. She was tired. The press had broken down, and she had spent the entire day trying to figure out what was wrong with it. She pushed the door open and began the ritual of feeding the dog and the cats. They milled around her feet until Kelly chased Lystra and Sadie from the room, asserting her right to be fed first. Jessie set Kelly's bowl on the floor and then spooned cat food into a dish as the two cats sneaked cautiously past the dog.

The air was unexpectedly chilly, even for late September. Jessie went into the study, deciding she would build a small fire in the woodstove. Absently, her mind still on the problems with the press, she crumpled newspaper and placed it inside the stove, adding kindling and small logs. Then, lighting the paper, she closed the door to the stove and sat down in the armchair to wait for the warmth. She was hungry but was too tired to think about cooking. Maybe she would make a sandwich later.

She had started into the kitchen when she heard a car pull up the long driveway. Checking to make sure the rifle was handy, she pulled back the corner of the curtain and peered out. It was Kate, walking towards the house in much the same way someone might walk to their own execution—her steps slow and heavy, head down, hands shoved into the pockets of her peacoat. Jessie took a deep breath and went to open the door, aware that all of her defenses had risen.

Kate came into the house, her smile tentative and cautious. Jessie motioned her into the study, then went back into the kitchen. When she joined Kate by the stove, she held two large mugs of tea in her hands. She gave one to Kate who accepted it silently. They drank without speaking. Jessie was determined to wait Kate out on this one.

Kate stood close to the woodstove, absorbing the heat, wondering what to say first. "I didn't come here to apologize," she blurted out finally.

Jessie looked at her squarely. "I would hope not."

"Can we talk?" Kate asked after another long silence.

"If we could manage to do that it might be helpful," Jessie answered, her voice soft but tight.

Kate sighed audibly. It was not going to be an easy conversation; she could already see that. She unbuttoned her jacket but did not take it off. "Jessie, I meant what I said to you."

"So did I."

"I know. But I also want you to know that I am very frightened. Not just for you but for everyone involved in this."

"People have to make their own choices, Kate. I'm not forcing anyone to do anything. And we do discuss risks. No one is doing this without being aware that there are some very real potential dangers involved."

"I'm glad to hear you're doing that." Kate sat down on the sofa, tucking her legs under her for warmth. "Jess, I care about you very much. I don't want to see you get hurt."

"We've been over this and over this. I take that risk by simply getting out of bed every morning."

Kate tried to head off the anger she heard in Jessie's voice. "I know. We all do. What I came here to say is that I know you're doing what you feel you have to do. I won't do anything else to try to make you change your mind. But I will raise objections, loudly, if I feel you're overlooking something. I won't maintain silence."

"All right." Jessie watched her carefully as she stroked the cat who had jumped into her lap.

"I will go right on doing what I've been doing which is working on the shelter. That's all I want to do. It's where I feel the most personal urgency. I don't want to fight the Ku Klux Klan right now. And I don't want to take to the streets."

"That's your choice, Kate. I'm not going to judge you for that."

"It felt like you were the other night."

Jessie was silent for a moment. "I didn't mean to do that, and I'm sorry if I sounded that way. I care about you, too, but you are only one part of my life. There are other things I need to do, and I won't if I'm always worrying about our relationship, worrying about what you think of my decisions. We don't have to agree. You have a right to your thoughts and feelings even when you totally disagree with me. I will try to listen to what you think and feel, but I won't always take your advice, or even welcome it. And I won't change for you. You need to know that now. I also won't defend myself to you. I would like to think you're basically on my side whether or not we agree, that you're my friend in spite of the differences."

"But if we're lovers. . ." Kate began.

"I want us to also be friends," Jessie said quietly.

"Aren't we?"

"I hope so. It's what I want."

"And lovers, too?"

"Both. Greedy woman, aren't I?"

"Yes. But so am I."

"Good. I was hoping you were."

Kate stared into her cup then looked up. "Much as I hate to admit it, the newsletter is really well done."

"Thanks. Everyone is working very hard on it."

Silence lingered in the room as Jessie and Kate studied the floor. Jessie didn't know what to say. She wasn't used to fighting and did not know exactly what one did when it was time to become friends again.

"I shouldn't have grabbed you like I did the other night."

It was an evening of confessions. Jessie looked at Kate. "No, you shouldn't have. And I shouldn't have reacted the way I did either. I don't want it to happen again. We were both scared and angry. It's too easy to take it out on each other."

"I'm sorry."

Jessie smiled quietly. "Don't be sorry. I learned something about myself the other night. I have a lot of anger, and there's violence right along with it. That's unnerving because I've always thought of myself as a nonviolent person. But that's not true. It's there. Since the demonstration, I've found myself drifting into some very violent fantasies. When you and I were fighting and you grabbed me, I was very close to hitting you. Too close."

"I'm still a little scared. I don't know where all of this will take us or how we will be able to be together. I've never had a relationship like this one."

"Neither have I. But it could be exciting."

Kate crossed the room and sat down on the arm of the chair. Jessie reached up and touched her face gently. "Actually, Kate, I think we're doing pretty well."

Kate's voice was light. "Does that mean we go on seeing each other?"

"I guess so. What do you think?"

"I think I'd like that."

Jessie raised an eyebrow, imitating one of Kate's mannerisms. "You *think*? Would you like to stay here tonight and make sure?"

"Are you going to help me make up my mind?"

"I am certainly going to do my best to be helpful."

Kate laughed softly and slid onto Jessie's lap. "Maybe we can just sit like this for a little while."

Jessie wrapped her arms around Kate and breathed in the scent of her. "For a while."

7

Beth hurried from the bathroom to the bedroom clutching her robe around her, her hair wrapped in a towel wound turban-style on her head. She could hear the two boys in their rooms in bed according to Hank's orders, but making just enough noise to communicate their dissatisfaction over the decision. It was Friday night and usually they would be allowed to stay up until nine-thirty. But it was only a little after eight, and they had been in bed for almost half an hour.

Beth toweled her hair briskly, staring at her reflection in the mirror. There were dark circles under her eyes, probably from lack of sleep. Hank had been in a horrible mood ever since that meeting on Monday, yelling at every little thing, slapping the children, not eating well, grinding his teeth in his sleep. This last created a sound that grated so heavily on Beth's nerves that she was unable to sleep through the noise. But she didn't dare get up, knowing how angry Hank would be if she got out of bed for anything other than to check on the children or make a quick trip to the bathroom. So she had not slept except for a few hours all week. Then tonight, Hank had abruptly ordered her to put the kids to bed and to make herself scarce. Tom and Edgar were coming over, and the three of them had business to discuss. Beth didn't mind being excluded. She didn't like Edgar. He was always dirty, smelled of beer, and had a whining voice which drove Beth crazy. But she especially did not like Tom. In fact, she was desperately afraid of Tom. He was always very nice to her, but there was something about him—Beth didn't know exactly what it was—that made her think he was. . .evil. That was the only word she thought fit him. Mean all the way through, and evil. She stayed as far from him as she could.

Hank chugged his beer and chain-smoked as he sat at the kitchen table and waited. Tom and Edgar would be there soon. But it would be just like Tom to be late deliberately just to irritate Hank. The man had no respect for anything or anyone. And he was dangerous; Hank knew that. He hated the man. Hank grinned. One of these days, Tom Riley would step out of line somewhere, and Hank would have the pleasure of blowing the sonofabitch clear to kingdom come. One of these days.

Hank had heard Tom's stories of what he did in Viet Nam. The boy was proud of himself. Hank scratched his chin thoughtfully. He had not gone to Nam, even though he had volunteered. Damn the Army anyway. Tom liked to rub Hank's face in the fact that the Army wouldn't let him go, that Hank had had a cushy supply job in the states while the *real* men were out killing Congs. Tom claimed to have kept count of how many men he had killed, most of whom he claimed to have shot up close. Hank didn't totally believe him. On the other hand, Tom seemed to be exactly the kind of man to do the things he claimed to have done, to men and to women.

Hank glanced at the clock. They were twenty minutes late. He lit another cigarette. Tom had put him in a very bad position. Much as he wanted to be an active member of the organization, his job meant too much to him. He had a rep around town—a very tough, mean cop, the kind folks didn't argue with. Punks stayed out of his way, and judges usually ruled in his favor when cases came to trial. Mostly, Hank liked the power the uniform gave him. He liked the fact that almost everyone got a little bit nervous when they saw him. And he loved the feel of the equipment against his hips—the gun, the cuffs, the nightstick. He had a chance at another promotion in the spring, if nothing went wrong. He was going to make damned sure nothing went wrong in spite of that bastard Riley. He would break him, too, one of these days. Tom was a mean, temperamental shit, but Hank knew he was meaner. Nobody crossed him and got away with it. Not people on the streets, not men on the force, not even his own wife.

His thoughts shifted briefly to Beth. He was going to have to get tougher with her. He had been so busy lately, he hadn't had much time to think about her. Things were getting slack around here. He had had to wait almost twenty minutes for dinner tonight. But then, she was a woman, and you had to stay on top of women. These liberal, pantywaist men might not think so, but Hank knew better. He knew women were sneaky, conniving little bitches, and he just wasn't willing to put up with much from them. You had to watch them every second. He had broken Beth in right, from the beginning. She had never doubted he was the boss.

Opening another beer, Hank wondered what it would be like to be a bachelor, to have no ties or responsibilities. He sighed. If Beth hadn't gone and gotten herself knocked up when they were dating, he wouldn't have all these worries. She had probably done it on purpose. All women wanted to be married, to have a chokehold on some poor guy, wrap him around their fingers, and try to control his life. Well, he might've had to marry her, but he sure hadn't let her bother him very much. That was never going to change either. She was his, and he was in control. She might've trapped him, but she would never own or control him. He'd see to that.

The doorbell rang and Hank rose. About time they arrived.

Beth heard the doorbell and then heard the sound of voices. Hank was leading the men into the kitchen; she caught a glimpse of them as they crossed the hall. She pushed the door shut quickly, not wanting Tom to see her.

When she started to take off her bathrobe, Beth realized that the door had not latched. Crossing to it, she listened for sounds from the boys' rooms. They were both quiet. She started to push the door closed when words drifted down the hallway.

Beth frowned. They had been talking about some girl last time, too. She wondered what was going on. Suddenly Hank's voice was louder, and Beth quickly, silently, closed the door. Better mind her own business and stay out of trouble.

Hank glanced down the hall to make sure Beth was not around. The door to the bedroom was closed. Stepping back into the kitchen, he lit a cigarette and studied the two men who sat at the table. "It's got to be done. There's no way she can be allowed to testify in court. Even if I rig the evidence, Baker doesn't want her to testify."

"You know the deal, Hank."

Hank knew the deal. When he had called Baker earlier to try to back out as carefully as he could, Baker had been very clear about what would happen if Hank failed. Hank nodded towards Tom. "I've been thinking about that. I've decided it probably would be better if I did go along. That way, I can keep an eye on things and make sure they go like they're supposed to."

"Yeah?"

"Yeah. I can make sure you don't fuck things up."

"You'd better watch your mouth, Parrish," came Tom's tight response.

"And you can go fuck yourself, Riley. You'll do exactly as I say." Hank leaned over the table as he spoke.

Tom sprang to his feet, fists clenched as he twisted to free himself from the chair. Edgar jumped up and slammed a restraining hand against Tom's chest.

"Ease off, Tom. You too, Hank."

"I don't want to ease off," Tom said through clenched teeth. "I want a piece of that mother."

"That'll be the day."

The two men glared at each other for a long, tense moment. Edgar maintained his position between them, knowing that if either of them struck the first blow, he was running for cover. Finally, Tom grinned tightly and sat down, his body taut. "I'll give you this one, Hank. We got work to do. But one of these days, I'll catch you, man. I'll catch you."

"Would you quit your bickering and let's get to it? I'm tired of sitting around talking. I want something to happen!" Edgar slapped an open palm on the table. Tom nodded in agreement, his gaze never leaving Hank's face.

'I agree. But first we have to figure out what we're going to do." Hank opened the refrigerator door and took out three beers which he handed around. Opening his, he sipped and waited for suggestions.

"You're supposed to be our fearless leader," Tom drawled. "I thought you would have it all figured out."

"Well, I don't. I do know that no matter how we come down on her, we have to be damned careful. This is going to take some planning." Hank resisted the urge to light yet another cigarette. He didn't want Tom to see his nervousness.

Hank kept his free hand in his pocket, his fingers curled tightly around his pocket knife. If anything should go wrong, anything, he could be in deep trouble. He'd be off the police force. No way he'd ever get a job as a cop anywhere.

"Baker wants us to scare the piss out of her," Hank said, his voice carefully controlled.

"So, how do we do that? All this shit over some girl is stupid. She ain't nobody worth worrying about. Let's just beat the hell out of her and be done with it," Tom said angrily.

"That's one option," Hank answered, "but don't you think we can find some other way to start? Save that for just in case she doesn't take a potent hint?" More than anything, Hank wanted to avoid a face-to-face confrontation with Jessie Pyne. No matter how badly they frightened her, she still might go straight to the police. They had to be *careful,* dammit. Very careful.

"Personally, I don't want to spend a whole lot of time messing with this broad. Let's just do it right the first time and get it over with." Tom drummed his fingers on the table top.

Edgar spoke up. "Well, if Baker wants to keep a low profile, I think we should do something pretty hard and straight but keep our faces outta that girl's line of sight."

Hank's knees went weak with relief. "You got an idea?"

Edgar nodded thoughtfully. "I think we ought to find out where she lives and pay a visit while she's at work. You can get her address, Hank. And we can redecorate the place for her, leave a note. She should be able to understand what we're telling her from that."

"And if it doesn't work?" Tom asked.

"Then we beat the hell out of her."

"I'll get the address tomorrow," Hank said.

Tom and Edgar nodded. Then Hank handed out another round of beer. This would work. And this would be the end of it.

Laura poked her head into the back room and shouted over the noise of the press. "Hey, Jessie! You have a phone call!"

"Do me a favor, Laura, and take a message?"

Laura shook her head. "It's Denny, and she sounds real upset. You'd better talk to her yourself."

Jessie muttered as she turned off the press. Work was still

backed up from last week when the press had broken down for two days, and she didn't want to waste precious time on telephone calls. The small shop had suddenly been flooded with jobs, all rush. She crossed the room to the extension phone and jerked the receiver off the hook. "What is it, Denny? I'm really. . ."

"Jess, I'm at your house, and I think you need to come home right now." Denny's voice was tight.

"Denny, I'm backed up to my ears with work," Jessie said impatiently. "I won't be able to leave here before midnight. It'll have to wait."

"Somebody broke into your place, and they completely wrecked it. You need to come home!"

Jessie held the phone in stunned silence. Finally, she found her voice. "I'll come home."

"Good. Kate's here, too."

"Why. . ."

"We came to start painting the kitchen." Denny cut her off impatiently.

"I'll be there in half an hour," Jessie said, and then hung up slowly. Who would break into her house? Almost two years there and she had never had any trouble before. Laura came around the corner and peered at Jessie.

"What's going on?"

"Denny says somebody broke in and wrecked my house."

Laura stared at her. "Burglars?"

Jessie shook her head. "I don't know. I have to go home. Can you handle things here?"

"Go on. I'll be fine."

Jessie nodded her thanks and headed for the door.

She climbed slowly out of the car, uncertain as to what to expect. Denny was waiting for her in the yard, and Jessie could see Kate standing on the porch.

"Jess," Denny said hurriedly, "I didn't want to get into all of it over the phone, but there's something you need to know before you go in there."

Jessie looked at her, alerted by the nervousness in Denny's voice. "Is it that bad?"

Denny nodded. "It's really a mess. They've torn up furniture, scattered trash all over the place. They even wrote stuff on the walls. And. . ." Denny hesitated, not looking at Jessie.

"Go on," Jessie prompted, feeling a sudden surge of alarm.

"It's Kelly, Jessie."

Jessie stared at her. "Oh, shit!" She ran towards the house, ignoring Kate as she burst inside.

Nothing Denny had said prepared Jessie for the chaos in front of her. Nothing seemed to be standing, or even in one piece. Tables and chairs were smashed, dishes broken. Trash was everywhere, the smell sickening. She could see the overturned woodstove in the other room, the room she had so recently changed into a "study," a place in which to write. Now ashes were scattered all over the floor. Then Jessie looked up. Written across the faded blue walls in large, red spray-painted letters were the words *nigger lover, queer.* Jessie could only stare. She felt nothing.

Finally, she started into the study, but Denny pulled her back. "Don't go in there."

"What happened to Kelly? Did they hurt her?" Jessie's voice was hushed. Denny nodded. Jessie brushed past her and walked into the other room. It was as bad as the rest of the house. The sofa and chair had been slashed and cotton stuffing was strewn around the room. Her desk had been overturned, and her papers had been scattered and trampled on. Jessie glanced at Denny as she gestured towards the closed bedroom door.

"Did they wreck that room, too? Or is Kelly in there?" Denny didn't answer. Jessie opened the door and stepped in.

For some reason, they had not touched this room. Everything was exactly as Jessie had left it, the bed neatly made, clothes in their proper places, a book still open on the bedside table, the lamp upright.

Kelly lay in the middle of the floor. Jessie knelt down beside her. No blood, she thought to herself as she touched the cold, stiff body. The dog's eyes were open and fixed. Jessie wished she could read the final expression. She rocked back and forth on her knees, not understanding. Pain was beginning to replace the numbness and she fought it; there was too much to do to give into it now. Too much to do. Denny touched her on the shoulder.

"What happened, Denny? What did they do to her?"

There was a long pause before Denny answered, her voice a pinched whisper. "They hung her."

Jessie turned to stare at her, a stunned expression of disbelief in her eyes. "They *hung* her? Hung her? Where?"

"From the tree by the porch."

"Oh, for. . .hung her. Goddamn, Denny, who would do that?" Jessie's voice cracked. She grabbed a shoe and threw it as hard as she could. It hit the wall with a loud thump and crashed to the floor. She leaned back on her heels and stared at the dead setter.

"I'll bury her for you, Jessie."

Jessie stood up abruptly. "I need to do it. Just go home, Denny, and take Kate with you. I need to be alone for a while."

Denny shook her head. "We'll stay out of your way, but we're not leaving. We can start cleaning up. Call if you need us." Denny touched her sleeve and then left the room. Jessie didn't move.

She put the shovel in the shed and stood at the edge of the pasture smoking a cigarette, watching the sunset. Digging had been hard. Kelly was a large dog. Had been. *Had* been a large dog. She wiped the sweat from her face and shivered as the chilly night air penetrated her damp clothes. Her hands shook and her stomach was in knots. She felt as though she might throw up. Where were the cats? Were they all right?

Jessie threw the cigarette on the ground and crushed it under her heel. She walked to the other side of the house, not wanting to go in to the mess and the people. Jessie paced around the huge sweet gum tree studying the branches, trying to find a sign of what had happened to Kelly, of why. The circle tightened as she walked, faster and faster, her hands clenched into tight fists deep in her pockets. There was no sign, not a broken branch, not. . . An indentation in the ground caught her eye. Jessie knelt and studied the footprint. Anger was immediate, surging. Jessie stood up, hands dangling at her sides, stifling the urge to scream the rage. As she started towards the house, she tripped over a log. Dogwood. The thought registered unsummoned. Dogwood. A killer to split. A killer. . .to split. She placed the log against the old stump she used as a block and picked up the heavy maul. She tapped a wedge into place then stepped back and brought the maul down with a loud crash of metal on metal. The log cracked. She worked in another wedge, rolling the log onto its side. Three strokes and the log split. She tossed it aside and reached for another. Over and over again she brought the maul down, faster, as she swung her grief into each blow. Down. Metal against metal. Sparks flew when her aim was off. Down, metal retorts like shots in the dark.

"I could," she muttered, "I could. I could kill them. I. . .could. . .kill. . .them." Her voice grew louder as she chanted.

She worked for almost an hour, until the muscles in her shoulders and arms felt torn from place, until she was hoarse from the words she had forced from her throat. Blisters rose on her hands. The pile of split wood grew. Jessie didn't notice the darkness, the blisters, the tears, the fierce ache in her body. She swung the maul, driving her anger into the wood, harder and harder, hearing only the shell-like retorts. She didn't feel the skin shredding on her hands. She didn't hear Denny's car leave or Kate coming onto the porch.

She turned to grab another log, but there were none left. She dropped the maul on the ground and stared at the woodpile. Kate came down the steps, took Jessie's arm, and led her inside without saying a word.

There was a fire in the woodstove. Denny and Kate had managed to get it upright and had replaced the ventpipe. Pillows from Jessie's bed were on the floor in front of the stove. Kate motioned for Jessie to sit down so she could hand her a cup of coffee. Jessie dropped onto a pillow and accepted the hot cup, then almost dropped it. She turned her hands over. They were raw and bleeding. Kate's face tightened, but she said nothing. She left the room and returned with a pan. Setting it on the floor, she rolled back Jessie's sleeves and immersed her hands in the water.

"Denny and I got most of the mess up. Some things can be fixed. Most of the dishes will have to be replaced. The cats came home a little while ago. They seem fine. I fed them." Kate's tone was quiet and conversational. She sat close to Jessie but did not touch her.

"Who would do this, Kate? Who would tear my house up and. . .kill my dog?"

Kate hesitated for a moment then reached into her pocket, bringing out a slip of paper. "This was hanging on the door when Denny and I arrived here this afternoon." She held it out so Jessie could read the words. *"You didn't see anybody. You can't identify anybody. But we know who you are, and we can come back again. Tell the D.A. you have nothing to say in court."*

"Oh, god." Jessie's tone was even and low. "I guess that answers my question."

"Yeah."

Kate carefully dried and bandaged Jessie's hands. Then she

slipped her arm around her lover's shoulders and pulled her close.

Kate pushed her own terror down. If they would do this, wreck a house and hang a dog, what would they do to Jessie?

Jessie's voice was shaking. "They're trying to scare me off. They're trying to get me to say I lied, trying to scare me into not testifying in January. Kate. . .they killed my dog. They hung her."

"I know, Jess. I know, baby." Kate lit a cigarette and tried to steady her hands. She had to be calm right now. "Are you going to stay here?"

"What?" Jessie seemed confused.

"Jessie, have you thought what might have happened if you had been home when those men came?"

"No."

"I'm not asking you to make any kind of decision right now. I know you can't. But please, honey, think about that. Those men obviously thought they had nothing to fear. They came in broad daylight. It could've been you instead of Kelly. I really believe that."

Jessie picked up her cup awkwardly and sipped the cooling coffee. "I love this old place. I don't want to give it up."

"I know," Kate whispered, "but I'm so afraid for you. I'm so scared they'll do something to you. I know how horrible men can be. Please don't stay here. Come to my house tonight and just think about it. Please, Jessie."

Kate's hands were shaking visibly. She was scared to leave Jessie alone, and terrified at the thought of staying there with her. What if they came back? She watched Jessie's pale face silently, willing herself to be quiet, forcing herself not to bodily carry Jessie out to the car and drive her away, drive them both away from the danger Kate felt throughout the house. She could feel Jessie's anger, pain, confusion, not spoken out loud but filling the room, surrounding them both.

Kate felt a wild urge to run, to leave and not come back. She couldn't take this. She couldn't just stand by and watch Jessie get hurt. And she couldn't put herself into the position to get hurt either. She had been hurt enough, too much. She knew about men. She knew what they could do. They had shown her over and over. And there was nothing she could do to protect Jessie. Nothing.

Jessie was numb. All she wanted was to sleep. She looked at Kate quietly. "I'll get some clothes, and we can go to your house."

Kate sighed with relief as Jessie rose and went into the bedroom. Once she got her into town, once Jessie got some sleep, then maybe she would understand. Jessie had to leave this house. She *had* to.

"You've got to move into town, Jessie. It's very dangerous for you to be way out there alone. It's too damned far from everybody and everything."

"I don't want to be forced out of my home, Val."

"You've got to protect yourself."

"It's like admitting defeat."

"It's like being alive!"

Val, Laura, Denny, Kate, and Jessie were all crowded into the small back room of the print shop. Jessie was exhausted. She had not slept much the night before, and the bandages on her hands made it nearly impossible for her to work. She was tired and irritable, sick of this line of argument, having heard it already from Kate.

"So I run away. The next thing they'll be trying to tell me is that I can't do the newsletter anymore. And what about the trial?"

"Ignoring what happened is just plain stupid." It was Val again. Jessie glanced at Laura who leaned against the wall, arms folded over her chest, a silent, watchful expression on her face. Finally she straightened, stretched, and spoke for the first time.

"You remember that story I told you about my grandparents, Jessie?" Jessie nodded. "Well, it was every bit true." Laura turned and left the room, quietly closing the door to the shop behind her.

"Next time," Denny said, "they might wreck more than just your house, Jessie."

Jessie jumped to her feet. "And just where would I go? They can find me if they want to, no matter where I am."

Val's answer was quick. "You can live with Denny and me. God knows, we've got enough room in that old house. The idea is to discourage them. Knowing you're not alone in some house way out in the country just might do that."

Jessie turned her back and picked up her knapsack. "I have to think about it."

Val kicked at a case of paper. "I hope you live long enough to make up your mind! Are you going back out there tonight?"

"Yes!" Jessie shouted, tears filling her eyes. "Now if you will be so kind as to get out of here, I'll lock up and go home!"

The women left silently, not looking at Jessie. She locked the door tiredly. Maybe they were right. She tried to brush the tears away, but it was futile. She felt a surge of pain and moaned quietly. She couldn't stop thinking about Kelly, hanging from that tree. She was glad she hadn't found her there. Jessie looked at the lights and the buildings and felt the surroundings close in on her. She hated the city. Hated it. The need to break down and cry nearly choked her as she climbed into the car and drove away.

Jessie rolled over and looked at the clock with a sleep-swelled eye. Four-thirty in the morning. She stretched, pulling the covers up under her chin. She could have sworn she heard voices. Maybe she had been dreaming.

The crash of glass breaking brought her straight to her feet. She jerked on jeans and a shirt and went carefully into the front room, staying away from the windows and trying to avoid the broken glass she knew must be all over the floor.

A brick lay in the middle of the room. She heard the sound of a car engine starting up and then the car drove away. She stood in front of the broken window, her gaze fixed on a burning cross in the front yard.

Val, Denny, and Kate arrived in less than twenty minutes. They piled out of the car and stood in the yard. They could see Jessie standing by the porch, her face lighted eerily by the flames that were slowly burning down.

Finally, Jessie crossed the yard to join them, wrapping her arms around Kate and burying her face in Kate's shoulder. Kate held her, feeling rigid muscles, feeling her tremble.

"I can't even put it out," she muttered. "There's no hose to use to put it out."

No one answered her. The women stayed close together, watching the flames die out.

All of them jumped when Ben Carpenter's voice sounded from the corner of the yard. "I wanta talk to you, Jessie."

"What do you want, Ben?" she asked tiredly.

Carpenter drew closer, glancing from the cross to Jessie to the women holding onto her. A frown creased his face. "I cain't have this. I cain't."

"What do you mean?"

"I got to have you gone. Today. I want you to pack up and move outta here. Cain't be having the Klan burnin' crosses on my property. You be gone from here, I mean it. You hear me now?" There was no friendliness in Carpenter's voice. He peered at her nearsightedly.

"Ben, look. . ."

"Don't argue with me, girl! I been thinkin' there was somethin' strange about you for a long time. I let you stay because my wife liked you. But I cain't have this. I ain't gonna tell you but just this once. You ain't outta here by this evenin', I'll get the sheriff to throw you out. You understand me?"

"A day isn't enough time to. . ."

"By evenin'. That's my final word. Get your friends here to help you." He gestured towards the group.

The blue light caught Jessie's attention as the sheriff's car pulled into the driveway followed by the highway patrol.

"What the hell are the cops doing here?" Jessie asked angrily.

"I called 'em, that's why. I gotta protect my property." Ben's voice was hostile as he walked across the yard to meet the men getting out of their cars. The women looked at each other.

"I guess we'd better get busy," Kate said briskly. "We can start packing and get a truck later today."

"Guess we'd better," Val agreed.

Jessie stood for a moment longer watching the flames dying on the cross and listening to the laughter from the men at the corner of the yard. Then she slowly followed the others inside.

Jessie sat on the sofa and read the brief article in the county newspaper. She tossed aside in disgust. The paper said that the Klan denied all knowledge of the incident, and that the police were convinced it was a prank played by locals. They had written it off as a hostile joke. Even the District Attorney's office had told her not to worry, that she had to expect some hostility. Jessie grabbed her jacket and headed for the door. She was going to be late for work.

Jessie took the mail from the box and looked through it. A small envelope addressed to her, the handwriting unfamiliar, caught her attention. Opening the door, she dropped the rest of the mail on the table and opened the letter. As she read, she sat down abruptly.

Nigger-lover. Queer. We don't need your kind around here. There won't be any more warnings. To you or your friends.

"So what if she moved into town? What does that prove? She hasn't contacted the District Attorney's office. The trial is still going to happen. So let's just stop bullshitting around and really let her know we mean business."

Beth stood just inside the bedroom door and listened to Tom's voice as it drifted down the silent hall. It was beginning to make some sense to her. They were doing something bad to somebody, a woman called Jessie. She crossed her arms over her chest and hugged herself tightly. Hank was going to hurt somebody; he was going to hurt this woman.

Hank glared at Tom. "I suppose you still want to beat the hell out of her, don't you?"

"Damn right. Nothing else is going to work. Sometimes, you have to make your point in person, face to face."

Edgar looked at Tom thoughtfully. "Risky. She could identify us if she sees us."

"She won't be talking to anybody when we get through with her," Tom answered with a slow smile.

"I guess you'd be happy just to kill her?" Hank's voice dripped sarcasm.

"I wouldn't mind. But we don't have to kill her. We can put some righteous fear into her, so much she won't open her mouth to a soul. She'll agree to anything just to make us leave her alone. I guarantee it." Tom's last sentence was spoken so softly Hank almost could not hear it. For the first time, he felt a slight jolt of fear when he looked at Tom. The man is crazy, he thought to himself.

"I'd like to get my hands on her for just a few minutes," Edgar said, a tight grin on his face. "I know exactly what she needs."

"I'll bet you would show her a thing or two," Tom said, also grinning. His face was flushed from the beer, from anticipation.

"Damn queer cunt," Edgar muttered. "I know what she needs."

"I still don't like it," Hank persisted. "If we go after her, people are going to know exactly where to start looking. It's too risky. I'd say yes if she weren't a witness and if the D.A.'s office didn't already have a handle on her."

"You know what I think, Hank?" Tom's voice was taunting. "I think you're scared of this broad."

"Shut up, Tom."

"I didn't hear him deny it. Did you, Edgar?"

Edgar studied Hank for a moment. "Nope. That true, Hank? You scared of this girl?"

"You're fucking bananas, both of you. Why should I be scared of some little homo like this?"

Tom leaned forward, resting his elbows on the table. "Then prove it, man."

Beth closed her eyes and leaned her head back against the wall. Oh lord, she thought to herself, let him say no. Just let him say no.

Hank rose and took a beer from the refrigerator. He opened it and drank half in one long gulp.

"You two are crazy," he said, wiping his mouth with the back of his hand.

"And you," Tom said softly, "are a chickenshit."

He ducked as the beer can sailed by his head, missing him by mere inches. Edgar jumped up, putting himself between the two men.

"Now just hold it! We ain't gonna get anywhere with you two fighting like a couple of bitching old women. Hank, what we tried didn't work. Now unless you got a better plan, I say we go with Tom's idea. I don't want to keep messing around with this girl forever."

"I don't have anything better."

Tom laughed. "Now you're talking! We'll scare the pure bejesus out of her." He winked at Hank. "Ever had a genuine lesbian before, Hank, my man?"

Hank shook his head. "No."

"Well, this will be the first. Don't expect a whole lot. After all, a cunt's a cunt. C'mon Edgar, let's get out of here so Hank can get back to his little woman." Tom stopped in front of Hank. "Edgar and I will check it out, and we'll be back in touch in a couple of days. Don't go getting cold feet on me now." He laughed and left the room, Edgar close behind him.

Beth bit her lip as she slumped against the wall. She strained to hear what was said next, but there were no other sounds from the kitchen. She leaned closer to the door. Suddenly, Hank was there filling the doorway, his face livid with rage when he saw her. He grabbed her by the arm and jerked her up against him.

"What the hell are you doing?" he roared into her face. "You were spying on me! Just what did you hear?"

Beth hung in his grip, trying not to cry out. "Hank. . .the kids."

"The hell with the kids!" He threw her onto the bed and stood over her, his face drawn into an ugly mask of hatred, his fists clenched at his sides. "What did you hear?"

"Nothing. . .I didn't hear anything, Hank. Honestly."

"You're lying! You heard it all, didn't you? You fucking bitch! How many times do I have to tell you to keep your nose out of my business?" He drew back his hand and slapped her across the face, knocking her back on the bed.

"I'll teach you to go listening at doors!" He glanced wildly around the room, then seized a belt from the chair. He wrapped the leather around his fist. Beth covered her face with her arms as she saw the wide, flat buckle flash through the air and towards her.

The grey light in the room let her know it was dawn. Hank had not moved all night, sleeping on his side, his back to her, one arm thrown over his head. As she turned over, Beth had to bite her lip to keep from crying out. Her body screamed protest with every movement. Last night had been the worst yet. He had hit her before but never like that. She finally got into a sitting position and thought she might faint. Through her thin nightgown, she could see the livid bruises and smears of blood where the belt buckle had struck her. Slowly, she pulled herself to her feet. Beth made it into the bathroom and swallowed some aspirin. She gagged repeatedly as she tried to force them down, and she ended up hanging over the toilet bowl retching until she felt her insides would shred. Then she slowly slid to the floor and burst into tears, her hand clamped over her mouth, her other arm wrapped around her shrieking body.

Jessie dried her hands and tossed the grimy rag into the cannister. She was finally caught up. She didn't know if it was good or bad, but she felt a huge sense of relief. It meant she could have the whole weekend to herself. Maybe she and Kate could go to a movie. Or a picnic on the Eno River. The weather was supposed to be nice. She wiped a smear of ink from the side of the press. This would be her first full weekend off in nearly two months.

Laura came into the back room and sat down on the stool. "Are we really caught up?"

Jessie nodded. "Amazing as that seems. What are you going to do with your weekend?"

"Sleep." Laura's answer was quick and definite.

"Doesn't sound half bad," Jessie answered with a grin.

"I thought I might write up that story about my grandparents for the newsletter. What do you think?"

"I think it sounds like a great idea."

"Well, I'll see what comes out on paper. Have a good weekend, Jessie. I'll see you Monday morning."

Val pulled the cord to signal her stop. She had almost an hour to kill before she met Jessie for dinner and their weekly newsletter meeting. She sighed softly, thinking how much better she felt since Jessie had moved into her house. So far, there had been no more trouble. Maybe that was the end of it. Standing up, she made her way down the aisle of the bus.

The three men waited at the back corner of the small parking lot. They had been there since six and had seen Laura leave. Tom leaned casually against the streetlight pole, smoking a cigarette. Edgar paced in small, endless circles.

"Calm down, Edgar. You're as nervous as a cat."

"I ain't nervous! I'm just tired of waiting." Edgar's voice was snappish. Tom smiled at him.

"You won't have to wait much longer. She should be coming out to empty the trash any minute now. She and that nigger broad are as regular as clockwork."

Hank shoved his hands into his pockets. The temperature was dropping rapidly as the sun set. He didn't want to be there. What if she remembered their faces? He would rather these two idiots handled this, leave him out of it. At least he had thought to bring sunglasses. That was better than nothing.

Tom seemed to read his thoughts. "Want to back out, Hank? Just say the word."

"Go to hell," Hank muttered.

"There she is!" Edgar's voice was a harsh whisper. Tom dropped his cigarette on the ground.

"Let's do it."

Jessie strained to lift the heavy can over the edge of the dumpster. She should have gotten Laura to help before Laura had dashed out for her much-awaited dinner with Moon. The last time Jessie had attempted to empty the trash barrel alone the entire can had gone over the edge, and she had had to climb inside the dumpster to retrieve it. Getting in had been relatively easy; getting out had been a little more difficult.

She set the empty can on the ground and bent down to pick up the loose paper that had scattered on the sparse grass. Stretching muscles stiff from standing all day, she watched the thin cirrus clouds whip across the sky. Val would be there soon. Jessie stifled a yawn; she would just as soon go home to bed. It had already been an exhausting day. She also needed to go to the grocery store. She was out of cat food, and she didn't dare appear at home empty-handed.

"I want to have a word with you, girl." His voice was soft. Jessie jumped back instinctively and slammed into yet another man who grabbed her arm. She jerked free from his grasp but there was nowhere to go. The dumpster was directly behind her.

"What do you want?" Her voice was strained to a whisper.

"Just to have a little talk with you. For now. So you just keep your mouth shut and listen, and maybe that's all we'll want."

Jessie heard the threat clearly. She watched their faces, searching her memory for some clue, some recognition of them. Nothing came.

"It must be real lonely for you with your dog dead," Tom said softly, smiling at her. "We know how much you loved that old dog of yours."

Jessie stared at him. The fear that surged through her was immediate, bitter. Her stomach knotted, and for a moment she was afraid she might vomit.

"Now, we tried to make a point when we visited your house. We thought you would understand what we were trying to tell you. But you're awful stubborn. You know that? Moving into town didn't solve a thing, girl. This ain't no game we're playing here." Tom's voice became harsh. "This is the real thing, Jessie Pyne. And you'd better back down right now or your friends will be finding pieces of you a week from next Christmas."

"Or maybe you'll be finding pieces of *them*," Edgar added with a low giggle.

Jessie would have been less afraid if Tom had shown some outward sign of anger. But his face held an oddly blank expression that chilled her. Edgar stepped forward suddenly and grabbed the front of her shirt. Several buttons popped loose, and Jessie was acutely aware that her breasts were visible.

"Ain't you got nothing to say? You been talking big up 'til now. I seen those interviews with you in the newspaper, and I even seen you on TV. You speak when you're spoken to, girl!" Edgar shook her.

"I heard you." Jessie spoke through clenched teeth.

"Good. I heard once that there ain't no cure for stupidity, and I'm hoping that's wrong. Now it's simple, so you listen up. One, you shut up tight as a clam. Two, you stop putting out that fucking newsletter of yours. It's a pack of lies. Three, you tell the D.A. that you made a mistake, that it was dark, and that you really can't identify nobody. You didn't see nobody kick no nigger woman. You hear me?" Edgar was staring at her breasts.

Jessie said nothing, too afraid to speak, too proud to give in.

Tom glanced skyward and sighed. "Maybe that saying was right after all, man. Look, we're trying to give you a second chance here. There won't be a third."

Edgar ran his hand down her chest. There were no choices left. Jessie kicked out as hard as she could, catching Edgar squarely on the shin.

"Goddam!" he yelled. He released her abruptly and clutched his leg. "Goddam, you bitch!"

Jessie feinted to the left, seeing one slim chance to make it past them to the door of the shop.

But Tom had seen it, too. Suddenly he was in front of her, blocking her way. His arms hung loosely at his sides. Jessie knew the danger in the way he held his body, in the calm stare, the beginnings of a smile on his lips. She lowered her head and catapulted her body forward, anger mixing with the intense fear. She *had* to get to that door.

She didn't see the fist coming. She felt it instead, bony and unyielding against the side of her face. The blow slammed her back and shoulders into the dumpster. Her head cracked against the cold metal. There was blood in her mouth, a ringing in her ears. Her face felt numb; there was no pain in her jaw, only blinding jolts in the back of her head. Tom jerked her to him, his breath warm on her cheek.

"You're not talking so big now, are you? Go on. Fight back. I like that."

All clarity vanished as he hit her again. Dazed, Jessie tried to kick him, to break his grip with her hands.

Tom laughed. "You can fight harder than that. Better yet, why don't you ask me to stop? C'mon, beg me to stop. Say it real nice."

Jessie clamped her mouth shut. She would not say a word.

He beat her methodically, forehand, backhand, holding her upright by the front of her shirt. Vaguely, Jessie was aware of her shirt tearing, of the laughter of one of the other men. She hung in Tom's grip, feeling the pain as it raced through her, sharp, shooting pain that increased with each blow and brought sickening nausea rolling to the back of her throat. Blackness swam through her head, and she yearned for it, grasped for it with all the strength she had left. Tom shoved her back against the dumpster and aimed his blows at her body, using his fists on her breasts, ribs, and belly. He would not let her faint.

"What the hell are you doing, Tom. . ."

The blows stopped abruptly, and Jessie slid to the ground, her back still against the dumpster, her legs unable to support any of her weight.

"I don't want you to kill her," Edgar said as he pushed Tom away. "I want a crack at her."

"We'll all get a crack at her, old buddy. Don't you worry about that."

"Now's the time then. Why don't you go first, Tom? After all, you been doing all the work. What about you, Hank? You gonna get in on the fun?"

Jessie heard the voices dimly but the words made no real sense to her. Names. She heard names.

There was laughter, then hands grabbed her and pulled her onto her knees. Someone locked rough fingers into her hair and pulled her head up. She felt cloth brush her face and heard the sound of a zipper sliding down its short track. She tried to raise her arms to ward off what she suddenly knew was about to happen, but she couldn't move. Keeping her eyes closed, she fixed her spinning thoughts on some blank space she found in her mind. Hold on. *Hold on.* Choking her, Tom came with the same violence that was in his fist when he hit her. She tried to spit when he withdrew, but she was too weak for even that.

She tried to concentrate on the cold, damp grass against her buttocks as they pushed her down onto the ground and pulled her jeans to her ankles. Pain shifted, changed, lessened, increased, as one man finished and another took his place. She didn't know how long it lasted or how many times. At one point, she was aware of the heavy pressure of a body on top of her but felt nothing between her legs. Her wonder was brief; she could find no answers. She felt them shift in turn. Time seemed to stop, isolating each thrust into an eternity of fear and agony.

Then a voice spoke close to her ear. "You just got a second chance. You remember what we told you."

Jessie could hear them laughing, talking, as they walked away. She lay on the wet grass, her pants still around her ankles, shivering from the cold. She managed to roll onto her side, and she threw up weakly, coughing and choking, her hands groping uselessly for her jeans. Val. Val was coming. . .she would help. Jessie tried to pull up her pants. She didn't want Val to see her like this.

She had heard names. Numbly, she tried to fix them in her mind. Tom. . .Tom and Edgar. Tom and Edgar and. . . .

Val pushed open the door to the shop and stepped inside. It was really getting cold outside. Maybe an early winter. She stuck her head through the doorway to the back room and called out, "Jessie? Jess, you back here?"

There was no answer. That was odd. They had a definite

date for dinner. Jessie would never just not show up. Then Val noticed the back door ajar. Jessie was probably at the dumpster. Val wandered around the room. She didn't know the first thing about presses, and she was intimidated by them. She walked around the machine, peering at it carefully, trying to figure out exactly how it worked.

She glanced at her watch. Jessie was certainly taking her time out there. She walked to the door and stepped outside. "Jessie?"

She wasn't sure it was Jessie at first. Then she looked more closely and gasped. Kneeling beside her friend, Val put her hand on Jessie's shoulder. There was blood all over Jessie's face, and she was not moving. Val touched her chest and felt an immediate surge of relief when the slow motion assured her that Jessie was alive. She jerked off her coat and covered Jessie with it, then ran inside to the telephone.

Kate did not rush into the hospital. She closed the door to her car and walked slowly across the parking lot, starting whenever a light cast her shadow on the ground near her.

Val had not given her any details over the telephone, saying only that Jessie was hurt very badly, and she thought Kate should come to the hospital right away. Val had hung up before Kate could ask any questions. Kate forced her mind to blankness as she walked towards the brightly lit emergency entrance; she could not give in to her imagination.

Kate stopped short of the doors. Puffs of hazy smoke rose in front of her face as her breath quickened, condensed, and whitened in the cool night air. She hesitated so long that the security guard approached to ask if anything was wrong. She shook her head and pushed through the door.

It took all of Kate's will power to keep her from turning around and running from the building. Sheer terror filled her as she watched the activity around her—patients being transported on gurneys, portable X-ray machines being wheeled down the corridor, carts loaded with mysteriously covered trays pushed by her. There was little curiosity, only tiredness, in the eyes that met hers as she walked down the hall, willing herself to move forward.

The smell always made her feel sick. Disease, blood, and antiseptic—a revolting combination, even if some of the smells were manufactured by Kate's imagination. But they brought back memories of being a child. No matter how much she steeled herself not to think, it came back.

Seven years old, lying on a stretcher in a cubicle, green curtains drawn around her, screaming from the pain in her broken shoulder and ribs. Her mother squeezing her arm, desperately explaining to the suspicious doctors and nurses that Kate had fallen from a tree. Kate's terror when her father had walked in, his eyes bloodshot from drinking, his hand almost crushing her thigh as he leaned close and told her what would happen if she said a word to anyone. Her mother trying to make him leave, saying Kate wouldn't tell them; she wouldn't want those awful strangers to take her away from her family and put her into an orphanage.

Kate tried to shake the memory away. Three times they had brought her to emergency rooms. Three times her mother had managed to convince hospital staffs and caseworkers that Kate had had accidents. Kate remembered lying on a narrow bed in the pediatric ward, the rails surrounding her like prison bars, her mother close by watching as Kate lay stone-faced and staring at the ceiling; her mother swearing that *this* time, when Kate was well, they were going to pack their bags and go away, just the two of them, far away from her father and her older brother. Just mama and her. She never believed her. And it never happened.

An arm dropped over her shoulders, breaking her free from the painful thoughts. Val. There was a bitter taste in Kate's mouth, and she was trembling. She thought she could smell blood.

Val led her to an uncomfortable plastic chair and handed her a paper cup filled with lukewarm coffee. Kate looked at her, noting the deep, hard lines in Val's face. *Exhaustion? Fear?* Kate groped in her pocket for a cigarette.

"Let me tell you what I know," Val said quietly.

"Is she okay?" Kate's voice was surprisingly steady.

"No. But she is alive, and she will be all right in time. I don't know all the details. I haven't seen a doctor in over two hours. Kate, Jessie was beaten up very badly. Her nose and several ribs are broken. She lost a couple of teeth. They said she would need stitches in her eyebrow and mouth. Her spleen is ruptured. They have her in surgery now. It's going to take time for those things alone to heal."

Kate stared at her. "What do you mean, *those* things alone? Is there more?"

Val nodded slowly. "Jessie was raped, maybe several times

and maybe by more than one man. So far there's no way of knowing details of what happened to her. She was unconscious when I found her, and even if she came to while they had her in the E.R., I doubt she could've said much that would be coherent."

"When did all this happen?" Kate felt her stomach start to churn sickeningly, and she spilled coffee on her pants as she tried to set the cup on the table beside her.

"I found her around seven. I don't know how long she had been lying there before I came."

Kate glanced at her watch. Ten o'clock. At six she had been working on a painting. At six-thirty she had taken a break for dinner. Maybe if she had. . .Kate stood up abruptly, staring out the dark window. Val began pacing the length of the long, narrow waiting room.

Her feet were mired. She moved, forcing her body against hands she could not see, trying to run towards the open door, but she moved only a few slow, thick inches. Her shout for help was deep and drawn, a low rumbling whisper that fell from her mouth to the ground, words shattering at her feet. Men surrounded her, their enormous heads cracked with silent smiles. She could see the fist as it came slowly through the air, hours to reach her face, hours until she tumbled back against the coldness of something metallic and unyielding, and then felt the ground beneath her. Her mouth made no sound this time when she opened it, spilling warm blood instead of words.

Jessie fought against the dream, her hands flailing the air, jerking at the IV tubing. Kate leaned over the bed, careful not to touch her but getting close to Jessie's ear.

"Jessie, wake up. It's a dream, baby. Wake up." Kate continued to call her softly until Jessie lurched into wakefulness, her eyes bright with terror and pain.

Kate was quietly insistent. "It's okay, Jessie. It's over. It was a dream, baby, a dream. You're in the hospital. There's no one else in this room except me and you. Nobody else." She repeated the words over and over, like an incantation, until Jessie's body relaxed somewhat and her breathing slowed. Finally, Kate touched her, placing a gentle hand on Jessie's shoulders. "I'm right here with you, Jess. I'm going to stay here. Nobody's going to hurt you anymore."

Kate's voice droned on. She wasn't aware of what she was saying. She was watching the expression in Jessie's eyes. And she knew the moment Jessie remembered. She felt it like a hot, piercing pain in her chest as Jessie's eyes filled with tears, and she turned her head away.

The shock of memory jarred Jessie, sending cold shards of fear through her as she clamped her eyes shut against the vision. But it was behind her eyelids, too, and for a moment she thought she might scream.

She felt Kate's hand close around her fingers, and she gripped it tightly. Breathing was agony, and she panicked at the tight constriction of something wound around her chest. Kate was talking to her, stroking her shoulder. Blackness swirled on the edge of her consciousness and she welcomed it, invited it. From a great distance, she heard Kate's voice.

"Sleep if you want to, Jess. If the dreams come back, I'll be right here."

Tom whooped loudly and dropped into the armchair, propping his feet on the scarred coffee table. He cracked his knuckles and stretched his arms over his head. Edgar sat on a kitchen chair, the back against his chest, whistling softly, tunelessly, and grinning from time to time.

Hank leaned against the wall near the door, an unsmoked cigarette between his fingers. He had said nothing since they left Jessie Pyne lying in the grass. He looked at his two companions as he fished around in his pocket for a match. There was no way they could know. No way to tell.

"Do you think we killed her?" Hank asked flatly.

Tom rolled his eyes towards the ceiling and fingered his moustache. "No. But I guarantee we shut her up."

"I don't think she'll have anything to say," Edgar added with his leering grin.

His face was still flushed, and his hands moved constantly, drumming his knee, rubbing his crotch, jingling the change in his pockets. He could still feel the adrenalin surge, soaring along on the power he felt in his body. Strong. He could go out and do it all over again. Edgar wished Tom had not hit her so much. He liked for women to know, to know *clearly,* what was happening to them. Yeah, he'd done that. Slapped a broad silly when he was through with her. Make sure she'd never forget Edgar Davis. But Tom did have the right idea; if they weren't scared of you, make them scared. Make them piss-in-their-pants scared. So scared they'd do anything you say. Edgar didn't want Jessie Pyne to die. Nope. He wanted her to live, and to remember.

He rubbed his shin gingerly. Hard to walk without limping. Hell, she probably cracked the bone, hard as she kicked him. He chuckled softly to himself. The way she kept trying to pull her pants up when they were leaving. He hoped she was awake when people found her, awake so she'd know how stupid she looked, lying there with her bare ass hanging out for everybody to see. Edgar laughed out loud.

"You're awful quiet over there, Hank. You got nothing to say?" Tom asked, his voice tinged with sarcasm.

Hank glanced at him. "I think we've said it all."

"Hell, you haven't said a word. I want to hear what you think. What's the matter? Didn't you have a good time? You sure dropped your pants fast enough. What did you think of your first queer?"

"It was okay," Hank answered with an uneasy smile. They didn't know.

"Yeah, well, like I said before, a cunt's a cunt."

Beth was frightened. Where was he? He had worn old clothes when he left, faded jeans and a torn shirt, that old, ragged windbreaker he refused to throw away. Hank was always so careful about how he looked when he went out. Where would he have gone, looking like that?

Beth sat at the kitchen table working a crossword puzzle. Hank always laughed at her. He said she was too stupid to work those things. But she always finished them, and they were always right. She had made straight A's in high school. Hank didn't. He couldn't work the puzzles, so Beth never let him see her finish any of them.

She studied the list of clues, her dark head bent over the folded newspaper. Three across, belonging to or occurring each day, seven letters, starts with D. Beth picked up her pencil, D-I-U-R-N-A-L. Where was Hank? Beth wondered if it had anything to do with the woman he had been discussing with the other men. She wondered if he was with Edgar and that Tom. She rubbed her face carefully. It was still very bruised and swollen from the beating he had given her, and she carefully remained at home, hidden away. She didn't want anyone to see her like this. It made her ashamed.

Hank slammed the car door with a violent gesture. What had happened? Tom and Edgar thought they had won. Stupid idiots. She never backed down an inch. Hank didn't believe she would remain silent. She would run straight to the D.A. and tell him everything. Stupid idea! He should know better than to listen to Tom.

He started up the short sidewalk to the front door. More importantly, what had happened to *him?* Was he getting soft? He had faked it pretty good back there, lying on that girl and humping away like he was really enjoying himself. Watching Tom beat her up had turned him on. But something had happened as soon as he unzipped his pants and climbed on top of her. He went limp and soft. Never did get it up again. What did that mean? His mood was vicious as he jammed his key into the lock and let himself into the house.

Beth knew the moment she saw Hank's face that she had made a serious mistake by waiting up for him. She took a tentative step in his direction but stopped when she saw his expression. There was blood on his jacket.

"Are you all right, Hank? I was worried. . ."

Hank grabbed her with a choked cry and slammed her against the refrigerator. Beth screamed, her body too tender and battered to withstand anymore abuse. With one quick motion, Hank slapped her across the mouth. Beth could smell the liquor on his breath, but he wasn't drunk. She knew that.

"You just can't stop shoving your nose in, can you? I'm not a boy, and I don't need a mama to wait up for me. You're supposed to be in bed! Where I go, what I do, and when I come home is *my* business! One of these days you're going to make me so mad, I'm gonna kill you!" He shoved her towards the door. "Get in the bedroom! Get in there where you belong! Get out of my sight!"

Beth ran down the hall and into the bathroom. She locked the door behind her. She wouldn't come out, not this time. He would have to beat the door down to get her out. She sat down on the edge of the bathtub and leaned her folded arms on her knees.

Hank finished the beer with a last long swallow. He was beginning to feel the effects of the alcohol. He was a *man,* by god, and it was high time she learned that. This was *his* house and she was *his* wife and she would do whatever *he* told her to do. Waiting up for him. Hank snorted. He dropped the beer can into the trash and turned out the kitchen light. She should've been in bed, minding her own business, either sleeping or waiting for him. Hank's eyes narrowed. Yeah, waiting for him, in bed.

He opened the bedroom door. Beth was not there. His fury surged as he tried the bathroom door and found it locked.

"Open this door, Beth!"

"I'm scared of you, Hank! Leave me alone. Please!"

"I'll give you a reason to be scared," he muttered as he slammed his shoulder into the door. He heard wood crack. "Teach you to be a decent wife. I should've done this a long time ago."

The door gave, and the lock broke when he hit it for the third time. Beth huddled in the corner, her eyes wide with terror. Hank grabbed her by the arm and dragged her into the bedroom, throwing her onto the bed. He ripped buttons off his shirt as he wrenched it free from his body.

"Teach you to talk back to me. Teach you to be minding my business. I'm the man of this house, and you're about to learn how much of a man I am. Take that gown off!"

"Hank. . .no. . ."

Hank pulled his underwear off and dropped it on the floor. He loomed over Beth, swollen, hard, and angry. With one quick gesture, he ripped her gown open and dropped on top of her. Beth's screams were muffled by his shoulder, and after a few moments, she stopped fighting.

All she ever wanted was her own newspaper, she thought fleetingly. Then she closed her eyes against the pain and tried not to think at all.

10

Val let herself into the house quietly. She closed the door behind her and turned on the lamp by the sofa. Dropping her coat onto the chair, she headed into the kitchen and to the refrigerator. She poured a glass of wine and stood by the table, sipping it rapidly. For the first time in years, she felt like getting quickly and quietly drunk.

She glanced at the clock. It was almost three. She would have to wake Denny and tell her what had happened. Maybe she should wait until morning. Val refilled her glass. Denny would be furious if she didn't wake her up. Val knew she wasn't going to sleep anyway, so she might as well have company. Kate was supposed to call if Jessie came to. Val had made her promise that.

She hadn't wanted to leave the hospital, but Kate had convinced her it would be better for Jessie if not too many people were around her when she finally woke up. It had been hard to look at Jessie. Her face was swollen almost beyond recognition—bandaged, bruised horribly. Still, Val had not wanted to go, especially after she had seen how shaky Kate was once she reached the hospital.

Val carried the glass of wine into the living room. The sound of a key in the lock startled her. She turned to see Denny come through the doorway.

"I didn't expect to find you up. It's late." Denny kissed her lightly on the cheek as she passed Val on her way to the closet. She hung up her coat and closed the closet door. "I had a great time tonight. I'll tell you, Laura and Moon are quite a combination. Say, were they ever lovers?"

"Yes," Val answered absently.

"That figures. They look like they might be again." Denny stopped suddenly and stared at Val. "Val, are you okay?"

Val shook her head. "No."

"Hey, what's wrong?" Denny's voice was soft as she put her arms around Val and hugged her gently. "What is it?"

"Jessie was beaten up and raped last night, Denny. She's in the hospital."

"Jessie?" Denny's voice was confused. Her arms dropped away, and she stepped back from Val, a look of disbelief on her face. "Jessie?"

"Yeah, Jessie."

"But. . .what happened? How did you find out?"

"I found her when I went by the shop to meet her for dinner. She's really hurt, Denny."

"Is she going to be all right?"

Val nodded. "Yes. They had to do surgery on her. Whoever did this knew what they were doing. She's going to be a while recovering from it."

"She was raped, too?" Denny's voice was toneless.

"Maybe several times. They don't know for sure. They had brought her back to the room after surgery, and Kate is with her. I came home because Kate thought it would be better if only one person was with Jessie when she woke up. Maybe she's right. I don't know."

"Is there any more wine?"

"A little."

"I think I'll get some."

Denny came back into the living room a few minutes later with a small glass in her hand. She sat down beside Val on the sofa and put her hand on Val's knee, squeezing lightly. "We need to tell Laura," she said.

"I know. But it's so late, and there's nothing anyone can do right now."

"How badly hurt is she?"

"Oh hell, Denny. Broken nose, broken teeth, concussion, stitches in her mouth and face, bruised, ruptured spleen, broken ribs. And raped."

"And you say Kate is with her?"

Val nodded. "She's supposed to call as soon as Jessie wakes up and let me know what's going on."

"Gonna be a long night."

"Yeah. I think so."

Jessie drifted in and out of reality. Now, instead of welcoming sleep, she fought to stay awake. When she slept, the dreams came, nightmares that terrified her. But when she was awake, very little around her made any clear sense. She had trouble focusing her eyes. One of the nurses said that was because she had hit her head. She didn't remember.

The police came. She told them to go away. Jessie didn't want to talk; she didn't want to remember for them. She said she didn't know who the men were. The police didn't believe her but they left. Val had stayed with her, quietly furious, until Jessie had drifted off to sleep in spite of herself, exhaustion outweighing fear.

Kate threw herself into work for the shelter. They had a building now, donated rent free for the first year, and they were moving furniture in, each woman feeling the need to get it open as soon as possible. Kate moved in an ever-present circle of fear. What if they knew who all of Jessie's friends were? What if they came looking for everyone else, too? From the trunk in the spare room, Kate took out the gun she had stolen from her father's drawer when she ran away from home. She knew how to use it. Her hands shook as she loaded the shells into the heavy revolver. But she kept it with her, wherever she went.

It didn't hurt quite so badly to walk. A few days had made a difference. But Beth's body was still sore and stiff, the bruises blue and purple. She moved around the small kitchen in silence, gritting her teeth against the pain whenever she had to reach or bend. Walking and sitting were different agonies, and she still felt torn inside. She was afraid Hank had really hurt her. . .there . . .but she was too afraid and ashamed to go to the doctor. He would want to know what happened and she couldn't tell him.

She now avoided Hank's angry, brooding gaze. She did not

speak to him any more than she had to. She did what was required of her around the house, but she did it mechanically, woodenly, her mind often a blank. Hank had not touched her again but she was watchful of him, starting violently if he came up behind her unexpectedly.

They were all at the table. Even the boys seemed subdued in Hank's presence. Beth carried bowls of food to them, helping the younger boy serve his plate, cutting his meat for him. When she stroked his hair as she straightened up, he pushed her hand away, glancing fearfully at his father as though expecting Hank to disapprove of Beth's gesture.

Hank was watching his youngest son quietly. "Whose boy are you?"

"I'm your boy, Daddy," Mark answered nervously.

Timmy chimed in from the other side of the table. "I'm not anybody's boy. I'm a man. You said so, Dad. Said I acted like a man."

Hank frowned at him. "Don't get too big for your britches, Timmy. Eat your dinner."

Timmy turned a crestfallen face back to his food. Mark looked from his brother to his father, his expression puzzled. Beth sat down and sipped her iced tea, her face a carefully composed blank, her stomach a knot of tension.

Hank chewed and swallowed a mouthful of food before speaking again. "You haven't had any more trouble at school, have you, Timmy?"

"No, sir. You really musta told that principal a thing or two."

"I don't want them giving you a hard time for doing exactly what I tell you to do. I'm the boss, not them. I don't ever want to hear tell of you sitting next to any nigger kid, or playing with one, or eating at the same table with one. It's bad enough they're even in the same school. Decent white kids shouldn't have to be thrown in with trash. And I want you to watch out for Mark here. You're the oldest, so you're responsible for him. Nigger gives you trouble, you go right ahead and punch him out. Never mind the principal. I'll take care of him."

"Okay, Dad. Does that mean Mark has to do what I tell him?" Timmy was eyeing his brother with obvious glee. Mark looked at his father in alarm.

"He's not my boss, Daddy! He can't tell me what to do. It's not fair! He pushes me around enough!"

Hank leaned forward, frowning. "I'll tell you what's fair, young man. Timmy is the oldest, and he knows more than you do. And I trust him. Hell, I've seen you talking to kids I told you to stay away from. I can't trust you. I do trust Timmy. I want him to watch out for you and make sure you do what I tell you. And if those niggers start picking on you, you'll be glad to have your big brother around to help out. Won't just one jump you. They always jump in packs, just like dogs."

"But they don't mess around with me, Daddy," said Mark, stirring his potatoes with his fork. "I don't want Timmy telling me what to do."

Hank's hand flashed with amazing speed as he slapped the younger boy across the face. Mark dropped his fork and grabbed his cheek, but he didn't make a sound. He blinked rapidly as his eyes filled with tears.

"Watch your mouth," Hank snapped. "I'll tell you what you can want and not want. You'll do as I say and that's that. Now if you'd like to argue with me, we can go into the bedroom with my belt and see who wins the fight. You want to do that?"

"No, Daddy," Mark whispered.

There was a long silence at the table. Beth saw the quick, smug look that passed across Timmy's face. He's just like his father, she thought to herself. She rose and poured herself a cup of coffee. There was an excruciating pain in her stomach—hot, burning stabs of agony. Her hands trembled, and she spilled coffee as she poured. Hank snickered. Mark pushed his plate back abruptly and stood up.

"May I please be excused?" he asked.

"You haven't finished your dinner. Sit down, Mark," Hank commanded. "And you sit down, too, Beth! I get sick and tired of watching you jump up every few minutes. No wonder the kids don't eat. You're probably driving them nuts."

"I'm not the one doing the yelling, Hank," Beth answered softly as she sat down, both hands holding the cup tightly.

"I suppose you think I should coddle them the way you do?"

"Kids need kindness, once in a while."

Hank looked at the children. "Both of you are playing in your food. Get out of here! Go to your rooms!" The boys jumped up and left the room without a word of protest. Hank turned his gaze back to his wife. "Don't talk back to me in front of the kids, Beth."

Beth flinched. She started to stand up but changed her

mind. She couldn't help either of the boys. If she left it alone, Hank would probably forget it much quicker than if she interfered. She stared into her coffee cup.

"I'm taking Timmy bow hunting next week," Hank said in a conversational tone.

"He's just a little boy, Hank. Don't teach him to kill things."

"If I say he's old enough, then he's old enough. I won't have you ruining him, too, Beth. You've already made a sissy out of Mark, but you aren't going to do it to Timmy. He's going to be a man. I'll see to it, even if I have to break his neck in the process. If I want to take him hunting I'll take him. One of these days he'll thank me for it. What will he ever thank you for? You don't know the first thing about being a mother just like you don't know the first thing about being a wife."

Unfamiliar anger flared in Beth, and she spoke before she thought. "Then why did you marry me?"

"I'll be damned if I know," Hank said as he rose from the chair. "You sure ain't no prize."

Beth sat very still, gingerly probing her anger like one would probe a sore tooth. She heard Hank turn on the television in the living room. Her whole body began to shake, harder and harder, until she felt she might crack from the vibrations inside, until she felt she might choke on the words that rose in her mouth, pushing at her lips. Her hands clenched the cup, sliding it around in small circles that grew wider and wider as her anger surged. Then, unexpectedly, she threw the cup on the floor, throwing as hard as she could. All anger left abruptly as she watched with horror. Hopelessly, she grabbed for it, but she was too late. The cup smashed against the tile floor shattering completely, shattering loudly. Beth jumped up from her chair, horrified by what she had done, fear replacing anger in great waves through her body. She crossed her arms protectively over her chest.

Hank stepped into the kitchen and looked at the broken cup. Then he looked carefully at Beth, his voice tautly controlled. "You did *drop* that cup, didn't you, Beth?"

"Yes. I dropped it," Beth whispered, her hand covering her mouth.

"Good. I didn't think you would ever throw anything, would you?"

"No, Hank."

He studied her for a long, tense moment then left the room.

Beth took a deep breath and leaned against the counter. She shouldn't have thrown that cup. It wasn't right to break things. It wasn't right to be angry. Bad things happened when people got angry. A good wife didn't get angry. She wasn't angry. No, she wasn't. Beth grabbed the broom and started sweeping up the slivers of glass. As she knelt to pick up the larger pieces, a razor sharp edge sliced deeply into her finger. Beth stared as the blood welled up and began to drip onto the floor. Red blood on the green tile floor. She wiped at it hastily with her other hand, smearing it, afraid Hank would come back into the room and see what she had done. Bad to be angry, she thought silently as she reached frantically for the sponge. Bad, bad, *bad*. . . .

Jessie was uncomfortable. The plastic bottom of the chair stuck to her skin, pulling and chafing at her thighs. She silently cursed the backless hospital gown and tried to shift her position enough to pull some of the flimsy material beneath her. The effort made her lightheaded and dizzy. Finally, she gave up, resigning herself to the torture of the plastic against her legs until the nurses came back to help her into bed.

It was her first time up in the five days she had been in the hospital. She had been eager to get up, to change locations, even if it was only a few feet from the bed to the chair. Jessie hadn't realized how weak she really was while she was confined to the bed. The five steps to the chair had been made with her leaning heavily on the arm of a sympathetic nurse, and when Jessie finally sat down, she was out of breath. It had felt like miles to the chair.

It scared her to know that she could not move herself around the small room without a great deal of help. She stared out the low window. It would pass as she healed; the weakness would pass. But she felt very vulnerable. Anyone could walk into a hospital. Anyone.

Val popped her head through the partially opened door and grinned in surprise. "Look at you, hotshot. When did they let you out of bed?"

Jessie smiled as best she could, relieved to have company. "About fifteen minutes ago. They practically had to carry me." It was still extremely difficult for her to talk. The swelling in her face and mouth had gone down some but not enough for her to speak very clearly. And she had to talk quite slowly in order to form the words. It was so frustrating that Jessie did not talk very much at all.

Val put the small bag of food she was carrying on the bureau and kissed Jessie on the forehead. "It'll get better as you do."

"I hate it. I hate not being able to do things for myself."

"I know. You're so independent, it's probably driving you crazy." Val sat on the edge of the bed, swinging her long legs back and forth as she watched Jessie trying to shift her body in the chair. "How long are you supposed to be up?"

"As long as I feel okay."

"Do you feel okay?"

"Except for this chair I do."

"What's wrong?"

"Plastic. Nothing between my ass and the plastic."

Val glanced around the room and saw a towel on the chair near the bathroom door. She brought it to Jessie. "See if you can lift your rear up far enough for me to slide this towel under you."

Jessie leaned her weight against the arm of the chair, straining to raise up from the seat. Val slid the white towel into the minute space Jessie was able to clear for her, and Jessie sank down, the strain evident on her face. It took a minute for her breathing to return to normal.

"Better?" Val asked.

"Thanks."

"Sure." Val sat on the bed again, resuming her leg swinging. "So, how are you doing?"

"Okay. I don't like people doing everything for me." Jessie's words were slurred, and Val leaned forward slightly, a frown of concentration on her face as she tried to make out what Jessie was saying.

"Relax and take it as it comes. You've been through a lot. Maybe you deserve to take it easy for a little while."

Jessie didn't answer. She looked out the window. She had not talked about what had happened to her, had not said a word to anyone. She worked very hard not to even think about it, trying to keep her mind carefully blank. She felt the blankness slip in now, with Val watching her so intently as if waiting for her to say something.

"Talk to me, Jess."

"No." The answer was quick and terse.

"Jessie. . ."

"It hurts."

"I know." Val's voice was gentle. She found herself wanting to wrap her arms around Jessie and rock her like a baby, have her feel okay again, without pain, without fear. Just like she had been before.

"You've got to talk sometime."

"I don't even think about it." Jessie's expression was defiant. "I think about going home, going back to work. Laura must be going crazy by now."

"Laura is fine. She told me to tell you things at work are under control, and that she'll be in to see you tomorrow. She said not to worry."

"I have to worry. I don't have insurance. This is costing me. . .I can't afford it. . .I can't pay."

"Jessie," Val interrupted softly.

Jessie looked at her, a tortured expression in her eyes. "I'm afraid that if I start, I won't stop. Ever."

"I know. You will stop when it's time to stop, though. But if you don't start, it will never go away."

Jessie struggled to push away the sudden flash of memory, the sounds of male laughter, the fist in front of her face, the cold ground beneath her. The pain. Always the pain.

"I can't cry," she gasped, her eyes full of tears. "I can't breathe when I cry. My ribs. . ."

Val knelt beside her and slid her arms carefully around Jessie, holding her as closely as she could without hurting her further. "It's okay. You don't have to say it all, feel it all. Not at once. Just don't deny it."

"Playing therapist, Val?" There was bitterness in Jessie's voice. She felt captive; she couldn't even leave the room to escape the conversation.

Val shook her head. "You know better than that."

"Kate said you found me," Jessie said suddenly.

Val nodded. "I did. I called for an ambulance. At first, I wasn't sure you were alive." Her voice was matter of fact.

"How did you find me?"

Val frowned, puzzled by the words, uncertain that she had understood Jessie's question. "I came by to have dinner with you before the meeting. I found you by the dumpster."

Jessie shook her head. "I know that. How did you find *me*?"

Suddenly, Val understood. "You were lying on the ground, on your side. There was a lot of blood. Your shirt was ripped open. Your pants were down. I thought you were dead," Val answered evenly.

"I tried to pull my pants up," Jessie said softly. "I didn't want anybody to see me. . .like that."

"I don't think anyone would want that. You were very cold. I covered you with my coat and went inside to call an ambulance. Then I came back and sat with you."

Val could see Jessie's distress as she stared at her hands, clenching and unclenching in her lap. Jessie's lips were white as she pressed them together, a gesture Val knew must hurt her. For the first time since she had known Jessie, Val found herself hating the young woman's self-control.

Jessie closed her eyes and leaned her head back. "They were the same men who trashed my house."

"How do you know that?"

"They practically told me. They said they had tried to make a point but that I wouldn't listen."

"And so they came in person," Val finished for her.

"They said all I had to do was. . .to not testify at the trial and to stop the newsletter. They said if I promised them that, they would go away and leave me alone."

"Would they have?"

Jessie shook her head. "I doubt it."

"Did you promise anything?"

"No."

Val waited, wanting to say something reassuring but there was nothing but lies to offer. She didn't really believe everything would be all right, that it was really over, whether or not Jessie testified at the trial.

"There were three men."

"The doctors figured there was more than one."

"Three. Tom, Edgar, and. . .I can't remember the name of the other one."

Val stared at her in amazement. "Do you know them?"

"No. They called each other by name." Jessie's voice became a monotone as she spoke.

Softly, Val said, "Tell me what you remember."

"I don't know how much I remember. A lot of it is hazy, like a dream. They hurt me. . .one of them beat me. Tom. The guy called Tom. The other two stayed out of the way for a while. . .At one point, before he. . .hit me the first time, I thought I had a chance to make it to the door of the shop. I didn't get very far. . .He used his fists, Val, and he liked it. If you could've seen the expression on his face. . .He liked beating the hell out of me."

"I'm sure he did," Val said, the low anger carrying through her words to Jessie.

"I was almost unconscious when. . .Edgar, I think, stopped him. Said he didn't want Tom to kill me. I knew if he hit me one more time, I would pass out. I wanted to. I really wanted to. Then they got me on my knees. Tom made me. . .They all raped me, several times. I don't know how many, maybe only once each. Maybe more. I couldn't do anything to stop them. I tried, Val." Jessie looked at her. "I really tried. But my arms wouldn't move. I wanted to faint but I was there, for all of it."

In Val's mind, she filled in what Jessie could not say. *Tom made me. . .*Val had a good idea what Tom had made her do.

"I'm scared, Val." Jessie was whispering, her eyes wide and dark in the dimly lighted room. "I'm scared they'll come here. What if they do? I can't do anything alone."

Val kept her close, patting her lightly on the shoulder. "I don't think they will. They may believe they've scared you enough to keep you quiet. And we can stay with you—me, Kate, Denny, Laura. We can stay with you all the time."

Jessie leaned into the circle of Val's arms, rocking back and forth. "They left it all with me. They beat off all their hate and left it with me."

"Hang onto that anger, baby. That's what will pull you through this. You need it. Pour it right back at them. They deserve all you can give and then some. Don't lock it away. Throw it right back."

"I'm scared. Scared to go home. The thought of being outside. . ."

"We'll be with you. Count on that. We'll be with you for as long as you need us to be there. We'll help. Denny and I will do all we can. And you know Kate will help. She loves you."

"Then why won't she talk to me?" Jessie's words were pouring out now, streams of bitterness and uncertainty. "And why won't she come to see me when I'm awake? It's like she can't take it, like she can't deal with me now."

"Jess, when a woman is raped, it doesn't just happen to her alone. It puts every woman who knows her through some pretty big changes. It scares the hell out of us all."

"But right before the demonstration, we had this big fight. What happened to me was exactly what Kate was afraid would happen, what she warned me about. I feel like she's pulling away from me."

"Are you afraid she'll leave you?"

There was a long silence.

"I'm just as afraid she'll stay."

11

Kate had begun slipping into Jessie's hospital room very late at night and spending the dark hours there, curled up in the armchair, only half-sleeping as she smoked endless cigarettes and kept a self-appointed vigil. They talked very little. When Jessie woke during the night, Kate would sit on the side of the bed and give her news about the print shop, word of the battered women's shelter, anything she could think to say that would not bring up the subject of what had happened to Jessie. Jessie spoke of herself in terms of pain level and mobility. Kate seemed content with only that information.

After ten days in the hospital, Jessie was able to move around a little on her own, although she still required help from time to time. Her strength was returning slowly. Kate watched her progress silently, wanting her out of the hospital, wanting her home in some familiar environment that did not hold such terrifying memories for Kate. She hated being there, even for Jessie's sake. But Jessie never asked her to come or to stay. As far as Kate knew, Jessie never asked that of anyone.

The hard chair made it nearly impossible for Kate to sleep deeply or soundly, and she welcomed the wakefulness even though she was slowly drifting towards complete exhaustion. Jessie's beating and rape had brought back Kate's dreams, nightmares she had thought long forgotten, dreams she had not had in years: her father, her brother, her mother's swollen, terrified face, the sounds of men laughing, the sound of a fist striking flesh, the green antiseptic of emergency rooms, lights in her eyes.

Kate had worked with battered women for nearly two years. Those women had not set loose the memories Kate so carefully locked away. Jessie had. And she not only brought back the memories themselves but all of the feelings that came with them—the fear, the pain, and the helplessness. Kate wanted to tell her. She wanted to tell Jessie that she knew, really *knew,* what Jessie was going through, but she could not find the words.

During the days while Jessie was in the hospital, a pattern quickly developed for Kate. She would drink coffee all during the daylight hours, cup after cup, until every nerve in her body screamed in protest. Then she would go home, take a shower, have one or two drinks, and go to the hospital. She did not sleep for more than a couple of hours each night.

Kate twisted her body in the chair, trying to find a comfortable position. She pulled the lightweight blanket higher under her chin. Jessie was dreaming; Kate could always tell. Jessie's hands were clenching and relaxing, her breathing labored as if in a race. Her legs beneath the covers twitched spasmodically. Kate watched, giving Jessie time to wake herself up. When she didn't, Kate stood up and went to her, calling her by name before she touched her shoulder.

Jessie's eyes flew open, containing the terror Kate had come to expect. She found herself remembering how Jessie used to wake up, her eyes soft and sleepy, friendly. Now she looked at her as though Kate were a complete stranger. And when she recognized her, the softness was still not there, only a memory of fear. Kate sat on the bed, holding Jessie's hand, waiting for her to calm down from the dream, to stop trembling.

"Are you okay now? Are you out of it?"

"Yes," Jessie nodded. "How long have you been here?"

"Since eleven. It's around two now, I think."

"Why don't you ever come when I'm awake, Kate?"

Kate looked at her. "This way, I'm here during the night. I'm here when you have the dreams."

"And when we don't have to talk to each other." There was bitterness in Jessie's voice.

"I didn't say that, Jessie."

"You didn't have to." Jessie looked away. "When I was still living in the farmhouse, Mrs. Carpenter told me a story about one of her aunts who died in a mental hospital. The woman had clenched her fists so tightly and for so many years that the nails had grown through her flesh so that they came through the backs of her hands."

"Was that story true?"

"I think so. It's become part of my dream. Sometimes lately I catch myself clenching my fists so tightly that I cut the skin on my hands. I dream about being like that woman, my fists always tight and useless, and my not being able to open them anymore."

"That's a terrible dream." Kate did not look at her.

"Yeah. It changes. It changes then to a man hitting me, and I want to hit him back but I can't because my hands are so twisted that they aren't really fists anymore. I try to call for help, but I have no voice. I keep thinking that if I could just open my hands, I could push him away and my voice would come. . ." Jessie trailed off and Kate started to stand up. But Jessie suddenly, harshly, gripped Kate's arm. "I don't know how to talk to you about any of this."

"Jess, we don't have to talk yet. You need to heal your body first and then we can talk. One step at a time, baby. It doesn't have to all be done at once."

"What is wrong, Kate?" Jessie demanded in a quiet tone.

Kate pushed her hair back with a quick gesture and reached for a cigarette. "Being here, in a hospital. . .it's hard for me. Not just being with you, knowing you are hurt and in pain. Just being in a hospital, period."

"Why?"

Kate exhaled a white cloud into the air and studied the book of matches she was holding. She offered a cigarette to Jessie who shook her head. Kate slipped the matches into her shirt pocket. "There's a whole lot about me that you don't know. I've never told you because there didn't seem to be any reason for me to say anything. I don't think now is a good time to get into it. . ."

"Tell me." Jessie was staring at her intently.

"It's just that I was in the hospital several times when I was a kid, and there are a lot of bad associations for me, a lot of painful memories. I don't usually think about them very much."

"But you are now." Jessie was grateful for a chance to think about someone other than herself. And she thought Kate was withholding something important, something Jessie very much needed to know.

"Yes, I am now."

"What happened to you?"

She looked at Jessie, her eyes narrowed and angry. "My father beat the hell out of me. He put me in the hospital three times, and those were only the absolute worst times when there was no way to keep me at home and take care of me there. So I know how it feels to have someone do that to you. I don't know how different it is being a child and being an adult. Or how different it is when it's done to you by someone you love or by someone you don't know. It's just that being with you has brought it all back."

The silence in the room lingered for a long time. Jessie watched while Kate smoked and forced herself not to pace.

She didn't want to talk about this, did not want to think about it right now. Jessie did not need to hear about *her* past; she had her own problems to deal with. She needed time to heal herself. Talking would come later when the time was right. Much later. Kate put out her cigarette.

"Were you ever raped, Kate?" The question hit Kate like a physical blow. She set the ashtray down, carefully keeping her back to Jessie, her eyes closed.

"Jessie, probably fifty percent of the women you know have been raped. Maybe even more than that. It happens constantly. But I don't think this is the time or the place. . . "

"Dammit, Kate, I'm not discussing the subject of rape. I don't want statistics. I'm asking about *you.* And I'm trying to tell you about me. It happened to *me,* not to someone else out there you don't know." Jessie gestured outward from her body. The words were there rushing to come out, the need to say them to Kate, pushing them forward, tumbling them into Jessie's mouth.

Kate turned to face her. "It's almost three in the morning, Jess. Let it be for now. I know what you're going through. But you have time, baby. You do have time. Just get better and then we can talk, then we can work this through."

Jessie turned onto her side, her back to Kate. The words silenced Jessie as effectively as a gag. She closed her eyes, pretending to go to sleep. When she felt Kate return to the chair, Jessie rolled onto her back again, her gaze locked on the far wall of the room. Kate did not want to hear about it. Maybe no one wanted to hear about it. She felt completely alone, and an icy fear spread through her. People wanted to forget; they didn't want to be reminded. They wanted her to get well and get back to her life, not to talk about pain and fear, not to remind them about death. She felt a sickening rush of apprehension. They would try to make it seem like it had never happened.

Maybe Kate was right. She should worry about healing her body. Maybe it would start to go away when she was able to do things for herself, when she didn't feel so helpless and vulnerable. There was lots to be done. No time for dwelling on something she couldn't change.

For the first time, Jessie considered not testifying at the trial, wondering if that would make them leave her alone. Everyone would understand. No one would blame her.

Jessie choked back sudden tears. She would not let anyone see her cry anymore over this, most especially Kate Robbins. Then she felt a stab of pain in her hands. Abruptly, she straightened her fingers. Small half-moons on her palms. The nails had cut through to blood.

Kate set cups of coffee in front of Val and Denny, then pulled out a chair for herself. The morning sun cut bright yellow patterns across the old, polished wood table, and Denny traced them with her fingertip. They could hear Laura in the next apartment humming to herself.

Kate glanced at Val. "Have you been able to talk to Jessie?"

"Some. She told me part of what happened."

"How is she?" Denny asked, her eyes lowered.

"Physically, I think she's doing remarkably well. Emotionally, I'm not sure." Val shrugged. "She did talk, and that was good. I think she needs to talk."

"Not everybody talks," Kate said quietly, "and she needs to heal her body before she tries to work through anything else. She can't do it all at once."

"No, she can't," Val agreed, "but her body is pretty much healing itself. Only Jessie can heal the rest of it. She won't do that by not talking."

"What did she say happened?" Denny asked as she picked up her coffee cup and rose to stand by the window, her back to the other two women.

Val watched her. "I think they were Klansmen. At least, it sounds like it. Three men. Jessie said they called each other by name. She can only remember two of the names so far. I think the other will come to her eventually."

"That was pretty careless," Kate said in surprise.

"Maybe they thought she couldn't hear or understand them. Anyway, from what she told me things sounded planned out, like the whole incident had been well set up. And they were the same men who broke into her house. They told her that. She said only one of the men did the actual beating, but that all of them raped her. She doesn't remember how many times. She never lost consciousness, not until after it was over."

"Oh, hell," Denny breathed softly.

"I think she's lying there feeling helpless, feeling very vulnerable to another attack, worried that they might come back. Even though she can get around by herself now, she still couldn't do anything to defend herself. But I haven't asked too many questions. I didn't want to push her. She does need some time."

"She has that," Kate said, a bit too firmly. "She has all the time she needs."

"I know that. But I wanted her to know that her friends are willing to listen if she needs to talk. I don't think it's safe to assume that she will know we are here and willing. Especially as many times as she may need to go through it."

"I wish you wouldn't say anything else to her, Val."

Val looked at Kate, a shocked expression on her face. "What are you talking about?"

"I just think she needs to be left alone." Kate's hands were trembling as she lifted her coffee cup.

"Well, I'm sorry, Kate, but I can't honor that request. I was raped a few years ago. What I remember most was the feeling that I had to go looking for women I could talk to, that no one else would bring up the subject. They all talked about how willing they were to listen whenever I needed to talk. The whole responsibility was on me. And they weren't even very good listeners for the most part. They wanted me to say it so they could nod and be sympathetic and then get on with whatever they were doing. Sometimes when I brought it up, women would pat me on the shoulder and change the subject, like they were protecting me from something by not talking about it. Most women stopped touching me. They wouldn't even look me in the eye. They wanted me to just get over it. I felt almost completely alone and isolated. Only a couple of my friends really stuck by me and worked with me. My lover left me. She couldn't deal with it."

The sudden crash startled them as Denny slammed her coffee cup onto the counter, spilling the hot liquid all over the floor. She turned to face them, gripping the edge of the counter behind her, her eyes narrowed.

"So what are we going to do?" she demanded.

"Whatever we can, Denny. As much as we can," Val answered.

"We can't just sit back like this."

"I don't follow you," Kate said, watching Denny carefully.

"I'm not dealing very well with any of this. I never have. Almost every woman I've ever been close to has been raped. It makes me so angry I want to hurt somebody. Now it's happened to Jessie. Only they almost beat her to death, too. I can't just sit and listen. Every time I hear about it, all those women go through my head. She's got her whole life to put back together now, and she shouldn't have to!" Denny's voice became increasingly loud as she spoke, and her hands sliced the air with quick gestures.

"She's got to live with those men for the rest of her life, in one way or another. Even when she's worked through it all to the point where she's not in immediate pain or fear, they will still be there. Things will happen to bring them back. I can't sit here knowing that and talk calmly. I want to take a crowbar and beat their fucking brains in! I want it to have never happened!"

"We all want it to have never happened," Val said softly, "but it did. Now we have to figure out how to be there for her."

"And they will be there, too!" Denny shouted. "How do we replace them with ourselves? How do we offer her more security, enough to offset what they've done to her? Will sitting around a kitchen table make her feel safe? What about the next time she has to walk down the street or go out to the dumpster? Are you going to be there, Val? What about you, Kate? You're so into being cool, saying she can take all the time she needs. What are you doing for her? I've listened to you, and you always sound like you're talking about a complete stranger!"

"Denny. . ."

"Don't take that tone of voice with me, Val!" Denny answered, glaring at her.

"I'm sorry. But I don't think jumping on Kate will get us anywhere at all."

"Where are we supposed to get us?" Denny snapped, smashing her fist on the table. "That woman is the closest thing to a sister I've ever had. I won't act like I feel calm and rational about this because I don't. I want to hurt them as bad as they hurt her." Denny's face was drawn, and her body trembled as she leaned over the table. There were tears in her eyes. Val couldn't separate the different expressions she saw there.

"So what do we do now? There's no way we could ever hurt them the way they hurt Jessie. We can never hurt them that bad."

Denny grabbed her jacket from the chair and pulled it on, her gestures abrupt and jerky. "I have to go for a walk," she said as she left the room, slamming the door to the apartment behind her.

A heavy silence filled the room as both Kate and Val stared at their coffee cups, each filled with her own thoughts.

Val sighed quietly. "I'm glad she finally lost her temper. It's been building all week, but she wouldn't say anything."

"Maybe it's better to just get mad like she does," Kate said. "Maybe it would be better if we all just got mad."

"Maybe."

"I have to go over to the shelter." Kate rose to her feet.

"I think I'll go to the hospital. Just check in and make sure Jessie is okay."

Kate studied Val for a long moment, her expression guarded. She felt a surge of resentment but quickly pushed it down. If Val was willing to go through the listening, willing to go through the pain, then more power to her. Kate wiped up the spilled coffee and put the cups in the sink. She couldn't do it; she couldn't listen to what Jessie had to say. Maybe it would be better to have someone else, someone not so intimately involved. When Kate looked up, Val was staring at her curiously. Kate shook her head and left the room in silence.

Denny stepped into Jessie's room, somewhat calmer, and tired. She kept her hands shoved into the pockets of her jacket as she leaned over and kissed Jessie on the cheek.

"You sure look better in your own pajamas. That little gown they gave you did nothing for your image."

Jessie smiled lopsidedly. "I know."

"I checked at the desk on my way in, and they said you can take a ride to the coffee shop with me. What do you say?"

"Oh my god, yes! Anything to get out of this room."

Denny pushed a wheelchair into the room. "They insist you ride, but this isn't so bad. All I can buy you is coffee or a Coke, but I'll treat you to a beer as soon as you get out of here. I think they frown at the consumption of alcohol on hospital premises."

"Stuffy bunch," Jessie said, maneuvering herself into the chair. "You know how to drive one of these things?"

"Sure do. You're in the hands of an expert. I worked for one summer as a nurse's assistant while I was in college. Here we go."

Denny pushed the wheelchair down the hall and onto the elevator. The two women were silent as they watched the green numbers on the panel announce the passing floors.

Denny bought Cokes and brought the drinks back to the table. She sat down opposite Jessie and stirred her drink absently with a straw. "I hear they may let you come home in a couple of days."

"That's what they said this morning. I'll be very glad to get out of here."

"Would it be easier for you if Val and I moved your stuff into that downstairs bedroom? That way you wouldn't have to. . ."

"No, Denny. I want to be closer to you and Val than that."

"Sure. I just thought. . ."

Jessie touched her on the arm. "I know. And I appreciate it. But I don't think I could take being downstairs and have both of you upstairs. I think it would scare me to death every time I heard a noise."

"I see your point. Do you think you'll be able to handle the stairs okay?"

"I don't know. Probably, if I move slow."

"Well, I guess we'll have to wait and see. How are you feeling?"

"Much better. I can get around pretty well now. They've taken out all of my stitches, but I have to keep the rib binding on for a while yet. That's my main concern. I still can't take a deep breath."

"Well, the swelling on your face has nearly disappeared, and the bruises are almost gone. You look like you feel a lot better."

"Yeah. I think if it hadn't been for the head injury, I could have come home several days ago. But they wouldn't let me leave until I had had three or four days with no dizziness."

"Better safe, I suppose."

"I suppose."

"Jessie. . ."Denny began awkwardly. "I'm having a hard time with what happened to you. I want to be here for you but I get so mad every time I think about it. . .I walked out, well, I should say I *stormed* out, of Kate's place earlier because I just couldn't stand talking about it. I want to listen and help, but I can't without losing my temper."

"I'm glad you told me."

"It's not you. It's them, the men. It's just that it has happened to so many women I care about. It's hard for me. I love you, Jessie. You're my best friend, my sister. I can't stand to see you hurt. It makes me want to jump on every guy I see."

"Yeah." Jessie's voice was soft. "I need you to be here, Denny. I'm scared to death. I'm afraid to go back to work, afraid they'll come back. I know they know where I'm living in town. I'm scared they'll hurt you or Val." She hesitated. "I've been thinking about not testifying."

Denny stared at her in surprise. "You're going to back down?"

"I don't know what to do. But I have been thinking about it."

"Well, everyone would probably understand it if you did. Except maybe for the D.A. You could go to jail, I think." Denny tried to disguise the disappointment she knew was in her voice. Now was not the time to argue with Jessie.

"I don't want to be hurt again. And I don't think I could take it if they hurt anyone else. One of the men threatened that."

Denny's answer was slow. "I think you have to worry only about yourself, Jess, and let the rest of us make our own decisions. You felt so strongly about what happened at the demonstration, I can't see you backing down. I won't judge you if you do. I'm just saying I can't see you doing that. I think you would hate yourself for it."

"That may be, but I'm scared."

Denny covered Jessie's hand with her own. "I know."

Beth dropped the newspaper into the trashcan and put her cup in the sink. She would finish the dishes later. As she walked towards the door, her eye fell on the folded pages and the headline seemed to leap out at her, *SHELTER FOR BATTERED WOM-*

EN OPEN IN DURHAM. She paused, hesitating, her hands held stiffly at her sides as she read the opening paragraphs of the article.

"Durham's first shelter for victims of physical abuse and rape opened its doors this week at an undisclosed location in town. The shelter, called Refuge, is designed to temporarily house battered women and children, as well as victims of rape, while sources of aid are explored and new housing can be found for those in need. Refuge features living quarters for those who go there, as well as a small, mostly volunteer staff to provide counseling and to act as contacts to other related agencies.

"In a brief news conference earlier today, director Kate Robbins stated that the location of the shelter is not being revealed to the public at large in order to offer as much safety and security as possible for those women and children who utilize the shelter. Arrangements have been made with local hospitals and law enforcement officials to provide information about and transport to the shelter for any woman and/or child who needs a place to stay until satisfactory arrangements for their well-being can be made.

"Consultants for Refuge include several local doctors, lawyers, and counselors. Ms. Robbins stated that the network which has been structured with other agencies in the area, such as Welfare, Rape Crisis, Traveler's Aid, and Legal Aid, will enable staff members to provide immediate and varying resources for many different needs.

"Ms. Robbins was quoted as saying that with the increasing number of reported cases of marital abuse and rape in this area, the existence of such a shelter is vital to the welfare and safety of many women."

A fold hid the rest of the article. Beth reached out a tentative hand and picked up the paper. A shelter. She had never heard of such a thing before.

She tried so hard—so hard—to be a good wife. She pulled her robe more tightly around her as she stared at the paper. *SHELTER FOR BATTERED WOMEN OPEN IN DURHAM.*

Spreading the newspaper on the kitchen table, Beth slowly ripped the article free. After a moment's thought, she hid it in a cookbook and placed the book far back on the shelf. Just in case. Just in case.

12

Kate pushed the chair back and rubbed her tired eyes. She had been doing paperwork since early morning. It was now nearly nine at night. She made a face as she downed cold coffee and emptied the overflowing ashtray into the wastebasket.

She had spent the day trying to make the operating budget she had drawn up in the beginning fit the actual money she had received for the center. It wasn't being easy. When she originally designed a budget for Refuge, she had gone through and trimmed every possible corner, paring the budget to the bone. The money she had at the moment showed that she needed to trim some more, but she didn't know where or how.

Kate was the only full-time salaried employee. As the Director of Refuge, she was being paid $9,000 a year. But even that money didn't come out of the budget; it was being paid by a Junior League group in town, at least for the first year. Some of those women were also on the Board of Directors. Kate's fund-raising tactics had been instrumental in getting the shelter open. She had literally pounded the streets, approaching civic groups, churches, public service organizations; she had brought money in from many of them. She had written grants, backed the United Way into a corner, organized bake sales, yard sales, and auctions. She had begged from individuals. And she had done well. But it was going to be a tight first year nonetheless.

She still had to hunt for money. Opening the doors provided the shelter, but it did not bring in money. Most of the women who came through would have little or no money to donate. Indeed, many of them would need money themselves.

Kate sighed tiredly.

The light touch on her shoulder startled her. Kate whirled around to find Denny standing behind her.

"What are you doing here?" Kate asked in surprise.

"Val has been trying to reach you all afternoon, but the line's been busy. The doctor released Jessie today. She's at home."

"How is she?"

Denny shrugged. "Getting around pretty well. She seems to be healing very fast."

"She's a strong woman," Kate said softly.

"Yeah." Denny's reply was short and flat.

"I guess she's probably asleep by now."

"I just don't get you, Kate," Denny said tersely. She leaned forward, resting her hands on the desk. "How can you be so laid back about all of this?"

Kate pushed her hair away from her face. "I don't feel very laid back, Denny, believe me."

"Then you've got a damned good act together. You sure had me fooled."

"Look, I don't need. . ."

"To be perfectly honest with you, I don't particularly care what *you* need. I care what Jessie needs."

"And just who appointed you her guardian angel?" Kate exploded. "I won't have you on my back, Denny. So get off!"

Denny stared at her for a long, tense moment, anger sparking in her eyes. "She's my friend."

"And she's my lover!" Kate blazed. She fumbled for a cigarette, lighting it with shaking hands. She threw the pack onto the desk and went to stand by the window.

Denny watched Kate's reflection in the glass. "So what is it? What's eating you?"

"I feel completely helpless! I can't even separate the realities, where I stop and Jessie starts. How can I deal with her when I can't even deal with myself?"

"I don't follow you."

"It's a long story."

Denny's face was set, her expression hard. "Look, Kate, Val talked to Jessie quite a lot while Jess was still in the hospital. Jessie is afraid you'll leave her. But she's also afraid you'll stay, that the two of you will just fight and never work it out. She doesn't know how to relate to you right now. And it doesn't sound like you've given her much reason to feel secure. Maybe you're scared, too. But withdrawing like this is going to have only one result. If you want to talk some before you see Jessie, I'll listen. I don't pretend to be the slightest bit objective but I'll listen."

Denny leaned against the desk and folded her arms across her chest. Kate stared at her for a moment, resentful and torn. It had been a long time since she talked to anyone about what had happened. She resented the need to talk, hated the whole series of events which brought it all up. She knew none of Jessie's friends understood why she was acting like she was. But maybe talking to them would help. Maybe it would calm her down, help her not feel so vulnerable herself. And god knows it would be better than dumping it on Jessie. She glanced at Denny again, wishing the expression on Denny's face was friendlier. She took a deep breath and forced the words out.

"One of the reasons I work so hard for this shelter is because I was a battered child. Every time I went to the hospital to see Jessie, it all came back. I realized that I had never dealt with any of that, had merely pushed it down. It's been so long now, I don't even know how to begin. The fear is still there. So I went to Jessie's room late at night so I wouldn't have to talk, so I wouldn't have to remember very much. Jessie is quite smart. She would've known something was going on, and she can draw it out of me. She already has pulled a lot out of me. She has enough to cope with, and all I can offer her is my own fear. I'm terrified for her, but I'm also terrified for me."

"Why don't you tell her that?" Denny demanded, not willing to back down.

"I have, in various ways. I don't want to get into it right now, with Jessie or with myself."

"But how can you work with these women and children if you haven't dealt with yourself? It seems to me it would eventually tear you apart."

Kate shook her head. "So far I've managed to keep a certain distance from them because they're strangers. That may be surprising, but it's true. I can't do that with Jessie. She's too close, too important. I told her some of it because she pushed me one night, and I didn't know what else to do. But she hasn't heard the half of it, and I don't think I can listen to her without going through everything that's happened to me. At least, in my own head.

How's that going to help her? The last thing she needs to be dealing with is my garbage."

"Maybe what Jessie needs is for you to be completely honest with her, and a little vulnerable. She thinks you don't want her anymore. True, maybe she can't really deal with what you call your garbage, but you're playing some kind of halfway game with her, staying there at night and not being there when she's awake, scared and lonely. I know there's got to be some comfort in knowing you're there, watching her while she sleeps. But what about when she's awake and wants you to hold her? What about then, Kate?" Denny's voice was hard. Clearly, Kate's explanation was not adequate to her.

"Look, Jessie needs good things right now. I'm not sure I'm a good thing for her."

"Do you want her?"

Kate answered softly, "I'm not sure what I want."

Denny drew back abruptly. "Then maybe you'd better figure that out first. I thought you loved her."

"I do, Denny. It's just that. . ."

"It's just that nothing! Sometimes you have to let go of yourself a little and just be there for people who mean something to you. What do you think is going to happen? Probably Jessie would be so relieved to feel she could do something for someone else. She feels so totally helpless. To be a little selfishly honest here, Val and I could use some help, too. We're doing all we can, but we can't give her some of the things you *can* give her. And she needs them from you. If you can't, or won't, then just say so and get out of her life. But stop taking two steps forward and six steps back. Jessie is in no shape for that. She needs so much she doesn't even know how to ask."

"Stop lecturing me, Denny!" Kate snapped. "We're all trying to do the best we can."

"Well, I don't think some of us are trying enough." She stared Kate down after several long moments. "Look, Kate, I didn't come here to lecture or to be nasty. But right now, I don't care about anyone else's feelings except Jessie Pyne's. As far as I'm concerned, I'll do or say whatever I have to to make things as easy for her as possible. I'm sorry if I upset you. But I kinda figure whatever any of us feel, it can't be half as bad as what Jess is going through. That makes me pretty unsympathetic. You figure it out, but for Jessie's sake, I hope you don't hurt her. I don't think she can take it."

Denny turned and quietly left the room. Kate wanted to stop her but she made no move to call her back. She dropped into a chair, leaned her head back, and closed her eyes.

Laura sat down on the edge of Jessie's bed and kicked off her shoes, a blissful expression settling over her face.

"That feels soooo good. Feet were not meant to be stood on for fourteen hours a day." She eyed Jessie. "You look pretty good, woman. How are you getting around?"

"The stairs are hard, but other than that I'm making it okay. How are things at work?"

"Well," Laura answered with a chuckle, "I can't say I mind a bit bringing the paperwork over here for you to do. Business is good. A lot of orders coming in."

"That's good to hear. How are you holding out?"

"I'm doing all right. I don't know as much about the press as you, but this is one way to learn. I've figured a lot of stuff out for myself since you've been gone from the shop."

"Well, I'm glad it's not driving you completely crazy." Jessie paused for a moment, then said in a very low voice, "There hasn't been any trouble there?"

Laura looked puzzled. "Trouble? No. Should there be?"

"I was worried that those men might come back. They threatened my friends, too."

Laura put her hand on Jessie's knee. "Everything is fine. No one has come around or bothered me in any way. Don't worry about me."

"It's hard not to."

"I know. But I'm okay. You need to be putting all your energy into yourself, and the account books."

Jessie smiled. "I'm glad you brought them over. Gives me something to do. I'm already so sick of reading, I could scream."

"And just think. Not a month ago you were moaning about how you never got to read these days."

"I know."

"Just can't be pleased, huh?"

"Circumstances. . ."

Laura leaned forward. "Hey, Jessie, I know it's hard for you.

I really know that. But I guess the reason I came over here was to just pass some time with you, see how you were doing, talk, give and get some moral support. I want you to get well. I need you. It's not the same being at work, at meetings, without you."

Jessie looked at her. "I miss being there."

"Don't you miss me?"

"Of course I do. What kind of question is that?"

Laura laughed. "Just thought I'd ask. I'm real glad you feel up to doing the paperwork. If you do that, then I can take a good deep breath again. I'm afraid it's in a bit of a mess. I haven't had time to do very much with it over the past couple of weeks. Things are a little slower now, so I can get caught up on the other stuff I'm behind on. Did that make any sense?"

"Yep. It sure did." Jessie stared at the pile of papers at Laura's feet. "Looks like I'll have enough to do there for a couple of days."

"Honey, I brought you the bills, the checkbook, the accounts, the invoices, the orders; I brought you everything. You just have yourself a ball."

"I never thought I would be happy to see the checkbook."

"Everything was up to date until two weeks ago. I haven't touched any of it since then. Feel free to call me fifty times a day if you have any questions."

"Okay. You just remember you said that."

"I will."

"Yeah?"

Jessie reached for a cigarette. Her stay in the hospital had almost stopped her smoking. Once she arrived at home, she found herself going back to cigarettes, fighting her tense nerves. But she was only smoking five or six a day, a drastic change from the pack and a half she had been smoking before. . .the accident. "I'm scared about coming back to work. The doctor says I can probably come back under limited conditions sometime next week. Half days, no lifting, twisting, or bending."

"You can be queen of the front office. Me and that old press are about to come to an understanding. Can't have you messing around with a budding relationship."

"Yeah, I know, but. . ."

Laura reached out and caught Jessie's hand. "Honey, *I* know. You'll be nervous and scared. I'll be there with you. Until you're ready, we're not going to let you be caught alone at home or at work. Not even on the streets. But this is your business, your work. If it's too much for you, if the associations are too bad, then let's look for another place for the shop. But we'll all be there for you in every way we can. Lots of women have been raped and beaten. We have to start watching out for each other."

"It makes me feel so damned helpless sometimes."

"I guess so. But look at it this way; we're not doing it just for you. We're also learning how to protect ourselves."

"I keep thinking I should be able to do it all."

"Wouldn't that be nice?" Laura smiled. "Sometimes we have to do it all, and alone. But it feels pretty good, from time to time, to know that there are women who can and will help. Jess, you're going to have to do a lot of this on your own, most of it. So let us be there for you when and as we can."

"Yeah."

Laura reached for her jacket. "Well, I have to get going. Oh, by the way, Moon told me to say hello to you from her."

Jessie smiled. "How is she?"

"Doing fine. Just as opinionated, ornery, and sweet as she ever was. I'm supposed to have dinner with her later tonight."

"I'd love to see her again sometime soon."

"I'll tell her. She's been wanting to stop by, but she wasn't sure you would welcome a visit from a stranger."

"It would tickle the hell out of me. She doesn't seem much like a stranger."

"I'll pass that along, too." Laura leaned down and gave Jessie a careful hug. "I sure will be glad when I can squeeze you again without worrying if I'm going to pop one of your stitches. See ya."

Jessie watched Laura go out the door. The room felt strangely empty after she had left. Jessie finished the cigarette and ground it out in the ashtray. Suddenly, she wanted to be with Kate very badly.

13

"I can't believe this!" Hank said as he waved the newsletter in front of Tom's nose. "That stupid broad! Does she think we're just blowing our horns?"

Tom scratched his head. "She does learn slow."

"So much for your bright ideas," Hank said, tossing the paper onto the table. "All that for nothing. And you were so sure it would work, so sure we would shut her up."

Tom spread his hands, palms up. "The girl is obviously crazy, man. Nobody would open their mouths after something like that."

"Yeah, well, what happens if she's crazy enough to start talking?"

"She hasn't said anything. And she won't either."

Hank sat down and opened the paper, reading parts of it aloud. "Listen to this. 'Unite Against Klan Activities.' They're talking about pulling a bunch of different groups together for a mass demonstration. They say they're going to come back to the farm and protest our next rally. Didn't they learn anything? And there's the usual bunch of history in here. And some garbage about Klan terrorism, personal recollections by some local niggers, civil rights shit. There's even some stuff in here about a Klan hit-squad, a terrorist group. And a whole thing about the junior KKK club at one of the high schools. She's getting too close to some things now."

"She doesn't do this newsletter alone, Hank. There are several other women who do it with her. Have you talked. . ."

"Hands off, is the word I get. Leave her alone. Do not make any personal contact with her or with any of her friends. We can do whatever we need to to scare her, but we cannot personally do anything to her. No physical damage, low profile. Don't show our faces. It's getting too close to trial time. That's what Baker told me." Hank rose and went to the refrigerator. He tossed a can of Miller's to Tom, then opened one for himself.

Tom stretched, cracking his knuckles loudly. "Well, we already know she doesn't scare so easy. We've done everything short of killing her, and she's still at it."

"I know that. But I get so pissed every time I see a copy of this rag that I want to. . .Wait a minute!" Hank said, staring at the newsletter. "Jessie Pyne owns a printing business. I'm pretty sure this thing is printed there and put together by that bunch of broads who are with her in this group. Maybe, instead of worrying about the people involved, we should take care of the machinery."

Tom glanced at him, a puzzled expression on his face. "What are you talking about?"

"It's not going to hurt Pyne to know that we know all about her. Okay, we did a number on her house. Then we did a number on her. She's out of the hospital, and she's pushing her luck by continuing to put out this newsletter. My guess is she's scared but getting a little nervy because she hasn't heard from us. So, a message to the house where she's living now and a torch to her business. We know all about her, and she is not safe, no matter what she thinks."

"You mean burn her printing business?"

"Exactly. Let her know we are all around her."

A slow grin spread across Tom's face as he took in what Hank was saying. "You know, that's not half bad, Hank. I worked in a printshop once. There are usually enough chemicals to make the whole place go up. It would be one hell of a bonfire."

"Will you see Edgar soon?"

"Tomorrow night," Tom answered.

"Bring him by and let's talk this out. We need to move soon. I don't want her to start getting too calm."

Jessie stacked the ledgers and account books into a pile and set them on the floor by the desk. It was all beginning to blur, and she couldn't make sense of the figures anymore. She leaned back in the chair and rubbed her eyes tiredly. It was nearly eleven; she had been at it for almost four hours.

She could hear voices in the living room but paid no attention to them. Val and Denny seemed to have an almost constant stream of visitors, and Jessie had come to ignore the activity. It usually didn't relate to her in any way unless she chose to participate.

She would be going back to work at the first of the week. Three days. Jessie pushed down the sudden surge of fear she felt when she thought about leaving the house, being out on the streets, in the shop. She didn't know if they knew exactly where she lived, but they did know exactly where she worked. What if they came back? The newsletter was out again. Maybe they had seen a copy. Probably, she thought quietly. It was one of the things they told her she had to stop. Jessie lit a cigarette. She rubbed her belly gingerly, feeling the ridge of fresh scar tissue where she had surgery. The incision itched, and now it ached from tension, from sitting too long in the chair, leaning over the books.

Jessie moved from the chair to the bed, pressing back against the pillows. What was she trying to prove? She had fought the depression for days, rationalizing that it came only from being confined, inactive. But it crept into her constantly, every time she dropped her guard the slightest bit. What was she going to prove? Maybe they were all just spinning their wheels. Who could stop those men? Kate might have had a point. A few women against so many men? Men who would batter and even kill. What would they do next time? Jessie knew there were few options left to them. If the beating and the. . .rape didn't stop her, then what would? She shuddered in spite of herself.

When Val had asked her about continuing the newsletter, Jessie had wanted to say no. Now, she wasn't sure if she was being brave or foolish. Since she had said to go on, put out another issue, she had had terrible dreams about the men coming for Val, for Denny, for Laura. She dreamed she was there, watching, but could do nothing to stop what was happening. All her movements were in slow motion as she tried to intercede. It was not an unlikely consequence; Jessie knew that now.

And what would she do if indeed that happened? Someone might get killed next time. *Next time.*

Jessie put out the cigarette in the ashtray and slowly swung her legs over the side of the bed as she sat upright. It was something they all needed to discuss. In fact, an attack on one of the other women felt very probable considering all that had happened already.

A brief knock on the door was quickly followed by Val's head as she peered around to see if Jessie was sleeping. "Is this racket bothering you at all? We can ask them to leave if it is."

Jessie shook her head. "No. It's fine."

"Thought I'd check. How're the books coming?"

"I'm almost finished. Feels good to be doing something instead of just sitting around."

"I'll bet it does. I forgot to bring up your mail before, so I thought I would run it up. Here you go." Val dropped a handful of envelopes on Jessie's lap. "I'm going back down. Yell if you need me for anything."

"Sure. Enjoy yourself."

Val glanced upward. "What I would most enjoy right now is some quiet time." With that, she left the room and closed the door behind her.

Jessie glanced through her mail, an assortment of advertisements, solicitations, announcements. One envelope caught her attention. It was hand-addressed to her in a block print that looked familiar. There was no return address on it. She ripped open the flap and pulled out a single folded sheet of paper.

We visited your house and tried to make you understand. We visited you and tried to make you understand. We are always here, even if you don't see us. The newsletter is out again, and you haven't spoken with the D.A. You've had your last warning.

There was no signature. It was the same print that had been on the other notes. Jessie stared at the paper for a long time, her hands shaking, her mouth dry. Then she balled up the sheet and threw it across the room. Rubbing her forehead anxiously, she suddenly clenched her fists and rose to her feet.

"I can't stand this!" she shouted. "I can't stand it anymore!"

She did not hear the knock on the door or hear Kate enter the room. When she turned, Kate stood there with one hand on the knob, a frown on her face. "Jess, are you all right?"

"No!" Jessie screamed at her. "I am not all right! I am *not* all right! I haven't been all right in a long time. My house was trashed. My dog was killed. I was beaten up. I was raped. I am scared shitless to go outside. There are men threatening to kill me and hurt my friends. I have a lover who won't even talk about what's happening. And I have to testify at a trial against a fucking murderer. I am not all right!"

"It'll be okay, Jess. . ."

Jessie whirled around, her fists clenched and her face drawn in rage and fear. "Don't mouth platitudes at me, Kate Robbins! I'm not some damned Pollyanna. I have a very good sense of reality right now. I had it beaten into me three weeks ago. And if you came here to just sit and stare and not talk, then you can just get the hell out of my room. Get out of my house! If that's all we can do together, then we don't need to even try. I can't deal with your silence. I feel like you're holding me personally responsible for everything that's happened. You sit there, and it feels like you're passing some kind of judgment. I can't stand it!"

Kate pulled away from Jessie's anger as if Jessie had struck her. She leaned against the door and watched Jessie pace across the room, her arms folded tightly against her stomach. For a moment she wanted to leave, to run from the room and never come back. She didn't want to deal with this, with what had happened to this woman who was her lover. And Kate loved Jessie more than she had ever loved anyone else. She knew that if she left the room, Jessie would never allow her to come back.

Jessie had stopped pacing, and now she stood staring at Kate, aware that Kate was making some kind of decision. The pain Jessie was feeling had little to do with her injuries; it hurt to see that Kate had to think about what to do. Silently, stonily, Jessie steeled herself to watch Kate walk out the door.

"Goddamn them!" Kate hissed suddenly. "Goddamn them all! Every last fucking one of them! They're going to do it to us. They *have* done it. There's no sense in even trying to pretend we can have something they can't destroy." She turned and walked to the window, her movements abrupt and jerky.

Jessie listened. She heard what Kate said, but her own pain was too great to consider fully what she had just been told. "Are you saying that we have nothing left? That they've taken it all? I don't believe that, Kate, but I don't have the strength to argue with you about it. They can take nothing unless we give it to them! But if that's the way you feel, then you should just leave. I can fight them or I can fight you, but I can't do both." Jessie lit another cigarette, burning her finger in the process. "Do you know what it's like to lay here night after night and wonder about every sound? Every squeak? Always wondering if they're here, if they're coming after you? Do you have any idea. . ."

"Yes!" Kate shouted as she whirled around. "Yes, dammit, I do know! You don't have any monopoly, you know. I have a brother, Jessie. A brother who is five years older than me. When I was twelve years old, he came home from a date one night drunk and mad because the girl wouldn't sleep with him. He came into my room and he raped me. He pinned me down to my bed, held his hand over my mouth, and he raped me! And it wasn't just once. He raped me many times, over and over, until he left home three years later. I was terrified. He convinced me that *I* would be held responsible if I told anyone. He said no one would ever believe me, that it was his word against mine. So every night, for three years, I lay in my bed, and I listened to every sound. I jumped at every noise. I never knew when he would suddenly show up. He left home when I found out I was pregnant, and I threatened to tell my folks that he was the father. He left in the middle of the night. And when I did tell mama that I was going to have a baby, and when I tried to tell her Rick was the father, she slapped me so hard I saw stars. She told me if I ever said that again, she would ship me off to a home somewhere. So I had to keep quiet. I had the baby, and she was put up for adoption. So yes, I know damned well how you feel! And right now, I relive it every time you mention what happened to you.

"I survived being beaten by my father and raped by my brother. Val survived being gang-raped. Laura survived a severe beating. Moon was shot and left for dead. We all survived! You will survive what happened to you, too. But dammit it, Jessie, I don't know what to do for you or say to you because it hurts so much. It hurts to know it happened to you because I love you. But it also hurts because I cry for me, too."

The tension left Jessie's body so quickly that she nearly sagged. A strange silence filled her as she reached out and pulled Kate to her, burying her face in the softness of Kate's neck, breathing in the scent of her, feeling Kate's tension also ease as she held Jessie tightly.

Then it was all there, sitting on the edge of everything—the hurt, the fear, the total terror—bringing the memories she had pushed down, the feelings she had not allowed herself to vent or experience. Her body became rigid as Jessie fought for control, fought not to give in.

Kate held her as tightly as she dared, trying to remember the injured body, wanting only to draw her inside, wanting to rub away all that had happened, wanting to heal her mind, heal her soul.

"No, Jess," she whispered. "Please don't hold it back. Please don't do that. Let it go, baby. Let it go."

The wrenching cry was painful as everything broke loose in Jessie. The tears came, not restrained, but hard and deep, pulling loose with tearing sobs that shook her entire body, turning her inside out through her feelings, then back again slowly as she reached for the hurt she had not touched before.

Jessie leaned into the circle of Kate's arms, weak and shaken, her body convulsed in spasms from muscles strained from crying. She could feel wetness on her shoulder and knew Kate was crying, too.

Finally, it eased. There were more tears, but her body refused. Exhausted, Jessie held onto Kate's shoulders, her lips pressed tightly together against the pain that rose in waves from her belly. She looked wordlessly at Kate, wanting to talk to her, wanting to explain the tears. Then she realized that she did not have to speak. Kate's eyes were soft with understanding and quiet.

Without undressing, the two women lay down across the bed, arms wrapped firmly around each other. Jessie quickly, almost instantly, drifted into a deep dreamless sleep, while Kate held her fiercely close and rubbed her back gently.

14

"Now that is what I call a good meal, Valerie," Moon said as she rose from the table and started stacking dishes.

Val laughed. "Lord, Moon, no one has called me that in years. It sounds so strange."

"I'll bet. I remember Bob calling you Valerie. *Valerie,* he would say in that authoritative voice of his, *Valerie, I think you should. . .* and then he would proceed to tell you what and how to do everything."

"It was pretty awful, wasn't it?"

Moon grinned at her. "Well, I did often wonder how you put up with him, especially when I saw how mad he made you."

Laura took the dishes from Moon's hand and placed them in the sink. "We were so bad in those days, Val. After one of those meetings where Bob did all the talking, corrected you in everything you ventured to say, told you everything you were supposed to do, Moon and I would go home and lay in bed, thinking all sorts of things we'd like to do to him."

"Like what?" Val asked, her interest piqued.

"Oh, things like tying his beard in a thousand little knots. Or kidnapping him and putting him in a room where he was told everything to do and exactly how he had to do it. Or gagging him so he couldn't talk for at least a week."

"And those were the *nice* fantasies," Moon added with a deep laugh.

"Nicer than mine," Val said with a nod. "I must have thought about castrating him at least a dozen times a week."

"He was so obviously gay, Val. I wonder whatever became of him?" Laura mused, running hot water over the dishes.

"I have no idea, but I hope he didn't find another woman to hide behind."

"Come out, come out," Moon sang as she shouldered Laura aside and reached for the sponge to wash the dishes. "I wonder how many men bully women in order to hide their lust for other men?"

"That would make a fascinating study, Moon," Laura said, pouring herself another cup of coffee.

"Wouldn't it though?"

The silence was comfortable in the warm kitchen. Moon washed dishes, and Val dried them and put them away. Laura lit a cigarette, ignoring Moon's look of protest. The dishes finished, Moon leaned over her and gave her a resounding kiss on the mouth.

"I love you in spite of your awful habits."

"That's good to know," Laura grinned, continuing to smoke.

"So how is Jessie doing?" Moon asked Val, who was hanging the dish towel on the door handle of the refrigerator.

Val picked up her coffee cup and refilled it. "She seems to be doing a little better. Not so jumpy as she was. The trial is only a month away, and I've sort of been expecting her to say something about it but she hasn't."

"I expect she's pretty nervous, whether or not she's saying anything."

"I agree," Val answered. "She got a letter in the mail last week, obviously from the same men. It was another threat telling her she had had her last warning."

Moon whistled softly. "How did she handle that?"

"I'm not completely sure how she's dealing with the threat itself. She's scared something is going to happen to one of us."

"Have she and Kate even begun to get it together?" Laura asked.

"That's the interesting thing. The night Jessie got the threatening note, Kate came to her room. Jessie was in a state, very freaked out and very angry, and she let loose at Kate, telling her that they were either going to have to deal with it, or she wanted Kate to get out and leave her alone."

"It, meaning the note, or it, meaning Jessie and Kate?" Moon interjected the question.

"It, meaning Jessie and Kate. She didn't tell Kate about the note that night. Well, it seems Kate got really pissed, too, because Kate thought Jessie assumed Kate didn't know what it was like to be raped and afraid and Kate let fly at Jessie."

"Whew. Sounds like a mess."

"Sure could've been," Val agreed, "but it wasn't. Kate finally told Jessie why she had been so closed up the whole time Jessie was in the hospital."

"Why?" Laura wanted to know.

"Kate was a battered child, but she was also an incest victim, raped repeatedly by her older brother for several years. Seems she even had a baby by him. Kate was having a hard time with all that in addition to trying to deal with the fact that her lover had almost been killed and raped. Moon is right: it is a mess. But from what Jessie told me, everything came out that night, and they are talking it through. Slowly, she said. Neither of them really knows exactly what to say or do to help the other, but Jess said she feels like just knowing is pretty powerful to them right now."

"I'm glad to hear it," Moon said quietly. "They could give each other a lot of suport."

"Is Jessie still planning to come back to work on Monday?"

Val glanced at Laura. "As far as I know. We talked a little about that. She is scared to death to go to the shop. Too many associations there for her. It's perfectly understandable, but she wants to go anyway. She showed me that last note. I know she's worried that the men may show up at work. We talked a little about security, and she seemed relieved to know someone else was thinking about it, too. I don't think she ought to be left alone for a while, at least not until after this damned trial is over."

"Jessie's pretty independent. How does she feel about having one of us trailing around after her?"

"Right now, I think she wants it. I don't blame her. If it were me, I wouldn't want to be left alone. She knows that once it looks like things have really cooled off, we'll stop. I'm feeling pretty protective of her, and of myself, too. It doesn't seem at all unlikely that those men would try to get to her through one of us."

"Well, this way we can all look out for one another," Moon said with finality. "I'm not too old to enjoy the possibility of kicking a few asses myself."

Val laughed. She had seen Moon 'kick asses' before, years ago. "How old are you, Moon?"

"Forty-seven and proud of every second," Moon answered with satisfaction.

"You should be. I'll be forty next month," Val said.

Moon leaned over the table and patted Val's hand. "Just you wait."

Jessie wiped the ink from her hands with a dirty rag and dropped it on top of a paper box. She lit her third cigarette of the day, sat down on the stool, and stared at the press as she smoked.

She had been back at work for almost two weeks, and she was finally beginning to stop jumping at every sound. Maybe the men would not return. Maybe. Laura, quietly and without mentioning the reason behind it, had started carrying the trash out to the dumpster every night, making the daily trip that Jessie had usually made in the past. Both of them unobtrusively checked the lock on the back door several times a day. Jessie often found herself staring at the lock, filled with a sudden panic that would temporarily immobilize her, leaving her body stiff with fear, her breathing short and ragged. After noticing this reaction, Laura had taken to announcing the source of sudden noises, the dropping of a package of paper, the slamming of a door or drawer, the characteristic tapping of her metal ruler on the side of the light table.

Jessie could hear Laura locking up the front office. It was after six, time to go home. Jessie took off her denim printer's apron and draped it over the press. She no longer stayed late hours working alone. She knew Val or Denny or Kate would be waiting outside to drive her home and that Laura would walk her to the car before heading off to her own.

Jessie was already feeling restrained in her movements. She was rarely alone, except when sleeping, a fact that she both welcomed and resented at the same time. She craved isolation, and she feared it.

Jessie rode home with Kate in silence, her mind elsewhere, her body tired from standing over the press almost all day. She was comfortable with Kate's presence as she watched passing sights without really seeing anything. There were Christmas decorations everywhere, and she blanked them out. The season depressed and angered her, making her feel even more the outsider for her rejection of it.

Shaking her head, Jessie turned her thoughts to what she wanted to do when she got home. Evenings at home now were given to all the things she had had no time for in the past—things such as writing, playing her guitar, talking with Val and Denny, planning the newsletter, even cooking, something Jessie dearly loved but had not done in a long time because of work and meetings. Val and Denny were wonderful to cook for because they were so open to trying new foods and got very excited over Jessie's experimentations. Kate preferred tried-and-true dishes and was frequently skeptical when Jessie suggested variations.

Kate stopped the car in the driveway. The house was dark. She reached for Jessie's hand and squeezed it lightly. "Can I come in for a while?"

Jessie glanced at the dark windows and nodded. "I wish you would. It doesn't look like anyone else is at home yet."

"Want me to stay until Val or Denny gets here?"

"Yes." Jessie was silent for a moment, and then she sighed. "I feel silly sometimes always wanting to have someone around. And yet, I want to be alone, too."

"I don't think it's silly, Jess."

Jessie smiled an acknowledgment and got out of the car. Kate followed closely and waited on the top step while Jessie unlocked the door. She watched the motion of Jessie's wide shoulders as she pulled the mail from the box and bent to pick up the newspaper. Then Kate looked away, trying to ignore the warm ache in her lower stomach. It had been almost two months since they had made love. But it was completely up to Jessie she reminded herself. Completely. She did not have the right to make that demand.

Kate stood by the small, cluttered desk in Jessie's room, glancing at the pile of papers balanced precariously next to the old typewriter. She could hear water running in the bathroom and the sounds of Jessie brushing her teeth.

"Are you writing again?" she called out.

Jessie stepped into the room. "I'm trying to."

"What are you working on?"

"Nothing very coherent. Lots of thoughts. Nothing that quite fits together. Mostly, I've been keeping a journal and going back through some of the stuff I wrote several years ago. But the journal is especially nice because things don't have to fit together there."

"That's true."

Jessie pulled off her sweater and tossed it on the bed. She caught Kate looking at her as she unbuttoned her shirt. Crossing the room, she pulled Kate close and kissed her cheek.

"I love you, Kate."

There was a long silence. Kate was stunned by the words. She pulled back so she could see Jessie's face. "You've never told me that before."

"I know." Jessie's voice was quiet.

"Did you just decide?"

"No," Jessie answered, rubbing her face against Kate's collar. "I've known it for a while."

"Why didn't you tell me?"

"I wanted to know what it meant when I said it."

"What does it mean?" Kate asked softly. She stroked Jessie's back then reached under the shirt to feel her ribs under her fingertips. She kissed Jessie's ear and waited, willing herself to be still and quiet.

"I was very idealistic, Kate," Jessie answered finally. "I wanted you to share that idealism with me and was pretty upset when I found out you didn't, and probably wouldn't. And then you were my first real lover, the first woman I had ever been to bed with. I wanted to care about you, love you, but I didn't want to be too involved. And I didn't want to be in love. I wanted to avoid that huge emotional upheaval almost every woman I've ever talked to said she had over and with her first lover. I wanted us to be radically different from everyone else, find completely new ways of being together."

"So are we just like everyone else?"

"No," Jessie said as she shook her head, "but I think we're only now beginning to find the new ways. Perhaps because of what's happened recently. You're my friend, Kate, my best friend."

"I'm glad. We almost weren't friends at all."

"I know. But everyone has their limitations. I'm just glad that wasn't one of yours."

Kate again leaned back so she could see Jessie's face. "You don't believe in forevers, do you?"

"I just hope for them. I am enough of an idealist to hope that they exist."

Kate felt relieved. Jessie had always been demonstratively loving and caring but had never been verbally expressive at all. Kate had often wondered exactly what Jessie was feeling but had never had the courage to ask. She trusted the overt physical signs as much as she dared rather than risk hearing truths she wasn't prepared to hear.

"Well then," Kate said with a grin, "if you don't believe in forevers, how long do you think we're good for? Any projections?"

Jessie rolled her dark eyes towards the ceiling, a glint of humor on her face. "For at least the next few hours."

Only Jessie's quick movement prevented Kate from nipping her ear. Laughing, she pulled Jessie tightly against her, nuzzling her neck playfully.

Jessie felt the sudden change in Kate. She felt the slight flutter in the other woman's stomach, the small tightening of her fingers, the deeper breathing. A momentary chill spread through Jessie. Kate wanted her. She didn't know if she could let Kate touch her, caress her. How could she tell Kate that?

She rubbed the small of Kate's back, circling wider to touch shoulder blades, hips, pressing Kate gently closer. Then Jessie felt her own ripple of wanting and the stab of fear. It was too soon, too soon for her. Kate drew back and looked at her, as though she had felt it, too.

There was an unusual stillness in Kate as she waited, a stillness Jessie could almost touch. She trailed her hands lightly up Kate's belly, pausing to feel the familiar curve of breasts against her palms, then down over the slight ridges of ribs, to pull once more at Kate's hips. She could feel Kate tremble as she leaned closer to Jessie, her body softening under Jessie's fingers. Jessie stroked her, remembering the fierceness of their lovemaking, the give and take that left them both breathless and exhausted afterwards. It did not ease the knot in her stomach when she felt Kate's hands moving on her back.

Shyly, they undressed and lay down together on the bed. Kate was silent and restrained, watching the expressions on Jessie's face as the younger woman leaned over her, her hand stroking lightly, insistently, uncertainty flickering in her eyes from time to time. Finally, Kate closed her own eyes and concentrated only on the growing urgency in her body, the heavy ache in her thighs. Jessie's hand slid into her softly, lightly coaxing her out, slowly, carefully drawing her to the crest, holding her there, then cupping her tightly as the waves broke and Kate cried out, her hand over Jessie's, pressing her fingers closer and holding them until she stopped shaking.

Jessie sighed softly as she leaned down and kissed Kate. Kate's grip was firm as she pulled Jessie close to her and whispered, her mouth against Jessie's ear, "I want to make love to you, too."

Jessie was still, her face resting on Kate's shoulder. She felt the fear, the twist of panic, the sudden move that could bring it all back, the weight of a body that would make her feel cold grass beneath her, the movement of a hand turning into a fist. She felt Kate's hand softly stroking her back, the touches light, careful. Jessie shook her head gently, no.

"I need more time, Kate. I don't think I'm ready for that yet. I'm sorry. . ."

Kate hushed her with a finger pressed softly against her mouth. "Don't be sorry. It's okay."

Kate was conscious of every movement she made, of every motion of hand and body. She wanted to press herself into Jessie's flesh and remove the hurt when she pulled away, like removing the mold from the newly cast form, fresh, untouched. Instead, she rubbed Jessie's back, shifting her position slightly so their bodies fit together. As she felt Jessie relax into sleep, Kate pulled the blankets over them, carefully reached for the lamp, and turned out the light.

15

"Look, why don't *I* just pick up the copy proofs and bring them to you later? I'll be over that way, and I'm already closer to the shop than you are . . .No, I'm not particularly thrilled about it but it's the simplest arrangement, and it won't take but just a few minutes. . .That's fine, Val. I have to get off now. I still have to take a shower, and I don't want to be late for the beginning of the film. . .That one is towards the end of the film festival. I'll pick up a schedule for you while I'm there. . .Okay. 'Bye." Laura replaced the receiver in the cradle with a little more force than was necessary to break the connection. She hated to talk on the telephone anyway, but was especially impatient when she was trying to get out of the house. Muttering to herself, she stood up and headed towards the bathroom. She was going to be late. And she was slightly grumpy that she had hooked herself into an extra chore. Damn, she thought as she leaned into the shower and turned on the hot water. Waiting for the steam, she glanced into the mirror.

"Damn," she complained to her reflection who nodded back sympathetically.

The streets were crowded with parked cars, and Laura had to circle the block twice to find an empty space. Even the parking area at the shop was full. Her muttering intensified as she fought to fit her car into a space made almost too small by the vehicle behind. Moon sat passively in the passenger seat, knowing from past experience that saying nothing was vastly more important at a moment like this than having any sort of alternative suggestion. She also knew Laura was completely exasperated with the Afro Film Festival because of the emphasis on African men and the male traditions. She maintained her silence, only occasionally giving Laura long looks from the corner of her eye.

"I'll be right back," Laura said shortly, as she removed the keys from the ignition.

"Afraid I'm gonna steal the car?" Moon asked mildly.

"No!" Laura's tone was one of exasperation. "It's just that I'm so used to. . .Oh, forget it." She got out of the car and slammed the door. Moon watched as Laura stood tapping her foot, waiting for the traffic to clear so she could cross the street.

Jaywalking, Moon thought, remembering being arrested on that very trumped up charge during a demonstration in Mississippi. Ridiculous as it had been, Moon had never jaywalked again, crossing instead at marked intersections and always with the lights. "I do learn, oh yes, I do," she said softly to herself. Then she settled back in the seat to wait.

She could see the shop from where she sat in the car. Lights were on inside.

"That's odd," she mused aloud. "Laura is going to be some kind of pissed off if she finds one of the other women there to pick up those page proofs." Moon watched the building, humming tunelessly to herself. Something about it bothered her. Just a feeling. Like something wasn't just quite right.

Laura approached the building slowly. No one was supposed to be there, she thought angrily. That was the whole reason for *her* coming to the shop. She started to insert the key into the lock, but a small alarm went off inside her head. Maybe she should just check first. Peek in the side window. Quietly, she went around the building.

Moon had spotted her and was already pulling herself out of the car when Laura skidded to a stop beside the door.

"There are three men in there!" she said breathlessly.

"What are they doing?"

"They've got a whole lot of paper piled in the middle of the floor. It looks like they're going to set fire to the place. They have cans of solvent sitting next to the paper."

Moon was reaching into the back floorboard of the car. "Call the cops," she said as she stood upright, an ax handle in her hand.

"What are you going to do?" Laura gasped.

Moon grinned at her. "Just gonna keep an eye on things until the cops get here is all. Go on and call them. And call Jessie, too," she said over her shoulder, starting to cross the street.

Laura watched her, indecision all over her face. "Girl!" she said to herself, then ran down the street to the telephone booth.

"Let's do it and get out of here!" Edgar said angrily. "We can't hang around this place all night."

"All right, all right. Just pour this solvent all over the paper and scatter it around on the equipment too. Hank, you got matches?"

Hank nodded. "I've got plenty of matches. Let's go, boys!"

Moon watched quietly through the window, staying back as far as she could. There was no way to go inside and stop them without the risk of being seriously hurt. She hefted the ax handle from her left hand to her right. But just wait until they came through the door, she thought. A small smile crossed her mouth as she remembered the face of the Kluxer who had ripped off his hood so he could aim better at her that night. She remembered the way the bullet had felt when it slammed into her shoulder, knocking her to the ground with a force she had never felt before. Yeah, she remembered how bad it had hurt before she passed out. Just wait until they came out the door. Her grip on the handle tightened with anticipation.

She heard the sound of the siren. Obviously the men inside heard it, too. Their movements picked up speed as they scattered the flammable chemical around the room. They all lit matches and tossed them onto the pile of paper. It caught almost immediately.

"Let's get out of here!" Moon heard one of them say. She glanced in once more to make sure she knew which door they would use as an exit and then, smiling, she grabbed the ax handle with both hands and crouched down.

Moon heard Laura behind her and did not look back when Laura touched her shoulder. "It's me, Moon."

"Ssshhhh! Give me room, honey. Give me room!" Moon whispered.

Laura moved back a step, glancing around for something to use as a weapon should she need one. There was nothing. She crouched, waiting.

The door to the shop flew open, and a tall man charged out, the flames back-lighting him so Moon's aim was perfect. She swung the ax handle. It cracked into the man's ribs with a jolting thump. The man screamed with pain and fell to the ground, drawn up and out cold. Probably broke 'em all, Moon thought with satisfaction. Drawing back, she waited for the other two. But no one came out.

The fire was spreading rapidly. Soon the whole room would be in flames. Edgar looked at Hank, terror spreading all over his face.

"We gotta get out of here!"

"Go!"

"You crazy? Someone just keeled Tom over like he was a goddam matchstick!"

Hank shoved him towards the door. "You want to burn to death, you idiot? Get out of here!" Hank pushed him through the open door, hoping Edgar would draw the attention of whoever was out there so that he could make a run for it. He watched as Edgar landed on top of Tom, out like a light. Who the hell was out there? Hank broke into a sweat, undecided. The heat from the fire seared his face when he turned back towards the room. But he didn't want his skull fractured either. He could hear the wail of the police siren as it drew close to the building. He had to get out before they got there. If they saw him. . . The flames were pushing him towards the door. He backed away from them. No choice.

"Hey!" he shouted. "Hey! I'm coming out! Don't hit me! I'm coming out! I'm not armed or anything, I swear! But I have to come out!"

A loud laugh answered him. Then, "You'd better crawl, mister. You'd better crawl out of there."

Hank stared through the doorway, straining to see who was there. "I'm not crawling!"

"Then burn, fella. Your life is not worth a damned thing to me."

Something singed his elbow. With a shout of fear and rage, Hank jerked off his jacket and threw it on the floor, aware that the sleeve of his shirt was smoking. "I'm coming out!" he shouted in desperation. He dropped to his hands and knees. "I'm crawling out!"

Even on his hands and knees, Hank was out of the building in a matter of seconds. He leapt over Tom and Edgar who lay, unmoving, on the ground. Still in forward motion, over which he had little control, Hank felt someone grab his shirt collar and haul him to his feet. Then he felt cold metal through his shirt as he was pushed roughly over the hood of a car and searched. Handcuffs dug painfully into his wrists, and he was shoved through an open door. It was a police car and, thank god, it wasn't on fire. Hank looked up to see a massive woman standing by the door, a huge grin on her face. She held a stick of some sort in her hands. She leaned forward and studied him for a moment.

"You know, I'm almost sorry you didn't come out of there standing on your feet. It would've given me the greatest of pleasure to help you join your friends." Then she laughed and walked away in the company of a serious-looking young officer.

Hank began to tremble. He was cold. And he was scared. He could go to jail for a long time for arson. At the very least, they would kick him off the force. Trying to get hold of himself, he began mentally running down his list of contacts. Someone could help him. Someone. He had to get his story straight, make it look like it was all Tom and Edgar. Think, he told himself silently. *Think*!

Jessie studied the ruins. That was already how she mentally thought of the business. It was still smoking, even though the fire had been put out twelve hours ago. The insurance claims adjuster was supposed to meet her there at ten o'clock. She had a few minutes left to wait.

There was a detached calm to her as she walked slowly around the building. Maybe if the police department had called a fire unit when they received the emergency call, maybe then the place could have been saved. If, if, if. If wouldn't buy her a thing. It would take a while to get a settlement. What would she do now? What would Laura do? The business was a total loss. Between the fire itself and the water damage nothing could be salvaged. She poked at the smoking rubble with the toe of her shoe. She had cried last night. No tears today. Today, she needed to think.

Kate stayed a discreet distance away, unwilling to let Jessie out of her sight. She remembered the expression on Jessie's face when they had arrived the night before only a few seconds after the fire department, the look as Jessie helplessly watched the fire, the look of utter horror and terror as Jessie saw the faces of the men who had done this damage. Kate had thought Jessie was going to faint and had grabbed her fearfully. All Jessie could get out was "those men, those men," over and over until Kate finally understood: they were the men who had beaten and raped her. At that, Kate and Val had taken Jessie to the car to wait.

The police had insisted that Moon and Laura come to the station with them so they could give statements. Two of the men who started the fire had to be taken to the hospital. The other had shot looks of complete hatred at them through the window of the police car. Jessie had also gone to the police station, although the officers had little to say to her once they established her identity other than that they were sorry, and that they had the men in custody with positive identification and eyewitnesses to their actually dropping the matches. Kate had stayed with Jessie while they waited for several long hours for Laura and Moon to finish giving their statements.

Then they had gone home. Jessie had not slept. She was too numb to sleep, too numb to talk. Kate had finally dropped off from sheer exhaustion on the sofa while Jessie sat in the chair, smoking and drinking beer.

Laura's car pulled up, and she and Moon got out. Laura looked worried. They stood beside Kate, and the three of them watched Jessie silently for a moment.

"Is she okay?" Laura asked.

"I think so," Kate answered. "How are you holding up?"

"Tired, child. I am tired. This is bad enough. I can't even imagine what it must feel like for this to be happening to Jessie on top of everything else that's already gone down."

"It's not easy for you either," Kate said.

"No," Laura agreed. "It definitely is not."

"Maybe the claim won't take too long," Moon offered. "Then you two can get set up again."

"That's what I'm hoping." Laura did not look convinced.

"I am so glad the police caught those three guys last night. They were the same three men who beat up and raped Jessie. And one of them is a cop."

Moon looked hard at Kate. "Really?"

"Yeah."

"If I had known that," Moon said softly, "I would've hit them even harder. And I sure would've nailed that last one, too."

The look on Kate's face was puzzled. "What are you talking about?"

Laura smiled, nudging Moon with her elbow. "This one got to play out one of her life-long fantasies last night. She got to pole-ax two of those three men."

"Pole-ax? I don't get it."

"Simple. I waited outside the door with an ax handle. I got the first guy right in the ribs. I got the second guy right over the top of the head. And I made the third guy crawl out on all fours to keep me from popping him, too. And woman, it felt soooo good."

"You're the one who laid them out?"

None of them had heard Jessie's approach. She stared at Moon, the beginnings of a delighted smile playing across her face. "You did that, all by yourself?"

"With unlimited pleasure."

"Moon, you absolutely amaze me sometimes. Why don't you let me buy you and Laura a drink tonight?"

"You got it. Well, I think that's your man over there. He's got the looks of an insurance guy."

Jessie and Laura both grinned as they turned and walked towards a young man in a grey overcoat. Moon glanced at Kate.

"Let's wait in the car. It's freezing out here."

16

The room was crowded and conversation was animated as Jessie pushed her way through to the kitchen. Val had said she wanted a good party for the solstice, and it looked like she was getting her wish. Kate was operating the tap on the beer keg and gestured to Jessie, asking if she wanted a refill. Jessie shook her head. She had been drinking entirely too much over the past four months. She needed to cut down.

Jessie was enjoying herself in spite of her earlier doubts about being in a party mood. The thought of so many women crowding her home had been disturbing at first. But she had loosened up as the evening progressed, talking with many women she rarely saw anywhere other than parties. And even though she still didn't quite feel fit enough to dance, it was very pleasant to watch everyone else.

Jessie found an ashtray and worked her way back through the crowd into the living room. Leaning against the stair railing, she smoked and indulged the moment of isolation in the middle of the crowd. She remembered the other parties she had come to in this house. And she felt like an entirely different woman.

Kate's mouth was warm on her ear. "Want to dance with me?"

Someone had put a slow record on the stereo, a pace Jessie felt she could handle. She smiled at Kate.

"Sure," she answered.

They found an unoccupied corner and moved slowly together, enjoying the close feeling, the gentle touching of their bodies.

Jessie pulled Kate closer to her, letting her lead as she leaned into her, content to close her eyes and follow. It was odd to Jessie that they danced together so well. They rarely went dancing and when they did, it was at the bar, where disco music pulsated.

Jessie concentrated on the rhythm of Kate's body, the slow sway and slight dip, the feeling of Kate's breasts against her own. It was only when they danced that Jessie was ever really aware that they were almost exactly the same height. Jessie relaxed, letting the sensual closeness seep into her, feeling her body warm and begin to open to Kate. She did not open her eyes, afraid that the feeling would go away if she acknowledged the surroundings. It seemed like a long time since she had felt like this.

Kate felt the change, too. She breathed lightly into Jessie's ear, holding her close, her hands pressed firmly against the small of Jessie's back. She wanted to whisk her away to some private corner. But instead she danced, barely moving, all her attention locked onto the woman she held against her.

The sudden shift to hard-driving disco music momentarily stunned them both, abruptly breaking the mood between them. Jessie stepped back with a rueful grin.

"I think I need to put a little distance between me and this music for a while," she said.

Kate glanced uncertainly at the door. "I would suggest a walk, but it's awfully cold out there."

"I was thinking I would just go up to my room for a little while." Jessie practically had to shout to be heard over the music. She wondered how long the neighbors would be willing to put up with the noise before starting to complain.

"Oh," was all Kate said.

"You could come with me."

Kate grinned. "I would like to."

Jessie grabbed her hand and they went up the stairs hastily, both vibrating from the noise neither was used to or particularly cared for. It was not completely quiet in Jessie's room, but the decibel level was lowered considerably when she closed the door. Jessie carefully locked it behind her and smiled at Kate.

"I've already tried to come up here once before, and there were two women in here obviously also seeking privacy."

"Bet they weren't happy to see you."

Jessie laughed and pointed at the rumpled bed. "I don't think they even noticed me."

Kate laughed, too, as she dropped onto the foot of the bed. "This is much better. The noise was getting to me."

"I liked dancing with you. I wouldn't have minded if they had played another slow song."

Kate looked at Jessie, very much aware that they were talking to one another like women just getting to know each other, almost like they were seeing each other for the first time. It felt odd, but it was not completely unexpected. It was also obvious to Kate that Jessie was feeling somewhat shy and uncertain.

Very slowly, without touching her with her hands, Kate kissed Jessie. Kate felt the tension in her own body, but she held it firmly at bay, knowing that if Jessie sensed it, she might pull away. Finally, she lifted her hands to Jessie's shoulders, then ran them lightly down her arms, softly crossing the palms of Jessie's hands. Kate moved more firmly into the kiss, and she rested her hands on Jessie's thighs, unmoving for a long moment. She slowly began to unbutton the younger woman's shirt, pausing to touch soft flesh as her fingers moved upward.

The tremors that ran through Jessie were only partly desire. She fought the momentary surges of fear, wanting Kate and afraid at the same time. She tried to rationalize the fear away. But it wouldn't leave.

As they lay back on the bed, Kate leaned over Jessie and kissed her eyelids. "What do you want me to do?" she whispered.

"Go very slow. And keep your hands where I can see them."

"I love you, Jessie."

Jessie's eyes opened, and she looked at Kate. "Touch me."

Kate had never been so aware of every movement, every gesture, as she was then. When she eased Jessie's clothes off, she saw that her hands were trembling. She did as she was asked; she moved slowly, gently, carefully keeping her hands where Jessie could see them. When she finally slipped to her knees on the floor and pressed her mouth against Jessie, she reached up Jessie's body to cup her breasts. Then she slowly savored the taste and the smell of her, fighting the urge to cry.

Jessie waited for her breathing to return to normal, her fingers still locked in Kate's hair, Kate's face against her thigh. She tugged lightly at Kate's hair, urging her upward, but Kate didn't move. Then Jessie felt tears against her leg, and she sat up abruptly, pulling Kate's face up so she could see her.

"What is it? What's wrong?"

"Nothing's wrong," Kate managed to say. "I didn't think you would ever want me to love you again."

Jessie wrapped her arms around Kate and rocked her slowly.

"I wasn't sure you would ever want to," she whispered.

One of the young graduate student interns was waiting for Kate as she entered the office and immediately dropped into the chair. Five hours of sleep. Her eyes felt swollen and gritty.

Betsy waited silently, just inside the door, wanting Kate to notice her before she spoke. It was a habit that grated on Kate's nerves. She sighed softly.

"What is it, Betsy?"

"A woman came in here early this morning with two children. She's in the living room. The kids are still asleep, I think. All she would tell me was her first name and the names of the two kids and that she has to stay here. She says she can't leave this building or *he,* presumably her husband, might see her. No. She said he might *kill* her. She won't answer any questions. I thought maybe you could get more out of her since I'm not having any luck."

Kate almost groaned from tiredness. She had come in hoping almost desperately for a quiet, uneventful day, and wanting there to be someone who could take her place for a few days. She rose and retrieved the white index card from Betsy's hand without a glance at what was written on it.

"I wish these women who come here would realize that we have responsibilities and procedures and that they can't come in and expect us to change everything just for them. I mean, we're supposed to keep records. It's necessary to have records. We can't change everything to make one woman happy."

Kate stared at her. "I can't believe you said that."

"Women like her are a lot of trouble. They just plain make trouble for everyone. I have a job to do, and she's not making it easy for me to do it. I tried to tell her that but she. . ."

Kate looked at the card. On it, Betsy had written, Name: Beth. 2 male children, app. 6 and 8 yrs. old. Names: Mark and Timmy. Client refused to give *any* additional info. Withdrawn and uncooperative.

Kate glanced at her as she ripped the card in half and headed towards the door. "You have a lot to learn."

"But. . ." Betsy sputtered.

"I'll talk to you later," Kate snapped as she left the room.

Kate leaned back in the armchair and studied the small woman seated on the sofa. One child sat beside her, a sullen expression on his face. The other boy, obviously younger, sat on the floor playing with a small car.

The woman had not told her much other than she was running away from an extremely violent husband who beat her up frequently and that he had been arrested for something the woman would not reveal.

"Beth, I'm assuming you live here in Durham. Is that true?"

Beth eyed her nervously. "What difference does it make?"

"You say your husband beat you up, that he's in jail right now, but that he might be out soon. You also say you're afraid he might kill you if he finds you. The reason I asked was because I'm wondering if you think there's a chance he might find out where this shelter is located and come here looking for you. We have several women in the area who have opened their homes for us to use as hideaways for other women who are critically endangered until we can make arrangements to get them out of this area. If you feel your husband might come here looking for you, I can. . ."

"No," Beth interrupted. "I want to stay here. I couldn't go to a complete stranger's home."

Kate knew not to push. "That's fine. It's completely your decision to make, however you feel the most comfortable. Let me tell you a little bit about the shelter. Usually, women stay here for not more than ten days. By then, we normally have had the time to make arrangements for them to go elsewhere, or they leave on their own. There are three women living here now. One of them also has a son so your boys will have some company for a while." Kate shifted her position slightly. "There's food in the kitchen, and you can prepare your own meals. There's no one to do the cooking or the cleaning up, so we ask that you do the dishes and put things away after you finish. There's also a washing machine. There's no dryer, but there is a line out back. The telephone is for local calls only. If you need to make a long-distance call, you'll have to see one of the staff members."

"I don't know anyone long distance," Beth said softly.

"Okay. The only other thing I can think to tell you has to do with leaving the shelter. We ask that you do not leave. But if you must, then please tell us that you are leaving, where you are going, and when you expect to return. That way we'll know whether or not we should be worried if you aren't back in what we consider to be a reasonable amount of time."

"Not so very many rules," Beth commented.

"We don't need rules."

Beth stared at her for a moment. "Ha. . .my husband," she corrected herself quickly, "he had a rule for everything. . .And he was always changing them without telling me."

"Well, we don't do that here. I'll show you to your rooms. There's a radio and television upstairs, but you'll need to work out the use of them with the other women. We don't get involved in any disputes between women who are staying here unless it's absolutely impossible for you to settle it yourselves. You can sleep as late as you like, stay up as late as you like, eat whenever you like. One other thing. Since the kitchen is downstairs, you'll probably be downstairs fairly frequently. Refuge is staffed at all times, mostly with volunteers. The door stays locked. Please do not open it for anyone, most especially not for men. Some women's lives may depend on your following this rule. If *anyone* comes to the door, call a staff member immediately. This rule is the one we are rigid about. It's for everyone's safety. Okay?"

Beth nodded. Kate rose from the chair and led Beth and her sons to the stairway.

Beth unpacked her suitcase, carefully arranging her clothes in the drawer. Underwear was meticulously folded and placed in the order in which Beth put them on. Two sweaters went into the next drawer. Hesitating, Beth stared at the third and fourth drawers. She had always only had two for herself, the bottom two. Hank hated to have to bend down for his clothes. She didn't really have enough to warrant using a third drawer. Then, with a quick gesture, she pulled the drawer open and placed her nightgown and a sweater side by side. She closed it gently and glanced around her as though half expecting someone to question or reprove her.

Timmy sat on the edge of Beth's bed, his face drawn into a scowl as he swung his legs back and forth and stared at the floor. Beth tried to ignore him, hoping he would go back into the next room and unpack without having to be reminded.

"I don't want to stay here," he said finally, his eyes defiant as he glared at his mother.

"I know you don't."

"Then why do I have to?" he demanded.

Beth sighed as she glanced at him. She continued to put clothes on hangers and place them in the tiny closet. "Because we have no other place to go, Timmy."

Mark looked up from his play in the corner. "It's nice here. I like it."

Timmy looked at him disdainfully. "Ah, you don't know nothing. You're just a kid."

"Anything," Beth corrected him absently.

"I hate it when you tell me how to talk," he shot back.

Beth glanced at him again, hearing the baiting tone of his voice, knowing Timmy was spoiling for a fight. "We are going to stay here for a few days. There's no other place," she said.

"There is, too. There's home."

Mark looked at his mother in alarm. "I don't want to go home."

Timmy jumped off the bed and stood over his younger brother, hands on hips. "We got a home and that's where we're supposed to be."

"I've already explained this to you, Timmy. There's no reason to get into it again."

"Is my daddy in jail? Was that woman down there saying the truth?"

Beth nodded. "Yes. Your daddy is in jail. He did a very bad thing, and they put him in jail."

"But you said he would be out soon. Maybe even today," he persisted.

"That's right."

"Then we should be home when he gets there. Dad's gonna be real mad if he gets home and we aren't there."

"I'll bet he will be," Beth said softly, "but he would be just as mad if we were. Your dad is mad all the time, Timmy. It doesn't matter what we do for him. There's nothing I can do about it."

Timmy's eyes danced as he contemplated Beth, obviously

enjoying the moment. "You'll be in a lot of trouble if he gets there, and there's no supper, and the house is dark, and we're gone. He'll be madder than ever then. He'll come looking for us."

Beth turned back to him. "Timmy, I asked you to unpack your things and put them away. Do that now, please."

"Don't you tell me what to do!" he shouted angrily.

"And don't you raise your voice to me, young man! Get in there, and do what I told you!"

"You wouldn't do that if my daddy was here," he said, glowering at her.

Beth took a step towards him then stopped abruptly. "No, I probably wouldn't. But he's not here and I am. Do what I told you to do. Now, Timmy Parrish. And not another word."

Timmy stalked past her and went into the adjoining room, slamming the door behind him. Beth sat down on the edge of the bed, her body leaning forward, her hands over her face. She could feel herself trembling as she rocked slowly to and fro. Then she felt a small hand on her arm.

"Are you crying, Mom?" Mark asked.

"No, honey. I'm not crying. I just don't like to fight with your brother. I don't like to fight with anyone."

"Mom? Will you hold me?"

Beth looked at him. "Are you scared?"

Mark nodded. "A little."

"So am I," she sighed. Beth reached out and pulled him onto her lap, wrapping her arms around him and holding him close, her chin resting on the top of his head. He curled in her arms, almost like he had done when he was a baby. If only she had been able to raise them alone, maybe things would be different with Timmy. He had once been like Mark, soft and gentle, sweet as daybreak. Then Hank got hold of him. Beth kissed Mark's hair and set him on his feet.

"You'd better go help your brother unpack the suitcase. It's not fair for him to have to do it all."

"Okay." Mark turned and walked towards the other room, his steps slow. Beth could hear the two boys talking after Mark closed the door. Then the talk escalated into shouts. Beth rose to her feet. She wished just one night would pass without the two of them having a fight about something. She waited for a moment, hoping they would settle it without her becoming involved.

". . .always get what you want. . .not fair!"

"I'm the oldest. . .top bunk. . ."

". . .not fair! I want it!"

". . .do what I say, you little. . ."

Beth could hear the sounds of the scuffle, and she turned towards the door. As she opened it, she gasped. Timmy had Mark pinned against the wall and was holding him by the collar, his fist raised in the air. He looked just like Hank, his young face twisted into an ugly, killing scowl. Hearing Beth enter, Timmy released his younger brother abruptly, giving him a warning look as Mark scampered away out of reach.

"It's okay, Mom. I'm gonna have the top bunk, aren't I, Mark?"

Mark raised a tearful face to his mother. "Do I have to let him, Mom?"

"Tonight. You can have it tomorrow night."

Mark nodded and turned away, his body slumped from her betrayal. Beth left the room. As she began to close the door, she heard Timmy's voice.

"I don't care what she says. The top bunk is mine. You try to get up there and I'll break your neck. You hear me?"

Beth closed the door. She could not listen to any more of what Timmy was saying. She was afraid she might grab him and . . . She didn't know what she might do.

Sitting down on the bed, she felt her hands tremble. "He's just like Hank," she whispered to herself.

17

Hank stood on the sidewalk and stared at the dark house. No wonder he hadn't been able to get Beth on the telephone. The bus ride from the police station had been terrible. Only niggers and white trash rode those damned buses.

Searching through his pockets, Hank finally located his key. There'd better be a good reason for why she wasn't home, he thought grimly to himself. Four days, four lousy days he'd spent in jail and not a word from her. *His wife,* for god's sake, hadn't even come to see him, hadn't even come to help get him released. None of the other officers would look at him or talk to him. If it hadn't been for his friends, he might still be there. Hank thrust the door open and stepped inside, fumbling for a light switch.

"Beth!" he yelled, kicking the door closed. No one was there. He turned on lights as he went through the house. Everything was neat and clean. No note. Nothing. Maybe she had just gone to her mother's for a while.

Hank peered into the kitchen. The dishes were washed and put away. Only one cup sat in the spotless sink. He walked down the hall. The boys' rooms were empty, the beds made. Puzzled, Hank went into the bedroom he shared with Beth. It was also neat and clean, like she expected to be back any moment. Suddenly suspicious, Hank opened the closet door. Beth's clothes were gone. Cursing loudly, he yanked open drawers. Empty. He charged into Timmy's room. Gone. Beth had left and had taken the kids. Momentarily stunned, Hank sat on the edge of his oldest son's bed and stared at the floor. Where would she have gone?

He went back to the kitchen and took a beer from the refrigerator. Lighting a cigarette, he tried to think. She wouldn't have gone to her mother's house. It would be too easy for him to find her there. She had no friends, no place to hide out. Where could she have gone?

Hank drank steadily for nearly an hour, his mind plunging from Beth to his own plight. He could deal with Beth later. And he *would* deal with her, he thought, his eyes narrowing. She had some fucking nerve trying to leave him. She would never leave *him.* If anybody walked around here, *he* would be the one doing the walking.

He stubbed out his cigarette into the rapidly filling ashtray. That goddamned Jessie Pyne had come to the police station the day after they had busted him for the fire and had gotten him on the beating and rape thing, too. Got Tom and Edgar. From what Hank had been able to gather, whoever that broad with the ax handle had been had really done a number on Tom, broke nine ribs clean as a whistle. Edgar was okay, just a concussion. Hank was glad they were in the hospital. It was easier for him to think and plan with them out of the way.

Hank ran through the options. They had them clean on the fire. Eyewitnesses and everything. But the other. . .that was Jessie Pyne's word against theirs. Quickly, Hank went through his mental list of friends and allies. He could set it up with some of his buddies to get them all covered for the night they had surprised that little cunt outside her shop. They would swear on a stack of bibles that Hank had been with them all evening. Hank smiled. That's what friends were for. And besides, some of them owed him. He had saved their asses often enough. He would have to think about the arson charge later. That one was harder. He had no ideas. He would just stick to his story that he had seen the two men inside and had gone in to investigate. Hell, cops stood by each other. It would work. It had to.

Hank was scared. It made him angry because he wasn't used to being scared. His wife had run off on him. He was suspended from the force. His stomach rumbled with hunger. She should be here to make dinner. When he finally got his hands on her, he would teach her a lesson she would never forget. If she thought he had been tough before, just let her see how really tough he could be. He jerked open the refrigerator and took out coldcuts. Snorting with disgust, he made a sandwich and wolfed it down hastily. A sandwich for supper! No matter what a man had done, he deserved a hot meal when he came home.

Hank turned off the lights and went back to the bedroom. He had phone calls to make, and he needed some sleep. He hadn't slept much in four days. It was hard to sleep in the lock-up. Too much noise and too many interruptions. Stripping down to his underwear, Hank sat on the edge of the bed and reached for the telephone. A slip of paper caught his eye. Still in the process of dialing, he picked it up. It was torn from the newspaper. *SHELTER FOR BATTERED WOMEN OPEN IN DURHAM.*

Hank replaced the receiver as he scanned the article quickly. . . .*the location of the shelter is not being revealed. . .arrangements have been made. . .law enforcement officials will provide information about and transport to the shelter any woman and/or child who needs a place to stay until. . .*Maybe that's where she went, Hank thought to himself. A smile crossed his face as he picked up the telephone and dialed.

"Sergeant Bill Davis, please," he said. As he waited, Hank lit a cigarette and grinned. Thought she'd get away, did she? "Bill? Hank Parrish. . .Yeah, a bit of trouble but I'm not too worried about it. . .I appreciate that a lot. Listen, I need some information. My old lady took a walk while I was locked up, and I think she might have gone to that new shelter for women. Can you give me that address? I want to go down there and talk to her. . .That's great. Sure, I'll wait. Thanks, Bill."

Jessie turned up the collar of her coat and shoved her gloved hands deep in her pocket. The wind off the ocean was icy. The sea was grey-green with winter and an approaching storm, and she and Kate had the entire beach to themselves.

The wind made it hard for them to talk so they walked silently, their shoulders touching, until they came back to the cutoff back to the motel. There were no shells to gather; the roughness of the surf pounded them nearly to dust before they ever reached the shore.

Jessie shed the layers of clothes, the heat of the room oppressive after the cold outside. Kate stood by the stove, dicing vegetables for stew. The tiny efficiency apartment had been incredibly cheap to rent in December, but Jessie was willing to bet the price tripled when tourist season arrived.

"Can I help?" she asked as she crossed the room.

"Nope," Kate answered with a shake of her head. "It won't take but a few minutes. Then we just have to let it cook for a while."

Jessie sat down at the table, propping her feet in the chair opposite her.

"It feels good to be away for a while," she said.

"I know," Kate agreed, wiping her hands on a paper towel as she reached for the carrots and onions.

"Why don't you let me cut up the onions?"

Kate grinned. "Okay."

Jessie sat upright and began to peel. The onions were strong. Within seconds, she could feel the build-up of tears in her eyes. "I'm glad you suggested this."

"So am I. I wasn't sure I could get someone to cover for me, especially after Betsy left the shelter in such a huff. We can't afford to lose people, but I'm glad she left."

"Why?" Jessie asked, wiping her eyes gingerly on the flannel sleeve of her shirt.

"Her attitude. She was so caught up in the bureaucracy of the shelter that she didn't see the women as human beings. They were people to be catalogued, and she got pretty hot if they didn't cooperate with her paperwork. She seemed very judgmental about the women, sometimes almost like she thought they had gotten what they deserved, like she didn't always believe them. She never said that outright, but there was just something about her attitude that conveyed it. Anyway, after that last woman came to the shelter and Betsy labeled her 'uncooperative' on her card, I lost my temper. It was obvious that the woman was terrified and worried that her husband might try to kill her if he found her. It seemed completely understandable to me that she wouldn't want to give out much information about herself. She had no reason to consider us trustworthy. We're perfect strangers to her."

"Why did Betsy think she was being uncooperative?" Jessie sniffed, her nose beginning to run from the onions.

"Because all she would give us was her first name and the first names of her two boys. Nothing more. Absolutely nothing. I guess it messed up Betsy's system of order and paperwork. It's true that we do have to keep records. But identities are not part of those records. Actually, we have to keep statistics, and we can gather those without knowing a single name. I was never quite able to get that across to Betsy."

Jessie rose and added the pile of chopped onions to the simmering stew. She was hungry, wanting dinner to be ready instantly. Peering inside the refrigerator, she took out the cheese and began slicing it. Putting it on a plate and adding crackers, she opened two beers, then set everything on the table. Kate washed her hands and sat down next to Jessie, reaching hungrily for the food.

"This was a good idea. I don't think I could just wait for the stew to cook. It'll take at least a couple of hours."

Jessie grinned at her as she ate. Kate's appetite never ceased to amaze her.

She sat quietly beside Kate, comfortable with the small talk and the silence. Things felt more natural, more normal, between them now. It was a relief to Jessie. She didn't feel like she was always fighting a battle. She sipped her beer and relaxed. Coming to the beach was a good idea. They both needed the rest, and they needed time alone together, away from interruptions and responsibilities.

"Are you still wanting just a part-time job?" Kate asked.

Jessie nodded, "Yeah. I may have to take something full-time though. The college students have most of the part-time jobs already."

"If the insurance company would just get it together and pay off."

Jessie smiled. "That would help. Laura and I are still trying to decide if we want to attempt to set up the business again. It was wearing us both out completely. Laura likes the temporary typesetting jobs she's gotten, says it leaves her with enough free time to feel like a human being. So I don't know what we'll do. I think we're sort of waiting until after the trial, to see what happens."

Kate was silent for a moment. "You had nightmares again last night."

"I know."

"Do you remember what you dream?"

Jessie nodded. "Yes."

"They'll go away eventually, Jessie."

"Did yours?"

"Pretty much. I still have them once in a while but not often."

"How long?" Jessie watched her face.

Kate looked at her. "A long time."

"I thought so."

"But I never talked to anyone about what happened to me," Kate said. "I've often wondered if the dreams would've gone away sooner if I could've talked about it all."

"I called Carol Sloane last week. I have an appointment with her for next Tuesday."

"I thought you didn't want to see a therapist," Kate said, surprised.

"'I didn't. But I need some help that I don't think I can get from friends. I ran into Leslie the other day, and she asked how I was. When I said fine, she asked if I wasn't furious? I realized that I have felt almost no anger. So I called Carol. I walk around feeling like I want to cry all the time. I get uneasy talking to my friends constantly. I get tired of hearing me say the same things over and over."

"Well, I'm glad you called her."

"I think I am, too. I'll let you know after I've seen her a couple of times."

Jessie's expression was reflective. Kate watched her for a moment, then asked quietly, "What is it, Jess?"

"One of the reasons I hesitated calling Carol at first," Jessie said slowly, "was because she is a straight woman. I was worried that I couldn't talk to her about this."

"Why would that matter?"

"I know it shouldn't matter. I guess it does because those men knew they were raping a lesbian. They made sure I knew that. That was a big part of it for them. Except for one guy."

Jessie rose and went to the stove, stirring the pot of stew. Kate watched her, trying to phrase her next question carefully. Jessie still had not told her exactly what had happened. She had gotten what information she had from Val.

"What about that one guy?"

Jessie leaned against the stove and folded her arms over her chest, a frown furrowing her face. "A lot of what happened is still foggy to me. I remember lying there on the ground. I was hurting so much, I just wanted them to get it over with and go away. I don't think I had considered that they might kill me. I'm not sure it even mattered at that point. One of the men, the one called Hank, I don't think he actually raped me. It might have been my imagination, or maybe the pain level was already so high I just couldn't feel anymore. But I could almost swear he was faking it."

"Does that make you feel he was less guilty?"

Jessie shook her head immediately. "No way. I feel the same about him as I do about the other two. If he didn't actually rape me, I know he would have if he could have gotten it up. And *if* my perception of what happened is indeed accurate, he went through a pretty elaborate hoax to convince the other guys that he was in on it."

"Did he hit you?"

"No. One guy did all the hitting. Tom. He was the one who got his ribs broken by Moon. I have to admit that I never thought I would enjoy, even a little, seeing another human being hurt. But I didn't mind a bit when they carried those two off on stretchers."

"If Laura and Moon hadn't been there, they might've gotten away completely."

"Probably. But there's a huge part of me that really wishes I had been the one holding the ax handle when they came through the door."

Kate nodded. "I can understand that. I'm really glad you decided to go down and swear out warrants on all of them for what they did to you."

"Well, the cops weren't completely convinced, especially since that guy Hank turned out to be a cop himself. The hospital records are probably the only thing that will ever get it to court."

"You know," Kate mused quietly, "I overheard the new woman at the shelter tell one of the other women that her husband beat her with the buckle-end of a leather belt in addition to using his fists."

"And they wonder why women sometimes kill their husbands." With a snort, Jessie turned back to the pot of stew. Kate watched her, her mind dwelling on the small, nervous woman who was now living in the shelter.

"She won't really talk much to anyone," Kate said. "I mean Beth, the new woman. She keeps to herself, stays with her kids mostly. One of those boys, the younger one, is really a sweetie. The other one, Timmy, gives me chills. Unreasonable as it may sound, I don't turn my back on him when he's around."

"Trust your instincts," Jessie said as she reached over Kate for her cigarettes. "Who knows what sort of life he's led or what he's seen? He might just be scared to death, but I don't think being cautious around him is paranoid."

"The little one, Mark, came into the office yesterday and wanted to know if he could look at the books. I showed him a carton of kids books we got in a while ago and haven't had time to put on the shelves. He got out a stack and curled up in the chair in the corner and read for hours. I almost didn't know he was there. He and his brother are completely different."

"But how will they grow up?"

"I know," Kate sighed, "But I can keep hoping that somewhere along the line, women will be able to change their sons, that there can be a different kind of man."

"Not in our lifetimes."

"Maybe not. But women still give birth to sons, and there's nothing anyone can do about it except try to help affect that change from the moment they come into the world."

"Maybe," Jessie said, only half-believing or wanting to understand.

"Jessie, I have a great idea." Kate sat on the edge of the bed, holding a steaming cup of coffee in her hands. Jessie groaned and opened one eye.

"I'm asleep," she mumbled, pulling the covers over her head.

"No, you're not. I just woke you up. I have an idea about a temporary job for you." Kate pulled the covers down so she could see Jessie's face. "Aren't you even going to listen?"

"How long have you been up?" Jessie asked in a whisper.

"About an hour."

"Well, I haven't. I'm not awake. I haven't even had any coffee yet."

Kate pressed the cup into Jessie hands. "Here. Take this one. I can get more."

Jessie forced herself to sit upright, balancing the coffee precariously as she tried to shove a pillow behind her back. It was chilly in the room. She pulled the covers up under her chin and sipped the hot liquid from the cup. Kate returned with her own coffee and sat down once again.

"Want to hear my idea?" she asked.

"Sure," Jessie muttered into her cup.

"We just got a building fund at the shelter, for repairs and things like that. There's enough money in it to pay someone for part-time temporary work to get things fixed around the place. It's not a whole lot, a few hundred dollars, but there's enough work and enough money to keep you busy for a while."

"I'm not a carpenter, Kate."

"We don't need a carpenter. We need someone who knows how to do things practically and cheaply. You know that. Part of that money may have to go for materials, too, not just for labor. Maybe by the time you finished at the shelter, the insurance money will have come through for you and Laura. Well, what do you think?"

Jessie looked at her. "I think I see potential for an endless number of problems."

"Why?" Kate asked, her voice puzzled.

Jessie climbed out of bed and began to put on her clothes, fully awake much more quickly than was usual for her. "The main reason is that we are lovers."

"I don't understand what that has to do with anything. This is a business arrangement."

"Come on, Kate. Think about it. I would, in effect, be working for you. You would be my boss, for crying out loud. It wouldn't work. I'm not saying I'm not touched that you thought this up with me in mind but I don't think. . ."

"There's got to be a way we can think up somehow to make this work."

Jessie only half-listened to Kate's jumbled sentence. "Well, I can't think of a way right offhand."

"I don't like thinking that the fact we're lovers should influence this."

"Maybe it would be a little easier for you to understand if you were at the receiving end rather than being the one to make the offer. It gives me the shakes just to think about it." Jessie pulled the grey top to her sweat suit over her head, still shivering a little.

"Well, it's only a suggestion right now anyway. I don't administer the building fund."

"Who does?"

"Carla. After all, she's donating it."

"So I wouldn't be working for you? I would be working for her?"

"I think so."

Jessie considered it for a moment. Doing odd jobs at the shelter was a much more enjoyable thought than going back into a male-controlled printing business, even briefly. "I might consider working for Carla. Provided," she added in a definite tone of voice, "you kept strictly out of it and that we did not discuss it outside the shelter."

Kate grinned delightedly. "Deal! I'll talk to Carla as soon as we get back."

18

Kate circled the playground, one hand shielding her eyes from the sun as she peered at the children milling around the swings. No sign of him. She hadn't the vaguest idea where he could have gone. Beth had been no help, saying she didn't think Timmy knew his way around at all. He could be anywhere. Probably trying to find his way home.

"Lost someone, Kate?"

"Betsy!" Kate said, surprised to see her.

"I was just on my way to talk with you, Kate."

"Good. I'm looking for one of Beth's boys. I could use a little help."

"Timmy?"

"That's the one." Kate was exasperated.

"Did he run away?"

"He sure did. We don't have any idea where he could be so we're just sort of combing the area hoping we'll spot him."

"I'll keep an eye out, too."

Kate looked at her. "Thanks, Betsy."

Kate watched the younger woman as Betsy strolled off. The new semester had begun. Maybe that's why Betsy looked so tired. Damn him, Kate thought angrily. She had better things to do than freeze to death looking for a nasty-tempered little boy. The trial started tomorrow. Turning, she headed back across the playground. Maybe someone had found him already.

Betsy spotted him near the restrooms. Casually, she pulled her cap lower so he couldn't see her face and then slowly ambled in his direction.

Timmy sat on the ground. He was tired. He didn't know which way to go to get home. He could ask a policeman; they were supposed to help if you were lost. But if his daddy was in trouble and in jail, maybe he shouldn't talk to a policeman. And those women from that place were all looking for him. He'd seen *them,* all right. He watched the large city buses go by. He wondered if he got on and told the driver he was lost if the driver would take him home? But buses cost money, didn't they? He felt his pockets. No money. Not even a penny. But maybe if he was lost. . .Maybe if he cried and everything. He wasn't far from crying anyway.

"Hi, Timmy."

The voice in his ear almost scared him to death. He tried to get up, but his legs just wouldn't work. Then a firm hand caught his shoulder and held him still.

"I know you ran away. I know you hate that place. But your mom is probably worried sick, and you have to go back. Now you can either walk with me, or I can carry you. Your choice."

He looked up at Betsy. "My mom doesn't miss me. She has Mark."

"Mark isn't you."

"She loves him best anyway."

"Why do you think that?"

"I can tell." His voice was defiant, but his eyes were uncertain.

"How?" Betsy sat down beside him, seeming relaxed as she broke off a blade of grass and shoved it into her mouth. But she was watching him very carefully, ready to grab him if he tried to bolt away.

"The way she treats him. She's always hugging him and kissing him. She's always nice to him. She's never nice to me."

"Are you ever nice to her?"

Timmy stared at her and began to frown. "I want to go home. I want to go home to my dad. *He* loves *me* best. He said so. He says Mark is a sissy and Mom spoils him. Dad says I'm a man, tough like him." His look dared Betsy to challenge him.

Betsy shook her head. "Even men need to be loved and hugged sometimes, Timmy."

"Not my dad," he boasted. "He's the toughest. He don't need that sissy stuff. I don't want to be like Mark. Dad says that if I'm like Mark, I'll grow up to be a faggot."

Betsy blinked, her composure momentarily challenged. Her eyes narrowed as she contemplated the boy beside her. "Do you know what a faggot is?"

"Not exactly. But I do know it's almost as bad as being a nigger! And nobody wants to be a nigger. Or a faggot," he added quickly.

"Where on earth did you learn to talk like that?" Betsy asked incredulously.

"My dad. He says. . ."

Betsy stood up abruptly. "I think I've heard all about your dad that I can stand. Do you also know that your dad beats up your mom? What do you think about that?"

Timmy glared up at her. "Dad says. . ."

"That's it. Let's go." Betsy grabbed his arm and hauled him to his feet. "March, young man. And not another word out of you."

Betsy locked the door behind her and watched Timmy run up the stairs, taking the steps two at a time. Kate touched Betsy's shoulder briefly. "Thank you. Where did you find him?"

"Outside the restrooms on the other side of the park. After talking to him, I really feel sorry for Beth."

"Why is that?"

"The kid's old man is obviously one of the worst examples of a bigoted human being who ever walked the earth, and that little boy worships the ground he walks on. 'My dad says' this and 'my dad says' that. I couldn't believe what I was hearing. His father told him that if he let his mother hold him or hug him that he would grow up to be a faggot." Betsy followed Kate into the office and accepted the cup of coffee Kate handed to her. "When I asked him what a faggot was, he didn't know, but he said his dad had told him it was almost as bad as being a nigger. Can you believe that?"

"I can believe almost anything. I'm glad you found him."

"This time. But how are you going to keep him here?"

"A locksmith is coming tomorrow. We're going to have a deadbolt lock put on the door that has to be opened with a key. We should have done that a long time ago."

Betsy sat down and sipped her coffee. "That sounds like a good idea. All you have to do now is keep him in until the locksmith gets here."

Kate smiled wryly. "And that should keep us all quite busy for the next twenty-four hours."

It was quiet in the tiny office as Betsy drank her coffee and Kate smoked, staring through the window. Betsy sat her cup down on the desk and watched Kate for a moment.

"Kate, what would you say if I told you that I want to come back to Refuge to finish up my internship?"

Kate met her gaze evenly. "I guess I would ask you why."

"I want to be here."

"That's not enough, Betsy. You know that. These women come here, needing desperately to trust someone. They have to know we are on their side, that we believe them, that we don't hold them responsible for what has happened to them regardless of circumstances. This place is usually a last resort for women. They don't come here if they have any sort of alternative. The women are more important than any records or forms or statistics."

Betsy leaned forward. "Kate, I *know* that, in my head at least. But we are raised not to believe it. We are told over and over to doubt ourselves, our perceptions. We are taught to hate each other, to compete with each other, and always, always, to consider each other liars. A lot of that has to be unlearned. I know when I doubt another woman that a large part of the doubt comes from that conditioning."

"But the women at Refuge are not at a place in their lives where they can educate you, Betsy."

"I don't expect them to. But I've got a lot to learn, and unlearn, and some of that process can happen by just being here and listening."

Kate was still dubious. "I don't know. . ."

"Can we just try it? I don't even mind a probationary period."

Kate laughed. "Well, I certainly do. I object a lot to that word. Betsy, you can come back, if that's what you really want to do. But. . ."

Betsy held up her hand. "I know what that but is, Kate. You don't even have to say it."

"Okay. When will you be here?"

"When do you need me?"

"How about tomorrow? Jessie is supposed to testify at the KKK trial, and I really want to be there."

"How is she doing?"

"Scared to death."

"I'll be here."

Kate smiled at her. Tomorrow was going to be a long day.

Jessie sat as quietly as she could. She felt out of place in the large room, crowded by people, wearing a pantsuit that made her feel ridiculous. Her hands drummed nervously on her knee. Kate reached over and squeezed her wrist reassuringly. Jessie gave her a desperate look. She just wanted to get it over with.

"The state calls Jessie Pyne."

Jessie jumped when she heard her name. Kate's smile of encouragement was anything but encouraging. Kate looked sick.

Jessie started to stand up but the defense attorney rose to his feet. "Your honor, the defense requests that Jessie Pyne be excused on the grounds of extreme prejudice."

"Approach the bench," the judge said wearily, glancing at his watch. The attorney and the assistant district attorney leaned their heads close to the judge's, and all Jessie could hear were whispers. She sat down, her stomach rolling from tension.

"What is going on up there?" she whispered to Kate.

"I don't know. But they have a copy of the newsletter."

The judge was indeed looking at a copy of the newsletter Jessie helped put out. She groaned audibly and wondered if they would let her leave the courtroom if she threw up. There was obviously an animated discussion going on up there, complete with hand gestures and emphatic nods of various heads. Finally, the lawyers went back to their respective places, with the defense attorney's face a study in fury. He shot Jessie a dirty look and sat down. The judge nodded to the assistant D.A.

"Call your witness."

"The state calls Jessie Pyne."

Jessie rose and walked down the short aisle.

"So, what was it like?" Moon demanded as soon as Jessie sat down. She took a sip from the drink Moon had ordered for her and made a face.

"What is this?"

Moon glanced at the glass. "A Tom Collins. You said to order you something. I don't know what you drink. Most people can handle a Tom Collins."

"It's awful."

"Take a few more sips. Then you won't care as much. Come on, Jessie. Denny and I were the only ones who couldn't be there. Tell us what happened."

Denny nodded, her glasses slipping down to the end of her nose. "Talk, Jess."

"It was terrible. I don't ever want to have to do that again."

Moon shot her a look of total exasperation. "That tells us a whole lot. Give us details, girl. The nitty-gritty. The gore. I want a blow-by-blow accounting here."

The other women at the table laughed at Moon's antics. Jessie took another sip of the drink. It was true; it didn't taste as bad now as when she first started.

"They called me, and then the defense attorney tried to have me dismissed because I was 'extremely prejudiced,' as he put it. They had this little conference with the judge, during which the guy gave the judge a copy of the newsletter to look at. But the judge said to call me anyway. Then as soon as I got up there the defense attorney asked that I be dismissed on some other grounds. I don't remember what they were. So they had another conference during which I got a lot of dirty looks. Then the judge told the jury that they were to ignore Martin's objections and told the D.A. to proceed. As soon as Parks started to ask me questions, Martin interrupted again, saying the defense needed a recess for two hours. The judge granted it."

"Yuck, Jessie," Denny said, frowning. "Sounds awful."

"It got worse. We came back after lunch, and I went back up there. Martin objected to almost every question Parks asked me. It seemed like he was trying to play on the jury. But hell, I don't know. I know nothing about law or courtrooms. But he was after my ass. I didn't realize how bad until he started to cross-examine me. He pulled every dirty trick in the book. He brought up my association with Communist coalitions. He brought up my being arrested for civil disobedience in D.C. He brought up my being a lesbian, a *perversion* he called it. Every time he did it, Parks would object, and the judge would have it stricken from the record and told the jury to disregard it. But you could tell by the looks on their faces that they weren't about to forget one word of it."

"It was as if he were trying to prove that no matter what a bad sort his client was, Jessie was worse," Kate commented.

"He did a pretty good job of it, too."

Laura swirled her drink around in the glass. "I'll tell you what kind of lawyer he is. He's the kind that wins. If I had done something bad and I wanted to get off at all costs, he's just the sort of guy I would hire. He's dirty, unethical, and crafty—and he wins."

"Then it's over for you?" Denny asked. "That's all you have to do?"

"There's a chance I may be recalled, but it's slim. I don't want to go back. It was bad. The absolute worst thing for me is that I really think the jury will let those men go. I can't tell you exactly why I feel that way. Just the looks on their faces. They felt sorry for him, and the rest of them, too, and they hated me."

Tom sat in the chair, his feet propped on the coffee table. He moved very slowly, obviously still in a great deal of pain.

"So what did you come over here to tell me?" he asked.

Hank rubbed his hands together. "Charlie, Dave, and Jim are all prepared to swear in court that we were with them the night Jessie Pyne was beaten up and raped. We're covered on that one. There's no way she'll make those charges stick."

Tom eyed him. "What about the other?"

"The arson thing?"

Tom nodded coldly. "That's the one."

"I'm still working on it."

Tom leaned forward, his face white from the pain the movement cost him. "You'd better work real hard, Hank, old boy. You'd better get us out of this one."

"I didn't get us into it all by myself," he shot back defensively.

"It was your bright idea to torch the place."

"And you were all for it," Hank replied angrily.

Tom leaned back, pressing his arm to his ribs. "Well, fearless leader, you'd better come up with a real good plan for this one. You'd better get us off. Because if you don't, I'll kill you. And don't you forget that for a minute."

19

Jessie checked the angle of the cabinet door to see if it was level. It wasn't. She had put the hinges on in the wrong place. Again. Exasperated, she took the door off and laid it across the kitchen table. She had never done any repair work like this before. Why Kate had thought Jessie knew all about it was beyond her. She could build shelves, bookcases, do a pretty decent job repairing windows and frames. But she had never hung any kind of door before, not even on a cabinet.

Jessie was so caught up in measuring, she didn't hear Beth come into the kitchen. Beth hesitated in the doorway, surprised by the tools spread out all over the room.

"Excuse me," she said.

Jessie looked up. "Oh, hi. I'm just trying to fix this door. Let me know if I'm in your way and I'll move my stuff."

"I thought I might be getting in your way if I came in," Beth said softly.

"No. Come on and do whatever you need to do. I'm trying to figure out how to get this door on straight. I'm not very good at this."

Beth opened the refrigerator and took out a loaf of bread. "You look like you know what you're doing."

Jessie winked at her and grinned. "That's half the secret. I'm supposed to look like I know, even when I don't. Actually, I'm not a carpenter or a cabinetmaker. Some things I do well but I missed doors somewhere along the way." Jessie put the door back on and began to tighten down the screws, bracing the door with her elbow. She watched Beth from the corner of her eye as Beth spread peanut butter on slices of bread and then reached for jelly.

"Lunch for your kids?"

Beth nodded. "Yes. I don't feel like arguing about nutrition today. They're watching cartoons on TV, and they're quiet, and they aren't fighting. If peanut butter and jelly sandwiches will keep them that way, then peanut butter and jelly is what they will get." Smiling at Jessie, she left the room with the two saucers in her hands.

Jessie stepped down from the chair and surveyed the door.

"It's straight," she muttered delightedly. She opened and closed it several times. "It's by god straight. What do you know?"

"It looks very nice for someone who says she doesn't know what she's doing." Beth had come back in and was putting away the jelly. Jessie smiled at her.

"Thank you. I was about to make some tea. Would you like some?"

A look of gratitude briefly crossed Beth's plain face. "I would love some. If it's not too much trouble."

"No trouble." Jessie set the kettle on the stove and turned on the burner. Then she began to pick up her tools, humming quietly as she loaded them back into the cardboard box that served as a tool chest. Beth sat down at the table, watching her silently.

"You treat everyone around here so normally. Isn't that hard for you?"

Jessie looked at her, puzzled. "Why should it be hard? You are normal. So are the other women. It's just your circumstances and your men that aren't normal."

"The other women talk a lot about what their husbands and boyfriends do to them."

"You don't talk about it?"

Beth shook her head. "No. I'm not proud of it."

"I doubt they are either. But it's nothing to be ashamed of. You never asked for it, no matter what you did or didn't do. It's not your fault."

Beth stared at her hands. "That's hard for me to believe," she said, her tone of voice wistful. "I kept thinking, for years and years, that if I just did things better, if I were smarter, that he wouldn't hit me anymore, that he would be nice. I knew it was my fault. Other women kept their husbands happy. I never saw them with bruises or acting scared. But Ha. . .my husband was never happy."

"Maybe he was just mean," Jessie said softly as she poured boiling water into the cups. "What kind of tea do you want? I recommend the Earl Grey, with honey."

"That sounds nice," Beth answered with a smile. No one had ever made tea for her before.

"I think it's hard for women to believe that it's not their fault. But it's not." Jessie set the cups on the table and drew up a chair. "Would it bother you very much if I smoked?"

Beth looked startled, unused to being consulted. "No. Go ahead. My husband smoked. He smoked a lot. A lot bothers me."

"I used to smoke a lot, but I cut down when I was in the hospital. Almost stopped completely. But it's a hard habit to break."

"Why were you in the hospital?" Beth asked as she waited for the tea to cool a bit.

Jessie lit the cigarette and exhaled slowly. "A group of men beat me up and raped me," she said finally, looking directly at Beth.

"Oh lord," Beth whispered. "I'm sorry."

"So was I," Jessie answered briefly.

"What is your name? I'm Beth."

"Jessie. Jessie Pyne."

Jessie was startled by Beth's reaction. The woman drew back, her face drained of color, and stared at her as though afraid.

"I. . .I saw your picture. . .in the newspaper. Several months ago. You were. . .helping a black woman, a black woman who was hurt."

Jessie watched her closely. "She died. Were you at that march?"

"No. No, I. . .Hank, I mean, my husband would never allow me to. . .I've got to go check on the children." She left the room, almost running. Jessie stared after her. Hank? Her husband's name was Hank? It couldn't be the same man. Hank wasn't that uncommon a name. She sipped her tea slowly and finished her cigarette. Then she rose to her feet. She hesitated for a moment, wondering what to do with Beth's cup. Then, with a shrug, she poured the cold tea down the sink and washed the two cups, leaving them in the drainer.

She heard the scream of brakes being released and looked out the window. There was Jake with the load of wood he had promised. She saw him wave from the cab of the semi when he spotted her face at the window. Better go outside and show him where to drop the load. No telling where he might leave it otherwise. Forgetting Beth momentarily, Jessie went out the back door.

Kate stuck her head out and shouted to be heard over the chainsaw. "Jessie? Jessie!"

Jessie looked up and slowed the saw to idle. "Yeah?"

"I have to go to the store. The locksmith still hasn't shown up, and there are no other staff people here. If he comes while I'm gone, will you show him what needs to be done?"

"Sure," Jessie yelled.

Kate blew her a kiss and disappeared. Jessie wiped the wood chips from her goggles and revved up the saw.

Timmy huffed down the stairs, stomping loudly. "I won't do it," he shouted upwards. "I won't wash dishes! Only girls wash dishes!" He stormed into the kitchen and put the plates on the counter by the sink. His dad would have a fit if he ever caught him washing dishes. His mom was trying to make a sissy out of him. Well, she wouldn't do it, not to him. Mark was sure a sissy, crying over everything. He raised a fuss over that little black eye Timmy had given him. But he warned that sneak. If Mark tried to get into the upper bunk, he would pop him one. He didn't even hit him that hard, for crying out loud. You would have thought he bopped him with a baseball bat or something.

Timmy shuffled into the living room, his hands in the pockets of his sagging jeans. His mom had tried to make him put on a belt, but he was tired of her always telling him what to do. It sure was a bother, though, to have to keep pulling his pants up all the time.

The face at the window in the door scared him at first. Then he looked closer. Excitement welled up in the boy, and he ran to the door, struggling with the lock. He threw the door open and threw himself into his father's arms.

"Dad! I knew you would come!"

Hank hugged the boy briefly and then set him on his feet, stooping in front of him so they were eye level.

"Is your mom here?"

Timmy nodded. "Yeah, she's upstairs. Boy, is she ever. . ."

"Ssshhhh. Don't make so much noise."

"Oh yeah. You're not supposed to be in here, are you?"

"Says who?" Hank growled.

"Not me," Timmy answered with a happy smile. "Are we going home now, Daddy?"

"Damned right. *All* of us. Where your mother got the big idea to waltz out with the two of you is beyond me. But I'll take care of her big ideas once and for all when we get home. Now you go upstairs and get your things together. And you tell your mother I want her down here right now."

"I heard you, Hank." Beth stood on the steps, her eyes wide with fright. "You're not supposed to be here. Get out."

Hank blinked in surprise. Then his eyes narrowed in anger. "You don't tell me what to do! Pack your things, and let's get out of this place."

Beth stopped Timmy as he tried to race up the stairs past her. "We're staying, Hank. I'm not coming home, and I won't let the children come back either."

"Let go of me!" Timmy tried to break Beth's grip on his shirt.

"No! You are staying right here. I want you to see just what kind of man your daddy really is. Be still, Timmy!"

"Come down from there, Beth," Hank said softly.

"You're not going to hurt me anymore. I won't let you."

"Be reasonable, Beth," Hank smiled at her, carefully keeping an eye on the other doors to make sure no one else entered without his knowledge. "I never did anything you didn't bring on yourself. Come home and act like a wife should act, and I promise I'll never hit you again. It's all your fault. You know that, don't you?"

"None of it is my fault."

Hank took a step towards her, and Beth backed up the stairs. "Don't come up here, Hank. I'm not alone."

Hank laughed. "If you think I'm scared of the other broads here, you sure are stupid. You hear that, Timmy? Your mom thinks I'm scared of a bunch of women."

Timmy laughed uncertainly, looking from his father to his mother who had not loosened her grip on his shirt. "You're in enough trouble already, Hank. Don't make it any worse."

"I'm not in half the trouble you're gonna be in if you don't let go of my son and come down here right now!"

"It wasn't enough you hit me. You had to beat on the kids. And then you had to pick a woman out to beat up and rape. Then you had to set fire to her business. Where do you stop? Where do you draw the line?" For a moment, Beth thought she might throw up; her fear was so churning inside her. But she clung to the banister and to her son, making herself hold her ground.

Suddenly, Timmy twisted and lunged down the stairs. Beth grabbed for him but Hank was faster, jerking the boy into the living room and grabbing her arm. Beth lost her balance as he hauled her down the steps. Hank threw her on the sofa and stood over her, breathing hard.

"Let's hear some more of that tough talk!"

Beth kicked without thinking, narrowly missing his groin. She wouldn't, she couldn't let him beat her up again. If he did it again, she would go crazy. She would lose her mind.

Hank jumped back, more amazed than hurt. He laughed and grabbed her by the front of her blouse, and drew back his hand. "I'll beat the living hell out of you for that!" He slapped her, then slapped her again, his face contorted with fury. Timmy stood frozen in the corner.

Hank didn't see Jessie enter the room, the ax and the maul in her hands. She stood in the doorway, unable to move for a long moment. Then she got a good look at the man's face.

Without thinking, she gave in to the surge of fury. She swung the maul with a shriek. Hank caught the motion from the corner of his eye, released Beth, and jumped back as the maul swung by inches from his face. The blade buried itself in the wall with a loud thump and crack of plaster. Hank backed away, tripping over a hassock as he tried to get some distance between himself and the woman coming at him with an ax. On one knee, he looked around desperately for something with which to defend himself. He grabbed the poker from beside the fireplace. Jessie swung the ax and knocked it from his hands, the shock of metal on metal numbing Hank's arm to the shoulder.

Hank could have sworn he heard the blade whistle as she swung the ax again and again, never missing him by more than two or three inches. Hank crawled backwards across the floor, looking for escape. But Jessie had him pinned in a corner, swinging the ax back and forth in front of his face, across his groin, close to his chest. Every time she swung, she yelled. The sound drove itself into Hank.

"Beth!" he screamed desperately. "Beth, get her away from me! Get her away!"

Beth sat on the sofa where he had dropped her, mesmerized by what was happening in front of her. Horrified, she still didn't move.

"Dad? Daddy?" Timmy's voice was soft as he watched.

"Get her away from me!" Hank was in tears, his face a pasty white as he tried to press his back through the wall. "Somebody do something! She's gonna kill me! Please! Oh god!" His voice broke off as he cried, his body drawn into a knot on the floor.

Jessie stood over him, feeling nothing. "Get in the closet. Crawl into that closet and close the door behind you."

Hank uncurled himself and shot into the closet, watching Jessie every minute. He was convinced she would sink the ax into him the moment he turned his back. When the door closed, Jessie flipped the lock and dropped the ax onto the floor, unable to hold it any longer. Her hands shook, and her mouth was dry. She hadn't noticed she was crying.

Kate stood at the edge of the room, her mouth open, two bags of groceries clutched to her chest. Finally she spoke, her voice a rasp. "Jessie. . .are you all right?"

Kate looked around the room, seeing the maul sticking out of the wall. Jessie nodded slowly as she walked towards Beth, her steps as unsteady as a drunk's. "Beth, are *you* all right?"

Jessie knelt in front of her, putting her hands on Beth's thin shoulders. "Are you okay? Did he hurt you?"

"I'm fine," Beth said, her voice cracking. Jessie held onto her, feeling faint.

Then Beth started to laugh. Leaning forward, arms crossed over her belly, she laid her head on Jessie's shoulder and laughed. Kate had still not moved. Jessie continued to hold Beth, a bewildered expression on her face. Finally, Beth straightened up and looked at Jessie.

"You. . ." she gasped, still laughing. "You made him *crawl* into that closet. You made him. . .if you only knew how many times I wanted to see him have to crawl, how many times I wanted to see him have to ask someone for something. . .if you only knew how long I had wanted him to ask me to help him. . .If you only knew." Beth ended in a whisper, and her laughter slowly changed into tears. Jessie pulled her close and rocked her back and forth while Kate watched. "If you only knew. If you only knew. If you only. . ."

Jessie sat down at the desk and leaned her head against the back of the chair. The police had come. Hank was locked away in jail once more. Beth was upstairs with the boys. Timmy seemed like a changed child, numbed from the experience and completely subdued.

Kate brought in a cup of tea and pressed it into Jessie's hands. Then she lit a cigarette and gave it to her. "You were truly amazing," she said softly.

Jessie looked at her tiredly. "I didn't even know what I was doing, Kate. I just reacted."

"You may very well have saved Beth's life."

"I'm just glad it's over."

Kate took Jessie's hand and held it, her finger tracing the pattern of veins under the pale skin. "I called a friend of mine in Asheville, a friend who told me a long time ago that she wanted to help in any way she could. I asked her if Beth and the children could come there for a few weeks, until things get sorted out here and Beth can decide what she wants to do. Jane said yes. The boys should love the farm. Beth will have some peace and quiet. I think she needs it. And I don't think there's any way her husband can find out where she is. There won't be any records kept."

"I'm glad to hear that. She needs to be a long way away from here."

"I just told her about it. She cried. I think she's packing up right now. I'll put her on a bus this afternoon."

"Good. She needs to know the whole world isn't like the one she's had to live in all these years. I wish I had a farm to go to right now."

"What do you need other than a farm right now?" Kate asked softly.

"Right now?" Jessie looked up at her with a small smile. "I need about fifteen hours of sleep. But I'm too tense to lie down."

"How are you feeling about what happened?"

"Scared. I think I could've killed him if he had come at me."

"He would've deserved it," Kate said vehemently.

Jessie glanced at her cup. "But I wouldn't have. It's scary for me to know I wasn't thinking, just reacting."

"You were thinking. Otherwise, you probably would have killed him. It seemed pretty clear that you were in full control of that ax."

"Maybe." Jessie looked up at her, a grin spreading over her face. "Did you see the expression on that cop's face when he found out I had used the ax? And when he saw the maul buried in the wall? Lizzie Borden!"

Kate laughed. "I think he felt safer with Hank than with you."

"He sure gave me hell for it though."

"Well, you just used what was at hand. I'm proud of you, Jess. You fought back. That's something I have always fantasized about doing. It feels good to know it can really be done."

Kate ran her fingers through Jessie's tousled hair, then rose from her stooped position. "Are you going to be all right by yourself for a while? I have to get Beth ready for the bus. I think I can probably get Betsy to take her to the bus station."

"I'll be fine," Jessie answered.

"Okay. The locksmith should be finishing up soon. After that, you could just sack out here on the sofa if you'd like."

"How's the little boy doing?" Jessie asked.

"Timmy?" Kate shrugged. "I'm not sure. He thought his dad was the toughest man who ever lived, worshipped him. This has been quite a shock to the kid, I think. Beth was going to try to get him to take a nap before we left for the bus. She said she didn't know what else to do for him right now. He's not talking to anyone. Or at least, he wasn't a little while ago."

"How does she seem to be doing?" Jessie persisted. Kate reached out and stroked her hair. "She seems to be doing fine. A little numb, but she acts like she feels safe for the first time. There's a spark in her I haven't seen before."

"Good." Jessie closed her eyes, suddenly exhausted. Over and over, she replayed the scene in her mind; she *had* known exactly what she was doing. She hadn't wanted to hurt Hank, only make him feel the same helpless terror she had felt. She had wanted to frighten him, cower him, humiliate him. She had done that. Jessie smiled up at Kate as Kate touched her cheek and turned to leave the room.

Jessie stood quietly in the living room, studying the hole in the wall she had made with the eight-pound maul. A large chunk of plaster was missing, and a crack ran almost to the ceiling. She would have to fix that. She touched the hole, almost not believing she could have done it. She looked at her hand. In the palm, pale but visible, were crescent-shaped scars made by her fingernails. Jessie stretched her fingers, feeling them flex easily for the first time in months.

Beth saw Jessie as she carried her suitcases down the stairs and put them by the door. She stepped up as close as she dared, her gaze fixed on the hole in the wall.

"Jessie?"

Jessie turned, a smile breaking across her face. "How are you?"

"Good. I'm good. I was hoping I would see you before I left. I want to say thank you."

Jessie shifted uncomfortably. "I wish you wouldn't. I did it mostly for me. I'm sorry he had to be your husband. I'm sorry for both of us."

Beth sat down in a chair and stared at the backs of her hands. "I know what Hank and his friends did to you. Kate told me the whole story. I knew something was going on. I only wish I had known how to stop them. But I was afraid, afraid of what he would do to me if I interfered."

"It wasn't your fault. Chances are you wouldn't have been able to do a thing anyway."

"I *will* come back and testify if my statement isn't enough."

"I appreciate that. I hope you won't have to."

"Me, too."

They sat quietly together, enjoying the silence in the room. Finally, Beth spoke again. "I guess I'll never figure him out. I guess I'll never understand what makes a man like him hate so much."

Jessie looked at her. "I know."

Jessie must have dozed sitting in the chair. When she opened her eyes, the room was dark and there was a hard pounding on the door. Lifting the shade cautiously, she peered out. Moon, Laura, Val, and Denny stood on the porch.

Jessie unlocked the door, relief surging through her. She wondered briefly how long it would take her to calm down completely.

Moon grabbed Jessie and swung her around the room. "What a woman! What a woman!"

Jessie let herself go limp in Moon's arms, knowing it was useless to struggle until Moon decided to put her down. Finally, Moon set her down with a jarring thump and turned Jessie to face her, a tight grip on Jessie's shoulders. "You are something else. I wish I could have been here!"

"You can do better than that. You can take me out for dinner and a drink. Then take me home and tuck me in bed. I am tired and hungry."

"You got it," Moon agreed enthusiastically.

A voice close behind Jessie startled her. "Jess," Kate said. "It sounds good to have Moon treat you to dinner and a drink, but I would like to stake a claim on the tucking into bed part."

Jessie could feel the flush starting on her chest. She turned with a moan, hoping it wouldn't turn into a full-fledged blush. But the others saw the creeping red and shouted laughter across the room. Finally, Laura was able to speak. "The insurance check came through today, Jessie."

Jessie looked at her carefully. "What do you want to do?"

"Well, we should talk tomorrow, I guess."

"All right," Jessie agreed.

"Jessie," Laura said reflectively, "have you ever considered owning a bar?"

Jessie stared at her in disbelief. "I don't know the first thing about bars."

"There's one for sale," Laura said, a wicked grin spreading across her face. "Just think about it, okay?"

Jessie shook her head and laughed. "Okay. Let's get out of here, please?"

Kate closed the door and locked it behind them. It was cold outside. Jessie zipped her jacket and turned up the collar, slowing down to wait for Kate.

"Y'know, Jess, I don't think we should fix the wall."

Jessie glanced at Kate. "No?"

Kate grinned. "Nope. I think we should leave it just the way it is."

Betsy handed Beth the tickets and a twenty dollar bill. Beth had already slipped the small bag of food into Mark's knapsack. Carefully herding the children in front of her, she checked their suitcases at the baggage area, then found seats for the two boys in the waiting room.

"Stay right here and don't move," she said as she headed towards the snack shop. She bought cartons of milk and some cookies. Then she pushed through the crowd, hoping the children were where she left them. As she worked her way through the people milling about the ticket counter, she noticed a newspaper rack. Inserting a quarter, she removed the top paper and allowed the door to snap shut.

Beth handed the milk to the boys and sat down beside them.

"Can we really ride horses, Mom?" Mark asked excitedly.

"That's what Kate said. But you'll have to listen to Jane and do what she tells you so you can learn the right way."

Beth glanced at the two boys. Mark looked eager, ready for what he saw as an adventure. Timmy stared quietly at the wall, his expression far away. Beth sighed. It would take time, a lot of time. She crossed her legs, ankle on knee, and leaned back. It would be better this way, no matter what happened. Settling herself more comfortably into the plastic chair, she smiled.

Then, she opened her newspaper and began to read.

Clenched Fists, Burning Crosses is part of The Crossing Press Feminist Series. Other titles in this Series include:

Abeng, A Novel by Michelle Cliff

Folly, A Novel by Maureen Brady

Learning Our Way: Essays in Feminist Education, edited by Charlotte Bunch and Sandra Pollack

Lesbian Images, Literary Commentary by Jane Rule

Mother, Sister, Daughter, Lover, Stories by Jan Clausen

Mother Wit: A Feminist Guide to Psychic Development by Diane Mariechild

Movement, A Novel by Valerie Miner

Movement In Black, Poetry by Pat Parker

Natural Birth, Poetry by Toi Derricotte

Nice Jewish Girls: A Lesbian Anthology, edited by Evelyn Torton Beck

The Notebooks of Leni Clare and Other Short Stories by Sandy Boucher

The Politics of Reality: Essays in Feminist Theory by Marilyn Frye

The Queen of Wands, Poetry by Judy Grahn

Sister Outsider, Essays and Speeches by Audre Lorde

Triangles, A Novel by Ruth Geller

True to Life Adventure Stories, Volumes I and II, edited by Judy Grahn

The Work of a Common Woman, Poetry by Judy Grahn

Zami: A New Spelling of My Name, Biomythography by Audre Lorde